A Year at Marshywood

Marina McLune

First published in the UK 2023 by Ark & Wyndham
a registered publisher name for Marina McLune
www.marinamclune.com

ISBN 978-1-7393137-0-8

Cataloguing in Publication Data for this book is available
from the British Library

Chapter 1

Drapers Lane looked different today. Amanda had walked down this street countless times but now all was set to change. Could this be the reason she felt she was looking at it with fresh eyes, noticing things she had never seen before? That alleyway, for instance. She ambled past and stopped to take a look, wondering where it led. On either side were tall grey stone walls, softened on the right by the green leaves of a laurel hedge peering over a wooden fence. Beyond, she could see the roofs and upper windows of terraced houses. The passage veered towards the left, leaving only a solid block of wooden fencing visible in the distance.

Suddenly, soft cumulus clouds separated in the sky, allowing the spring sun to light up the paving stones. She watched for a moment, now even more tempted to venture in and explore, but she didn't have the time, not today. She felt a tightening in her stomach, knowing this could be her last chance to find out where it would lead.

This unexpected pathway to an unknown destination perfectly summed up Amanda's life right now. She knew the chances of finding hidden and mysterious places in East London were small, but there was always something new, if you were prepared to look. Yet Amanda didn't have to do anything to experience novelty and change. Her life was going to get very interesting, whether she liked it or not. Nothing would ever be the same again, which both frightened and excited her. Very soon she would break the news, making it official. What would the reaction be?

In front of her stood a small silver birch, and she looked up to see several goldfinches, sporting flashes of red and yellow, chirping energetically. This greatly helped settle her nerves. She loved this tree, and it always held her interest, whatever time of year she passed by. It was now April, and she stopped to look at the long male catkins, hanging down like lambs' tails, in close proximity to the smaller pale-green female ones, standing upright beside the leaves. Catkins were a beautiful sign that spring was here, as was the frenetic activity of goldfinches preparing their nests. Males, females and nest-building – even the natural world echoed her desire.

* * *

Sam had just finished talking about a new guy at work when Amanda finally broke the news.

'You're definitely leaving London and moving to a village?' Sam held back an uneasy laugh. 'Can't you just stay here and leave them to it?' Amanda shook her head. 'Okay, I get it. Your dad's taking early retirement, but has he thought for a second about you? You'll miss all your friends, and you'll be bored stiff.' Amanda wasn't so sure a few work colleagues and former classmates qualified as friends. Samantha – Sam for short – was the only person she could always rely on.

'And what about Mark?' Sam added with a knowing smile.

She certainly knew how to get Amanda's attention. As well as being Sam's cousin, Mark just happened to be Amanda's dream date. He lived south of the river in East Dulwich, and after not being in touch for several years, Sam had been meeting up with him since his father had contacted hers to break the news of his terminal illness. It was at the funeral that Amanda met Mark for the first time. Sam had invited her, explaining that Ghanaian funerals were big social occasions. 'Sometimes hundreds come along. In fact, the more people the better.' Amanda had felt reassured, hoping the experience would leave her feeling positive, despite it being an unhappy event.

She thought back to that day. It started with the girls making their way by train, to allow for a quick stop-over at Petticoat Lane market, while Sam's parents were coming later in the car. The aim was for Amanda to pick up a pair of shiny red Sandy-in-*Grease* shoes, but after she eventually tracked them down, she changed her mind.

'Standing in these all day at Woolies would do me in – not that they'd let me wear them,' she said, her shoulders dropping.

'Yes, they're definitely more suitable for clubbing,' Sam agreed. 'But if you're planning a night out on the town, you'll just have to go without me. You know what my mum thinks about those "dens of iniquity."' She gave Amanda a snarky smile.

'I'd trip over and do myself a serious injury, so it's just as well,' Amanda said, reluctantly placing them back on the market stall table.

'Yeh, there's a good reason they're called killer heels. Let's go shall we?' Sam gestured for her friend to get a move on.

Amanda had enjoyed *Grease*, but unlike most people she wouldn't describe it as a feel-good movie. When it came out the previous year the queue had snaked around the street and extended for almost as far as the eye could see. Many girls fancied themselves as Sandy, but not Amanda. She didn't want to light up a cigarette or don sexy gear in order to get her man. Surely any guy worth his salt wouldn't be impressed by that. She hoped that Mark was a man able to look beyond the superficial.

Within minutes of arriving at the church hall, she had noticed Mark's heart-warming smile. He was tall, dark and handsome. Like his cousin Sam he had a Ghanaian father, but whereas Sam's father had married a lively Nigerian lady, Mark's mother was an Irish lass from Dublin, and his toffee-coloured skin tone reflected this mix. The moment she introduced them, Sam saw her best friend's eyes light up and she immediately set about trying to matchmake. Perhaps the distraction of an understanding girlfriend would help Mark cope with his grief.

'Amanda, this is Mark, my cousin. Mark, this is Amanda, a friend of mine I've known since school – I'm not sure if your mum mentioned she was coming.'

'Yes,' Mark replied, smiling warmly and turning towards her, 'she did say you were bringing a friend. Hi, Amanda.'

'Hello Mark, I'm really sorry about your loss.' Amanda felt her words were feeble and pressed her lips tightly before returning his smile. Couldn't she think of something slightly more original to say?

'Thank you,' he said, sounding relaxed and with a momentary distant look in his eyes. 'We were so grateful that Dad's last days were free from suffering, and Guy's hospital was amazing.'

A long pause followed, and Sam felt obliged to step in. 'Mark, your mum looks really ... how can I put it ... calm and peaceful today. When Mum and Dad went to see her a few weeks ago, they said things were very difficult for her during your dad's last days.'

'That's right, they were,' Mark said. 'Reconnecting with you all, after all these years, has been a great support for Mum. My sister worries that she hasn't been able to look after her in the way she would have liked, since becoming a mum herself, so we can't thank your parents enough, especially Aunt Precious for ringing Mum almost every day.'

That's so typical of Sam's mum, Amanda thought. She knew from personal experience how caring she could be. Mark was soon distracted by a relative, and they wouldn't get the chance to talk again for a good few hours.

* * *

'I told you there'd be vol-au-vents,' Sam said, swallowing a mouthful of pastry and prawns. But Amanda was only picking at her food. Sam saw that her friend kept glancing towards the other side of the room. 'I'll have to get you two talking again, won't I,

Mand? Let's go over to him.' She tugged at Amanda's sleeve and soon Amanda and Mark were face to face once more, but before they could strike up another conversation, Mark's mother interrupted them.

'Mark, a friend of mine wants to ask you a quick question about a boundary issue with her neighbour,' she uttered in her soft Irish accent.

Mark looked uncomfortable. 'I'll try my best, but I've only just started working for Cartwright Berrington, and they don't teach you everything in the Law Society exams.'

It was getting late and everything was drawing to a close. Before walking away to respond to this request, Mark said goodbye. He extended his hand to Amanda, and she took it, thinking it would be a brief handshake, but instead he didn't let go. Starting to become too aware of herself, she felt her breathing quicken and hoped it wasn't obvious. Was he just seeking consolation, or was it something more? All she knew was, she never wanted to let go.

In reality, the physical contact was brief, but it seemed like an age. Amanda suddenly noticed that several pairs of eyes were watching them – Sam's, of course, Mark's mother, even his sister, who was trying to soothe her crying baby. Amanda's face glowed from the heat of embarrassment, but she also felt flushed for another reason. After holding his hand, she knew she wanted to see him again and hoped he felt the same way.

The journey home began with Sam's little brother carefully positioning himself on her lap, while she sat next to the eldest one on the back seat of the family's Austin Allegro. Now they'd have no problem having four people in the back.

'Get in, Mand!' Sam said, giving the seat a whack.

There was just enough room for Amanda to squeeze onto the seat. They set off across London, leaving East Dulwich and crossing over the Thames towards Leytonstone. The two friends, although keen to chat about the day's events, had little opportunity to talk, since gospel music was ringing out through the newly installed cassette player, to which Sam's mother

Precious sang along heartily, encouraging the young people in the back to join in.

Amanda sat in silence watching the sights of London whizz by to Precious' musical backdrop, and in her heart of hearts she knew saying goodbye to all of this was not going to be easy.

* * *

Reality was slowly sinking in and Amanda's excitement began to grow. She adored the countryside, and the coast too. Even so, it was disconcerting to be moving to a totally new area where there was no one she or her parents knew – apart from her father's brother and his wife.

Uncle Charles and Aunt Pauline had settled in Pevensey Bay on the East Sussex coast, following a life of jet-setting. After living the dream in Toulouse for five years, they had decided there was no place like home, and somewhere on the south coast, the warmest part of the UK, seemed a natural choice. '1066 country is the home of the most famous battle ever,' Charles would crow at his jaded brother and sister-in-law. Although they struggled to understand his morbid fascination with war, Amanda's parents, Joan and Robert, made an effort to tolerate his interest in all things heroic and bloody.

Little surprise then that Charles would enjoy recounting memories of his time as a young man in the navy during the second world war. Robert, on the other hand, chose never to speak about his service. Although Amanda had tried to get him to open up and would occasionally broach the subject, in recent years she had all but given up, accepting that her father would never talk openly about his experiences to her or anyone else, perhaps not even to Joan. All he was prepared to say was that war was a very ugly thing, he was too young to handle it, and that he had lost friends. Amanda wondered if needing time to recover was a reason he remained single until he finally met Joan at the age of 33.

Trips down to Sussex to find the perfect new home, exciting as they were, came at a price – the obligatory visit to Charles and Pauline's house.

'So Rob, have you decided where around Hailsham you're going to settle?' Charles asked, frowning. 'It's very inland, and I thought Joan suffered terribly from hay fever. Wouldn't the coast be a better bet?'

Robert sat in his brother's lounge and found himself silently agreeing with him. The coast might well be a better choice, but there was only one problem: his wife found Charles even more intolerable than he did. Because they were the only close family members left, and could be a means of support one day, she had conceded that it would be good to live within striking distance of them, but she didn't want them too close. Since they lived by the sea, she wanted something different. Of course there were other areas of coastline nearby – further along westwards towards Seaford, for example – but Joan liked the idea of having country lanes, farmland and fields on her doorstep.

Robert, momentarily distracted by visions of Joan sneezing uncontrollably, was brought back to the presence of his hosts when Pauline gently prodded him with a plate.

'Here Rob, have a slice. Where near Hailsham exactly?' she asked.

'Magham Down village,' he said, picking up some Swiss roll, 'we were thinking, looks like a nice area, close enough to town but also far enough to enjoy the best views and scenic walks. It's been on the radar for us ever since I saw it featured in a book on Sussex walks.'

'Magham Down?' Charles guffawed. 'Sounds awfully provincial to me. Have you checked there's anyone living there who's actually left the village?' Robert clenched his jaw. 'Not wishing to pour cold water over your plans,' Charles continued, tipping a teaspoon of sugar into his cup and stirring, 'but you know me, I couldn't cope without the sea and the sailing club, especially since selling our yacht. Are you, Joan and Amanda sure you can handle living next door to a bunch of backward country bumpkins?'

Robert just wasn't in the mood for his brother's clumsy attempts at humour. He knew his exaggerated words were a veiled attempt to irritate him, so now was probably a good time to make his excuses and leave. He had also discovered a long time ago that getting annoyed was fruitless. His mind travelled back to when he was nine and Charles was eleven, recalling a rare occasion when he decided to fight back. It was 1928, and Charles had accused Robert of stealing a marble which had gone missing. Robert's dismay at being unjustly blamed turned into fury when Charles started teasing him after their mother confiscated Robert's halfpenny-an-ounce bag of aniseed balls and gobstoppers as a punishment. That was the last straw. Robert lashed out at Charles in a tearful fit of anger. As a result he was swiftly punished with the strap from his father, and even when Charles' marble was found under the Welsh dresser several weeks later, Robert received no apologies from either his mother or his father, and certainly not from Charles.

'Thanks for the tea and cake,' Robert said, rising to his feet. 'We'll keep you posted, and as I said before, I'm sorry Joan couldn't make it.'

Charles saw Pauline's fixed smile, and he knew precisely what she was thinking: that Joan usually developed a migraine or something similar just before visiting them.

'And just one other thing,' Robert continued, 'we're staying at a guest house for a couple of nights, and we're only here until Sunday morning, so I don't suppose we'll see you again before going back to London, but if house hunting goes well this weekend, we'll let you know. No need to come to the door, I'll let myself out.'

Robert left Charles and Pauline's large beachfront house and shut the door behind him. Now at last they were alone, free to talk about what they really thought of Robert and Joan and their ridiculous decision to leave London to pursue the country dream.

* * *

'This place has seen better days.' Amanda looked around as Robert quietly muttered to himself. 'Definitely seen better days,' he repeated uneasily, looking up at the exposed dark-wood beams covered in layers of cobwebs.

'I know,' Amanda said, trying her best to sound encouraging, 'but Mum's been in the garden for ages and she's fallen in love with those views. You know she's always dreamed of somewhere like this, and she may even be right – a good clean, some fresh paint and thick carpets, and we'll be well on our way to a cosy home again.'

Robert nodded but then looked pained. 'Yes, she insists on carpeting throughout, only she seems to forget her asthma improves whenever we stay in that cottage in Wales with the flagstone floors. She claims it's the Welsh air.' Amanda smiled and nodded while her father vented his frustrations. 'Ever since I read that report about dust mites, she's been battling her desire for shagpile against her need to breathe easily, and as you know, the shagpile's won. Only here will be even worse than back home, since this house, being so old, is also damp. Carpets plus damp will be lethal for Mum's asthma, but what can I say?'

'I know, Dad, I know.' Amanda nodded.

At that moment, Joan dashed into the house, puffing and out of breath with excitement. 'Oh my goodness, it's absolutely breathtaking out there. And look!' she said, rushing to a window. 'From here you can see those fields and sheep. We have to buy it, Rob,' she urged, turning around swiftly. 'I know it's the place for us, I can just feel it.'

Robert knew his reservations wouldn't stop her. 'Where's Mr Brookes?' he asked.

'I think he's speaking to what will be our new neighbours. He'll be in soon.'

Right at that moment, in through the back door walked their estate agent, a tall well-dressed man in his early fifties. 'Did someone mention my name? Just talking to the nearby farmer, Cecil Appleby.'

Joan hurried upstairs again, this time taking Amanda with her, leaving Robert with Mr Brookes.

'Your wife is very taken with this cottage, Mr Fernsby,' Mr Brookes said, peering at him over his half moon glasses.

'I know,' Robert replied, his shoulders sagging, 'so there's not much point saying we need to sleep on it. Not when Joan's mind is firmly made up.'

'Excellent,' the agent said, grasping his clipboard. 'Old Miss Baldwin would have been delighted you're going to buy it. You seem such a lovely family. Being a probate sale, there's no onward chain, and since you already have a buyer for your London house, I'm sure we can get you in before the summer.' Looking uncomfortable, Robert offered up a reserved smile. 'Life here is slow and steady,' Mr Brookes continued, 'and folk look out for one another. But take it from me ...' He stopped short and looked him squarely in the eye. 'The people here will treat you very well, provided, of course, you do your bit.'

'I really hope we can,' Robert said, as he and Mr Brookes shook hands on the deal.

Chapter 2

'So, it's really happening then?'

'You know it is, Sam. You've known for ages.'

'Yes, I guess, but I didn't think it would actually go ahead. What I mean is, I hoped they'd change their minds, or that you'd decide to stay here. You *are* 19, so you're old enough to make your own decisions, you don't have to go.'

Amanda was sitting in the front room of Sam's house. On the mantelpiece were assorted ornaments, while on the wall a red wall hanging said: 'Christ is the head of this house, the unseen guest at every meal, the silent listener to every conversation'. On a small table in front of her was a bright blue mug and a plate with several Happy Faces biscuits looking up at her – jammy, creamy Happy Faces, but the biscuits didn't reflect the mood in the room.

'It's all happening much quicker than I thought it would, Sam,' Amanda said, her voice flat. 'We've got a completion date for the tenth of May, but Marshywood has a lot that needs doing to it, so it's probably best you wait until the summer to stay over.'

'Marshywood?' repeated Sam. 'Why's it called that?'

'No idea. There's a big sign over the door with the name – I don't think homes in the village have door numbers. An old lady died there. She was 95 and never left the village. She was born in the cottage, the estate agent said.'

'Died there? Aren't you spooked by that?' Sam said, looking unsettled.

'Not really,' Amanda shrugged. 'There are plenty of freaky cobwebs though. It's a good job I'm not a spider-phobe like you, Sam.'

'Spiders!' Sam shivered. 'That settles it, I won't ever visit.'

Laughter helped them momentarily forget the reality of their imminent separation.

'I think you've forgotten something, or rather someone.' Sam raised an eyebrow, pulling out her trump card.

Amanda had no doubt what was coming next. *Here we go again*, she thought.

'You may not think I'm worth staying for, but surely Mark is.'

Amanda recalled holding his hand and felt her cheeks glow. 'He hasn't asked me out, has he,' she replied, trying to sound unruffled, 'and anyway, he may already have a girlfriend.'

Sam smiled. 'His mum talks to mine about our respective love lives, so I know for sure he hasn't. And I know something else,' she said, pausing to create suspense.

'Oh really, what?'

'Geraldine thinks you're lovely,' Sam enthused. 'I kept quiet because you've got a big enough head already. No, seriously, with all that's been going on with you away in Sussex, and things hectic at work, I forgot to tell you.' Amanda's eyes lit up and Sam continued. 'Mum spoke to her last week and she said ...' Sam paused to put on her best southern Irish accent, 'Sam's friend was such a lovely young lady.' She saw you holding Mark's hand, so that can only mean one thing; she approves of you, which is quite something, since most mums don't think anyone's good enough for their only sons. Personally, I think your red hair won her over. It suggests you've got Gaelic roots like her.'

Amanda instinctively took a strand of her long hair and twisted it round her finger. 'There's no Irish blood in me, at least as far as I know, but I could be wrong. Anyway Sam, don't get carried away,' she exhorted. 'The funeral was two weeks ago, so wouldn't I know by now if he was interested?'

'I bet he's trying to muster up the courage. Give him time.'

Amanda could certainly do that, since she was used to waiting. So far, the men who'd asked her out just hadn't been right, or she didn't find them attractive. And the men she liked weren't interested or were already dating. Although her job at Woolworths brought her into contact with young men, most of them worked downstairs in the stock room and were as young as 16, fresh out of school. Attractive men came into the store from time to time, but her more typical customers were young mothers, school children or the elderly. Even if Mark bucked this trend, there was a further hurdle to overcome: her parents. While Amanda's mother Joan could have unsavoury attitudes, her father Robert prided himself on not being prejudiced, but the concept of a mixed marriage was going to be a challenge, even for a liberal-minded man like him. Still, such concerns were jumping the gun and possibly a waste of energy, especially now she had more pressing things to think about, not least of all, what she was going to do for work after moving to Sussex.

Amanda's manager Sheila was in her early forties, with short ash-blond hair, bright red nail varnish, and an unfortunate steely stare. Amanda knew that Sheila had thought her to be easily distracted, particularly in the early days, but she felt she had done a reasonable job since she'd started work there straight from school three years ago. However, despite maturing into her role and acquiring sufficient skills to make her a valuable member of the team, she very much doubted Sheila would go the extra mile to sing her praises, something which might be necessary in order to achieve a quick and easy transfer to another branch of Woolworths.

'What's up, Mand?' Sam noticed her friend had gone quiet.

'Nothing much, I was only wondering if Sheila might put in a good word for me for a transfer, that's all. Even if she does – and it's by no means guaranteed – will there be an opening in the local branch? I've seen it and it's a lot smaller than Walthamstow.' Amanda's voice wavered. 'Life seems scary at the moment, Sam. Soon I'll have no job, no London, no Sam down the road, and no boyfriend – although that's nothing new. I've no idea how this will all pan out. It's okay for Mum and Dad to take a punt, but will it all work out for me?' Amanda wriggled her shoulders pretending to dance and started to sing, 'I Will Survive'. She always found comfort in music. In spite of Amanda's attempts to make light of the situation, Sam could see genuine anxiety in her eyes. She didn't reply, but instead gave her friend a sympathetic smile, before passing her the plate on which lay a solitary biscuit.

'Gosh Sam,' Amanda said, looking at the plate in disbelief, 'how did we manage to scoff all those? I don't want to add my figure to that long list of things I'm going to leave behind.'

'Leaving your figure behind? Don't you mean you're going to end up with a massive behind!' Sam quipped, watching Amanda reach for the sweet treat. Amanda hesitated, popped the entire biscuit into her mouth and looked remorseful before breaking into a smile. Both girls laughed freely, enjoying what was to be the last opportunity they would have to be together for quite some time.

* * *

Amanda looked out of the car window. She had forgotten just how many trees there were once they had left London behind. It had been an extremely cold and snowy winter, and although it was now May, the whole of the UK was still experiencing unseasonably low temperatures and this was reflected in the scenery. Robert said that he had read in *The Telegraph* that the 4th of May set the record for the coldest May night recorded at a Scottish weather station, with a temperature reading of minus seven, but all the UK was affected by a cold arctic front, even as far south as the Channel Islands.

The dusting of white lit up the scenery outside, and Amanda was enthralled by it. As Robert drove through Kent to East Sussex, Joan sat animated in the passenger seat. They were all looking forward to their new life, which had now truly begun. The life they had always dreamed of – or more accurately, the one Joan had hankered after – was set to become a reality.

'Manda,' Joan would say every so often, 'look over there, isn't it gorgeous? Robert, please slow down love, the road's slippery.'

Amanda and her parents had travelled along this route before, but only as visitors. Today was different. It wasn't car sickness, but rather eagerness and uncertainty which were making Amanda's stomach churn. Identifying trees, many of which were showing signs of spring, calmed her. Oak, beech, ash, Amanda certainly knew her trees. She had always had a fascination with them. From an early age her parents would take her on holiday to the Gower peninsula in South Wales. It wasn't far by car, yet it was officially another country, with its own unique language, and therefore a good alternative to a foreign break. Trips away from home were usually in July or August, and knowing how easily their daughter burned, Joan and Robert would seek out the shelter of a tree when having a picnic, which was a regular highlight of their week away. Three years previously during an unusually hot summer when it was so dry there was water rationing, Amanda had never felt so grateful for the covering the fresh green canopy provided. She came to associate the cool shade of a tree, its patterned bark, the wind whistling through its branches, with tranquillity. Of course, London had its fair share of trees, including the majestic London plane, but now she anticipated so much more on her doorstep: hawthorn, willow and birch, to name just a few. And it wasn't only the trees that excited her, but also the Downs, the River Cuckmere and the nearby coast. She wondered if living here might feel like being on holiday forever.

Except life wasn't a holiday, and she still needed a job. She also thought how much she would miss having a close friend nearby. And, when it came to meeting the right man, if that was purely a numbers game, living in a small village wasn't exactly going to maximise her chances. Dare she put all her eggs in one basket and hope for Mark? Experience had taught her this was unwise. And what if they did fall in love? He lived and worked in London. Would that mean having to uproot herself yet again to return to the Big Smoke?

Stop building castles in the air, it'll probably never be an issue, she told herself. But what if it did become an issue? In a way, she'd be disappointed if it didn't, since she wanted Mark and she now hoped to settle in Sussex, but what if she couldn't have both? Amanda knew she was being unduly apprehensive, but old habits die hard, and she was no stranger to fretting about the future and allowing her nerves to get the better of her. This led to her recalling a battle with anxiety she had once lost.

Amanda was bright and had been on course to complete A levels, and perhaps then go on to university. She was predicted to get good results for her O levels, (as well as maths and French – her only CSEs). However, the pressure of study and the thought of what was at stake led to an emotional crisis. She failed to show up for her English exam, despite it being her favourite subject. Although she managed to turn things around and successfully resat the exam the following January, she decided after that experience she definitely didn't want to go on to study for A levels. The teachers may have thought her capable, but what was the point of university, and what did she want to do with her life? If she was honest, she wanted a family more than a career, and for that reason putting herself through more study and exams just didn't seem worth it.

Maybe she was making a mistake. Shouldn't she try to carve out an independent life, as so many women were doing today? Amanda wasn't interested in women's lib, but nevertheless she wondered if she should feel guilty, perhaps even pathetic for not being more ambitious. After all, this wasn't Austen's Regency

England, this was 1979 Britain with its first woman prime minister freshly at the helm. A woman could do anything and everything these days, if only they put their mind to it. However, thoughts of London and 10 Downing Street grew ever more distant with every passing mile, as did Amanda's wish to be anyone other than who she truly was. Her disquiet began to slowly evaporate as she began to revel in the beauty of her surroundings, and soon the car crunched to a halt on the gravel drive. They had arrived at Marshywood.

* * *

Robert was trying to light a fire for the fourth time, while Joan surveyed the cold, unfamiliar surroundings, unable to believe they were finally here. After a bracing stroll around the three acre grounds, it was now sunset and time to be cosy by the wood burner, if Robert could manage to get the logs he had found in the front porch to catch, that is.

'I hope we get some respite from this big freeze soon,' he muttered, feeling chilly but undeterred. Joan didn't reply, but a dispirited expression in her eyes spoke volumes as Robert's fifth attempt failed, or at least she thought it had, until a flicker that had disappeared began to rise up again. Soon there was a strong, warm glow, and the log burner was alight with yellow and orange flames. 'Success at last,' he piped up, falling exhausted into an armchair. Joan was delighted when she saw the fire ablaze, but her mind was elsewhere.

'Robert darling,' she said, after a while. 'We have made the right decision, haven't we?'

'What a question, love. Why are you asking?' Robert gave out a brief and nervous laugh, fearing the worst. He hadn't anticipated such a bombshell before they had even spent one night in their new home.

'What I mean is, have we done the right thing for Manda, Robert?' Joan continued. 'It's okay for us at our age, but she has her whole life ahead of her, and she's had to leave everything behind.'

Robert felt relieved Joan was talking about their daughter and wasn't having regrets herself. 'Joan, you know how much Amanda has been looking forward to this,' he whispered, not wishing the subject of discussion, who was upstairs unpacking, to overhear. 'She'll make new friends and get another job no problem.'

Joan nodded. 'Robert, love, there is one thing I don't regret about taking her away.'

Robert knew what Joan was about to say. 'We'd better keep our voices down, she's only upstairs,' he said, fearful that Amanda might hear what was inevitably coming next.

Joan resumed quietly, 'I can't believe how quickly she fell for that half-caste boy. Sam's lovely, and we've never been bothered about her having a coloured friend, have we?' Robert shook his head. 'But going out with one, well, that's different, isn't it?' She reached over to switch on a lamp, almost knocking over a pile of unpacked boxes in the process. 'I can't imagine that sort of thing would go down too well around here. I've seen that programme *Mixed Blessings*, and apart from it not being in the least bit funny, it's also not realistic, is it, Rob? The reality's much worse.'

Robert smiled to himself. Did anyone expect sitcoms to reflect reality?

'Robert, she'll have to forget about him now and be done with it,' Joan continued. 'Hopefully she'll find a nice English lad, I don't doubt it. She's young, with her whole life ahead of her.'

Robert thought carefully before responding. He knew Amanda well, and although she didn't say much about Mark, he could tell her heart lay in that direction. Most importantly, no admission from Amanda was necessary, because Joan confessed to him she had read her diary and learned all about Mark in there. Although disappointed at the invasion of privacy, Robert didn't reproach his wife, since Joan assured him she hadn't intended to read it but was searching Amanda's bedroom for a missing sewing kit. She was also worried that evening, because

Amanda was late home from work and she was seeking clues as to where she might be when she stumbled across the diary hidden under a pile of magazines in a dressing table drawer. Amanda remained blissfully unaware of all this. Nothing felt amiss, since openness and honesty between her and her mother was already lacking. She was more likely to confide in her father, who now had to carry the double burden of knowing about his wife's breach of trust and his daughter's private thoughts.

What's done is done, Robert rationalised, while reminding himself that for all her failings, Joan genuinely wanted the best for Amanda.

'It's different here at night, isn't it, Rob?' Joan clasped her hands tightly between her jiggling thighs, eager for the heat of the fire to flow through the room. 'Doesn't it feel strange not being able to see those lovely views or hear the birds sing?'

Robert wanted to say something encouraging, but words eluded him. However, Joan stepped in with some positive words of her own. 'The fire looks great, so thanks for persevering,' she smiled.

'My pleasure,' Robert replied, sighing deeply. 'It is looking good now, isn't it, love?'

He had seen sadness fall across her face more than once that evening and it was his heartfelt wish that her mood would improve, or at the very least stay on an even keel. Despite his own misgivings before buying Marshywood, he wanted her to love their new home, warts and all, and was keen to do what he could to prevent any negativity taking root. After all, he had seen it all before. Joan loved new beginnings but was no stranger to low spirits once reality set in, and not since they first got married and moved into their home together in London had they experienced a new start as big as this.

Robert thought back to the early years of their marriage and a time when he and his brother Charles found themselves comparing notes. Pauline had wanted a large family, but it became apparent that this wasn't going to happen. In contrast, Joan had decided from the outset that she didn't want any children. 'I'm just too selfish, and I'm not keen on babies,' she had said, within weeks of starting to date. By then, Robert had fallen head over heels for this independent young auburn-haired beauty, who at 19 years old was fourteen years his junior. Although he had always wanted children himself, he decided Joan mattered more, and so they were married within two years.

Robert was beside himself with joy when six years later, despite precautions, Joan fell pregnant and gave birth to Amanda. However, Joan's pregnancy and labour, culminating in a caesarean, was very difficult and was followed by severe postnatal depression. This made her swear she would never go through it again, and anyway, she felt that being a mother hadn't changed her one bit, she simply didn't feel any less selfish. So, after frog-marching a compliant Robert to the hospital, no more children was pretty much guaranteed. Robert remained philosophical and considered his family complete, grateful that he was a father.

'I've still got stuff to unpack but I'm taking a break,' Amanda said, entering the room. She looked over towards the sofa and saw her cat, curled up and asleep, and sitting herself down, the movement on the sofa was all it took to wake her pet from its slumber.

'Tabitha survived the journey well, didn't she?' Amanda smiled, stroking the cat's stripy fur. Tabitha lifted her head before stretching and yawning. She extended her paws and slowly climbed onto Amanda's lap.

'Yes, she did,' replied Joan. 'I wonder how well she'll get on with her new surroundings. The pet shop man advised me to keep her indoors for a while.'

Amanda looked down at Tabitha, thinking how easy and uncomplicated her life was.

'What about you, Manda love?' Robert asked. 'There are no such restrictions on you, so what are you planning to do tomorrow? Your mother and I are going to Hailsham to get some food in. Would you like to come with us?'

Amanda pondered. 'I will need to go to town at some point to visit the job centre and Woolies to speak to the manager, but tomorrow, if the snow has melted enough, I just want to walk around the village and country lanes and explore, if that's okay?'

'Of course it is, love. You go ahead and enjoy yourself.'

'Thanks, I hope I will,' Amanda smiled, feeling tired but happy and unsure what tomorrow would bring.

Chapter 3

Drawing the curtains wide, Amanda was delighted to see the ground had thawed. There was no pressure of work, which was quite a novelty, and it didn't feel at all like a weekday. Prior to today, Sundays had been her only guaranteed day off, having worked Monday to Friday, and three Saturdays out of four at Woolworths.

On her last day, the staff got together and presented her with a large teddy bear and a card. 'Hope you love your new life', and 'Visit us when you come back to London', were some of the messages scribbled within.

Despite it being Amanda's send-off, Sheila had remained aloof, but was considerate enough to state that she had spoken to the manager at Woolworths in Hailsham, and he was happy to meet Amanda and put her application on file. Amanda readily thanked her manager but felt inwardly dissatisfied, knowing that 'on file' could mean years. Doubtless, she'd need something else in the meantime, and she could even take the opportunity to explore another direction altogether. Since she wasn't a career girl she had flexibility, so why stick to retail? There was office, hotel

or bar work, maybe even childcare or working with the elderly –
in fact, many options, and Amanda wasn't too fussed.

She slipped on her dressing gown and considered turning on
the paraffin heater because it was still chilly for May. About to go
downstairs she decided against it, and judging by the sound of
the kettle whistling on the stove top, breakfast was already in
progress. Perhaps her mother was getting used to that rusty old
Aga. Amanda came downstairs to find Joan sitting at the table for
her breakfast –a bowl of Special K, followed by Slimcea toast and
marmalade. Robert was busy boiling eggs. 'Soft or hard, Manda?'
he asked, without looking up from the stove which he was clearly
finding tricky to use.

'Soft please, Dad. How was your night?' Amanda looked at
them both.

'Fantastic,' Joan responded, her strength renewed since the
previous evening. 'I'm looking forward to our trip to town and
shopping as a local.'

Joan seemed happy and relaxed and Amanda realised that
although her emotions would oscillate, this particular morning
she had an affinity towards her mother. Perhaps it had something
to do with sharing this new adventure together and waking up in
a new home with exciting days looming ahead. But there were
also the not so good days. Amanda often suspected something
was wrong with how Joan related to her. She remembered her
saying when she was younger, 'Amanda, I told your father I was
just too selfish to have children, but I'm not sorry you came
along.' To Amanda though, rather than selfish, self-absorbed felt
more accurate, especially those times Amanda found her cold
and distant, failing to somehow connect, share or feel. And then
there were the moments when she'd sense her mother was
somewhere else emotionally and mentally, and although she
knew both her parents loved her, she sometimes felt neglected
by Joan, and annoyed and frustrated that her father gave in to her
far too readily for the sake of an easy life.

Joan's relationship with her own mother, who died when
Amanda was seven, had been difficult. From what Amanda could

gather, being a widow and a single mother in the 1940s was extremely hard. After Joan's father died in the second world war, her mother worked five nights a week in an armaments factory to make ends meet, leaving Joan and her older brother with their grandmother, who was a widow herself and practically immobile. Amanda tried to understand how that must have affected Joan, so she did her best to accept her mother's struggle to relate. Perhaps the emotional detachment was a reason why Amanda had felt so secure and happy in the presence of Sam's mother, Precious, who in total contrast showered love and attention not just on her three children but on Amanda too. Things were different now. Precious and Sam were in London, and Amanda and her parents were here in Sussex, enjoying an optimistic start together. Everything felt new.

'Manda dear,' Joan repeated, 'I said, did you sleep well?'

'Not bad, but it did feel nippy so I threw on extra blankets,' Amanda said, remembering how quickly she fell asleep afterwards. 'I soon warmed up, but you can really feel the difference in a detached after living in a terraced.' She eagerly looked over towards the kitchen window. 'Before we know it, it'll be our first summer here, and I can't wait.'

* * *

'Enjoy yourselves!' Amanda stood in the front porch waving off her parents, watching the steam of her breath condense in the crisp morning air.

'You too, my dear,' Robert called back, and soon their car turned left on to the lane and was gone.

Amanda was alone.

It's wellies weather, so better get on an extra pair of socks. Within minutes Amanda had also popped on her coat and grabbed her leather satchel and woolly hat. She was a newcomer, but didn't want anyone to notice if she could help it.

She had a choice – walking along the country lane or cutting across the field. She decided to walk along the lane on the way there and return home via the field. The recent flurry of snow had turned to brown sludge along the grassy verge, and there she noticed clusters of a plant she hadn't come across before. It was green and uniquely fragrant, with tall stems and tiny cream-coloured flowers. She promptly took out her wildflower book and eventually found something which looked identical. *Alexanders. And they're edible.* She snapped off a stem, inhaled deeply and smiled, delighted by her discovery. A little further along, the more familiar and unmistakable aroma of hedge garlic reached her nose. She could definitely make something tasty with that.

Countryside foraging was a major item on her growing to-do list, her interest sparked by an article in *Country Life*. She had bought the publication from a man with a stall in Walthamstow market who sold out of date magazines for a fraction of the original price. He had all sorts. She would even grab wedding magazines if available. Once she was terribly embarrassed when a colleague, who knew she wasn't even dating, spotted her at a bus stop with a copy of *Brides* magazine peeking through her thin carrier bag. 'Getting married, Amanda?' was her snide comment.

Thoughts of work colleagues and London made Amanda think of Sam. What was she doing right now? Most likely sat at the counter dealing with customers in her role as a clerk for the Midland bank. Then her mind drifted to Mark. He'd be in the office at Cartwright, Berrington and Co. She thought about how smart he was to get a job as an articled clerk, and after completing his Articles and qualifying as a solicitor, Amanda had heard it was his ambition to eventually become a partner at the firm, and no one in Sam's family doubted he would. His mother was so proud of him, and his father would have been overjoyed to see how well he was doing. Sam said Mark was so clever that not even a bully at work who was giving no end of trouble could prevent him from impressing the partners. And they were not the only ones to be impressed. Amanda wasn't sure exactly what it was about him that she admired so much. His intellect? His thoughtful manner? It could easily be his dark brown eyes, or simply his handsome face. No, Amanda thought, if she had to decide what impressed her most it was his smile. Shy, but also quietly confident. It was hard to describe, but she had no trouble visualising it in her mind's eye.

It was a short walk into the village centre and she soon reached her destination. The busiest area was around the post office where she saw several people milling about. She smiled and said hello to a couple of elderly ladies waiting outside having a chat, so engrossed in conversation that she only received back a cursory 'good morning'. Beside them was an old gentleman sitting on a bench, wrapped up in a scarf, thick coat and woolly hat and sipping a hot drink from a chipped enamel mug. He remained seated once the ladies dispersed, firmly established in his position.

In the post office window were notices, including a local gardening service, a knitting and crochet club, and some recently born kittens needing a home. Amanda was thinking to herself how much she'd love to see those tiny moggies and wondering what colours they were, when the old man spoke.

'Good marning, young lady, not seen you around dese parrts before.'

'Oh hello,' replied Amanda, surprised by both the unexpected greeting and the broad accent.

'I'm Edward Walder, Eddie to everyone who knows me.'

Amanda smiled politely at the kindly gentleman with the toad-like figure. 'Hello Mr Walder, I'm Amanda. My parents and I have just moved into the village,' she said.

'Oh yes, my lurve,' Eddie smiled, holding firm the walking stick held upright between his legs. 'I recollect that old Miss Baldwin's house had sold and they say folk from Lunnun 'ave moved in. She were a fine lady and as good a person as ever lived in this village. I'd known her since I were a boy.'

Amanda sensed she would be spending some time talking to Eddie and was glad she wasn't in a hurry. His eyes sparkled as he spoke in his rolling Sussex accent, and she was happy not to rush away.

'It would have been lovely to have met her, Mr ...' Amanda tried to recollect the name she had just been told.

Eddie leaned forward and smiled broadly. 'Walder, it's Walder, but call me Eddie. You're living in Rosy's old home and so you're no stranger arrfter all.'

'Thanks Eddie,' Amanda said, her curiosity sparked. 'What was she like? Rosy, I mean.'

'Oh Rosy were always ...' Eddie paused to gather his thoughts, 'Rosy were always ... chipper.' He laughed warmly at the memory of her. Amanda didn't know what chipper meant, but guessed it was something good. 'She were the last of her eight brothers and sisters, and by and by that old woman were all alone in Marshywood, save for Tricky, her old German shepherd. Rosy died so sudden,' Eddie said with a faraway look. 'She were 95, but always so sprightly, sitting outside 'er front porch talking to all the good folks who'd be passing by – then one day, she were gone.' He sniffed and ran his hand across his nose. There was a pause and Eddie seemed lost in thought. Just as Amanda was thinking she wouldn't be disappointed if she managed to reach Rosy's age, he suddenly perked up. 'You're mighty purty, if you don't mind me saying,' he said looking animated. Amanda smiled self-consciously and Eddie extended his hand and looked slightly embarrassed. 'Oh, Miss Amanda, I didn't mean to make ya blush, young lady. I do beg your pardon.'

'It's fine, Eddie, really it is, and thanks for telling me about Rosy and the cottage.'

Eddie leaned on his stick and pushed himself up with a groan.

'I've been sitting 'ere far too long and it isn't the warmest of springs. Can't chat to all an' sundry all day, no matter how charming they aarr when there's chores to be done. It sure does keep me young doing all the sweepin' and washin' at home. Since my Ethel died I've lived with my darrter and son-in-law down the lane over that way.' He pointed with a nobbly finger. 'They look arf'er me, give me meat and two veg and the like, but they expect sup'n in return, so I don't get away with not doing my share o' the chores.'

Amanda thought Eddie must be 85 at least, so being fit enough to do chores was impressive. 'It was nice to meet you, Eddie. Hope to see you soon.'

'Yes, young lady, I hope so. Cheerio, my dear, and I wish you every happiness living 'ere – arrfter all, it's done me no harm, and plenty of good, I'd say.' He gave Amanda a warm smile and then slowly ambled away as she entered the post office.

The letter in her hand was to Sam. The phone was yet to be connected at Marshywood, and the nearest phone box was the other side of the village. Even if it was closer, standing in a telephone booth on a chilly evening shoving 10 pences into the slot every time the pips went didn't appeal. Writing also had the added advantage of having clear costs from the outset. Telephone bills were expensive, and now her father was retired, they had to budget tightly. The two friends would have no difficulty being on the phone for hours, if given the chance, but Amanda was free to ramble on as much as she wanted in a letter, all in the comfort of her bedroom. It was almost like having a penpal, and Amanda had always wanted one of those.

After purchasing a stamp, the matronly woman behind the counter promptly popped the sealed envelope into the post bag. 'You're the young lady who's just moved into Miss Baldwin's house, aren't you?' she stated with confidence, leaving Amanda wondering how on earth she knew. Welcome to Magham Down. Please pass on my regards to your parents. I'm Phyllis, Mrs Phyllis Stratton, postmistress since 1967.' Sounding very official she gave Amanda one last glance before looking straight over her shoulder to serve the next customer.

Making her departure, Amanda thought she could hear tittle-tattle in hushed tones, and she turned around to see the person who had been standing behind her, a tall thin-faced woman with small eyes at the counter, staring back at her, as was Phyllis. Seeing Amanda facing them, they immediately averted their gaze.

That's funny, she thought, brushing off her feelings of discomfort. She was sure it was nothing.

She soon approached an unorthodox-looking church. The sign revealed St Mark's was founded in 1890, and it called itself a mission hall, which sounded grand, considering its diminutive appearance. It appeared to be constructed of green painted corrugated iron, and although not a traditional building, was very endearing, reminding her of the church in *Little House on the Prairie*. Two churches in a village this size seemed unusual, she thought, knowing there to be another place of worship, the Ebenezer Strict Baptist Chapel, a little further along the road.

The door was wide open and she decided to peek inside. What she saw was underwhelming, an empty room with several chairs stacked around the edges and an old piano. Not wanting to stop in case someone wondered what she was up to, she continued on her way, noticing the church's bellcote with what looked like a cracked bell inside it.

The Red Lion was now in view. Both the village pub and the church provided scope for making new friends, but when it came to her parents' preferences, Amanda knew the pub would win hands down. She thought about her own limited church-going experience and one occasion stood out in particular – Sam's baptism. It was nothing like a christening. Sam gave a speech at the front, after which she was plunged into a deep pool and this was followed by a lively and noisy service. St Mark's was bound to be more traditional, and it crossed her mind there could be another compelling reason for her to attend one day. Contrary to her self-imposed rules, she now found herself slipping into fantasy mode again. St Mark's was just about big enough to host a wedding. Mark, getting married at his namesake – how fortuitous was that?

Her last stop, the village shop, was housed within a Grade 2 listed building and was chocolate-box beautiful. It was built in the traditional Sussex style of brick with tile elevations on its upper section and had freshly painted bright, creamy white walls. Amanda had seen many pretty cottages and properties in

Magham Down, but this was the first she was free to enter. Standing outside, she compared it to her new home. Marshywood, constructed in the mid 1800s out of flint and brick, was undeniably charming, but more rustic than pretty and quaint.

As soon as she entered, she could see a small range of basic everyday groceries: tinned soups, bread, milk and so on. However, she knew exactly what she had come in for and headed over to the counter where several chocolate bars were on display. The catchy jingles for television adverts came to mind. Should she choose Aero because 'biting bubbles is better', or was she in the mood for 'the crumbliest, flakiest chocolate', because only Flake 'tastes like chocolate never tasted before'? In the end, she chose Cadburys Fruit and Nut and walked up to the large man behind the till with 'everyone's a fruit and nutcase' to the tune of Tchaikovsky's 'Dance of the Reed Flutes' playing in her head.

Amanda noticed this heavy gentleman was keeping a close eye on others in the shop. There was a young mother with a small boy whom she kept scolding for touching everything. The other customer was a tall and thin middle-aged man, who looked like a vagrant. He had a long, unkempt beard with plenty of grey, and he was picking things up, looking at them and putting them down again. Amanda jumped when the shopkeeper rolled his eyes and bellowed, 'Hey, Pickwick – are you buying something?' The man replied sheepishly, 'Not today, sir,' and, quick as a flash, exited the shop. Shortly afterwards, the mother and her screaming child, who was having a tantrum at being denied sweets, were also gone. The shop bell rang behind them as the door slammed shut, and everything became quiet.

'That'll be 12p,' the man said, looking relieved to see them go.

Amanda thought 12p was expensive, but this was a village shop and not London, after all. She opened her satchel and dug deep for her purse before handing over the coins. The shopkeeper took her cash before immediately opening a little metal container which Amanda could see was a snuff box. He pinched out a small cluster of dark powdered tobacco, lifted it to his nostril and sniffed vigorously. Like the rest of him, his nose was large and also had many thread veins, and Amanda wondered if this was caused or merely exacerbated by his habit.

He looked at her intensely. 'Live around here or just visiting?' he asked.

'I live at Marshywood, just up by Hillbrook Farm,' she replied, happy that, finally, someone didn't appear to know who she was.

'Oh, I am well aware of the whereabouts of Marshywood, since I've lived in the village all me life,' the man said, as though her words were somehow impudent. Even at this point he wasn't smiling, but instead extended his large, tobacco-stained hand, took Amanda's, and shook it with great vigour. 'Nice to meet you, Miss ...'

'Amanda, Amanda Fernsby.'

'Nice to meet you, Miss Fernsby,' he said, still shaking her hand.

'Thank you,' Amanda replied, pleased when he eventually let go.

'I'm sorry about all that racket just now. That's Mrs Davis,' he said disapprovingly, shaking his head. 'She just can't control that littl'un. And as for Pickwick, keep alert when he's about. He's not a bad soul at heart, but has been known to take a thing or two and not pay – just gotta watch him.'

'Pickwick?' Amanda asked, intrigued.

For the first time since she'd walked in, the shopkeeper smiled. 'Sorry, I mustn't forget you're not from around these parts, so you don't know that quite a few village folk have earned themselves nicknames. Do you know why I call him that and why that name took off, Amanda?' he said, leaning in.

Amanda didn't reply since it was obvious the shopkeeper already knew the answer to that question and was eager to fill her in.

'I call him that 'cos he picks me groceries from time to time, if I'm not careful. Oh, nothing pricey mind. Last week he tried to snaffle a packet of Tooty Frooties – so that's the "pick" bit taken care of, and as for the "wick", well, because I can't relax anytime he's around, he gets on mine!'

If he was such a nuisance, why was he allowed in the shop? Amanda wondered.

'I suppose you know Pickwick is a character by Mr Charles Dickens, but he weren't named after him, not at all, and I don't think he favours him either, going by a picture in a book I've seen, in fact, I'd say Pickwick looks more like Fagin. He's light-fingered like him, that's for sure.' Amanda remained quiet but had to agree, Pickwick did have a look of Fagin, at least the one in the film *Oliver!*

The shopkeeper carried on with his long-winded explanation of how Pickwick got his name and reputation. 'Anyhow, one time many years ago at the Cuckoo Fair up in Heffle …' he paused to explain more fully, 'Heffle is Heathfield and the Cuckoo Fair happens every April, a grand tradition which dates to medieval times. 'You've only just missed it, that's a pity.'

He paused again, waiting for assurance of Amanda's continued interest. 'As I was saying, many years ago Pickwick – Leonard's his actual name – was found wandering around all the stalls stealing everything – cakes, chocolate, prizes what were sweets, I even heard he'd taken a half-eaten packet of crisps – always food, and would you know, not a soul seemed to notice until all his pockets were stuffed. The poor fella stood there with a look so guilty he just emptied them pockets and gave back everything he took – at least what he'd not eaten in the meantime. And furthermore, apart from a laddie who lost a toffee apple, no one caused a ruckus and folk went easy on him. That's cause he's harmless really, more a simpleton than a criminal. But I've a business to run, and can't afford to lose even a penny chew, because it all adds up.'

Amanda was surprised Pickwick was so scrawny, despite these strange habits, and having been entertained by this little anecdote, it was now time to leave. Holding her chocolate bar she thanked the shopkeeper, said goodbye and left, marvelling at how tolerant people were in the village, feeling sure that in London poor Pickwick would have been arrested or placed in an asylum long ago.

The time flew fly by as Amanda walked around, weaving in and out of gates and over stiles, exploring the village lanes. She loved each season, but spring had been a long time coming, and she took delight at the buds on the trees, a sure sign of new beginnings, while listening to the sound of woodpeckers battering tree trunks and the call of the cuckoo.

Heading home, she walked towards a stile, aware of a mechanical hum in the distance. The sound grew louder, and soon she could see a shiny green tractor, its paintwork reflecting the sun's rays. It worked its way through the field as she approached, the hum gradually increasing to a loud clatter. Edging closer, she could just make out the face of the person inside. Expecting her neighbour, Farmer Appleby, she was surprised instead to see someone who didn't fit the description. Rather than a mature individual, it was a younger man in the driving seat, resolute and content as he set about his work.

I wonder who he is? Amanda thought in passing, as she made her way across the field towards home.

Chapter 4

'Sounds like quite a character that Eddie,' Robert concluded, his pineapple upside down cake and custard almost gone, 'and as for Pickwick, well, a strange story for an even stranger man.' Turning to Joan, Robert placed a hand on his stomach. 'Thanks for another fantastic dinner, love. Your spag bol is the best, but of course you already know that. The beef from the Hailsham butchers probably made it tastier, and I never thought it could get any better.'

'Yes Mum, it was great,' Amanda agreed.

Joan, beaming with pleasure was always glad to delight her family with her homely but basic culinary skills. The trip to town had lifted her spirits no end, and the injection of positivity still remained. Seeing people on the go while she shopped was restorative, and this meant Robert also felt upbeat. For good or ill, his wife's moods rubbed off on him, and he found himself whistling a tune as he waited for the butler sink to fill with hot water. Amanda stood up.

'I'll help with the washing up.'

'No need, I've got it in hand,' Robert replied, squirting in some washing up liquid and rolling up his sleeves.

'At least dry then, there's not enough room to drain everything.'

'Oh, go on then,' he said, vigorously scrubbing the baked-on meaty sauce from the heavy saucepan, but the moment Amanda grabbed a tea towel, there was a loud knock on the front door.

Everyone paused.

'Are you expecting anyone?' Robert asked Joan, hesitantly.

'Oh Rob, of course not. Wouldn't I have said if we were having visitors? Besides, it's gone half seven, don't you think it's a bit late?' Her countenance rapidly changed, and she grew excitable. 'I wonder who it is,' she said, her eyes wide.

'There's only one way to find out,' Robert said with a wink 'Want me to get it?'

'No, that's okay, I'm going.'

Joan jumped to her feet and headed through the small hall to the large oak door. No car had arrived along the gravel drive, they would have heard it approaching. Whoever it was must have come on foot but they had only spoken to a few people since moving in, and it was rather late in the day for a travelling salesman. Although eager to see who it was, Joan was rather tentative as she opened the door.

On the doorstep was a woman around her age, with brown hair and friendly eyes. She was carrying a wicker basket and wearing a blue and white polka dot apron tied around a somewhat old fashioned brown, stripy dress.

'Hello, I'm Victoria Appleby from the farm next door. I hope it's not a bad time to call – I'm sorry if it's a tad too soon after your arrival.'

Joan's feet were itching to lead the way. 'Not at all, please come in,' she spluttered. 'We've just finished dinner, and it's really good of you to pop by.' Joan led Victoria into the kitchen where Amanda and Robert were waiting.

'Please, sit down. Would you like a cup of tea?' Robert asked, after introductions, pulling back a chair.

'Ooh, that would be lovely, thank you, and I've brought something to go with it.'

Victoria put her basket on the table and lifted out a package wrapped in a pretty gingham cloth. Opening it, she took out a Quality Street tin. Inside it was a large fruit cake. How quaint, thought Amanda. An aproned woman carrying a basket with a cake inside wrapped in gingham. She seemed the archetypal farmer's wife.

'It looks lovely,' beamed Joan. 'Thanks so much. I love fruit cake. Is it homemade?'

'Yes, I baked it this morning. I hope you like it.'

'Oh, we're bound to,' said Robert. 'We've just had dinner but I'm sure we can manage a slice.'

Forty-five minutes later Amanda and her parents had learned that Victoria was married to Cecil Appleby and they had two sons and a daughter. Stuart, 23, was a Cambridge graduate, his brother Dean, who was two years younger, worked full-time on the farm, and 14-year-old Millicent, known as Millie, was extremely bright and had earned a scholarship to Moira House, a private girls' school in Eastbourne. Victoria said she and Cecil were blessed to be able to rely on Dean to keep the family farm going. Amanda's mind drifted to the tractor and the young man at the wheel she had seen the day before. That must have been Dean, hard at work.

'That boy is a total godsend,' Victoria said, drawing her hands together with a single clap. 'We don't know what we'd do without him. He's up at the crack of dawn with the livestock or out in the fields, all through the year. We're a mixed farm and raise most of our animal feed ourselves. That's pretty unusual these days. Economies of scale and mega farming is increasingly what it's all about.'

She launched into a detailed explanation of how farming was changing. Neither Amanda nor her parents grasped everything that was said, but before they could seek clarification, Victoria looked at her watch. 'We've not had dinner yet, would you believe? I've got a stew in the oven so I'd better be off. The main reason I'm here is to ask you to Sunday lunch – if you're free, that is.'

Robert glanced at Joan, who was smiling happily.

'That would be lovely. What time should we come?' she asked.

'Shall we say one o'clock? The men at home always take Sunday afternoon off if they can, and they'll have done the muckspreading by then, so I'd say around one will be fine.'

Amanda was hoping the muck wouldn't spread to her meal.

'That's so kind of you, we'll be there,' said Robert.

'Oh, I almost forgot,' Victoria added. 'Millie has just left for a school trip to Bayeux, so she'll be in France unfortunately. The hours she spends at school, not just in lessons but also travelling there and back, takes up so much of her time, but it'll be worth it. She's got her heart set on becoming a surgeon, you know. Imagine that, my little girl a surgeon! Anyway, Cecil, the boys and I look forward to seeing you on Sunday.' She swiftly scooped up her Quality Street tin and bid her goodbyes.

'A surgeon. That's so impressive,' Amanda remarked, when they were alone again. Robert nodded his agreement. 'Victoria seems nice,' she added, thinking she might be a suitable friend for her mother.

'I guess,' said Joan doubtfully. 'She seems down to earth and friendly enough, but I really hope she isn't going to keep popping by uninvited. I'm not used to that sort of thing.'

Amanda wasn't totally surprised by her mother's reaction. Reconciling a desperate desire for company while being fiercely private wasn't always easy. Although Amanda was keen to make new friends herself, she didn't want to become anxious about it and instead focussed on the great opportunity she had to indulge in her favourite hobbies before landing a job.

Her new bedroom was larger than the one she had left behind, with plenty of space to store her partially squeezed tubes of oil paints, canvases, and her set of watercolours. She was itching to take out her paintbrush, but tonight she had other plans. On their trip into town, Joan and Robert had rented a TV set with a video cassette recorder. Amanda had always wanted a VCR, ever since seeing the one at her aunt and uncle's house, but they were ridiculously expensive. She was delighted when Uncle Charles had told her to record something. 'Anything you like, Amanda. Go on, test it out.' She had soon found herself rewinding and replaying Steve Harley and Cockney Rebel's 'Make Me Smile', which she had recorded from a glam rock programme. The only dampener was her parents were now renting a VHS recorder whereas her uncle and aunt owned a Betamax model outright, which was bound to prove itself better and longer lasting, like almost everything else they owned. Since they were only renting, however, Amanda decided that longevity didn't matter quite so much because they could get it replaced for free.

After a tuning hiccup, and several aerial adjustments, the TV was finally up and running, but Robert, having had his fill of technology, promised to tackle the video recorder the following day. Not having everything set up that evening didn't frustrate Amanda too much. There would be plenty of opportunities to watch television in the days ahead. She was particularly looking forward to indulging in daytime television: *The Sullivans*, *Crown Court* ... and for childhood nostalgia, she could revisit *Play School*, *Jackanory* and the schools programme *Picture Box* with its haunting enigmatic theme tune reminiscent of fairgrounds. Leaving her parents in front of the television, she walked upstairs to her room, clutching her favourite magazine *Jackie*, and shut the door behind her. There she lay down on her bed, stretched and then sat up, drawing her legs towards her and hugging them. She switched on her radio. Blondie's *Sunday Girl* was playing and singing along to the tinny sound, she opened her magazine at the agony aunts page and started to read.

Dear Cathy and Claire,

I get so depressed when I think about growing up and getting married – the thing all girls are supposed to want. My 19-year-old sister is married and I don't fancy her life at all. Her and Jim and the baby live in one room, she never cleans up and there are nappies drying everywhere. She used to be pretty and fun, now she's a mess and never stops moaning. Is this what I'm going to be like in four years' time?

This girl sounds terribly afraid of marriage, thought Amanda, and feeling unable to identify with her conundrum, she quickly moved on.

Dear Cathy and Claire,
My boyfriend's brother is 25 and he's married, he's really nice to me and puts his arm around me when we go to visit him and his wife. I keep hoping he's going to ask me out. Do you think he will?

Amanda couldn't believe what she was reading. 'She needs her head testing. A married man who's also her boyfriend's brother, for goodness sake!' she muttered. She moved on to the next letter.

Dear Cathy and Claire,
I'm 13 and have a boyfriend I've been going out with for the past four months, but he's never kissed me, in fact he hasn't even held my hand! What do you think I should do?

Thirteen? Amanda was horrified. Although she had already known it deep down, it suddenly hit her that the magazine in her hand was popular with 13 year olds. *What's wrong with me? I may as well be 13. I've never been kissed, or even held a boy's hand, apart from Mark's at the funeral. This 13-year-old is more experienced than me!* What did Cathy and Claire have to say?

Poor thing, he's probably dead scared to make the first move. It may be hard for you to believe when you're just sitting there waiting for things to happen, but imagine if you had to be the one to decide exactly when and where and how to show physical affection.

That's true enough, thought Amanda. *Boys have it hard too, but at least they don't have to be passive, meekly waiting for someone to ask them out, not like us girls, and it's incredibly frustrating.*

She thought back to when she was around that age, and recalled a school disco when she was twelve. It was Christmas, and her first year of junior high school. The boys' and girls' schools got together at Christmas discos, and Amanda had been looking forward to it for months, especially after seeing the disco scene in the film *Melody* starring Jack Wilde and Mark Lester.

She took ages to get ready and felt very pretty in her vibrant floral pink and orange mini dress with long white socks and white shoes. She remembered her father smiling proudly and saying, 'Manda, my dear, you do look bonny,' and she arrived, full of eagerness and trepidation, greeting her friends with giggles as they passed several pairs of male eyes. She desperately wanted to impress. While patiently waiting to be asked to dance, she giggled with her companions and when the chart topper, Little Jimmy Osmond's 'Long Haired Lover from Liverpool' started to play, she swayed happily along to the light-hearted tune with her friends. Then, the time came for the final song, 'Puppy Love',which was delivered by another Osmond brother, this time Donny. As the intro built up to a crescendo, peaking with 'puppy luh uh uh huv…' Amanda was surprised to see how quickly boys were pairing up with girls. Her fair-haired friend Karen had her hand immediately grabbed by a good-looking boy, and her other friend Anne, also popular with the lads, had gone to the toilet, so suddenly Amanda felt quite alone.

The music was loud, yet she couldn't help overhearing a boy who was standing behind her say to another, 'What about her? Are you going to ask her to dance?' Amanda stood upright, her young heart beating furiously, hoping, wondering what she was going to hear.

'What, the goofy, ginger girl? She's not my type. Anyway, she's a bit fat, don't you think?' came the reply. The next thing she heard was laughter.

Amanda felt almost unbearable pain welling up inside, so much so that Donny's repeated calls for help in the song became the desperate cry of her heart. It was obvious that they were talking about her. No one else in the room was without a partner, and she suddenly realised how she looked to boys. Rather than puppy love, all they could see was puppy fat.

When she got to 15, the chubbiness had all but disappeared, braces had straightened her teeth, and she began to embrace her red hair, which a friend of Joan's had described as 'russet and unusual'. By the time Amanda was 16 she was tall and slim, attracting male attention and wolf whistles by the truckload, but by then the damage had been done.

So here she was, seven years later, in the middle of the countryside, with just her mum, dad and cat for company. She'd had plenty of crushes. There was a chap in a youth club she had once summoned up the courage to attend, for instance, but with lots of girls chasing him, he had the pick of the bunch, and so he chose someone else. Would Mark also turn out to be a pipe dream, especially now she lived even further away? *He'll most likely forget me*, Amanda thought soberly, although if he did visit soon, perhaps, just perhaps ...

'Goodnight Manda,' called Robert as he and Joan walked past her closed door.

'Night Dad, night Mum.'

'Night love,' replied Joan.

Bedtime already! Amanda looked at her clock radio. Where did the time go? Would the days, months and years ahead, and perhaps her entire life, go by quickly too? Or would things drag, because she had nowhere to go, and no friends to do anything with? Amanda closed her eyes, feeling an ache starting to rise up within, before opening them again with a start. 'I won't let myself get low,' she mouthed furiously, 'I've seen what that does to Mum.' But something stopped her from getting ready for bed and her emotions still weighed heavily. Just a few days ago she was full of expectation and excited about the days ahead. She had loved exploring the village, and on Sunday she had an invitation to lunch. Maybe, just maybe, either Stuart or Dean would turn out to be gorgeous and available. You never know, it certainly wasn't impossible.

It tickled Amanda to imagine two chivalrous brothers fighting for her hand, yet her amusement was short-lived. Ever since she had known she was leaving London, emotions had been building with no release, and now, after recalling an unhappy event, past memories were becoming enmeshed with future fears. *Stop it Amanda. You're fine, you're absolutely fine.* She was determined not to give in, but then it came, like a dam bursting. She cupped her face in her hands, but that proved to be just the beginning. When she finally and fully gave way to her emotions, throwing herself down onto her bed, her copy of *Jackie* tossed aside, the barriers she had erected broke, like sea defences in a fierce storm. Burying her weary head in her arms, at last she began to feel comforted by the sound of her own voice as she sobbed into her pillow.

* * *

The letter dropped on the mat and Sam grabbed it from her younger brother's hands.

'Give it here!' she snapped.

'Don't snatch. That's rude!' he shouted back, but it was too late. Sam was already running up the stairs. She opened her bedroom door, sat on her bed under a poster of a smiling David Essex, and eagerly ripped open the envelope. She unfolded the pages and began to read.

Dear Sam,

How's things? Can't believe we're actually here and it's final! The journey was slower than usual with the roads still icy. Stopped off at a Little Chef on the way and had a ham, egg and chips. On the table next to us was a guy who looked like a trucker (think Yorkie advert!) who kept staring at me, even though Mum and Dad were right there. As we were leaving he puckered his lips as if kissing me, the cheeky blighter. What's worse, he looked at least 35, and suspiciously like he had a wife and kids at home!

It's really, really quiet around here and if it wasn't for an owl hooting last night it would have been silent after dark. I don't know when I'll manage to get a job, but I can wait – you know me, give me some trees, wildflowers, birds and creepy crawlies and I'm in seventh heaven.

How's all the family? Or should I say, one in particular? I won't mention any names, but hope your mum has been behaving herself and not singing my praises too much. He'll get suspicious and think, why is everyone trying to palm me off with this girl? There must be something wrong with her! Seriously, I can't wait for you to visit. If you bring a friend with you 'hint hint' you could share with me and he could have the spare room. Who am I trying to kid though, Sam? Mum and Dad won't want any male friends under the same roof overnight. They trust me, of course, and they're not too old-fashioned, but I just know they'd prefer a bloke get a room elsewhere (thankfully, there's a guest house in the village), especially as, to be honest, I get the feeling the penny's dropped and they already know I like Mark. There, Sam. I've now confessed, but don't you DARE show him this letter, but I know you're a good friend and wouldn't dream of doing something so cruel.

Anyway, our phone will be connected up next week so we can have a chat soon, but don't let that stop you writing back. I really want to write regularly, there's something really special about sending and receiving letters, don't you think? By the way, how are you getting on with that new guy at work? Paul, I think you said his name was. Has he asked you out yet? Did the flashing a bit of leg technique work, or is he oblivious to your numerous charms? (Hee hee). Can't wait to hear from you.

Love, your bestest friend,

Amanda

Sam put the letter down and smiled. *I must let her know I've gone off Paul since I got close and noticed he has the breath of a thousand camels,* she thought.

It was Saturday, and Sam could hear her brothers watching *Tiswas* on the television in the living room. She considered going out and then thought about staying in, and neither appealed. It wasn't as though she normally saw Amanda on Saturdays, but today Sam felt low, knowing her friend could no longer simply pop by. When should she visit Sussex? If Amanda got transferred to another Woolworths, she'd have to work Saturdays and book time off, just after starting a new job. So, travelling down sooner rather than later might be sensible. However, Sam didn't feel comfortable visiting too soon. Best to let them all settle in first, she reasoned.

She opened her diary. Booking time off work some months ahead should allow sufficient time for Amanda to settle into a new job before needing to request holiday leave, but it wasn't just their diaries which needed coordinating. Sam had taken seriously her friend's request to bring Mark along. Besides, Sam preferred to be with someone for the journey. She felt nervous travelling on her own to the countryside, wondering if her black skin might attract some unwanted attention. Five years ago, when Sam was 14, her family went away to Cornwall, the first holiday her parents had been able to afford. She was dismayed to find herself and her family the centre of attention for all the wrong reasons, and felt very uncomfortable throughout. In the end, she couldn't wait to go back home to London, and now Amanda was no longer there with her, she hoped the physical distance wouldn't also grow into an emotional one.

Thoughts of Cornwall reminded Sam how ironic it was that the first thing she saw on the television when she got home was the sitcom *Love Thy Neighbour*. It made Sam and her parents laugh to see the warring next door neighbours, one black man and one white, hurl insults at each other while their more amiable wives did their best to keep the peace and reduce racial tensions. Sam and Amanda joked about buying houses next door to each other when they got married, saying that, knowing their luck, their husbands would fight even more than the infamous TV characters. 'If he's good-looking and takes me out to dinner every week I can live with that,' Sam said, making Amanda smile. As she thought about the fun times they'd had, Sam's throat felt dry. There was no chance they'd be neighbours now.

Sam tried to talk herself out of feeling low. After all, Amanda could get on her nerves. She could be too soft for her own good and annoying when she got into a panic over some small thing. Sometimes Sam just wanted to shake her and tell her to get a grip. But Sam knew she wasn't perfect either, and somehow Amanda had the knack of bringing out the best in her friend, and knew how to help her see reason by curbing her tendency to fly off the handle and jump to the wrong conclusions. When Sam sat opposite a sour-faced woman at the Queen's Silver Jubilee street party she was irked by her rudeness and was all set to give her a piece of her mind. It was Amanda who calmed her down. 'You never know, maybe she's not feeling well,' she said, and Sam bit her tongue. Weeks later, not only was that same woman on the panel at her interview at the Midland Bank, Sam later found out she was going through a messy divorce. To this day, she couldn't thank her best friend 'Mand' enough.

Now to that letter. Sam searched a drawer for writing paper but all she could find was a pad with a picture of The Wombles at the top of each sheet. *That'll have to do,* she thought, and started to scribble a letter. She soon became distracted by the closing credits of *Tiswas*, and then hot on its heels was her mother Precious singing along to one of her favourite albums, Elvis Presley's *Sacred Gospel Songs.* 'There's always so much blinkin' noise in this house.' Sam muttered to herself. She took a deep breath and held it in for a second, wondering how she was supposed to concentrate, thinking she'd swap with Amanda for the peace and quiet of the countryside any day. But that wasn't going to work, since her noisy family would be there too.

As the record played, Sam braced herself for the scratched bit, and before long 'his hand in mine – his hand in mine – his hand in mine' repeated over and over. Sam sighed and looked upwards. *How long before Mum deals with it?*

Eventually Precious intervened by picking up the needle and setting it back down on the LP, moving the track forward.

Maybe, just maybe I'll start this letter, Sam thought, trying to block out Elvis' melodic voice. *I want Mand to get it before Wednesday so I can ask for some annual leave as soon as possible. Summer dates will get booked up really soon, and I imagine it'll be the same for Mark. It's May already, so we'd better get a move on.'*

Chapter 5

It was Sunday afternoon. Amanda looked in the mirror and made final adjustments to her hair, attaching a few colourful hairpins. After a tearful end to Friday, Saturday turned out to be much more positive, with much of her day spent at home. Looking over at the landscape painting now sitting on the chest of drawers in her bedroom, Amanda was reminded of her activities the previous day.

Prompted by the sunlight, she had taken out her watercolours to paint her first piece of Sussex art: the stunning view which was visible from the garden terrace. It was invigorating to be sitting outside, despite a fresh breeze, and she was kept extra warm by a thick knitted shawl wrapped around her.

The garden melodies gave a serene backdrop to her craft, and the song of a blackbird heralded summer in its own unique way. House sparrows, greenfinches and dunnocks fluttered and hopped, and the sighting of a green woodpecker on the lawn was the icing on the cake. Marshywood was clearly a haven for birds, and a perfect place to learn their songs and calls.

She had once borrowed from the library a birdsong LP by Victor C Lewis, and tried hard to learn the sounds, but despite there being no shortage of birds in Leytonstone, with regular sightings of collared doves, robins and starlings, the opportunity to attune herself to countryside birds such as bullfinches, redstarts and turtle doves, just wasn't there. *I really must listen to that LP again*, she thought, dipping her paintbrush into a jar of water. *Maybe I'll find it in the local town library.*

Now Sunday had arrived, Amanda was looking forward to joining her neighbours for lunch. She stood up and glanced at her reflection in the full-length mirror. The sundress with accompanying matching jacket accentuated her shapely figure. Joan had made the outfit for her from a Simplicity dress pattern. Now Amanda was at home during the day, she hoped to pick up sewing skills from her mother. The warm tangerine colour suited her complexion, and was perfectly offset by the darker tones in her hair.

Although not a fan of makeup, since this was a special occasion, with two young men present, she wanted to make a special effort, despite not having the faintest idea if they'd be worth it, or even available. Fortunately, she was able to convince herself she wasn't too fussed, whatever the case, in the same way she avoided getting her hopes up with Mark. However, just a little mascara, some rouge, and her sheer pink bubble-gum flavoured lip gloss would make her feel more dressed for the occasion. Eye shadow and bright lipstick were overkill, she mused. They could easily tip her over into clown territory. But, in any case, she didn't want to look like Miss World, all she wanted was to enjoy herself without feeling unduly self-conscious in the presence of new people.

* * *

Amanda, Joan and Robert left the country lane and walked up the drive to Hillbrook Farm. They passed impressive oak trees and a large pond with several ducks and geese, plus a few coots swimming contentedly. At first the farmhouse looked grand, but as they walked towards it they noticed that the traditional, timber-framed building, showed subtle signs of disrepair. Window frames were worn, roof tiles missing, and a few outbuildings had rotting doors and cracks running through the walls. Even so, none of this detracted from the overall sense of grandeur, and when Robert lifted the iron knocker, they all felt somewhat daunted as they stood, waiting for a response.

After some time, the door opened to reveal a man with a sober, earnest expression. He was tall, with eyes that squinted as though the sun was shining in his face. That same face gave away that he was an outdoor type, and although in his late forties to early fifties, his face was wrinkled. Despite being past his prime, there was something appealing about him. He reminded Amanda of Clint Eastwood. She could imagine him wearing a cowboy hat and poncho, and was sure that in his younger days he would have been attractive.

'I'm Cecil, please come in, lovely to have you over.'

He led the way through the house and Amanda eagerly took in her surroundings. In the same way some houses are deceptively spacious – like Sam's terraced house back in London – this period farmhouse was smaller than its outside would suggest, but was nonetheless much larger than Marshywood. As they were guided through the hall, Amanda noticed heavy exposed beams, old photographs and dark, antique furniture.

'Sit down, please.' Cecil motioned towards comfortable seats by a large inglenook fireplace. 'Victoria will be with you in a moment, she's just finishing up.'

'Thank you,' Robert and Joan said in unison, as Amanda settled into a stripy brown chair.

'Can I get you some tea or coffee, or something stronger while you wait? an aperitif perhaps?' His noble effort at hospitality couldn't hide an abrupt tone and a hint of awkwardness.

Joan opted for a glass of sherry, and Robert decided he'd join her. If there was going to be wine with the meal, Amanda wanted to save herself for that, since being only an occasional drinker, that would be more than enough for her. 'I'm fine for the moment, thank you,' she said and smiled politely as Cecil walked over to the well-stocked, teak drinks cabinet.

'Well, if you're sure,' he replied, turning briefly before picking up a bottle of Harvey's Bristol Cream and two small crystal glasses.

At that moment Victoria swiftly entered the sitting room with a rushed smile, wiping her hands on her apron. 'Hello, so glad you could make it. I'm sorry I was in the kitchen when you arrived.' Joan, presenting Victoria with a gift of Terry's All Gold, quickly assured her that wasn't a problem. However, after expressing her gratitude for the gift, Victoria still sounded flustered. 'Had to check on the Yorkshires but I think they're about done now. Let's proceed to the dining room, Stuart's already there. I asked him to finish setting the table.' She paused. 'Oh, and also, I'm sorry to say Dean couldn't make it. He told me just yesterday he was going to Carolyn's house for lunch with her family.'

Seeing curiosity on her guests' faces, Victoria explained. 'Sorry, I didn't mention it, did I? Carolyn is Dean's girlfriend. Typical of young folks, eh? He leaves it to the last minute to tell me he won't be here for lunch. So, we've no Millie and no Dean. Anyway, not to worry, at least Stuart's here. Come this way.'

Amanda and her parents were promptly led past the impressive open fire and ushered into the dining room. On the walls was wood panelling, and the floor was varnished and dark. Was it walnut? Amanda wasn't sure. Whatever it was, it looked lavish. In the centre of the room was another large fireplace, this time with a woodburning stove inside it. Eight chairs were set around an imposing oak dining table. At the end of the room was a tall window with floor-length red velvet curtains on either side. Looking out at the garden was a tall man with mid-brown hair, neatly styled, his hands clasped behind his back. Once he realised he had company, he spun around and faced the guests with interest, his eyes on Amanda in particular.

'Hello, I'm Stuart – which I assume you already know.' He greeted them with a smile which fell somewhere between his mother's vivacity and his father's restraint.

Amanda's first impressions were that Stuart was attractive, in that he was tall and in good shape, with a fanciable face, although she wasn't particularly attracted to him. He looked mature, and older than 23, but without doubt, it was his eyes that spoke volumes. Trying not to judge, she thought she could detect an air of flirtatiousness, suggesting he might be a player, and before long, Carly Simon's 'Nobody Does it Better,' Bond theme popped into Amanda's music loving mind.

In no time, lunch had begun, and apart from Victoria rushing to and from the kitchen, exclaiming 'hold on', and 'please excuse me, I forgot…', not much could be heard, apart from the gentle clattering of knives and forks.

'This is delicious roast beef,' Robert said between mouthfuls, genuinely impressed but also keen to break an awkward silence.

'Thanks so much, one of our own, you know,' Victoria replied looking pleased. 'We supply Bryant Family Butchers in Hailsham.'

Despite feeling disquieted that Robert had praised someone else's cooking, Joan added a few complimentary words of her own. 'Yes, it is good. We bought some wonderful lamb from that same butcher's on Friday, and minced beef which made a delicious bolognese, didn't we, Robert?'

'We did indeed, it was delicious.'

Victoria smiled proudly. 'The lamb is also ours and the mince was likely to be too, although, I can't completely vouch for that. Bryant's will sometimes get mince for their beef burgers from Stilehurst Farm in Herstmonceux, but generally we supply the meat for most of their prime cuts of beef and lamb.'

'You could really taste quality in that mince,' Robert added.

'Then it was most definitely ours,' said Stuart, with a cocky smile.

'What's the history of this house?' Joan enquired after a pause in the conversation. 'It looks old. Is it listed?'

'No, and it's not as old as it looks,' replied Cecil. 'In that sense, it's a bit like Victoria,' he smiled, wiping his mouth with a napkin.

Cecil's attempt at a joke fell flat, and although no one laughed, he was entertained by it. Fortunately, Victoria didn't seem in the least bothered, although Stuart looked distinctly unimpressed, and Joan and Robert squirmed a little in their seats. Only Amanda was quietly amused, finding Cecil a rather odd but interesting character.

Unfazed by the unspoken disapproval, Cecil continued, 'Hillbrook House is actually quite new. My father started building it when he bought the land in the late 1920s, a few years before I was born.'

'Oh really, was your father a builder?' Amanda asked, wanting to participate in the conversation.

'Oh no, not at all, he farmed, like myself. No, he didn't actually physically build it, but chose the style, which is based on a Wealden Hall House, a type of vernacular medieval timber-framed structure, which is traditional around here.'

Since Robert was interested in history and a former librarian, he knew what 'vernacular' meant, but he wasn't sure his wife or daughter did, so he chipped in: 'Sussex has so many historic buildings built from traditional and local building materials. It's wonderful to see.'

'I'll say,' replied Cecil, 'much of the oak used here was sourced from the nearby Hillbrook woods.'

'That would be a great place to visit,' Joan responded eagerly. 'We love woodlands, especially Amanda, don't you dear?' Amanda smiled and nodded.

'I'm afraid that particular woodland is now private,' Cecil replied, 'but there's plenty more, and we've got twelve acres of our own on the farm which you're welcome to access anytime. It's carpeted with bluebells at the moment, so looking particularly lovely.'

'We'd love to Cecil,' said Joan. She looked at Amanda and smiled.

Robert turned to Stuart. 'So you're at least the third generation of farmers at Hillbrook, and I hear you finished university just last year.'

'That's right,' Stuart replied, swallowing a mouthful of food. 'I was at King's College Cambridge reading philosophy, although, to be honest, I'm not really academic. I went thinking it'd be a hoot,' he sniffed nonchalantly. 'I never really thought about what I'd do afterwards, but after graduating and travelling for six months, I've decided on the army.'

Sadness briefly fell across Victoria's face, and she extended her hand towards the food. 'More wine or roast potatoes anyone? Or beef or vegetables?'

While extra portions were being served, Amanda felt uneasy, not only for Victoria after noticing her reaction, but also her father, knowing that the mere mention of the word 'army' was unsettling for Robert. She was surprised to hear him delve deeper.

'Oh really, that's interesting. What made you decide on the army, young man?' he asked.

After a swig of wine, Stuart responded, 'University left me disillusioned, if I'm to be honest, although I have to admit, it was fun, and most of my friends now have successful careers. Being at Cambridge felt like a meal ticket, but I didn't like the lack of purpose and sense of entitlement people seemed to have – taking everything for granted and all that. So I left, determined that I wanted to do something worthwhile.'

Victoria kept her eyes down, with Stuart either oblivious or indifferent to her discomfort.

'I'm not saying farming isn't worthwhile. I love the farm, I grew up here and it's been a big part of my life, but after university I travelled abroad and saw other places. After that, I knew I couldn't stay here forever. Travel opened up my eyes to so many new things – food, languages, not to mention people, plus the army teaches new skills too. At uni you work on your own, but in the army it's all about teamwork, and you also learn discipline and a good work ethic. And that's coming from someone who didn't do much work at university.' Suppressing a smile, Stuart cleared his throat, 'but I'm afraid that's a story for another day.'

Not having been to university herself, Amanda was soaking up his words like a sponge.

'It's not that farming is boring,' he added, 'there's too much bloody work to be bored.' Victoria flinched. 'I know. Language. Sorry Mum,' he apologised robotically.

Unlike Victoria, Cecil didn't appear bothered by Stuart's mild profanity, but nevertheless he was obviously angered by something. *Is he annoyed because Stuart won't stop talking?* Amanda thought, as she listened to him continue to extol the virtues of military life.

'Everyone likes a challenge, don't they, and I'm not sure farming will give me that, but in the armed forces I could literally be fighting for survival and that's something worth experiencing.'

By now Victoria was looking crestfallen, and Robert, feeling dangerously close to being asked about his time of service, thought the subject had gone on long enough. Although curious to know if Cecil had fought, he was happy to assume that he and his father had availed themselves of their farming exemptions. Much to Robert's relief, Stuart fell silent, and unlike his brother Charles, who would have jumped at the chance to discuss all things military, no one present wanted to prolong the topic. Once the meal had been eaten, the conversation turned once again to the farm woodland, after which Victoria returned from the kitchen with a large Black Forest gateau, which she sliced and began to serve up.

All appeared relatively peaceful until Stuart unexpectedly piped up again, much to Robert's dismay.

'The army's not all about fighting, you know. People forget, or fail to appreciate, it's also very much about peacekeeping and humanitarian efforts.' He appeared to be making one last ditch attempt to turn around the negativity he had perceived, but still failed to win anyone over.

Cecil finally stopped seething and spoke up. 'Stuart isn't really keen to keep the family farm going. Not like our Dean who works tirelessly day and night.'

You could hear a pin drop and Stuart looked furious, leaving Amanda with little doubt that Cecil had hit a raw nerve.

'True. Just like our Southdown sheep, there's always a black one in the family,' Stuart replied, attempting a smile, but his words came through gritted teeth. 'You know as well as I do how sorry I am to disappoint you, Father.'

Cecil held a spoon in his clenched fist and stared at Stuart who looked back disdainfully. Joan didn't know where to look. 'This is a delicious Black Forest gateau, Victoria. Did you make it yourself?' she said, in an effort to change the subject.

'I'm afraid not, I just didn't have the time. I grabbed it from the cash-and-carry.' Despite her solid reply, Victoria's voice wavered.

'Good choice anyhow,' Robert said encouragingly.

'Please, have another slice, there's plenty here.' Victoria smiled, keeping her eyes fixed on the cake rather than meeting anyone's gaze, and somehow a semblance of decorum was eventually restored.

After returning to the sitting room for tea and coffee, Stuart said his goodbyes. 'Because Dean is at Carolyn's, I've a few jobs to get on with, and the Border collies have been left alone for far too long, they'll be running riot. Got to go, I'm afraid, but it was really good meeting you all.' He gave Amanda a quick smile. 'I hope you enjoy living here. There's not many our age – by that I mean people in their twenties – but there's often something going on at the Old Sussex Tavern in Hailsham, especially on a Saturday night, so I'll try to keep you posted.'

'Thanks, that would be nice,' Amanda smiled, happy to have been included.

'Bye everyone, see you around.' Stuart was gone.

* * *

As they walked across the driveway past the outbuildings, Amanda spotted Stuart leaning against a dilapidated shed puffing away on a cigarette. *So much for looking after the dogs*, she thought. *No wonder he wanted to get away so desperately.* Then, acutely aware she was judging him yet again, she reprimanded herself.

The three talked as they walked, commenting on Hillbrook House's attractive yet somewhat run-down exterior, the warm welcome they had received, but also the air of tension which had put a slight dampener on things.

Amanda wondered what it would have been like if Dean and Millie had been there. Dean was clearly very different to Stuart. His dedication to the farm was commendable, of course, but favouritism, if that was what it was, wasn't a good thing. After all, nobody likes being a second-rate sibling.

'Mum and Dad, I'm coming out later to pick some of those,' Amanda said, pointing to the roadside. 'I'm going to have a crack at candied alexanders, using a recipe in my wildflower cookbook.'

Robert broke off a stem and sniffed. 'Careful love, make sure you know what you're doing, I'm guessing these are fine, but try not to poison yourself.'

Amanda gave a little laugh. 'I'll try to be sensible,' she replied.

Joan looked vaguely troubled. 'It's funny, isn't it,' she said. 'Walking along here with the high hedges on either side feels almost oppressive, like walking through a tunnel. We're so lucky to have such great views at home.'

At that moment a blue Land Rover slowly approached. Having not seen a single car on their way to Hillbrook House, Joan was surprised that this was now the second on their short walk back, adding to her disappointment over the absence of views. Robert could read her expressions perfectly. He knew what was going on in her head.

'Don't worry, love, it'll never get as busy as London,' he said reassuringly.

'I know that, Robert.'

Joan smiled in embarrassment that her unfounded concerns were obvious. Robert was trying to stay optimistic, but he knew full well that his wife's anxieties were rooted in her growing fear that their countryside reality would fail to live up to the dream.

The car edged closer, and soon they could see a young man behind the wheel. Amanda immediately knew she had seen him before, recognising him as the one in the tractor she had spotted just two days ago. He had a handsome, fresh face and a lovely smile, a smile which could possibly even rival Mark's, something she hadn't thought possible until now. As the Land Rover rolled past, he held up his hand to thank them for stopping and making way.

'This lane doesn't go anywhere,' Robert said, as they turned the corner and into the grounds of Marshywood. There are a few more houses and cottages down that way, but not many – and there's the farm, of course.'

'Do you think that was their younger son?' asked Joan.

'Quite possibly,' replied Robert, 'although you'd think his girlfriend would be with him, but not necessarily I suppose. Yes, that could well have been the Applebys' youngest lad.'

'I saw him driving a tractor on Friday,' said Amanda.

'Oh that's it then, most likely that's the son. Dean's his name, isn't it?'

'Yes,' Amanda said quickly, allowing her thoughts to wander as it crossed her mind that he was the first Dean she had ever met.

'Well, if that's him,' Robert replied, 'he seems like a pleasant young man.'

Amanda couldn't help but agree. He did look pleasant, but the hint of sibling rivalry over lunch was anything but pleasant. As Robert turned the key to open the door, the words 'seems like a pleasant young man,' echoed in her mind. *Yes, he really did*, she thought to herself, climbing the stairs to her room.

Chapter 6

Standing in Marshywood's small orchard, Amanda breathed in the heady sweet smell of the honeysuckle which weaved its way through the apple trees. She watched and listened, as industrious honeybees, fluffy, golden and black, flitted in and out of the tubular petals, their vibrant shades contrasting beautifully with the fuchsia-pink blooms. Had she ever, even for a moment, questioned the wisdom of her parents' bold decision to leave London and everything they had ever known, this feast for her senses would chase away any such doubts.

The orchard was largely taking care of itself, but other areas of the garden weren't doing so well. Beyond the small area of lawn by the terrace, most of the land had been left to grow wild, which wasn't surprising considering Miss Baldwin's advanced years. Brambles were aplenty, and Amanda got scratched constantly as she explored. Stinging nettles had also sprung up in various locations, and although she loved blackberries and wanted to make nettle soup, both plants were abundant in the wild so neither were an asset.

Further risk of injury came in the form of several unpruned rose bushes. Some had vicious-looking thorns, while others with less intimidating spikes had unruly, tangled branches, which acted as a trap for the unwary. Although no expert, Amanda had seen enough stunning rose gardens to know there was potential here, and even though digging the shrubs up and starting again might be the easiest thing to do, working with what was already there through patience, proper care and pruning was bound to be more rewarding.

Amanda knew that going from a low-maintenance courtyard garden to three acres had worried Robert. Charles and Pauline would be visiting soon, and since her uncle had more horticultural experience, she hoped her father could learn something from him. Charles had learned hard lessons – paid for in blood, sweat and tears – during his experimental years attempting to live off the land in Toulouse. However, she also knew that her father was probably too proud to receive guidance from his older brother. So now, with time on her hands, Amanda resolved to borrow a library book or two and learn the art of gardening herself. Her walk around the neglected three-acre plot culminated with lofty ideas of a kitchen and herb garden and other exciting projects.

Other non-gardening activities and projects were also taking shape. Joan had started teaching Amanda how to sew, and her parents had recently joined the East Sussex Ramblers Association, with their first walk, followed by a pub lunch, scheduled for Thursday. With unknown work commitments ahead, Amanda had decided against joining, but that wasn't the only reason. A photo of the group pinned to the noticeboard in the village shop revealed a posse of smiling, silver-haired retirees.

An absence of employment had failed to dampen Amanda's spirits. The recent national winter of discontent, with widespread strikes, trade union unrest, rubbish piling up in the streets, and a worrying increase in unemployment meant she could distinctly feel the nation's mood, but it didn't reflect her own. A job would come soon enough, she was confident of that, and in the meantime, she revelled in the opportunities and challenges that lay ahead.

* * *

Once again Amanda was at the Hailsham job centre. It was smaller than those she had seen in London, the orange and black signage all the more prominent in the high street of a small historic market town and its modern exterior a sharp contrast to the Unemployment Benefits Office's traditional building. She examined the cards from board to board, eliminating the vacancies one at a time, and tried her level best not to get discouraged. There were plainly fewer opportunities in this area, and those which did exist often required skills she didn't possess, such as fast typing speeds. Some were too far away or awkward to get to without transport. Other posts were male-orientated, such as bricklaying, and some were part-time, short-term or Saturday or weekend jobs. Amanda decided not to worry. Her weekly visits to the job centre and search of the classifieds in *The Sussex Express* were bound to result in something turning up.

Sam had written to say she had booked time off work and was all set to visit in August. And there was more – Mark was coming too. Amanda couldn't believe that not only Sam, but also Mark would be around for four days, and just the thought of that made her heart flutter with both intense excitement and uneasiness.

When she broke the news to her parents that Sam and Mark would be visiting, Joan's reaction was disappointingly predictable. 'Be cautious, love. You'll get yourself a reputation if you're not careful. Remember this is a small village and we're not in Leytonstone any more.' A sardonic thought crossed Amanda's mind. Had anyone told her mother this was 1979, not 1879? Although to a degree she appreciated her mother's concern, she could never allow it to influence her behaviour and was perfectly capable of making sensible decisions. She also knew that, given time, there was a good chance her mother would give in. Joan lacked the will or energy to grapple with situations, eventually becoming distracted before moving on to something else. Although striving to be a good mother, she found it hard to separate her own needs from her daughter's, and in the end, persevering through conflict was just too much effort. When it came to Mark, Amanda had no idea whether Joan's listlessness would ultimately overshadow her worries about what people might think, but at least she could hope.

* * *

It was a Tuesday in mid-June, and Joan had invited Victoria over to Marshywood for tea and a chat. It had soon become clear that Joan had nothing to fear from Victoria making herself a nuisance by popping in and out unannounced. Instead it was becoming apparent that Victoria was the one having to find time to squeeze her in. Joan needed company. As soon as Amanda found work, Robert would be her only source of companionship, and being retired and at home all day, this prospect scared her more than she cared to admit. Joan needed more than evenings in front of the telly together watching *Tales of the Unexpected* and *Blankety Blank*. What she really longed for was to become part of the county set, with their Barbour jackets, Hunter wellies and bridge afternoons.

'Another biscuit?' Joan asked. She cowered inside, embarrassed that she hadn't found time to bake and convinced her friend would have been more organised. Victoria, oblivious to Joan's insecurities, was full of smiles as she sipped her tea and nibbled on a chocolate finger.

'I have an announcement to make, Joan,' she said, beaming proudly. 'Dean's engaged to Carolyn.'

'Oh, that's great news, Victoria. Congratulations to the happy couple. I've yet to meet Dean but it sounds like he'll make a wonderful husband.'

'Absolutely he will. He's only 21 but so sensible.' Victoria's huge smile was unable to hide her pride. 'They've been dating solidly for about a year now, but it's always been a long-standing joke between Janice and me – Janice is Carolyn's mother, by the way – that they were betrothed before they even went to school.' She paused, picked up another biscuit and licked her fingers. 'Everyone knew they'd get married one day. Carolyn is one of five children and her family were already living in the village when Cecil and I got married. Our two families used to get together when the children were young, and we've been friends with Carolyn's parents, the Mitchams, ever since. They've now moved to Windmill Hill. Do you know it?' Joan looked doubtful and then shook her head. 'Windmill Hill village is … let me see … about three miles away. It's just five or six minutes in the car, so we still get to see them regularly. Anyway, Carolyn works as a receptionist at the Western Road doctors' surgery in Hailsham. I'm guessing you've registered there?' Joan nodded. 'She's such a lovely girl. Really quiet, a bit like her mother. My only worry is they don't have much saved up, and it can be hard for young people starting out these days. I'm not sure when they'll start a family because Carolyn loves her job, but when they do, she's probably going to have to give up work, at least for a while, so Dean will have a family to support. Apart from the fact that you don't get rich in farming, he's still very young, but we managed it in our day so I'm sure they'll be okay.'

'Oh yes, I'm sure they will be fine,' Joan agreed.

'Thank goodness there's a small cottage on the farm. A planning application was finally accepted last year, making it now officially a separate dwelling, and a perfect place for them to start married life. Way back in the day, Cecil and I lived there at the time Cecil's father farmed Hillbrook. We've done a great deal to it since, and it was far less polished and much more basic in those days, plus we've extended it. It now has two bedrooms, a bathroom, a kitchen and quite a big living space, in fact, everything a growing family needs.'

'That sounds fantastic, Victoria, they're very lucky. Have they set a date yet?' Joan hoped for an invitation although she knew the chances were slim.

'There's a fair bit of preparation to be done. Young people today, they have to have this, that and the other – a good photographer, special bridesmaids' dresses, you know the score. Dean said Carolyn was even making enquiries about getting the whole thing recorded on video but I doubt they'll be able to afford that.' Victoria paused to pour milk into her teacup. 'They're aiming for mid to late January, but as soon as I've got a firm date I'll let you know, so watch this space.'

'January? Interesting choice,' said Joan.

'I know,' Victoria replied, 'but it's too late to get married before the winter now, and since they don't want to hang about, they're unwilling to wait until next summer.'

After the two women had shared memories of their own weddings, Victoria asked, 'How's your Amanda? And more to the point, does she have a beau?' Joan, unfamiliar with the word 'beau' thought it sounded sweet but also a little pretentious.

'Not really, not at the moment, no. Amanda's quite shy really, and fussy – two things which are a rotten combination for getting a boyfriend.'

Victoria smiled. 'I'm sure it won't be long. She is a lovely-looking young lady and comes across as so polite and gentle. How about work, has she found something yet?'

'I'm afraid not. She hasn't found anything that's right for her so far. She seems to be enjoying her time off, but I worry that the novelty will wear off and she'll start to get bored before long.'

'Yes, I can see how that could be a danger,' Victoria replied reflectively. There was a lengthy pause before she suddenly spoke up again. 'I don't know what you think, or what Amanda will make of it, but we do need some help on the farm.'

'Oh,' replied Joan half-heartedly.

'We're family-run, as you know. Cecil isn't getting any younger, and I've told him I can't manage both the home and the farm. I think you also know Stuart isn't committed to farming and has other plans, and Millie is too young and studying for O levels, which leaves everything to Dean. I've told you about how hard he works. The wedding is coming up in a matter of months, but he can't afford to take time off to get things organised. So yesterday he was talking about trying to find a volunteer for the farm. We'd employ someone if we could, but at the moment we just don't have the resources.'

Joan could see where this was going.

'We were discussing the possibility of having a student from Plumpton Agricultural College, but I'm sure if Amanda is keen to learn, not worried about muck, and is happy to just roll up her sleeves, we can keep her busy. A few hours a day will really take the edge off during the run-up to the wedding, and if she doesn't get on with it, or gets a job in the meantime, there's no pressure to continue.'

'That does sound interesting,' Joan said, her chin resting in her hand and looking upward in thought. She was starting to warm to the idea. 'Amanda hasn't got any experience with farming, of course, but she loves the outdoors and she might very well be interested. I'll ask her tonight, and thanks so much, Victoria, for your kind suggestion.'

'No trouble at all, and it would be great to have Amanda on board. I'll need to run it past Cecil and Dean in the meantime, but I can't imagine they'll have any objections.'

* * *

When Amanda heard the news later that day her first thought was fear, thinking she had effectively been signed up in her absence and was now committed, but the more she thought about it, the more the proposal started to appeal. She had never worked on a farm before, or even visited one, so she was intrigued. *Why not?* she pondered. Victoria had suggested a couple of hours a day, but at the moment she could easily do four or five, and there was no long-term commitment. The forthcoming wedding also sparked her interest, not having yet met the bride or groom. Would she get to see how the bride looked on the day? With her mother and Victoria enjoying a growing friendship, an invitation was not impossible. And besides, wasn't a church wedding a public event, making her free to attend regardless? Even so, she simply couldn't imagine imposing herself without an invitation, despite loving weddings and having very few social events to attend.

She was soon visualising herself walking down the aisle on Robert's arm, guests on either side, and then … Mark, standing at the altar, tall and handsome turns around, excited and exuberant. Sam, her chief bridesmaid – possibly her only bridesmaid – is walking behind her with a dainty bouquet, and there are church flowers, hymns, and to her amazement and delight, Joan is crying tears of joy, having finally overcome her fears and prejudices.

'Manda!' Amanda was abruptly brought back to reality by her mother's voice, 'Dinner's ready.'

'Coming!' she called back, leaving her bedroom and daydream behind.

Chapter 7

'That's the turning,' Pauline said hurriedly, looking up from the road atlas. The car took a sharp left, and soon they arrived at their destination. Charles parked their shiny 1978 T Reg Triumph Stag convertible on the gravel drive next to Joan and Robert's Ford Escort, and after taking out the bunch of flowers and box of chocolates from the boot, they gave the outside of Marshywood a thorough inspection. Neither felt impressed by the simple exterior, which lacked the elegance of their beachside residence.

'It's better than their London house,' Pauline whispered.

'You could say that,' Charles muttered, 'it's certainly bigger, but when they said it needed work doing to it, I didn't think this much. I can't imagine Robert's up to it, to be honest.'

'Quite,' responded Pauline, as she extended a perfectly manicured hand to lift the knocker and then quickly decided against it. 'Oh you do it, Charles, will you darling? I'll chip my nail varnish.' Charles rapped the simple brass ring several times against the dark wooden door.

Within seconds the door flew open, and it crossed Pauline's mind that the apparent eagerness to welcome her and Charles inside was actually a clumsy effort to get the experience over and done with.

'Robert, my good man. Lovely to see you.'

Charles grasped his brother's hand and shook it vigorously. The two brothers often greeted each other with a formal handshake, which had at first seemed odd to both their wives. Robert couldn't remember how long they had been doing this, but believed it may have started the first time they saw each other after Charles had lived abroad for many years. From then on, they did it out of habit.

'Joan, my dear.' Pauline puckered up as she and Joan exchanged showy cheek kisses without actual contact. 'Mwah, how are you?' She stood back and examined her sister-in-law. 'Have you lost weight?'

Joan looked at Pauline's slim figure and gave her usual reply. 'Not that I know of.'

Pauline intended to encourage, but Joan was growing tired of being asked this question. As much as she would have loved it to be true, she found Pauline's words insincere, even mocking, especially as each time she saw her, she had actually put on a little more weight since the last time.

Pauline and Charles were ushered into the living room where Amanda was waiting to greet them. 'Uncle Charles, Aunty Pauline, lovely to see you.' Amanda wasn't being insincere. She didn't dislike her uncle and aunt, but she knew Robert and Joan didn't relish their company, and the sour atmosphere rubbed off on her.

A tour around the compact home didn't take long. Pauline and Charles were promised a leisurely walk around the grounds after lunch, but first it was time to sit down with a drink.

'So Robert, my old man,' Charles said, always happy to kickstart a conversation, 'how are you settling in? You know, village life and all that sort of thing.'

'Fine,' Robert replied. 'Joan has made a friend or two, including the farmer's wife next door. Amanda's yet to find work but she's not in a hurry, are you, Manda?'

'No,' said Amanda with a smile. 'It's beautiful around here, so quiet, but so much to see – if you love nature, that is.'

'And that's definitely you,' said Pauline with a light chuckle. 'Since you were a little girl I remember you would walk around pointing at trees and telling everyone which was which. So impressive! And now, most girls your age are out at parties looking for a boyfriend, but you have other priorities like the sensible girl you are. Don't get me wrong, we all know boyfriends have their uses,' she gave Charles a sideways glance, 'but they can come with a whole bunch of trouble too, so all in good time.'

Amanda responded with a reticent smile, leaving Joan and Robert trying to think of something to say, until Charles stepped in. 'This is a nice little place. I'm guessing you've plans to do it up in due course, but it's very cosy right now, especially in here with the lovely wood burner.'

'Yes, it is, now I've finally got the hang of lighting a fire. It took me a fair number of attempts before I succeeded but I think I've got the knack now,' Robert responded.

He appreciated the kind words. Perhaps his brother wasn't that bad after all, and maybe these days it wasn't so much Charles as his lifestyle which was grating.

Robert had never earned much as a librarian but had always believed it was better to have a little with less stress than a lot with a whole bunch of pressure. He had chosen his career because he felt it would be easy and enjoyable and he had seen how fraught Charles' job could get. Unfortunately for Robert he was only half right. Being a librarian could be a wonderful occupation for someone like him who adored books and learning, but after years of service he wasn't sorry to retire. Over time he began to find his work increasingly unchallenging, repetitive and boring. Even though he believed money was not important, if he were to be totally honest, he was just a little bit envious of his older and very successful brother who never seemed to want for anything. Of course, had he wanted to work long hours in commodities as Charles had done, he too could have enjoyed the same level of material success, but instead Robert had opted for a quiet life, enjoying as much time as possible with Joan and Amanda.

Just as Robert felt inclined to share a little more about their new life, he was disappointed to discover the interest his visiting relatives had shown had already come to an end. Pauline had an announcement to make.

'Charles and I have something to tell you,' she said with a big grin.

'Oh?' Joan replied, making minimal effort to hide her indifference.

'Well,' Pauline went on, 'it feels like ages since we went away on a proper trip – outside Europe, I mean.'

Joan and Robert wondered where they were planning to go, because there wasn't much left of the planet for them to explore. As well as living in France and touring Europe in their yacht, they had visited a host of countries – Australia and New Zealand, Bali, Fiji, Singapore, Thailand, the USA, Barbados and Brazil. Charles recently said his wanderlust had been well and truly satisfied and they were just happy to enjoy an annual trip to Greece, their favourite holiday destination, but Pauline wasn't so sure she had seen it all. There was a certain holiday experience they were yet to cross off the list.

'We're going on safari to Kenya,' she said with a self-satisfied smile.

Joan immediately felt her heart sink. She was taken aback by how severely she reacted to the news. 'That's great,' she said, trying to sound enthusiastic. She and Robert never cared much for foreign travel, and after experiencing a couple of package holiday disasters to places like Benidorm they happily settled for annual trips to Wales. However, there was one holiday experience that had fascinated Joan since her childhood, and that was a safari. British wildlife, lovely as it was, just didn't interest her in the way that the exotic animals of the savannah did, and having managed to convince herself that trips to the zoo and safari parks would do, she had all but forgotten about her longing … until today, that is. She pictured glowing sunsets as she sat on the veranda of a game lodge, sipping red wine with Robert by her side and she wistfully recollected how Kenya would be pronounced 'Keenya' by the rich upper classes in classic old films with fairy tale endings. To her credit Joan knew the reality was likely to be far less romantic, but this didn't stop her fantasising. With Robert retired, that once in a lifetime trip was now totally out of the question. Pauline and Charles would be the ones to come back with all the stories, photos and memories, with Joan receiving it all like a well-worn hand-me-down. Finally, pulling herself together, she reminded herself that she now had the lifestyle she had always dreamed of, right here in the English countryside.

'How exciting,' Robert said, sounding more sincere than his wife. 'When are you off?'

'Around September time,' replied Charles. 'The travel agent told us that by then the summer rush is over, but it's the dry season and therefore warm but pleasant and the peak time to spot migrating wildebeests, giraffes and zebras. We've got to go before the end of October, mind you, because that's when the rainy season starts, and it'll be much harder to see the wildlife.'

Amanda wasn't sure how keen she would be to go on safari. Pauline and Charles were sun worshippers, something the wrinkled, leathery skin on her aunt's chest gave away, but for Amanda, who had inherited her mother's fair skin, sunbathing was ill-advised. Not being able to tan had often frustrated her. Pictures of beach-bronzed models and deeply tanned movie stars, such as Farrah Fawcett with her ash-blonde mane, bright white teeth and red swimsuit, made her question whether she was attractive enough. It took her time, but slowly over the years, she began to believe she was beautiful in her own way, just as her best friend Sam, although the polar opposite, was beautiful in another.

Despite a preference for temperate rather than tropical climes, Amanda accepted that if she were ever to get serious with Mark, he might wish to visit his father's homeland, so perhaps she would get the opportunity to see Africa that way. Unlike Kenya, Ghana wasn't known for its tourism, but that didn't matter if the reason for going was to visit family. What was Africa like? she wondered. She had no idea how often Mark had visited. What if they married and he decided to settle there – how would she cope with that? Was she being foolish even thinking on these lines? After all, had Mark's parents been English like hers, there's still no guarantee he wouldn't want to up sticks and emigrate to Australia or something.

Love seemed to be the glue which held together all sorts of situations, and Amanda felt that if she were to find love, she was prepared to go wherever it took her. However, deep down she sincerely hoped that wouldn't be far, because she loved England – and Sussex, in particular. 'The Things We Do for Love' by 10CC entered her mind, but rather than deliberate over what *she* was prepared to do for love, she concluded that she probably had nothing to worry about. Culturally, Mark was very British – his mother was Irish – and he was clearly settled with a solid career path ahead of him. It was unlikely he would want to do something so drastic as to emigrate to Ghana.

Her faraway thoughts were interrupted by her father. 'Amanda, do you want me to take the casserole out the oven? I think you said it'd be ready about now.'

'Of course, sorry Dad. No, don't worry, I'll deal with it.'

After an enjoyable meal and a quick tour of the grounds, Charles and Pauline were ready to leave. 'Thanks for having us, and for a lovely meal. Joan, you're a wonderful cook, you know. I can barely stand I'm so stuffed,' Charles said, rising to his feet.

'It was a bit of a joint effort with Amanda,' Joan replied truthfully. 'I have to confess, since we moved here and she's been off work, we've eaten really well.'

'That's because you've taught me so much, Mum,' Amanda smiled.

She was pleasantly surprised by her mother's candour, but when she thought about it further, she realised Joan had little to lose by being honest and not taking all the credit. Although she had become an expert at hiding her vulnerabilities from Charles and Pauline – which included her battle with depression – she had given up trying to impress them a long time ago.

* * *

Pauline and Charles waved goodbye from their Triumph Stag, and set off for the journey home to Pevensey Bay. Meanwhile, in Central London, Mark Boateng had just finished a meeting with a client and returned to his desk with his managing partner, Peter Berrington.

'I see you've taken some thorough notes there,' Peter said, looking over at Mark's file. 'With such a ridiculous number of specific gifts, that's going to be a time-consuming will to draw up. For heaven's sake,' he rolled his eyes, 'why would anyone want his blasted pipes? A box of Havanas you could understand, but his old pipes? Perhaps he fancies himself as Harold Wilson, who knows.' Mark laughed and shook his head. Peter continued, 'We'll have to charge him more or he'll be the sort to call up every week to request amendments. You can guarantee he'll want a codicil every time he falls out with someone. That's when we start charging by the hour!' Then the senior solicitor's tone softened. 'Perhaps it'll all be worth it in the end, Mark. After all, he's 79 and not in the best of health. It'll all come out in the wash when we act as his executors.'

Mark was not only training to be a skilled lawyer but also learning how to run a successful business. His boss may have sounded heartless and mercenary, but Mark had already discovered there could be no progress without profit. Mr Berrington was usually a reasonable man, so he decided that his irritation with the client must be justified.

'Mark, you'll be moving over to the civil litigation department in August, and I have no doubt you'll be an asset there, as indeed you have been to me.'

Mark thanked his superior effusively.

'I will warn you, though, contentious matters require an entirely different approach. Try to learn all you can from Mr Reeve, who admittedly isn't very good at passing on what he knows to trainees. You have to prise things out of him, especially when he gets stressed and preoccupied, and that happens pretty much every time there's a court hearing, but as long as you spend plenty of time observing and reading up on the files, I'm sure you'll learn quickly.'

'Thanks Mr Berrington, I will take that on board.'

As his principal walked away, Mark began to feel apprehensive. He had heard on the grapevine that Mr Reeve could be a crabby, hard taskmaster, and he worried that despite glowing feedback so far, it would be a struggle to impress him, but he resolved to cross that bridge when he came to it.

Putting the file on his desk, he picked up his diary and viewed the appointments for the forthcoming week. Then, looking further ahead, he came to the month of August and his eyes fell on the words 'annual leave'. This was a break he was really looking forward to – his trip to East Sussex with Sam to visit Amanda.

Mark knew well enough that his mother, aunt and cousin were matchmaking and didn't know quite what to make of it. He certainly liked Amanda, but apart from meeting her at his father's funeral, and what he had been told, he knew so little about her. That wouldn't stop him finding out more, of course, but he didn't want anything too serious or too fast just yet, at least not while he was carving out a career after years of study and gruelling exams. He was attracted to her, and sensed she felt the same way, but she now lived in Sussex, and that could prove challenging. Perhaps everything would become clear after this trip.

During his Friday lunch break Mark would usually head out for a walk and stop by a bakery for a pasty or pie as a reward for his hard work all week. Today was no exception; he felt justified in taking a break from his desk to enjoy his lunch outdoors and watch the world go by. He needed to make the most of this relaxing Friday ritual since he wasn't sure how long it would last, once he'd moved departments. The civil litigation team didn't appear to take breaks, and were famous for being at the office at weekends, frantically preparing court bundles for upcoming hearings.

As Mark sat in Lincoln's Inn Fields holding a steak and kidney pie in one hand and *The Guardian* in the other, he paused to reflect on how much he loved his job and felt optimistic about the future. Taking another bite of his pie and turning a page of the newspaper, he lifted his face to the warm sunshine and experienced a moment of fulfilment. Then, all of a sudden, his contentment turned to sadness and longing. If only he could share all this with his father and tell him what he was thinking and feeling right now. He missed him so much.

Chapter 8

Walking up the stony track to Hillbrook Farm for a second time, Amanda was even more nervous than the first. This time she was alone and about to step into a new role, with no idea of what lay ahead of her. She noticed the pond again, today graced with slightly inelegant but beautiful green-legged moorhens, and armed with her wildlife book she soon identified Egyptian geese and mallards. *And what was that?* A small duck delighted her with a call which sounded like a whistle. Thumbing the pages of her book she soon found the answer: *A wigeon, and with that pink breast and orange head, I'm guessing it's a male.*

Stepping further towards the door, her nerves were temporarily soothed by the intermittent mooing of cows until the crowing of a cockerel, audible from a distance, but now loud and sharp, put her right back on high alert again. Before she could lift the weighty door knocker, she heard Victoria's pleasant voice calling her from around the side of the house near the outbuildings.

'Oh Amanda, you're here! Please, come this way.'

Amanda turned to see Victoria beckoning her. After hellos were exchanged, she accompanied her hostess, who looked down at her feet.

'Fantastic, you're wearing wellies – very sensible. You'll certainly need them here.'

They walked across the farmyard to a large cowshed where Amanda was excited to see several black and brown beauties with wet noses, poking their heads out through the opening.

'These are our ladies,' Victoria said with a smile.

Just then someone emerged from the bovine crowd who was neither a lady nor a cow. Instead, it was a tall, handsome lad, dressed in a checked shirt with sleeves rolled up and blue jeans. Amanda instantly recognised him, the images of a tractor and Land Rover quickly coming to mind.

'And here he is, the only one who can keep these ladies under control. Amanda, this is Dean.'

Dean extended a hand to shake Amanda's, but drew it back again when he noticed it was covered with something grimy. However, he didn't appear to have any qualms about using that same hand to flick back his floppy brown fringe.

'Hi Amanda. It's really great to meet you, and thanks so much for agreeing to volunteer.'

Amanda didn't think the genial look on his face was that of someone who was overwhelmed with work, yet at the same time he seemed slightly flustered.

'Mum said you'd like to help out until you get a job.'

'That's right,' Amanda replied, still feeling nervous, perhaps even more now.

'Well, that would be brilliant,' he said and smiled. 'It's not always easy to explain how we operate, but I'll try my best, and don't worry, you'll pick things up as you go along. How about I take you for a tour?'

This was Victoria's cue to depart. 'Right then, I'll leave you to it. Remember, Amanda, lunch is at one. We can't offer many perks here, but that is one thing I am able to provide. More often than not I'll bring it to you outside, a sandwich, Scotch eggs or something like that, but if it's raining or if you just want to sit down for five minutes and have a cup of tea indoors, you can always have lunch at the kitchen table.'

Victoria then left hurriedly, leaving Dean to lead the way. He took Amanda, who was trying not to look as apprehensive as she felt, to various parts of the farm. He led her through fields and to a range of outbuildings, while trying to explain what tasks might lie ahead. The conversation didn't always flow, and there were awkward moments when Dean would fall back on the weather – always a safe topic and especially important to a farmer.

'We were worried the late spring would cause issues, with it being so cold until recently, but we've been fortunate and lambing has been very successful this year. Can't say it's been easy though. We've had times when we've literally had to shovel snow from the accessway before we could transport the sheep and cattle in the trailer. You're here at a good time now the weather seems to be working with us not against us.'

Amanda was pleased to hear that, and to see Dean slowly growing more relaxed in her presence.

'How many hours do you work a day?' she asked.

'I'm usually up by six, although it's five thirty at lambing time. What I tend to do day to day depends on the time of year and whether calving or lambing is going on. All the livestock, including the chickens, need feeding and monitoring daily to check they're healthy. Dad and I also grow maize and produce our own hay and silage, and there are lots of maintenance jobs too.'

Amanda wondered where she fitted in and waited patiently for Dean to tell her. She didn't have to wait long.

'Please don't worry, we won't expect you to do everything, but we tell volunteers that the most common daily routines involve feeding the livestock, mucking out, and odd jobs like repairing buildings, animal housing and fences.' He raised a hand and with a finger touched his forehead and closed his eyes to aid recollection. 'Also, depending on the time of year, there's hedge laying, woodland maintenance, and even gardening, since we have an apple and pear orchard. Anything unfamiliar or that doesn't appeal can be crossed off the list. Sheep shearing, for instance, we'd expect you to pass on that.' He took a breath. 'And of course, we won't let you loose with the tractor!' he added with a mischievous smile.

Amanda allowed her face to relax a little at this reassurance but didn't feel confident enough to fully appreciate the humour. It all sounded interesting but challenging, and she was beginning to wonder if she was up to it. It was too late to back out now. She would just have to give it her best shot.

Cecil had been busy in the field since her arrival, and he was still there at lunchtime when Victoria brought out a pot of tea and a plate of cheese and pickle sandwiches.

'So Amanda,' she said, setting down the tray, 'has Dean completely put you off, or are you going to come back tomorrow?'

'I'm coming back, definitely,' Amanda replied without hesitation.

Dean bit into a sandwich. 'I was worried the smells might put you off.'

'Smells?'

'Yes, you see, when you work with animals 24/7 you become immune to it, but there have been people who've told us after visiting the farm for the first time they're surprised how smelly it is.'

Amanda couldn't imagine being that blunt, although she *had* noticed some odours, particularly around the cowshed, but nothing too off-putting. In any case, she was used to it. In recent days, the smell of silage had even reached the grounds of Marshywood.

'We're muckspreading at the moment,' Dean continued. 'That's what Dad's doing right now and it does pong, but, like I said, we're used to it.' He looked at her and smiled.

'It's not a problem at all,' Amanda said, her words quick and her tone bright. 'It really is a healthy, wholesome farmyard smell, at least that's what my dad always says, and I agree.'

'So true.' Dean laughed briefly, watching Amanda tuck in. 'And I'm glad it isn't putting you off your sandwiches.'

Victoria returned to the kitchen and Dean gave Amanda some more guidance. 'When you're here, just give Dad or me a shout if you need any help, or you can always track down Mum, who'll usually be in the house. Millie, well, as you would expect, is likely to be at school, and as for Stuart …' Dean paused, looking pensive, '… he's not usually around either.' Falling silent for a second, he perked up again. 'Anyway, I'm sure you'll get on fine.'

Amanda wasn't sure if she was reading too much into things or if she could sense tension again. 'How is Stuart?' she ventured to ask.

'He's okay … I guess,' Dean replied, sounding unsure. 'He's gone back to Cambridge for a few days to see some old university pals.'

'I imagine that must mean you're a man down.'

'Most definitely, but we're used to that.' Dean shrugged half-heartedly. 'While he was away at Cambridge, it was pretty much just Dad, Mum and me, with some help from Millie and the occasional volunteer. We just got on with it and have done ever since. Even before he went away, Stuart was never really the farming type. He does love the hunt though. His friends from Polestead Farm rear pheasants for the shoot, and he likes nothing better than to join them. Apart from that, when he's here he spends as much time as he can with Jess and Bess. He loves those dogs.'

Amanda had been entertained by the working sheep dogs running around at various points throughout her tour. She could see them carefully stationed outside the wire mesh surrounding the enclosure, watching the chickens in the hen house, while geese roamed free range in the vicinity. Attentive and protective, they looked like such reliable guardians, and although she'd always considered herself a cat person, she was drawn towards these intelligent, hardworking creatures.

'They seem very protective towards those chickens,' Amanda said, fascinated.

'They most certainly are, and with several foxes prowling about, even during the day, they really need to be. They also protect the geese, and make sure they don't wander off too far.' Then Dean suddenly had an idea. 'Amanda, how would you like to feed the chickens? I'll show you how we do it, and then that can be your job first thing tomorrow.'

'Yes, that would be great,' she replied, following Dean to the chicken coops.

After the hen feeding was over, Amanda also had a go at cleaning a couple of animal enclosures and was rewarded for her efforts with time spent in the fields with the sheep. She longed to paint the peaceful pastoral scene and was desperate to scoop up one of the adorable lambs in her arms. Although she didn't get to do either of those things, she did witness a mini crisis being averted. Jess and Bess came to Dean's rescue after two lambs accidentally wandered into the wrong field, and with Dean's instructions, the dogs effortlessly guided them home, back to their mothers. Amanda found their bleats of protest while being herded so entertaining, and Dean went on to thank Jess and Bess with affectionate pats and strokes.

'Without another person around, our dogs truly are an extra set of hands and I wouldn't be without them,' he said.

Time advanced, and when Amanda was ready to go home, she realised she was yet to speak to Cecil. Had he even stopped for lunch, she wondered. The tractor was now stationary, but he could still be seen busying himself in and around the field.

'Dean, I hope I didn't interrupt your work too much this morning,' she asked hesitantly before departing.

'No, not at all. In fact, you've been a great help. And besides, from tomorrow I'll start to get my money's worth,' he teased. 'I'm fully expecting you to know the ropes now.' Having raised a smile, he was ready to get back to his duties. 'See you in the morning?'

'Yes, all being well, I'll be here.' She stood for a moment, not knowing what else to say. 'Well, goodbye then, and have a nice evening.'

As she turned to leave, she heard her name being called.

'Amanda, I'm so sorry.' It was Cecil, limping as he approached her. 'I want to apologise that I didn't get the chance to speak to you today, it's been full on. I intended to see you later this afternoon, but an hour ago I stood on a nail which was stuck in some wood in the cowshed and it went right through my boot. Don't worry – I've moved everything out of the way so you'll be okay in there tomorrow.'

Dean didn't flinch but Amanda's mouth fell wide open. 'I'm so sorry, Mr Appleby.'

'Oh, not to worry, one of the many occupational hazards, although to be fair, that was more to do with carelessness and a failure to clear up than anything else.' He looked squarely at Dean.

'Don't blame me, Dad! I have no idea what those panels were doing on the floor. Are you sure Foggy didn't leave them there?' Dean turned to Amanda and said quietly, 'Foggy is a builder we use. He's not known for the quality of his work, but he's *very* cheap.'

Cecil didn't respond, but turning again to Amanda said, 'I gather from Victoria you're coming back so we'll see you tomorrow, and remember, if you need me at any point, just give me a shout.'

Amanda thought that might be easier said than done, judging by how busy he seemed. Also, how easy would it be for him to hear her shout for help from the other side of the farm? Nonetheless, appreciating his words, she replied, 'Thank you, Mr Appleby, I will do.'

'Just call me Cecil,' he said.

'Yes, of course,' Amanda replied. 'I'll see you both tomorrow. Goodbye.'

'Pleasant girl,' Cecil said, watching her leave. 'Do you think she'll be an asset, or has your mother made a mistake?'

Dean tucked in his bottom lip and frowned slightly, 'I don't know, Dad. We'll have to see. So far she seems keen and not afraid of hard work. I was impressed with her effort at cleaning and disinfecting the sheep pens, but she doesn't seem to have any experience.'

'She's from London so no surprises there. Anyway, time will tell,' Cecil concluded, as he and his son returned to work.

* * *

Sam opened the letter with the familiar postmark of Hailsham, East Sussex.

Dear Sam,

How are you, my gorgeous friend? Enjoying the sunnier days I'm sure. At last it's starting to get warmer and I'm looking forward to hotter days ahead (in more than one sense of the word!)

Still no joy at the job centre, but I've been volunteering at Hillbrook Farm for about three weeks now and I'm getting to know how things work on a farm. I'm pretty much left to my own devices, feeding the cows, sheep and chickens, and doing lots of cleaning and mucking out. It's dirty work at times, but I'm surprised at how much I'm enjoying it, and if I'm feeling fed up, or it starts to get tiring, looking at the cute animals cheers me up no end.

My boss Dean (well his Dad Cecil is technically my boss but I hardly see him) is so busy working I don't have much to do with him either, although he comes in and checks on me every now and again to see how I'm getting on, and we usually have lunch together which his mum provides (she's really nice). Dean is engaged to a girl called Carolyn (not met her yet) who works as a doctor's receptionist. He works really long hours, so I'm not sure how much he even sees her. His brother Stuart seems a bit of a flirt (I don't fancy him though – he loves his ciggies a bit too much!) He's hardly at the farm and plans to go into the army.

Everything is coming to life – nature, I mean. The garden and land at Marshywood is vast and interesting, but needs so much work doing to it. I'm hoping to spend any spare time I have doing it up a bit. How's your mum, dad and brothers? My aunt and uncle, Pauline and Charles, are going to Kenya and I can see the longing look in my mum's eyes wishing she could go too (but not with them – ha ha!). I know Kenya is east Africa and Ghana west, but I wonder how much wildlife you saw when you went to Ghana last? If I remember rightly it was some years ago now (were you 12 or something?) You'll have to tell me more about that trip because I can't remember you saying much about it before, apart from how terrified you were at the prospect of seeing massive spiders (which I know luckily you didn't!).

Have you heard from Debbie lately? Last time I spoke to her was just before we left London, and when I told her we were going, she couldn't believe it. Has she managed to get Jason to pop the question yet? Which reminds me, what about you? Any news on that front? What about that cool Jamaican guy at your church who seems interested?

Anyway got to go now. There's TV to watch because it's Friday night. I really miss Flambards. Fridays don't seem quite the same without it, and I'm not so keen on Mork and Mindy or Hawaii Five-O. Looking forward to a nice quiet Saturday again, with no Woolies to go to. There's also nowhere to go in the evening, because, as you can imagine, there's not much nightlife in the village, unless you count the owls and bats. So, I'll be watching TV again (sigh). Happy Days is on and Chachi (Scott Baio) is really cute (should I be embarrassed about that?), he's our age, isn't he? Whoops, sorry, I forgot, you go for old men don't you? (Is David Essex still on your wall? Hee hee.) I also don't know what you see in that Mexican-looking guy from Chips, what's his name? Eric something. Give me Chachi or John Boy Walton any day! Oh dear, Sam, here's me banging on again about hunky guys. Truly pathetic, isn't it? We're hardly schoolgirls any more. One day I'll stop dreaming and actually start living – hopefully with you-know-who.

I can't wait to see you in August. I've been counting the days. I really hope you end up falling in love with Sussex as much as I have, and

talking of love (apologies for sounding soppy) I may as well come straight out with it – I'm really looking forward to seeing Mark – goodness me, how could I not be? I know I can count on you not to let him anywhere near this (or any of my other letters). Getting strong hints from you is one thing, but I'll curl up and die if he hears straight from the horse's mouth just how much I really do fancy him.
Write soon won't you – I'm missing our chats. The cows and sheep at Hillbrook Farm don't tend to tell me what's going on around here (although I suspect not much!)

Lots of love,

Amanda

* * *

'This is incredibly beautiful,' Amanda said, after a gentle climb.

'Amazing,' replied Robert, 'the High Weald is exquisite. The landscape has hardly changed since medieval times.'

Joan, her eyes red and itchy, tried to respond, but instead sneezed.

'Mum, you need to get something for your hay fever. When are you going to the doctor?'

'I've been trying to hold off, but I don't think I can any longer. I'll have to go on Monday.'

As they ambled through the landscape, the beauty of a sparkling stream, wildflower meadows, picturesque oast houses and patches of ancient woodland helped Joan forget her allergies for a while. It was within one of these woods, where red campion, herb robert and greater stitchwort dotted areas of green with red, pink and white, that they came across a woodcutter. The man was probably in his early sixties and simply dressed. He was standing in the centre of a clearing, diligently chopping logs and looked up briefly as he saw them approach.

'Hello,' Robert said in his friendliest voice.

'Good marning,' the man replied in a heavy rural Sussex accent, possibly the strongest Amanda had heard so far. 'How are ye all today?'

'Oh fine, thank you,' Amanda said. 'Do you live nearby?'

'Yes, I do, in a cottage by that gurt oak tree up by the hill.'

He pointed westwards, and Amanda and her parents could just make out through the trees a section of a beautiful view.

'Have you always lived here?' Amanda asked, enthralled by his delightful accent.

'Lived here all me life and spec I'll die here, I will,' he replied nonchalantly, proceeding to chop another log. 'Goodbye to you good folk. It were a pleasure to pass the time o' day with you.'

Hoping she'd stumble across him again one day, Amanda felt grateful to have met this gentleman. It was like stepping back in time. Few people now had a Sussex accent, and even fewer still used Sussex dialect, and most of those were elderly. Hoping this charming way of speaking wouldn't die out, she couldn't help but wonder if its demise was partly due to TV, increasing car ownership, and incomers or 'Lunnun' folk like her.

She arrived home exuberant and refreshed after the walk, and her positive feelings didn't end there. She was getting stuck into many practical endeavours at home and feeling good about her progress at the farm. In stark contrast, her mother didn't appear to be faring so well. The bulk of Joan's hay fever symptoms had now subsided, although her eyes remained red and swollen. But instead of perking up at this improvement, she was instead unnervingly quiet and not for the first time in recent weeks. Although she couldn't help but fear her mother was on an emotional precipice yet again, Amanda tried to remain optimistic, hoping it would soon pass.

Chapter 9

'It's all hands on deck, but not yours, Amanda, although you're welcome to watch, of course. Sheep shearing is a skill that takes ages to master and some people just never do.'

Such were Dean's words when Amanda arrived on Monday to find, not just him and Cecil, but also Victoria in the sheep enclosure. They were armed with electric shearing equipment as they held bleating sheep steady between their knees, the animals lying with their legs in the air, their backs pressing against their shearer. It did look like tough work, and Cecil told Amanda that with a flock of over five hundred sheep, Victoria had also taken pains to learn the skill. Hiring sheep shearers was expensive.

'I'd better get on with cleaning the indoor pens.' Keen to make herself appear useful and as a mark of solidarity Amanda attempted to leave, but Dean stopped her.

'Hold on a minute, why not sit and watch for a while, you might learn something,' he said with a quick glance and a smile.

Amanda was only too happy to oblige, as she had to admit, their battle with large and wilful sheep was an entertaining sight. She noticed a few nicks and cuts, but Cecil assured her shearing didn't hurt, and the grazes would soon heal. He also said how much worse it would be for the sheep to be left unsheared. 'They'd die when the weather heats up, leaving fly strike and other nasties knocking at the door. It's for their benefit we're doing it, not for ours, and certainly not for the money the wool makes, that's for sure.'

The day was growing hotter, and there was hardly a cloud in the sky. It was thirsty work and it wasn't long before Dean took a swig from a bottle filled with water. Not being cooled sufficiently, he removed his shirt and as he wiped his hair away from his forehead Amanda was suddenly aware that for a moment she had stopped looking at him for the purpose of learning. She also realised that she hadn't known until then that sweat could be so attractive. Dean looked up briefly and catching her eye sent a warm and sensitive smile her way. She felt herself glow with embarrassment. She hoped he hadn't noticed anything untoward, and it crossed her mind, there and then, that Carolyn was a lucky girl. Would she strike it lucky too when Mark came to visit in just over a month's time? She hoped so.

Over lunch Amanda felt that if she had momentarily lost decorum she had now managed to recover it. Discussing jobs to be done with Dean, the conversation flowed as naturally as ever, reassuring her that she hadn't given anything away. Once the shearing was over, the next thing to tackle was the overgrown shrubbery around the public footpaths and stiles around the farm. They also talked about Jess and Bess being working dogs, which meant they were smelly, and so not permitted to enter the farmhouse, but were otherwise free roaming.

Amanda couldn't recollect how, but the conversation took a turn to more personal matters. Perhaps it began with Dean asking her if she had made any friends in the area yet.

'Not really, no. I've never had lots of friends and it takes me time to get used to new people. Having said that, I haven't seen many people my age, but I suppose I've not been living here long enough to know where to meet them. I miss my best friend Sam who's planning to visit in August with her cousin Mark.'

Amanda could see Dean was listening keenly, and although she didn't know him well, she was comfortable talking to him. He seemed genuine and trustworthy – someone safe to open up to, if she ever wanted to. Even so, when she heard herself sharing so much, she surprised herself. Perhaps the circumstances had something to do with it. They were thrown together several days a week, and it was relaxing to wind down over a simple meal after a shift of hard work. Cecil rarely joined them.

'That'll be nice for you, having your friends visit from London. I'm sure you'll have a lovely time and enjoy showing them around. I must say, Amanda,' he said casually, 'you sound a bit like me, someone who tends to have just one or two close friends. There's something about farming, I think. Because you're often working alone for hours on end, it can make you desperate to interact with people, but at the same time you get used to your own company and enjoy being alone. I've never been the life and soul of the party, and apart from a couple of farming friends I've met through Hailsham Young Farmers, and some old schoolmates, I don't know that many people either, even though I've lived here all my life.' Dean paused when a tiny grasshopper sprung onto his hand and instantly bounced onto the grass below, amusing them both. 'I used to go to the Young Farmers regularly,' he continued, 'but now it's just me and Dad doing most of the farming, I've less time to socialise. The admin and red tape is growing, so Dad's finding it harder to keep up with all the paperwork, and he's not as strong as he used to be, although he'd never admit it. Anyway, I'm finding the club a bit much these days. Some of them are only interested in wild parties or going out drinking, and getting drunk isn't really my thing.'

Amanda nodded. 'Mine neither, I don't think I've ever been drunk,' she said, biting into her sausage roll and brushing bits of flaky pastry from her lap.

'I wish I could say the same,' Dean confessed. 'I have, and I definitely don't recommend it. I thought it would make me more sociable – you know the sort of thing – I thought I'd feel less awkward, but I drank too much at the club's Christmas party last year and made a total idiot of myself. After that, I swore I'd never do it again.' He winced at the memory but then his face broke into a smile. 'As it happened, I needn't have worried, because just after that party I decided to get serious with Carolyn. We've been going out together since we were 16, but it was just a childish thing for years. After we started going steady, and with all the farm work, I hardly had time for the club.' Dean paused. 'But hey, you could go, Amanda. You don't have to be a farmer, you know.'

'Really? I didn't know that.'

'You may need your own transport though. They meet all over East Sussex, not just in Hailsham, and I don't know anyone in the village who still goes who could give you a lift.'

'Dad's my transport, although he is teaching me to drive, and Mum doesn't like driving after dark.'

Dean rubbed the back of his neck, trying to problem solve. 'That could be an issue,' he said, 'the meetings are usually in the evening, unless there's a special event going on.'

'Thanks for letting me know,' Amanda said, nodding with gratitude, 'but I'm not too sure it sounds like my sort of thing either, with all the drinking and partying, although I might give it a go some time.'

'Don't let me put you off, Amanda, they're not all like that, not by a long shot. Maybe it's changed since I last went. You should try it out.'

Amanda wondered how many of the members of the Young Farmer's club had the 'ooh arr' accent she imagined all the farmers in the locality would have. This raised a question in her mind. 'You don't have a Sussex accent, Dean. How come?'

Looking quietly amused, Dean was happy to fill her in. 'Granny and Grandad moved from Marlow in Buckinghamshire when Dad was fifteen. They were tenant farmers at the time but could just about afford to buy this farm, which in those days was only the land, a run down farmhouse and a cottage too small to swing a cat in.' He clasped his lips together, remembering Amanda was a fan of all things feline. 'Sorry,' he said, 'maybe not the best phrase to use,' but her smile and nods assured him there was nothing to worry about. 'By the time Dad moved to Sussex, he had a very Queen's English accent, you might say. He met Mum at a dinner and dance when she was visiting family in the area, but she had grown up in Surrey and was living in Woking at the time. So neither Mum nor Dad spoke like rural farmers.'

'That's interesting. Are your grandparents still alive?'

'No, unfortunately, Grandad died when I was little and Granny two years ago.'

Amanda's expression softened. 'I don't have any living grandparents either. My grandad on my mother's side died in the war.' There was a long pause before she asked, 'So you've always lived in Sussex?'

'Yes, right in this house. I didn't go to university, although I would have liked to, I guess.'

'Really? What would you have studied if you'd gone?'

'I'm not sure, something sciencey, I suppose.' Looking thoughtful, Dean bit into an apple. 'Probably chemistry, I enjoyed that at school. Stuart was very lucky, he was given an offer of just two E's to get into Cambridge. He always passed exams so easily. I don't know how, because he never seemed to study, I think he's just very bright. The distractions of uni life proved too much for him, though, and he left with a third class honours. He likes to call it a 'gentleman's degree'. Now he's going into the army, I wonder if there was any point in him going to university at all. It's different for Millie, she wants to be a doctor, but Stuart seems to have just wasted three years of his life doing nothing except gallivanting about – something he calls 'travel' – and partying with different women, even though he's supposed to be in a steady relationship.'

Amanda wasn't sure she felt comfortable hearing all this about Stuart, but just like herself earlier, Dean didn't seem to want to hold back, and she appreciated his willingness to talk.

'Do you have any regrets about not going to university?' she asked.

He shrugged his shoulders. 'No, not really. Even if I did, my future is here, so there wouldn't have been much point. Anyway, it's not a problem, my parents will be able to say they have two children who went to university and as Meat Loaf sang, 'Two Out Of Three Ain't Bad'.

Amanda's face lit up at the musical reference, and remembering Victoria had said he'd grown up with Carolyn, she was keen to hear more. 'Your mum said you've known Carolyn since you were little.'

'Yes, that's right. Our mums were friends.' Dean looked slightly dreamy. 'Carolyn says she knew she wanted to be my girlfriend since infant school, but you know what boys are like, well, perhaps you don't, but she was just a silly girl to me, and I had no interest in her whatsoever. No interest, that is, until we hit 16, and even then I didn't really want anything serious.'

'I'm not surprised,' Amanda replied, '16 is very young to be serious. Was your brother ever a contender? I mean, don't brothers sometimes fight for the same girl, especially when they're kids?'

'Stu? Nah, not really. I guess because Stuart was that bit older, my mum and Carolyn's mum would only joke about me and Carolyn. Besides, even from an early age, Stuart had girlfriends and was spoiled for choice, whereas I just mucked about being a kid. Then, one day, I started to see for myself that there was one girl in my life who was truly special.' Looking upwards in thought, hand on chin and elbow resting on the sturdy picnic bench, he took one last bite before tossing the apple core into a hedge. 'Carolyn has always been very grown up for her age, in fact, I think she was already a little woman at ten years old. At 16 she managed to land herself a good job as a receptionist at Western Road doctors' surgery, where she still works, and now at 21 she's been there for years, so she's really good at what she does.'

'Western Road? My mum went there this morning,' Amanda said, her voice bright, as she made the connection. 'We had a walk at the weekend in the High Weald and she ended up with terrible hay fever, so we persuaded her to go to the doctor. She may have met Carolyn then.'

'I'm sure she has,' Dean said buoyantly, 'I hope they liked each other. Most people take to her straight away, although she's quiet, and can come across as serious or no-nonsense, if you see what I mean, until you get to know her. It might have something to do with having to deal with demanding patients all day.' He looked at his watch. 'A quarter to two already. Better get cracking. It was nice to chat, Amanda and remember, if you want a Young Farmer's club programme, just shout – in fact, I think I've got one upstairs.'

'Thanks, Dean, I appreciate that,' Amanda replied, feeling refreshed as she rose to her feet. 'Time to feed the chickens.'

* * *

When Amanda arrived home, Robert met her at the door and spoke with a whisper, 'Mum's in bed with a migraine.'

'Oh no, poor old Mum. Did her trip to the doctor's go well?'

'I think so, but she went straight to bed when she got home so didn't say much. How's your day been, love?'

'Oh fine, and yours?'

'Apart from Mum being unwell, it's been good. She insisted on driving to town and going to the doctors' on her own, even though I offered to take her, but I think it was all a bit much for her after the hard time she had, what with being so unwell on Saturday. All that sneezing and itching really tired her out, making her asthma bad, and was probably also the trigger for this migraine. Anyway, I think the reason she wanted me home was so I could finish painting the living room.' Robert looked down at his hands, which were white with smudges of caulk. 'It's still not done, but at least I've made a start, with so much filling and repairs to do beforehand it's taking me ages.'

Amanda headed over to the kitchen and took some chicken out of the fridge. 'I'll sort out something to eat, Dad. You get back to your work, and hopefully Mum will want dinner later.'

At half past five Joan slowly descended the stairs with puffy eyes, wearing her dressing gown. Amanda couldn't help but notice her mother looked more exhausted and redder around the eyes than she normally did after a migraine attack, and she wondered if she'd been crying. Joan let out a huge breath when she saw her daughter busy at the Aga doing her best, despite the absence of temperature control. The heat emanating from the old oven, which was so welcome in the winter, now made the kitchen uncomfortably hot, and Joan, feeling another unpleasant hot flush come over her, removed her dressing gown before she sat down. 'You are a love, fixing dinner,' she said picking up a couple of Green Shield stamp books to fan herself. 'Don't know why I bother with these any more. Hardly any shops give out stamps these days, apart from a few petrol stations, so it'll take forever to fill these books.' She stopped, and took a moment to savour the aroma of garlic and thyme. 'That smells really delicious, what is it?'

'Chicken chasseur and roast potatoes,' Amanda replied, closing the roasting oven door. 'How are you feeling?'

'Much better now, pet, although it was an awful migraine today.'

'I'm so sorry, Mum. How was your day otherwise, and your visit to the surgery?'

'It was fine. Dr Wilson was pleasant enough, but it'll take me some getting used to not having Dr Rao any more. He knew us so well, didn't he? And it's funny, and I never thought I'd say this, but I'd really got used to having an Indian doctor.'

Amanda smiled to herself. Her mother was mildly amusing sometimes.

'I'm sure we'll get to know our new doctor too, but then again, I hope we won't need to see him,' Robert said, walking into the kitchen.

'He prescribed me Benadryl,' Joan said with a yawn. 'He said it's much better than those yearly steroid injections, which he thinks might be why I'm struggling to lose weight. He also said Benadryl might make me drowsy but I'll still be able to drive.'

'Did you mention the migraines?' Robert picked up a bottle of tablets and read the label. 'This Fiorinal doesn't seem to be working.'

Joan curled the fingers of one hand into a ball, 'Oh damn, I forgot to ask him about it, believe it or not. The attack came on after I left. How stupid and annoying is that?'

'Did you meet Carolyn?' Amanda asked.

'Carolyn? Oh yes, of course, Carolyn,' Joan said, her voice trailing off.

'What was she like?' Amanda, paused and listened, keen to hear more.

'*Well*,' Joan said, putting great emphasis on the word, 'she was quite short, or what you might call petite. I noticed that when she went to get my records she wasn't a great deal taller than the filing cabinet. She has dark brown hair,' Joan looked upwards to recall more details, 'and was wearing smart clothes and glasses, although I think she only needed them for reading. She's got quite a pretty face, but there was something a bit,' Joan paused, 'I don't know – official about her. I'm not sure how to put it, but I found her a bit 'off', shall we say.'

'Really?' Amanda raised her eyebrows.

'Well, yes, for instance, when I went in I said, "Hello Carolyn, I'm Joan Fernsby. I'm a friend of Victoria Appleby and have recently moved to the village." Well, she hardly responded. She just nodded and smiled and said, "Hello, Mrs Fernsby, please take a seat, Dr Wilson will be with you shortly." And that was it. I appreciate she's at work and, by the looks of it, very busy, but I thought she could be a tad friendlier.' Joan picked up a packet of Opal Fruits and popped one in her mouth. 'Maybe she was having a bad day,' she said, chewing loudly.

Amanda agreed that Carolyn did sound a bit off, but had her mother misjudged her, or was she indeed having a bad day? She tried to recollect what Dean had said, something about Carolyn coming across as rather serious.

'Dean told me a bit about her today,' she said. 'He said she's always been sensible and he knew she loved him from an early age. I guess that's just her way.'

'Maybe it is,' Joan said as she reached for a mug. 'Anyone else for a cuppa?'

* * *

Yes, I can definitely start next Wednesday. Thanks so much. It's really good to meet you.'

'And you, Amanda.'

Amanda was standing in Jimmy's, a greasy spoon café in Hailsham, and what's more, it did actually smell of grease. She had just finished talking to Jimmy himself, a rotund man with a paunch, wearing a grubby apron, and hoped she'd get used to the smell of rancid oil. Despite this obvious disadvantage to her new working environment, she felt triumphant as she stepped out of the café and into the sunshine. A job at long last! Thank you, Jobcentre for finally coming up trumps. With an early start and finish it was full-time, and at £1.30 an hour she felt it would earn her enough to become independent again. Finishing by 2pm, she'd have the rest of the day to herself, and today she could still do a stint at the farm and break the news to them at the same time.

* * *

Amanda arrived at Hillbrook Farm to find Dean waiting for her at the entrance, excited and out of breath.

'Amanda, it's great you're here. Dad told me you were coming in a bit later and I'm glad I caught you. I'm going to town for a couple of hours on some business, but I'm also ...' he paused and lowered his voice, 'I'm going down to Eastbourne to choose a ring for Carolyn.'

'Really?' Amanda looked at his hands which he was rubbing together excitedly. His enthusiasm was adorable.

'Yes, you see, when we got engaged back in May I was waiting for some cash to come through,' he explained. 'Just after I proposed, I borrowed her tiger eye and silver ring and promised I'd trade it in for something more valuable. I think she wants me to do the traditional thing, you know, go down on one knee and open the ring box to reveal something special inside.'

'Does she? I hope she really loves whatever you choose.'

Dean didn't respond and Amanda could tell he was eager to say something else.

'That's where you come in, Amanda. I need your help. It's ridiculous but despite knowing her for so long I really haven't a clue what she'd like, and when I saw what was available at the jeweller's I was blown away by the choice.' He paused, and began to count the options on his fingers. 'There are single rubies, emeralds, sapphires ... diamond clusters, single diamonds, double, triple ... I honestly don't have any idea what a girl wants, except for a man to correctly read her mind and surprise her.' He smiled roguishly.

Amanda, although flattered that Dean was seeking her advice, didn't think she could help. 'Dean, I can tell you what *I* might like but I'm afraid I don't know Carolyn and her tastes.'

'I know that,' he replied, his smile dropping slightly, 'and to be fair, not everything's within my price range, but I guessed if you really liked something, it would be surprising if she hated it, so I thought asking you might be a good place to start.'

'Okay, let me think.'

It wasn't hard. It's not as if Amanda hadn't already dreamed about the perfect engagement ring, wedding dress, flowers, you name it, but she hadn't settled on anything in particular, although she did know which gemstones were her favourites. She loved diamonds, which girl didn't? Rubies had depth and were fiery like her hair, sapphire was calming and felt regal, but the gemstone she always had a special fondness and affinity for was the emerald. Green reminded her of trees and her eyes were green – something her biology teacher, Miss Hodges, had said was quite rare. So she had already decided that if she ever had an engagement ring, she could do a lot worse than choose an emerald, surrounded by diamonds of course.

Having shared her choice with Dean, but without giving reasons, he seemed more than satisfied. 'I'm sure there will be something that fits the bill when I get there, and your insight will help narrow things down a bit. Thanks, Amanda.'

'No problem at all,' she replied. 'I'm sure that whatever happens Carolyn will think it a fair swap for the tiger eye.'

'I'm guessing she will,' Dean said, smiling.

'Not that tiger eye stones don't have their own beauty, I'm sure. I can't quite remember what they look like, although I know I've seen one before. They're reddish brown, aren't they?'

'Hers is a sort of mottled orangey yellow with a few brown streaks. Here, take a look.' Dean reached into his pocket and pulled out a silver ring with a single stone. He handed it to Amanda.

Without thinking, she slipped it on, extended her fingers and examined it. 'Interesting ring,' she said, 'I quite like the look of tiger eye actually, not bad at all.' Seeing Dean was keen to get going, she quickly took it off and handed it back.

Just as he was about to go, Amanda decided that now was as good a time as any to broach the subject of her leaving. 'Dean, I have to let you know something. I've got a job. It's at Jimmy's café in town. It's only mornings but enough work to keep me going for now at least.'

Dean didn't answer straight away and Amanda thought she briefly detected disappointment in his eyes. 'That's great, Amanda, congratulations.' he said brightly, 'We expected you to find work soon, I'm not surprised. You've been a real asset to the farm in the short time you've been here.'

'Thank you,' Amanda said, regretting that it had to end so soon. She really felt she was making a difference, and she was also starting to feel guilty for leaving them high and dry. Then it dawned on her. Since she finished work at 2 pm, there was no reason to stop entirely.

As Dean said goodbye and began to walk away, Amanda called after him, 'I can stay on for a bit! In fact I'm still able to work afternoons, if that suits you.'

Dean's face appeared to light up a little. 'That's very good of you, but don't put yourself out, please. It's now July, and after the rush of spring and early summer, things are starting to calm down, so don't feel obliged to carry on if it'll be too much for you.'

Amanda, unable to think of a good reason to stop immediately, was becoming increasingly aware that she wanted to stay on. She loved volunteering at the farm, it had helped her to feel even closer to nature, and she was amazed at how quickly she had taken to spending hours at a time outdoors.

'I really don't feel the need to leave just yet, but I'll see how it goes. If working at Jimmy's and staying here gets too much, then I can review things, so if your Dad's around, I'll tell him the news about my job *and* that he won't be waving me on just yet!'

Dean looked pleased, but was clearly itching to leave. 'Gotta go, Amanda, see you soon and thanks for your advice.'

As his Land Rover rolled slowly across the drive, he shouted after her, 'Oh, by the way, some of the eggs have started hatching. So far, eight beautiful chicks, and more are pipping too.'

Amanda, absolutely thrilled at the prospect of tiny chicks shouted back, 'Looking forward to seeing them.'

Once Dean was out of sight, she couldn't help but wonder if she had really seen disappointment when she told him she was leaving. Had she also imagined his shoulders falling slightly when she said she'd found a job? He said they were less busy, but she really couldn't see much evidence of that. Perhaps he only said that to stop her from feeling guilty about leaving. Thankfully that wasn't going to be an issue any more, and she felt relieved there was now no question of her leaving them in the lurch. It would be bad timing to stop now, and until they found a replacement volunteer, she resolved to stay.

Chapter 10

The loud, spirited worship music stopped. A man with a strong Nigerian voice, wearing a light grey suit, waistcoat and tie, spoke out a powerful prayer through the microphone, after which everyone sat down, including Sam, Mark and their parents. Precious loved her Ministry of Redemption International Pentecostal Church, more widely known as the Ministry of Redemption, and had been attending since Sam was young. Today she had invited Mark and his mother, determined to provide Geraldine with prayer support and encouragement, since she was struggling after Mark's father's death. Geraldine was a Catholic and found solace at mass, but Precious thought the warmth and energy of her church might offer something different.

It was now time for Pastor Randolph to deliver his sermon. Sam knew that their pastor, who hailed from Barbados, could preach for long stretches, and she glanced over at Mark to see how alert he was and how interested he looked. She was worried it could all go downhill from here if he already seemed bored, but was relieved to see him looking attentive and receptive to what Pastor Randolph might have to say.

'Thank you for your prayer, Brother Malachi. Welcome, everyone, to Ministry of Redemption. It is our hope that God will richly bless you here today. Please can you open your bibles and turn to Titus 2.'

Mark had no clue where Titus was, and seeing his struggle, Sam quickly helped him find it.

Similarly, encourage the young men to be self-controlled.

Hearing the words 'young men' and 'self-controlled,' Precious sat tight, hoping the sermon would have something to offer Geraldine. Soon after, the pastor was interrupted by a distortion to his microphone, which produced the most excruciating screech that appeared to wash over the congregation, who patiently waited for it to stop. After the noise recurred several times during the sermon, Mark came to the conclusion they were all used to it.

Pastor Randolph began to extol the virtues of being single, the joys of marriage, and being happy in either situation. A lot of what he said resonated with Mark, who although happy being single, was struggling with his thought life, so much so that when the preacher announced with a raised voice 'You have to repent of sexual immorality!' Mark felt as if he was speaking directly to him. But surely that couldn't be the case, he reasoned to himself. The preacher was only saying that because every man must struggle in that area. When, once again quoting from the Bible, the pastor said, 'It is better to marry than to burn with passion,' Mark thought about his situation. His main passion was his work, and he felt he didn't have time for much else – certainly not church. After five full days at the office working hard, trying to make a good impression, he was exhausted at the weekends. Sometimes he even wondered if he had the time or energy to look for a girlfriend, but perhaps he wouldn't have to. His visit to Sussex was coming up, and Amanda was attractive and available, plus she had already passed the test by being best friends with his cousin and he trusted Sam implicitly.

After the service, Precious was both surprised and delighted to hear that Geraldine had enjoyed it, even believing the sermon had blessed her.

'How about you, Mark?' Precious said, with her West African articulation, accompanied by a hearty smile. 'The message seemed to be good for a young man like you who might be contemplating marriage.'

Mark, not knowing quite what to say and how honest he should be, was relieved when Geraldine interposed, 'Please don't encourage him, Precious, all this talk of marriage is not easy for a mother to hear. He'll be gone before you know it, but where does that leave me? All alone after my baby boy has flown the nest.'

Despite these fatalistic words, spoken in a lilting Irish accent, her positive countenance reassured everyone she would indeed have the strength to cope.

After tea and coffee, it was time to leave. 'We'd better be off now,' Geraldine said, placing her empty cup on a table. She turned to Sam's parents and said, 'Thank you for inviting us today. Bless you both.' Hugging her in-laws she picked up her bag ready to set off for the bus stop with Mark, but before they could leave, Sam touched her cousin's arm.

'The next time I see you, we'll be catching a train to Sussex.'

'We will,' Mark replied, who had been thinking the same, 'and I for one can't wait.'

* * *

After her morning's work, Amanda sat down to lunch with Dean. She had noticed that he seemed quieter than usual.

'How was your weekend? Did you buy a ring for Carolyn?' she asked, trying to initiate conversation.

'It was fine thanks, we had a lovely time on Sunday. When things are busy we only get Sunday lunchtimes together, if we're lucky, but because the last few days have been quiet on the farm we spent yesterday afternoon walking in Abbot's Wood.'

'That sounds wonderful. I've never been to Abbot's Wood. What's it like?'

'Lovely … gorgeous, in fact. It's an ancient woodland, you must check it out.'

Amanda tilted her head to one side, 'And the ring?' she nudged gently.

'Yes, of course, the ring. This time I could do things properly, you know the right way. So I got down on one knee and proposed while opening the ring box.' Dean had a faraway smile. 'As if to serenade us, a blackcap was in an ash tree nearby, belting out a song.'

'A blackcap? Did you see it, or did you know it was a blackcap when you heard it?'

'I didn't spot it, but I could easily tell by its song.'

'Oh wow, I'd struggle with a blackcap. I'm trying to learn birdsong myself,' Amanda said enthusiastically.

'I'm sure you'll get the hang of it. I sometimes fancy myself as a bit of an expert, you see. Out in the fields you hear all sorts, skylarks, nightingales, whitethroats, bullfinches, plus I've had years to attune myself.'

Amanda thought it all sounded so romantic – the blackcap, the proposal, the beautiful woodland setting. 'I'm assuming she said yes?'

'I'm afraid not, she turned me down.' Pretending to look miserable, Dean sank his head low and then lifted it again with a broad smile. 'Actually, I think she really likes the ring, but …'

'But what?'

Dean ran his fingers through his hair before answering. 'While I was driving her home she asked me how I'd chosen it – what made me choose that particular one. I didn't know what to say. Telling her I asked a girl she didn't know for advice just didn't sound right in the moment.'

Amanda, unsure what to say and uncertain how she would feel in Carolyn's position, decided to keep quiet and just listen.

'She knows you volunteer here, and that you moved to the village from London. Oh, and by the way, she did meet your mum at the surgery last week.'

'Yes, that's right.'

'But, I suppose she doesn't know we talk,' Dean hesitated, 'by that I mean, quite a bit, so for me to tell her you gave me advice just didn't seem right. Am I making any sense?'

Dean looked to Amanda for validation. She returned his gaze with a smile which told him she understood.

'I'd hate her to think I'm hiding anything from her.' Dean straightened up. 'And anyway, I intend to tell her one day, perhaps once she's had a chance to meet you.'

Amanda was curious, she sensed there was more to tell. 'What did you say when she asked you what made you choose that particular ring?'

'Nothing,' Dean replied, shrugging his shoulders. 'I was unprepared because I didn't think she'd ask that question, in fact, I didn't really think at all before asking your opinion. It just seemed like a good idea at the time.' There was a crack in his voice and he cleared his throat. 'I want to be open and honest with her. She's going to be my wife so I'd like to start as I mean to go on, but something just didn't feel right about saying you'd said it was what you would have chosen.'

They sat in quiet contemplation for a while and Amanda took another bite of her ham and cucumber sandwich, realising that Dean had finished his.

'I'd better get back to helping Dad with the repairs to the weatherboarding on the barn. He's hoping we can manage on our own without getting Foggy in. Perhaps I'll see you before you knock off for the day?'

Amanda nodded and smiled, thinking, *That was new, he never usually makes a special effort to say goodbye when I leave.* She started to wonder if this was a special goodbye because soon she'd be starting at Jimmy's, which meant no more lunchtime chats. Would he miss it? She certainly would.

* * *

Amanda's first day at Jimmy's café came and went, and the weeks flew by. She soon learned her craft, but as far as she was concerned the jury was still out on whether or not she enjoyed waitressing. She got on well with everyone, not just her boss Jimmy and his wife Pat, known as 'Mrs Jimmy', but also the other waitressing staff. One of these was Maggie, a single mother who, in her words, had 'the most gorgeous five-year-old baby girl on the planet'. Maggie was talkative and friendly, but occasionally too chatty. And then there was Ray, also a talker, who reminded Amanda of a younger version of the comedian Larry Grayson, who had recently taken over from Bruce Forsyth to present *The Generation Game*. Ray would sometimes even use Grayson's camp catchphrase, 'Shut that door!' when someone entered the cafe, and this didn't always go down well with customers. He admitted to loving a good natter and often spoke at great length about his favourite movie stars especially Bette Davis and Katherine Hepburn.

Amanda couldn't make up her mind if she wanted to stay at Jimmy's long term. She wasn't finding being on her feet for the majority of her seven-hour shift easy. At least in Woolworths she had stints at the till. On the other hand, she finished work by 2pm, when most office workers still had hours to go. Another plus was that she was also being kept physically fit by constantly running around. She had learned the art of grabbing plates and bowls and piling up crockery without any breakages, not to mention avoiding spills when carrying several mugs of coffee and tea. There was no doubt she was usually rushed off her feet, but she coped admirably, finding that most of the customers, typically working men who enjoyed a cooked breakfast, were easy to please.

Then, one day, during her third week, work was to become even more challenging. Ray, after being employed at the café for just six months, suddenly announced he'd had enough of 'being sworn at and abused by customers', and walked out. Instantly Amanda's workload increased. Unquestionably, some customers could be offhand, even rude and demanding, but unlike Ray,

Amanda had never felt mistreated. However, there was a regular customer who made her feel uncomfortable. She started noticing him during her very first week. This wasn't difficult since he continually called her over, insisted on being served by her and her alone, and was over-friendly and intense. It wasn't as though Amanda thought he was loathsome – after all, he often left her large tips. It was just that she wasn't sure about him and felt uneasy in his presence. It was soon obvious that his full-on behaviour was because he fancied her, and after he started to call her 'babe', she was left with little doubt. With his short, spiky fair hair, upturned nose and piercing blue eyes, she wasn't bowled over, but neither was she repulsed. However, his personality was the main issue, and she was about to discover more of it the day he made his move.

'Hi again. I think it's time you told me your name, don't you?' He smiled audaciously. Amanda didn't want to say, but neither did she relish being called babe.

'Amanda,' she replied, finding it difficult to meet his gaze.

'Amanda, that's cute, I'm Nick.' He leaned back into his chair and smiled. 'You know, Amanda, since you started working here I've come to realise you brighten up my day. I reckon you've already guessed I'm a builder.'

Amanda had worked that out. His bright yellow safety helmet resting on the table and his heavy-duty boots had somewhat given it away.

'I've been working at the construction site on the new building in Vicarage Lane—'

Before he could continue, a woman called out from a nearby table, 'My bacon sandwich is stone cold. Get me another one please.'

'Yes, of course.'

Amanda ran over, grabbed the plate and took it back to Jimmy who, preoccupied with frying bacon, looked disgruntled when he saw the rejected food in her hand.

After replacing the woman's sandwich, and without even so much as a thank you in return, Amanda started to wipe down an empty table. Just as she finished, she spotted Nick out of the corner of her eye waving her goodbye, but she knew it wasn't going to be goodbye for long. Other builders would visit the café from time to time, but Nick was there consistently, like clockwork, almost every single day. So she wasn't surprised to see that he was there again the next morning.

Amanda had mentioned him to Robert and Joan the previous evening and their response was, 'Don't encourage him but be polite.' Also, days before that, she had written a few lines to Sam about 'the guy who's always there', and Sam wrote back with the words, 'I'd normally say "go girl" but since he's not your type that's just too bad because you can't run. He's got you cornered!'

Before long, others at Jimmy's café also started to notice something. While Nick was waiting for his cooked breakfast, Maggie whispered to Amanda, 'He keeps staring at you. Not a bad-looking fella if you like the rough and ready skinhead type.'

'Not sure I do.'

'I definitely do, or at least I did,' Maggie said. 'I had a boyfriend, a carpenter who did building work with blond hair just like him. I thought being a chippy he'd be strong and macho, you know what I mean, but guess what, he turned out to be sensitive and caring so I dumped him. Fancy me pigeonholing him like that.' She whacked a hand across her forehead and shook her head. 'I was pretty immature in them days.'

'Was that Becky's dad?' Amanda asked, hoping she wasn't sounding nosy.

'Nah, he was nice. Becky's dad was a prick!'

Maggie shook her head, smiled and returned to her work, leaving Amanda hesitating before taking Nick his coffee. As she approached she could see he was looking at her *that* way again.

'Hi Amanda, babe.'

'Hi Nick,' she replied reticently, thinking to herself, *So much for telling him my name so he'd stop calling me Babe.*

Nick drew the mug towards him and thanked her.

'I've been meaning to ask, do you live 'round here?'

'I'm fairly local,' Amanda replied uneasily.

Nick grinned. 'Me too. I used to live in London but I've been here for about a year working on this project as well as others. This town's booming for building work. And, you know, I really like it here so I just might stay longer.'

'I used to live in London too,' Amanda responded feeling annoyed with herself and wondering why on earth she was volunteering information.

'Ah! Something we've got in common. Which part?'

'East London, Leytonstone.'

'You're an Eastender, you don't sound like one, not a trace of cockney in your voice, babe. In fact you speak beautiful. Me, I'm from Crystal Palace, so a 'Saaf' London boy through and through. And of course, being from Crystal Palace I support the Eagles. When they beat Burnley two nil back in May, I could breeve again, what a relief! But why am I banging on about football? Beauties like you aren't usually into the beautiful game, are you?'

Amanda's disinterested face seemed to say, 'You're dead right.'

'So you're not into footie but what *are* you into, Amanda?'

Looking around and finding the café annoyingly quiet, she had no excuse to bow out now. 'I guess, nature, painting, cooking … plus, I volunteer on a farm.'

'Really?' Nick looked intrigued. 'I've got a good friend who's from a farming family. His name's Stuart. I call him Stewpot after that bloke off the telly but I'm not sure he likes it. Between you and me, he's a bit posh, went to Cambridge and goes hunting and shooting, you know, all that kinda stuff. He's not stuck up though and he lives up in Magham Down. Not a bad fella all round, I have to say.'

Amanda froze at the coincidence, and deliberated over whether or not to reveal the truth. *Isn't honesty always the best policy?*

'It's his farm, or rather his parents' farm I volunteer on,' she finally admitted.

'Well blow me flippin' down, that's amazing. A small world, ain't it.' Nick slapped the table hard, unable to contain his excitement. 'He's a crackin' mate, you know. I first met him down the pub last year, but I see him all the time when he's around, in fact, he's now one of me best drinking buddies. I know he'd be happy to vouch for me when it comes to you, babe.' Nick winked, and at that moment, the door opened and two customers walked in and sat down, looking around for assistance.

Amanda, grateful for the opportunity to get away, pulled out her small notebook and pen from her pocket. 'I've got to take an order, I'm afraid.'

'Gotta get back to work myself, babe. Bye for now, and see you very soon, I hope.'

You hope? thought Amanda. *It's almost guaranteed you'll be back tomorrow!*

Just as she was about to walk away, Nick called after her, 'Before you go, babe, I must let you into a bit of a secret. *Oh no, what's that?* thought Amanda, itching to go.

'I've already stashed up twenty grand in the bank and I'm planning to settle down and buy a house soon. Not a bad achievement at 22, d'you reckon? And I think you ought to know as well, builders can get a house, cheap as chips, and turn it into a palace fit for a queen.'

Amanda tried hard to keep a straight face. She decided that rather than thank him for informing her, she'd simply say goodbye again. Clearly oblivious to her amusement, Nick left the café, the contented look on his face showing he judged their conversation a success.

* * *

Just four days later, Amanda found herself unexpectedly talking to Stuart. She had only seen him twice at the farm, and neither time had they spoken to each other. On one occasion he was leaving, just as she arrived, and on the other, he was in an outbuilding, working on his motorbike. By now she was wondering if he ever had lunch with his family. Whenever they mentioned his name, it was usually to say he was visiting some friend or another. Today though, she was surprised to see him making a beeline for her as she was laying down fresh straw in the cowshed.

'Hi, Amanda. How's things?'

'Fine, thank you, Stuart. How are you?'

Stuart didn't waste any time getting straight to the point. 'Brilliant, Amanda. I've been chatting to a friend of mine who I think you know. He's a regular at Jimmy's.'

Amanda felt her heart sink, knowing what might be coming up next.

'First, I have to say sorry I've been so busy and not had the chance to speak to you all this time. I keep hearing so much about you though. Dad and Dean as well as Mum all sing your praises, and I can see you're doing a good job in here.'

'Thanks, Stuart,' Amanda said, wondering how much he could tell from a mere cursory glance how well she was doing. Clearly, he was preoccupied with something other than the state of the cowshed. 'It's a good thing it's dry and warm,' she added. 'I'd really have my work cut out if it was winter and the cows weren't out in the fields most of the time.'

Leaning up against a metal livestock enclosure, he had a glint in his eye and he gazed at Amanda intensely. Feeling on edge she put down her pitchfork and wheelbarrow and gave him her full attention.

'I don't want to interrupt what you're doing and I won't keep you for long, I just wanted to let you know that on Saturday 4th August there's an annual dance, well it's a disco really, at the Old Sussex Tavern, the pub I told you about in Hailsham.'

'Saturday 4th August,' Amanda repeated, soon realising what that meant. 'Thanks, but I've got some friends down from London with me that day.'

'Bring them along! The more the merrier,' Stuart said loudly, then he paused again, and much to Amanda's dismay, the odd smile returned and she could guess what that meant. 'Although it's not the first time I've invited you out to the pub, I have to confess I have slightly ulterior motives this time. No point pussy footing around, so let's just say I've had my orders from Nick.'

Seeing the horrified look on her face, Stuart immediately sought to reassure her. 'Don't worry, I know it's all in his head, at least at this stage. He's only just realised he didn't even bother to check you were single, but then again I don't think minor details like that bother him much. He called me on Wednesday demanding I speak to you, thinking that if he can twist my arm into inviting you he's in with a fighting chance.'

'Oh really?' Amanda replied nervously. This wasn't good news.

'By the way,' Stuart added, 'I'm happy to have a drink with him every now and then, but I don't remember giving him my telephone number. I think he probably looked the farm up in the Yellow Pages.'

Stuart noticed Amanda's hand was twitchy when she tucked hair that had come loose from her pony tail behind her ear. He decided to tone things down a bit. 'Look, Amanda, if you're not keen on him, don't feel you have to come. But then again, I'd also say, don't let him stop you either. It'll be worth going, it always is.' Amanda tried to smile, appreciating Stuart's efforts to let her off the hook, but he hadn't finished yet. 'Do you think you'll come? I'm not allowed to take no for an answer, even though he knows you're not interested. He told me as much, but he also says he's not about to give up on you just yet.'

Amanda was torn. She didn't want to do anything else to encourage Nick, who was clearly determined, but why should he stop her from going out and having a nice time?

'Thanks for the invitation, Stuart. I'll definitely consider it,' she answered at last.

'That's fantastic,' Stuart said, turning to walk away, before spinning back round. 'By the way, I wouldn't write Nick off completely, that is, if you're the remotest bit interested. Under that rough exterior he's not a bad chap, and he works hard. And, I know it sounds mad, but he told me to remind you that he has £20,000 saved up. He's obviously going all out to impress you.'

Amanda smiled, thinking, *Gosh, he really wants to hammer that home* and was reminded of Jane Austen's England, where any potential suitor's annual income was a matter of considerable importance.

'I can't imagine he tells everyone about his financial situation, so I think you must be right,' she replied, the smell of fresh hay calling her back to her work.

After saying goodbye, Amanda reflected on Nick's full-on approach, unable to decide whether on balance it was more flattering than creepy, but one thing was certain, he had no chance with her. Mark seemed all the more perfect in comparison. She wondered what he and Sam would feel about going to a disco. Sam, at least, would jump at the chance. A social event like this would also fit in well with all the other things she had planned for their visit, bringing variety and balance to the activities she had in mind and the more she thought about it, the more she grew excited about the prospect of a night out.

* * *

The skylark was flying high and twittering its morning song as Dean stepped down from his tractor onto the open field. He paused to take in the view. It wasn't every day he stopped like this to appreciate all that was around him, but today was special. Carolyn had some time off work and was spending the day with him at the farm, which was a rare treat and something they had been talking about and looking forward to for weeks.

Dean looked westwards towards the Downs, then southwards in the direction of the sea, and then finally turned to face east to Hillbrook Farm, thinking to himself that one day it would all be his. Well, his, Stuart's and Millie's, to be precise, but it was the plan that he would take over the running of the farm one day. Cecil had made it clear that he wanted to leave an inheritance for all his children but it just wasn't possible for everything to be split exactly three ways when passing down a working farm. Dean was aware that following professional legal advice, Cecil had made a will, and although he didn't know the details, the plan was that he would gradually take over the farm and Cecil would wind down. He was also aware that provision through some sort of trust, had been put in place for Stuart and Millie. Although at times Stuart had been a great disappointment to Cecil, Dean knew his father dearly loved all his children and wanted to take care of them all.

Looking at the farmhouse, Dean could see in his mind's eye small children running towards him, shouting, 'Daddy! Daddy!' while Carolyn hung out the washing on the line, contentedly humming a tune. Then he smiled, telling himself not to be silly. The truth was, his attractive and ambitious wife was more likely to be at the surgery than at home all day, and as long as she was happy and the children were being looked after somehow, that was absolutely fine by him.

* * *

Amanda was relieved to be spending another morning at work without Nick around waiting to pounce. Today was the third day in a row he hadn't visited the café. She hadn't seen him since speaking to Stuart and she wasn't sure why. Perhaps because she had told Stuart she would consider going to the disco he was now simply biding his time, or maybe he thought backing off would make her miss him, or it could be another reason altogether. Whatever the case, she found herself relieved as well as unnerved by the change in his pattern of behaviour. Although she wasn't interested, deep down her insecurities made her wonder if he'd even gone off her.

Sam and Mark's visit was now less than a fortnight away. Jimmy's 16-year-old daughter was off school for the holidays and had agreed to cover Amanda's shifts for a few days, and with volunteering on the farm on hold until her guests had returned home, Amanda could devote all her time to them. As she wiped down the tables she wondered how she would avoid coming across as awkward with Mark. She made the decision not to worry. Being thrown into the deep end by spending so much time with him was bound to break the ice, and if they ended up dating, the sooner she felt comfortable with him the better.

Amanda grabbed some used cutlery and collected up squeezy ketchup and brown sauce containers for a quick top-up. When she returned she was startled to see Nick standing at the café entrance. *He's back,* she thought, bizarrely relieved, which made her feel disappointed in herself.

'Hi, Amanda, not seen you for a while.'

'No, I guess not. How are you?' she asked politely.

'I've been doing really well but the guvnor's been giving me jip lately, watching me like an 'awk so I've not had time for my usual breakfast. There's been a bit of a setback with the building work and we've been expected to sort it out quick like, but I won't bore you with the details.'

'I hope it works out.'

'So do I, babe. I just popped by to let you know I'm on holiday next week. I booked a fortnight in Spain a few months ago. I'm not that fussed about going no more, but well, I couldn't just cancel, could I? The money's been paid up-front an' all. I thought if you didn't see me you might wonder where I was, so I've come to say goodbye. Also babe, here's my number for when I get back.'

'Enjoy your holiday.' Amanda apathetically took the piece of paper and crumpled it up before shoving it into her apron pocket. She then attempted to walk towards a customer who had beckoned her over, but Nick had more to say.

'When I get back, I look forward to seeing you at that disco. It should be good, I've never been before myself but I've heard—'

'Sorry, I really have to go,' Amanda interrupted, not wanting to leave the waiting customers a minute longer. As she swiftly walked away, ponytail swishing as she went, Nick thoroughly enjoyed the opportunity to admire her from behind.

* * *

Amanda kept her hair tied back for her afternoon stint at Hillbrook Farm. The sometimes dirty and smelly work meant she needed to keep it in check, since the thought of it trailing in cow dung and urine wasn't desirable. With a bucket in each hand she turned the corner to begin her next job, cleaning the water troughs and, just as she did, she saw Dean coming towards her with an attractive pint-sized girl by his side. She sported a neat page-boy hairstyle and was wearing wellies and a grey and brown tweed jacket. She certainly looked the part, dressed in classy farming attire and Amanda realised she was about to meet Carolyn at last.

'This is who I was telling you about,' Dean said enthusiastically as they approached. 'Carolyn, this is Amanda.'

Carolyn's eyes were attentive, and she had an understated but pleasant smile. 'Hello, Amanda, great to meet you at last. Dean told me you've become an invaluable member of the team. I met your mother at the surgery a few weeks back. How is she? And your father?'

'Not bad, thank you,' Amanda responded, thinking that her mother's words didn't tally with how Carolyn appeared now, she actually seemed very pleasant.

'Dean's been trying to get me to do some work today but I keep telling him it's my day off.' Carolyn smiled and looked up at him affectionately.

'I've been doing no such thing,' Dean said with mock indignation. 'Trying to get you to roll your sleeves up and muck in on the farm is like trying to make John Lennon kick Yoko out of bed.'

'Don't be so disgusting!' Carolyn whacked Dean playfully on the chest, as they both smiled and briefly embraced, quickly withdrawing so as not to make Amanda feel awkward.

'Dad's been looking after you today, I hope?' Dean asked Amanda.

'Yes, definitely, everything's been fine.'

'I'd better watch out then,' he smiled. 'Perhaps I'm not needed around here as much as I like to think I am. We'll leave you to it then, Amanda, but seriously, thanks for all you're doing, you're amazing.'

Amanda felt her face grow hot and knew she was blushing. 'Thanks, but really I'm not, I just enjoy working here.' She paused and looked around. 'The scenery's beautiful, and there's really no denying that the animals are gorgeous.'

As she walked away, Carolyn turned to Dean and give him a searching look.

'Amanda seems nice. She's also quite pretty, don't you think?'

Dean shrugged his shoulders, 'Oh, I dunno. We really must give her a gift when she leaves,' he said sounding rushed.

'Oh, is she leaving soon?'

For a second Dean was taken aback by his words. Why had he said Amanda was going to leave the farm? But then, he thought, it was perfectly logical. 'After our wedding it stands to reason you'll be around here so much more, and then she probably won't be needed, will she?'

'But I'll still be working,' Carolyn replied, mildly confused.

'Yes, but you'll be here evenings and weekends, and that counts for a lot.'

'I suppose so,' she replied, nodding sedately, 'plus we can always draft in extra help if we need to, can't we? In fact, didn't you say the plan was for Amanda to stay on until she could be replaced, perhaps with someone from the college?'

Dean smiled as he looked into his fiancée's eyes. 'Absolutely, that's exactly it, and a replacement might not even turn out to be necessary because you'll be here.'

'Ah, but will I prove to be as amazing as her?'

'You already are. There's no doubt about that, and not just on the farm but in every way.' Dean's smile was confident and reassuring as he took her by the hand.

Chapter 11

'For goodness sake, Pauline, our safari is a whole two months away and we really don't need to go to Selfridges to buy a whole load of gear, do we?'

'Oh yes, we most definitely do,' Pauline replied sternly. 'Charles, you know I love my vibrant colours, but it's simply not advisable to wear bright pink and orange on safari.'

'Can't you buy something more toned down from C&A or something? I'm not made of money, you know.'

'You bet you are. Why do you think I married you? Besides, it's not just about the colour but also the material. I've got to have natural cotton for that sort of heat, nothing synthetic.'

Charles, leaning back with his legs apart was too relaxed to argue. 'Perhaps you're right,' he sighed. 'Okay, you win.'

Charles and Pauline were settled down for the evening, on the sofa with a bottle of Blue Nun, watching *Shelley*.

'Not sure I find this funny, what do you think? I can see you're not laughing much yourself,' Charles remarked.

'It has its moments, but it's not as good as *George and Mildred*. What's on the Beeb?' Pauline slid her arm through his, and rested her head on his shoulder.

'I can't be bothered to check, love.'

They sat for a while, too lethargic to change the channel, before Pauline asked, 'Charles, don't you think we ought to be inviting Robert and Joan around again soon? I can't remember the last time they were here, but it's been absolutely ages.'

'I suppose we should, but you and I both know Joan will find an excuse not to come.'

'And what with Amanda working at that café as well as carrying on at the farm, I don't expect she'll come either,' her voice was monotone. 'Perhaps we won't bother then.'

Charles noticed Pauline's last sentence ended with a slur. 'How much wine have you had?' he asked, picking up the half-empty bottle. 'Where's it all gone?'

'I've only had a glass, it was already open when I took it out the fridge.'

Charles shook his head and snorted. 'The only time you knock back the booze is before a flight, but that's not for a while yet. It's funny you can't cope without, no one would guess you're a seasoned traveller, the way you still hate boarding an aeroplane.'

'I don't think I've had *that* much to drink, but for some reason it seems to be going straight to my head tonight,' she said slowly. 'I have to say, this Blue Nun is far too drinkable, so it might be best to avoid going past the off licence for a while, I'm tempted to get another bottle.'

'Sounds like a good plan, sweetheart, but then again,' Charles said with a smirk, 'if the booze will make you forget Selfridges, I'll buy several bottles.'

'It won't, Charles, not on your nelly,' Pauline smiled back at him. 'So, honey, are you going to change the channel or what?'

* * *

Amanda watched Jess and Bess effortlessly herd the sheep and lambs into their new pasture. Dean had once told her that, although cattle and sheep grazed in different ways, overgrazing was a risk with both, and the fields needed time to recover. Today it was the sheep who were on the move, and closing the farm gate behind them, Dean noticed Amanda coming towards him. He walked over to meet her, leaving his tractor behind, the dogs hot on his heels.

'Hi, have you just arrived?'

'Yes, Cecil thought that being in the biggest field, you might need help with rounding up the sheep.'

Dean looked around, pointed and smiled. 'As you can see, all the rounding up's been done. It's good of Dad, but he should know by now I can handle it on my own – with Jess and Bess's help, of course.'

Seeing the sheep happily settled, Amanda looked down fondly at the dogs. 'That's great, Dean. I'll let Cecil know.'

As she turned to head back to the outbuildings, Dean called after her, 'There is something you could help me with though.'

'Yes?' Amanda replied with bated breath.

'I have to make a trip to Northiam. It's a bit outside our usual area but there's a new butcher's shop wanting to do business with us. I'd normally drive down to Polegate and then along the main road to Hastings and up from there, but Mum's asked me to drop something off in Battle, so I'll be taking the scenic route. I should be fine until I get to Battle, but after that I'd prefer not to have to keep stopping to look at the map. If you wanted to come and navigate that would help a lot, and save me tons of time.'

'Of course,' Amanda said, her tentative smile growing. 'Northiam? I think I've seen it on the map, is it in the High Weald?'

'It's actually in the Rother District, but we'll need to pass through the High Weald to get there.'

'Great,' Amanda replied sounding increasingly eager, 'I won't be long. I just need to get my bag, although I have to confess I'm not that good at navigating.'

'I'm sure you'll be fine. I'll quickly tell Dad.'

As he walked past the farmhouse Dean decided against hunting down his father and instead darted into the kitchen to speak to his mother. 'I'm leaving now and Amanda's coming with me to navigate.'

Victoria looked up and stopped gliding the rolling pin over the pastry for a moment. 'Okay Dean, see you later,' she said, her voice jittery.

'Is something up?' he asked, sensing her disquiet.

'Not really but just be careful,' Victoria replied, dusting flour on to the rolling pin. 'You know people love to talk around here, and even if they didn't, do you think it's appropriate to spend such a long time alone with Amanda like that, away from the farm, when people might notice?'

'Oh come on, Mum!' Dean almost bellowed. 'If people want to talk, more fool them. Carolyn is everything to me and we're just months away from our wedding.'

'Yes,' Victoria replied, 'that's just it, you're engaged, so people will talk. If you weren't engaged they'd still talk, but at least that wouldn't create such a stir. What do you think Gwen Knowles – aka Mrs Know-it-all – will say if she sees you drive past with Amanda in the passenger seat?'

'Oh, I really couldn't give a toss what that miserable old bag says.'

'Dean, that's rather rude,' Victoria replied, suppressing a smile.

'Besides,' Dean continued, 'I won't drive past her house. I'm going in the opposite direction.'

'Yes, but I imagine you're going past the village shop and post office, and she spends a lot of time around there.'

'It'll be absolutely fine.' Just before leaving, Dean sought to clarify something. 'Mrs Know-It-All, that nickname really suits her. How long has she had it? It always reminds me of Stevie Wonder's "Misstra Know-It-All."'

'I'm not sure when it started but the name is pretty self-explanatory, and with a surname like Knowles it fitted perfectly. Her tendency to know everything and what's best for everyone has turned her into a living legend.'

Dean gave his mother a quick hug as she gave him one last message.

'I hope you both enjoy the trip, and don't forget to thank Olivia for lending me her book,' she said. 'Safe journey, and remember, please be sensible.'

Brushing the concern away with a flip of his hand, he bounded out to Amanda who was waiting patiently by the Land Rover.

'Is everything okay?' she asked, noticing a look of embarrassment in his eyes as he approached. He seemed flustered.

'Yeah, definitely. Mum was just saying, er … nothing important. Anyway, she'll pass on the message to Dad that you won't be around for an hour or two.'

'Is that how long we'll be away for?'

'Well, perhaps two to three hours, but I hope no longer than that.'

Once they were settled in the car, Dean handed Amanda a battered road map, which she readily accepted. The prospect of winding country lanes was appealing and she was looking forward to seeing more of the Weald, with its pretty views and historic architecture. She suddenly felt light-headed but put it down to the novelty of the experience and the hot temperature inside a car warmed by the sun. Dean turned the key in the ignition and the engine vroomed. 'Let's go!' he said with a smile.

As he drove onto the lane outside Hillbrook Farm, cool air began to circulate through the open windows, instantly making Amanda feel better, as did the flow of conversation, which further put her at ease. 'Are you going to the dance at the Old Sussex Tavern next weekend?' she asked, enjoying the feeling of the wind on her face.

'No, I'm afraid not. Carolyn doesn't really like discos, and we tend to be a bit protective about our Saturday nights in together. It's one of the few times in the week when neither of us is working, although for me there are no guarantees. She wouldn't enjoy herself anyway, so it makes the decision easy for us.'

'Doesn't Carolyn like dancing?'

Dean smiled briefly and he changed gears. 'I didn't mean to give the impression she doesn't like dancing, she's just not a fan of discos or disco music. She did try to get me to go ballroom dancing once, but I have to be honest, it didn't really appeal. Dad needed help with the calving so in the end I couldn't go, and I can't say I was too disappointed.' Amanda noticed a subtle smile as he turned the steering wheel.

'Do you like discos, Dean?'

'Me? Yes, I do, and I like all that disco music too – 'Boogie Wonderland', 'September', 'If I Can't Have You' ... all that kinda stuff.'

'I love all that too,' Amanda said, her eyes sparkling, 'what about other types of music?'

'I'm into all sorts, I've got quite an eclectic taste really, everything from classical to pop,' he slowed down to allow a pheasant to cross the road in front of them.

'I must be sounding like a broken record by now, but me too! My dad's really into classical and he introduced me to it.'

'So that's why you don't have an East London accent,' Dean said with a cheeky grin, 'your father's posh!' Despite having never thought of Robert in that way, Amanda didn't contradict him.

'I don't like music snobs,' he went on to say. 'Don't get me wrong, I'm not implying your dad's one of those, but some people think pop is trashy and classical is classy, but in my not so humble opinion I just think a good tune is a good tune,' he smiled.

'Couldn't agree more.' Amanda inhaled deeply. 'The last record I bought was 'Dance Away' by Roxy Music. Now, *that's* class.'

This kick-started a lengthy discussion about favourite songs, artists and bands – ELO, Heatwave, Andrew Gold, Gerry Rafferty ...

'I wonder what's on the radio?' Dean said. He started to fiddle with the knob. 'When I'm on the road, and if the weather's good, I'll chop and change between driving with the radio off and windows down to get some air, and cranking up the volume with the windows shut so I don't disturb the peace. Shall we see what's playing?'

'Yes please, but will that mean closing the windows?'

'Nah,' he smiled, 'stuff that for a game of soldiers. I can't see anyone around to disturb anyway.'

It wasn't disco but 'Are Friends' Electric?' by Tubeway Army which blasted through the airways. 'I love this song, so cool,' Amanda said, bobbing her head rhythmically.

'Definitely different. Yeah, I like it too. Not heard of Tubeway Army before and it sounds really futuristic with that synth. "Our Friends Electric" is a weird title for a song, though.'

'I believe it's "*Are* Friends Electric",' Amanda said, after pausing for thought.

'So even more bonkers then.' Dean smiled as he approached a quiet junction.

The next song was 'Hit Me With Your Rhythm Stick', by Ian Dury and the Blockheads, and Amanda and Dean were soon singing along, shouting out 'hit me!' three times with the emphasis on the final 'me'. This proved too distracting for someone in control of a vehicle. 'Better concentrate,' Dean said, approaching another junction. He stopped the Land Rover. 'I think I need your navigation now.'

'Really? But we haven't reached Battle yet, have we?' Amanda looked around her.

'I know, but I've not been concentrating. I think I took a wrong turn and I'm lost.'

After that, they agreed that Radio 3 was less distracting than Radio 1, and they soon managed to get back on track. Following a brief stop at Victoria's friend's house in Battle, Amanda continued to guide, and it wasn't too long before they arrived in Northiam. The beautiful historic buildings in the village filled her with awe, and as Dean pulled up near the butcher's shop she agreed to wait by the car while he went in to talk to the owner.

After about forty-five minutes of negotiations, he returned to find her examining the knapweed, hemp agrimony and wild marjoram on the grass verge. She beckoned him over. 'Look at this gorgeous orange butterfly with black spots.'

'That's the comma. Pretty, isn't it?' he said, sounding very knowledgeable.

'Comma? That seems a boring name for such a beautiful creature.'

Amanda and Dean crouched down to get a closer look, watching as the butterfly opened its wings, sunning itself on the knapweed.

'Its wings are so raggedy,' Amanda observed.

'They sure are.'

Before long, Amanda was distracted again.

'Hold on, that bird, listen … is that a great tit?'

Dean cocked his ear. 'Nope, Amanda, that's a nuthatch. The great tit sounds more like a bicycle pump.'

Amanda giggled. 'Bicycle pump? I think I'll stick with you, I'm sure you can teach me lots of little tricks like that.'

'There's plenty more where that came from. I always think the blue tit sounds like R2-D2, for instance.'

'That's a character from that film *Star Wars,* isn't it?'

'That's right. I can also teach you how to tell a chiffchaff from a chaffinch – their names may sound similar but their songs are very different.'

As Dean went on to describe their individual sounds, Amanda was so thrilled about the prospect of being tutored by him she had almost forgotten the reason for them being there in the first place. Then she remembered.

'By the way, how did your meeting go?'

'Very well thanks. Actually, really well. We're set to receive several orders from them. Now Amanda, if we end up standing here talking about birds all day, I'll have lost all that time you saved me. Best get back, don't you think?' Dean gave her a stern look. 'You've been a great help. I don't want to hear you put down your navigation skills again,' he said, wagging his finger, 'you did absolutely brilliantly.'

'Thanks,' Amanda said looking away briefly, 'although I don't know how I did it.'

'More Radio 1?' Dean asked, after they had got back into the car. 'I'm guessing it'll be easier not to get lost on the way back, but it's still a bit risky.'

'I'm happy to take the chance,' Amanda said, smiling broadly as she reached for the button.

* * *

The day of Sam and Mark's arrival had come at last, and Amanda sat in front of the dressing table mirror nervously combing her hair. She hadn't seen either in what seemed like an age, and having had so many new experiences since leaving London she wondered if Sam would find her changed. She hoped they would gel instantly, the way they used to.

An hour later, she and Robert were standing on the platform watching the train arrive and impatiently looking out for their guests. The doors began to open, as one by one, passengers pulled down the windows and reached through to turn the handles. 'Can you see any black people yet?' Robert smiled, nudging Amanda with his elbow. It wasn't long before they saw a pretty dark-skinned girl with dimples, her hair separated into several small plaits with red beads attached to the ends. She was accompanied by a tall good-looking man with coffee skin, carrying a small suitcase.

'Sam, Mark!'

'Mand!' The two friends were soon hugging while Robert shook Mark's hand and then grabbed the small suitcase and holdall he was carrying.

With the luggage now in the boot of the Ford Escort, the passengers climbed in, Mark in the front and the girls in the back. Robert turned the key and they set off on the short journey back to Magham Down.

'How was your trip?' Robert asked, glancing at Mark while keeping his eye on the road.

'Really good. It wasn't too long after we left London that we saw amazing views. By the time we got to …' Mark paused '… what station was it, Sam?'

Sam hesitated. 'Umm, Haywards Heath?'

'It was nice around there, but no, I think it was after that. Wivels something, or perhaps Lewes? Well, wherever it was, from there I thought the views were fantastic all the way to Polegate.' Mark lightly rubbed his hands together and looked out of the window at the views. 'You're really lucky living here.'

'We know, Mark. That's why we moved,' Robert said, sounding just a little bit smug.

In the back, Sam looked at her friend and cupped her hand in hers. 'Wow, you're looking good. The country air really agrees with you, Mand.'

'Thanks, Sam, you look great too. I can't wait to show you around.'

Amanda was relieved that so far she was feeling surprisingly relaxed with Mark present, even though the moment she saw him and was reminded how attractive he was, her heart flipped.

'We thought you'd appreciate a chance to relax tonight, so we're having an evening in,' she said. 'I've got chilli con carne with rice and salad for dinner, and there's some French bread to go with it. I hope you're both hungry.'

'You bet,' replied Mark.

'And for afters, it's Arctic roll,' added Robert, 'which was my small contribution to dinner, because I went out and bought it. By the way, an interesting fact for you both. Did you know that Arctic roll was invented fairly locally? A Czechoslovakian doctor, Ernest Velden I think his name was, moved to Eastbourne and set up a factory in the 1960s, after creating it in the 1950s.'

Amanda felt a little embarrassed. 'I'd be surprised if they knew that, and I hope you're not boring them silly, Dad.'

'That's actually an interesting fact,' Mark said politely, managing to sound sincere.

The car pulled up on the drive, wheels scraping across the gravel path. Having seen the car approaching from upstairs, Joan was soon waiting at the front door. Amanda was hoping with every fibre of her being that her mother would be tactful throughout her guests' stay. She needn't have worried. Joan was on top form, having felt particularly positive and well that day.

'Sam, how lovely to see you again, and you must be Mark. So good to meet you. Come in, won't you,' she beckoned warmly.

The conversation during dinner was varied, covering many topics including Mark's work as a trainee solicitor, Sam's job at the Midland Bank, life in a village, and favourite TV programmes and hobbies. After dessert, Robert suggested a game of Monopoly, with everyone agreeing Cluedo would be better as it was likely to finish sooner. This turned out to be a good choice because before long there was drowsiness in Sam's eyes, and Amanda noticed Mark was also looking tired.

'Sorry everyone, after a week at work I find it hard to stay up on a Friday,' Sam said, covering up a big yawn with her hand.

'Please don't apologise, you've done well to last this long after all that travelling,' Joan replied sympathetically.

'Dad will give you a lift to the guest house, or you can walk, if you prefer, and he'll walk with you,' Amanda told Mark confidently, before checking with her father, who was nodding. 'It's only a six or seven-minute walk, if that, but you'll need a torch.'

'I'm afraid I didn't think to pack one,' Mark replied.

'I wouldn't have expected you to. It's not a problem. Dad will lend you one so you're prepared, just in case you want to go out for any reason. We found not having street lights really weird at first and it took us time to adjust.'

'Thanks, Amanda. That's so good of you, Robert,' Mark said, smiling at them both. 'I'm happy to walk or drive, whatever suits you best.'

'What time is it?' Robert looked at the clock on the mantelpiece. 'Twelve minutes to ten, so not too late to walk, but still I think I'll drive you. That'll give you more time to settle in.'

'The plan for tomorrow,' said Amanda, 'was originally going to be the pictures in the morning and Eastbourne beach in the afternoon, but I'm not too sure now. We were listening to the radio on our way to the station and the forecast is heavy rain pretty much all day, so I suggest Sunday for the beach instead. This'll probably work out better anyway, as long as we go in the afternoon. That way we won't have to rush home for Sunday lunch.'

'Going to the beach on Sunday sounds good to me,' said Sam.

'Yes,' Amanda agreed, 'and now, thinking about it, the pictures, beach plus a disco all in one day sounds a bit much.'

'True,' Sam replied. 'Are we going to see the new James Bond film? Everyone's talking about it.'

'Yes, *Moonraker.* I thought you'd like that. You haven't seen it yet, have you?' Amanda asked, looking at Mark.

'No I haven't. I can't possibly miss the latest Bond film,' he replied.

'Will you be coming too, Mr and Mrs Fernsby?' Sam wanted to know.

'No,' Robert answered, 'we'll leave you youngsters to it, but I'm more than happy to be your taxi service again. You won't want to arrive at the cinema looking like drowned rats.'

* * *

When Robert returned after dropping Mark off, he and Joan could hear the faint murmurs of Amanda and Sam giggling and chatting upstairs.

'I assume they're talking about men again,' Joan said quietly.

'Yes, and I suspect one young man in particular. Mark is a nice chap, isn't he? Polite and friendly.'

'Yes, I suppose he is,' Joan said, tightening her lips, 'but I hope Amanda knows what she's doing. You can see by the way she acts around him she's smitten, although she does her best to hide it, which is pointless of course, since we've known for ages.'

'Yes, but she doesn't know that, does she?' Robert replied, in a hushed voice.

'No, she doesn't, and I do hope she listens to me, Robert,' Joan murmured. 'I've told her before and I'll tell her again: "Manda, this isn't London".'

Chapter 12

Mark took his seat first, followed by Amanda, who found herself positioned between him and Sam.

'It's ages since I've been to the pictures,' Sam said, jiggling with excitement as she sat down.

'It's been a long time for me too,' Amanda replied. 'What about you, Mark? What was the last film you saw?'

'Do you know, I think it might have been *Jaws 2* at the beginning of the year, as long ago as that.' He paused to think. 'Or perhaps it was *Superman*, one of the two. I saw them both within a week, so it's hard to remember.'

'Did you go with friends?' Amanda's voice lifted as she probed gently, wondering if he'd taken a woman with him.

'No, I went through a phase when I really got into films so I'd see one every month or so, but the Law Society Finals soon put a stop to that. *Superman* and *Jaws* were after I'd finished college and during the Christmas holidays, so I had more time then, but I went alone. By then I had kinda got into the habit of going on my own because it meant I could just go whenever I felt like it. Maybe if I'd known you then,' he smiled flirtatiously, 'we could have gone together.'

'True,' Amanda mumbled, feeling overwhelmed by his directness while sitting so close.

The seats began to fill and before long a tall man with a big mop of hair sat down in the scat in front of Sam.

'Oh great,' Sam's shoulders dropped, 'now I can't see.'

Amanda was torn. A good friend would offer to swap seats, but that would mean no longer sitting next to Mark. Among the hustle and bustle of the padded red seats being lifted and lowered as people found their places, Mark hadn't heard what Sam said and knew nothing of her disappointment.

Amanda filled him in. 'What a pain, that man in front is blocking Sam's view.'

Mark immediately stood up. 'I'll swap. Sam, come sit here and I'll sit where you are.'

Problem solved, thought Amanda, admiring Mark's gallantry, and very pleased that she was still sitting next to him. Everyone was happy.

Before long it was time for the intermission. In front of them hung the heavy, velvety red cinema curtains and the interval music played quietly. Mark had bought the girls Lyons Maid ice cream from one of the usherettes. He looked hesitantly at the small tub of strawberry ice in his hand. 'I'm not sure why I got this,' he whispered in Amanda's ear, 'there was so much breakfast at the guest house I don't fancy it now. Would you like it?'

'I've got plenty, thanks to you, so no, I'm fine, really I am,' Amanda said quickly, her skin tingling as she felt Mark's breath on her neck. Being able to smell his freshly washed and ironed shirt as she listened to his soft voice felt very intimate. She had to remind herself that her best friend – his cousin – was sitting right by her too, and not to let her emotions get carried away. Besides, had Mark given her any indication that he was 'proper interested', as they were inclined to say in East London? His earlier comment about going to the pictures with her was a clear sign that he was keen, as was offering her his ice cream, and then there was his warmth and attentiveness, not to mention the fact that he had come to Sussex. But Amanda felt she couldn't be totally sure, not just yet. She had been disappointed before, and she didn't want that to happen again.

'Your opinion so far?' Mark asked her.

'Oh, the film,' she replied, slightly flustered and taken off-guard, realising her mind had drifted, 'not bad, not bad at all.'

The second half seemed to be over in a flash, and as they left the cinema with the crowd, the three friends exchanged their verdicts. Sam thought it was one of the best Bond films she'd seen, although admittedly she hadn't seen that many, the one standing out most in her mind being *Live and Let Die*. Mark thought Roger Moore was on top form, and Amanda, who had been distracted throughout, simply said it was 'good'.

'Dad's not picking us up for half an hour yet, and the rain's not so heavy now,' she said. 'Fancy having a walk around town? We can go past Jimmy's café so you know where I work, but I'm keeping my head down, I don't want them to rope me in!'

'That sounds great, Amanda,' Sam replied. 'It's a bit windy so my brolly won't hold up well, though.'

'Living out here you get used to rain, wind and all sorts,' said Amanda. 'At the farm I've stopped caring about getting drenched. I just put on my waterproofs and get on with it. Even though I still get soaked to the skin, I'm used to it now.'

'Sounds grim,' Sam said, clutching her umbrella. 'Rather you than me.'

When Robert picked them up, the rain had become heavy once again. As the friends got into the car, they placed themselves on their seats tentatively, not wishing to leave big wet patches behind.

'I hope the weather cheers up before tonight,' said Amanda, staring at the long streams of water running down the window. 'I don't want to turn up at a disco looking like something the cat's dragged in.'

'Too late for that,' Sam said, her voice teasing.

'That's impossible,' Mark said softly.

'Impossible?' repeated Amanda.

'For you to look like something the cat's dragged in, unless it's a beautiful bird, of course.'

For a moment there was an embarrassing silence, and despite finding his comment just a little bit corny, Amanda felt an effusion of warmth inside. She wondered what her father was thinking, but he was keeping his eyes on the road, pretending not to have heard. Perhaps this was a sign Mark was more interested than she had even dared to believe.

After dropping Mark off, Sam and Amanda discussed a plan of action for the evening, starting with what they were going to wear.

'What about these instead of the red stilettos?' Amanda held up a pair of ankle strap tan and white shoes with a wedge heel.

'That depends on what you're wearing,' Sam replied.

Pulling a dress from the wardrobe, Amanda held it up against her.

'Definitely not the red shoes with royal blue,' Sam said, looking at the dress, 'the shoes don't go and the heels are too high. Light brown and white will look better with blue, unless you've got a red bag to match.'

'No I haven't,' Amanda said, pointing instead to a brown and cream handbag. 'I agree, Sam. Wedge heels are better than stilettos for a disco. There's an Oxfam in Hailsham, perhaps I'd better drop these off next time I'm in town. I don't remember the last time I wore them.'

'I know you, Mand. As long as you're comfortable, you couldn't care less what you're wearing or what people think. You'd be happy dancing in your wellies, and Mark wouldn't be put off in the slightest!' Sam giggled.

'D'you reckon?' Amanda smiled, her assurance of Mark's interest growing by the hour.

* * *

Before long Sam was ready and full of anticipation, perched on the edge of the spare room bed in her sophisticated burgundy halter dress with a thick, shiny black belt around her waist, patiently waiting for Amanda to knock. After a rap on the door, Amanda walked in wearing a royal blue lycra dress with a swishy wrap-around skirt which fell just below the knee, designed to swirl around when spinning. The straps held up the figure-hugging top which fitted her snugly, accentuating her bust and showing off her waist. Amanda hoped the overall look was respectable but feared it might fall slightly too much on the seductive side. Sam looked a little taken aback.

'Wow, Amanda, you're going to make me look like a bag lady wearing that!'

'Don't be silly, Sam, you look gorgeous and that colour really suits you.'

'That's nice of you to say, but seriously, Amanda, it's a lovely dress and I guarantee all eyes will be on you, girl.'

'Do you really think so, Sam? Perhaps it's a bit too much?'

'Don't be so bashful, you look great. Mark won't know what hit him tonight.'

'Sam stop it!' Amanda protested with a smile.

Suddenly Sam looked less cheerful and stared down at her hands.

'Is something wrong?' Amanda asked, concerned.

Initially unsure whether or not to share her thoughts, Sam spoke up. 'Well, it might just be me being paranoid, but did you notice a few people staring at me and Mark when we were walking around town today?'

Amanda thought hard. 'I suppose I did notice one woman who seemed stressed and was looking at Mark a bit funny, but people can be weird, so I just put it down to her own issues. Is it her you're thinking of? Did you see her?'

'Her and a couple of others,' sighed Sam. 'Don't get me wrong, most people we spoke to were lovely – like that woman in the cinema ticket office, she was really nice, but there were a couple of people that made me feel, how can I say it, a bit uncomfortable, staring and stuff like that. Oh Mand, I hope I don't get that tonight. I just want to enjoy the evening.'

Amanda put her arm around Sam and gave her a squeeze. 'Look, you're my best friend, and if I think you're brilliant, I bet most people you meet tonight will think the same. But I can't guarantee that, and I'm sorry in advance if anyone's an idiot, but all I can say is hold your head up high, just let your hair down and enjoy yourself. I hope I'll like it too, but to be honest I don't know if I'll fit in either.' She paused. 'I've never told you about this before, Sam,' Amanda said, sounding tense, 'but once, at a school disco when I was twelve, I overheard a boy say some nasty things about me. It really hurt and dented my confidence. Even though that was a long time ago, I'm afraid tonight might bring back those bad memories, so I'm not sure how much I'm looking forward to it either. But we're together and I feel a lot better for it.'

Sam maintained steady eye contact, her face softening. 'You've never mentioned that boy before. What did he say?'

'We'll chat about that some other time, Sam. Right now I think we'd better go downstairs to spend time with my parents before heading off. We've only got about a quarter of an hour before we need to think about leaving.'

They threw on their summer jackets and sliding their hands along the rickety banister hurried downstairs to find Joan and Robert watching TV.

'I see you're ready, girls. Let's go,' Robert said, jumping to his feet.

'Dad, we've got a bit of time, it's only a quarter to seven, we'll be early.'

'Not much. Anyway, I arranged to pick Mark up at ten to, it starts at seven, doesn't it?'

'Yes, but I'm not sure we want to be the first to arrive.'

'You won't be, pet. It's a pub so there's bound to be people there already,'

'You're right.' Amanda said, adjusting her necklace. 'Perhaps we'd better head off then if Mark's expecting us in less than five minutes. And I guess there's only one thing worse than getting there first.'

'What's that?' asked Sam.

'Turning up and finding everyone already there, staring at you when you arrive.' Amanda chuckled and Robert picked up his car keys.

'Have a nice time,' Joan called after them as they walked towards the front door.

'Thanks, Mrs Fernsby,' Sam shouted back.

Within minutes they had arrived at the guest house to find Mark waiting outside. Sam, having been offered the front passenger seat, got out of the car and Robert helped her pull the seat forward to allow Mark to slide into the back next to Amanda.

They greeted each other shyly. Amanda soon noticed she and Mark were colour coordinated with his blue open-neck shirt with a soft sheen, and barely visible stripes, and his lightly flared blue trousers and thin blue belt. She also detected he was wearing Old Spice aftershave, which had sold very well in Woolworths. Unlike Sam, who loved fragrance, her current favourite being Charlie, Amanda wasn't keen. Even so, because tonight was special she was wearing a dash of Joan's Chanel No 19, one of the few fragrances she could tolerate. She recollected that Robert had said the music in the advert for Old Spice was from *Carmina Burana*, by Carl Orff. Soon that rousing piece, which starts quietly and builds to a crescendo, was in her head, as was the image of the surfer mastering the gigantic waves.

'How was your dinner, Mark?' she asked, trying not to get distracted by his scent. 'Throwing in evening meals with the breakfasts makes it really good value, doesn't it?'

'Fine, in fact it was quite nice. Boeuf bourguignon, and a fruit salad for dessert, but it wasn't as good as your chilli last night.'

Amanda felt flattered. 'Thanks, I'm glad you liked it,' she said, trying not to bask too much in his words, 'but I'm not sure you would have been so impressed with tonight's meal. I usually help Mum in the kitchen but because I was rushing to get ready I told her to do something easy, so we had Spam, mushy peas and

Smash, so hardly cordon bleu. Mum had baked a Madeira cake while we were at the pictures today though, and we had that for afters. I've saved you a piece.'

Sam, overhearing, turned to face the back seat. 'The cake was really nice and I love Spam, especially Spam fritters, so I'm afraid you did miss out, Mark.'

Mark wrinkled his nose slightly as if to say *I don't think so*, but thanked Amanda for saving him some cake. Before long, Robert pulled up outside the entrance of the Old Sussex Tavern.

'Now, are you sure you don't want a lift back?' he asked.

'Thanks for offering again, Dad, but as I said, I've booked a taxi for a quarter past twelve. I don't want you having to stay up. I know how much you like your early nights.'

'Alright love. You youngsters all have a good time, and be good!'

It was just gone 7 o'clock when Sam, Mark and Amanda stepped through the pub door. In front of them was the bar with tables and chairs. Beyond the bar they could see a dark room with colourful flashing lights within, moving to a disco beat. From where they stood they couldn't tell whether anyone was dancing yet, although it seemed unlikely. Several people were sitting at tables in the bar, including two elderly gents holding pints, and a large group of middle-aged men who seemed quite rowdy. A number of them gave the three newcomers a glance, but nothing unwelcoming or intimidating. Because of the concerns Sam had voiced earlier, Amanda was keen to reassure her.

'They're probably looking at us because we're newbies. When my parents first visited the Red Lion in the village they said they got stared at when they walked in.'

'It's fine,' Sam replied positively, making Amanda feel much more relaxed.

Mark glanced at the barmaid, busy serving a middle-aged couple, then he turned to Amanda. 'Can I get you a drink?'

'What about me?' Sam asked, feigning sadness.

'You can get your own!' laughed Mark. 'Only joking. I don't think I need to ask what you'd like because I'm pretty sure you'll want a Martini.'

Amanda was surprised. 'I didn't know you drank Martini, Sam. You've always been a Cola person.'

'Shush!' Sam covered her lips with her forefinger. 'Don't let it slip out in front of my mum, please. She believes strong drink is the work of the Devil, although Dad has one now and again and she turns a blind eye to that. She wouldn't approve of me doing it, though. I got into Martini at the work Christmas party, so now Martini means *party time*. I was telling Mark all this on the train.'

'Sam,' Amanda said disapprovingly, 'I know I'm a fine one to talk because I hide things from my mum all the time, but if I had a mum like yours, I wouldn't be secretive, I'd want to share everything with her.' Amanda instantly regretted her words wondering if Mark might disapprove, but was relieved to see a warm look of acceptance on his face.

'Amanda's right, I'm sure Aunt Precious wouldn't mind at all, Sam,' he smiled. 'What can I get you, Amanda?'

'Do they have Babycham or Cherry B? If not, a white wine spritzer will be lovely. Thanks, Mark, that's kind of you.'

'No problem at all.'

While Mark was at the bar, Amanda and Sam found a table and it was time to check in.

'Mand, how do you think it's going – with Mark, I mean?'

Amanda dipped her head, 'Careful Sam, keep your voice down, will you? He's just over there.'

'Oh don't be so nervous, he can't hear us.'

At that moment Mark turned around, saw the girls chatting and beamed over a smile.

'See what I mean?' Amanda tried to hide her embarrassment. 'We're being obvious.'

'No we're not, and by the way, where are all the young people tonight?'

'I expect they'll get here soon enough. The night is young ...' Amanda paused, and Sam, picking up on the cue, looked at Amanda and then they said in unison, 'and so are we!' before falling into another fit of giggles.

By the time Mark returned with a Martini, Babycham and a pint of Carling, more people were piling into the pub, with some disappearing into the disco room.

'I can see things are livening up,' he said, placing the tray on the table.

'And heating up too. It's really warm in here.' Sam took off her jacket, quickly followed by Amanda.

'That's a beautiful dress. It really suits you,' said Mark, trying not to ogle.

'Thank you.'

'And my dress looks like a bit of old rag, I suppose,' said Sam, pouting. Mark didn't reply, but instead kept an admiring eye on Amanda as she sipped her drink.

'I get it,' Sam said, fully resigned to her fate. 'I should have guessed I'd end up being the biggest gooseberry on the planet today.'

Just at that moment, Amanda spotted a familiar face. It was Stuart, and next to him was a tall leggy blonde with skin-tight red lycra trousers, a matching boob tube and sultry heels. Amanda couldn't help but notice how fashionable she looked, thinking to herself that if anyone she knew was going to have a film star lookalike by his side, it would be Stuart. It was a little while before Stuart's eyes fell on Amanda, something his lady friend also very quickly noticed, but instead of coming over to say hello he gave her an official-looking salute, and after picking up their drinks he and his glamorous partner headed straight into the disco room.

'Who was that?' asked Sam.

'The farmer's son, the eldest one,' Amanda answered, thinking it a little odd that Stuart didn't come over to chat. Once the disco was truly under way it was going to be much harder to be heard above all the noise. Surely he should know that.

'Time for us to go in, don't you think?' Sam said eagerly. 'We came to boogie, not to sit. Come on, Mark, drink up.'

Mark took a swig of lager before gulping down the rest.

'I haven't finished my drink yet.' Amanda picked up her glass. 'I'll take it in and hope it doesn't get knocked over.' All three stood up, but at that moment the pub door opened and to her alarm Amanda spied Nick entering with two other men.

'Quick,' she whispered to Sam, grabbing her by the arm and pulling her in the direction of the disco lights. 'Nick – you know, the one I told you about at Jimmy's – has just arrived.' She'd been enjoying herself so much, she'd practically forgotten about him.

The moment Nick entered he started scanning the room for Amanda. Standing up and looking stunningly beautiful, she was not hard to spot. Unlike Stuart, Nick was like a man on a mission and immediately made a beeline for her, leaving behind his two thuggish companions, a pair of 'hard-nut' looking, tattooed men.

'Hi babe, I mean, hi Amanda.'

Amanda and Sam kept their heads down as he approached. Noting their body language, Mark swallowed visibly. Nick completely ignored Mark and Sam, having eyes only for Amanda, her figure in particular, and made no effort to be discreet with his lecherous looks.

'It's well cracking you made it, Amanda. Got your dancing shoes on?'

'Yes, we were just heading to the dance floor,' Amanda replied, trying to sound civil. 'When we arrived there was hardly anyone here, now it looks like people are dancing.'

'I arrive, the party starts!' Nick gave a hearty laugh and rocked back on his heels.

Amanda looked down to hide her amusement and managing to keep her face in check, lifted her head again. 'How was your holiday in Spain?' she asked.

Nick shrugged. 'So, so, and the weather weren't up to much. It was either belting heat or tipping it down. What are you drinking? Can I top it up?'

'I'm fine for now, thanks.' Amanda soon felt duty bound to introduce everyone. 'These are my friends, Sam and Mark. Sam and Mark, this is Nick.'

They exchanged awkward hellos. Sam and Mark were cordial but Nick showed little more than a passing interest.

'Is Stuart here yet?' he asked looking around.

'He is,' Amanda replied.

'Is he with his girlfriend, the one from Cambridge Uni? They've been on and off for a year, mostly off I'm told, but now it's on again.'

Amanda wasn't sure how to reply, and Nick interpreted her silence as a yes.

'As you can see, me good mates Wayne and Baz are 'ere with me. They're from London and tonight they're crashing out on the sofa and floor. There's not much room in my flat. If I had my way, I'd have someone more feminine than two burly blokes staying tonight, and though my place ain't bad, it could definitely do with a woman's touch.'

Amanda winced, especially as she noticed that when he said certain words like 'feminine' and 'woman' his eyes settled on parts of her body, making her wish she was hiding under a potato sack.

Oblivious to Amanda's discomfort and Sam and Mark's growing embarrassment, Nick continued unabashed. 'Well, if you're absolutely sure I can't get you anything I'll see you in there, and don't forget, if you fancy a drink, not to mention a dance, hunt me down. I'd better get back to Wayne and Baz. The London in 'em stops 'em from being willing to hang about too long, if you get my drift. I see they've wasted no time ordering, and I hope they've got me one as well, or I might change me mind about giving them free bed and board tonight!' Nick gave Amanda one more longing look before departing, saying nothing more to Sam or Mark.

'Umm,' Sam said once he was out of earshot, 'I see what you mean, Mand,' but Mark stayed silent.

* * *

Although it was much darker on the dance floor than in the bar, the bright flashing lights and the reflections bouncing off the disco ball gave extra illumination to the revellers. Amanda wasn't ready to dance just yet. It would take a few more records for her to relax and get into it. On the other hand, Sam was true to her word, and from the get-go started to groove, wasting no time in joining a sisterhood of women dancing around their handbags.

With Sam away, Mark relished being alone with Amanda, speaking mouth to ear as they communicated over the noise. But while they chatted and flirted, Amanda could sense beady eyes staring at her from the other side of the room. When Nick was illuminated by the lights, she could see him gripping a pint and chatting to friends, which at one point included Stuart, but his eyes never seemed to stray from her direction for very long.

A Taste of Honey's 'Boogie Oogie Oogie' was the tune which finally got Amanda dancing. As soon as she heard it, she grabbed Mark by the hand and soon they were on the dancefloor boogie oogie oogi-ing, and if the song was right, they'd be dancing until they simply couldn't groove any more. She immediately noticed Mark had two left feet, but that didn't put her off in the slightest. In fact, she thought it was rather sweet. His dancing certainly left much to be desired, but he was giving it his best shot and having fun, which was all that mattered to her.

'At last!' Sam breathed. She promptly left the group of ladies to join Amanda and Mark when she spotted them on the dance floor. The three friends were soon going crazy for Frantique's 'Strut Your Funky Stuff'. Watching Mark, Amanda smiled, and had to agree with the song that it really didn't matter if you couldn't do disco like John Travolta.

As they were dancing, she glanced over to see Stuart's on-off date gyrating in front of him, twisting her body with legs apart and rotating her hips, moving up and crouching down, right down to the floor as she pressed herself against him, and by the look on Stuart's face, he was enjoying every movement. Amanda couldn't help finding his girlfriend's dancing uncouth, and even a bit vulgar, but she didn't want to say anything to Sam in case she came across as a priggish modern-day version of Fanny Price in Jane Austen's *Mansfield Park*.

Suddenly Nick was right by her side trying his darned hardest to be like Travolta himself. He was going all out to impress, doing his level best to move his stocky, well-built body to the music. Another person also joined them, a young man who had been watching Sam all evening, something which hadn't escaped Amanda's attention. She thought now was a good time to check if Sam was remotely interested, even though she could anticipate what the answer would be.

'He definitely likes you, Sam.'

'He looks about 12, for goodness sake!'

'I think more like 16 or 17,' Amanda replied, 'which I agree is a bit young, but you never know, he may be a lot older than he looks, and anyway they wouldn't let him in if he was that young, would they?'

Sam didn't want to lead the youth on, so kept her eyes focussed on Amanda and Mark. At the same time, Amanda was desperately trying not to encourage Nick, and wanted to show Mark that she only had eyes for him. Seeing the undeniable closeness between Mark and Amanda, a sweaty and exhausted Nick appeared to finally admit defeat and walked away, much to Amanda's relief.

The next song was Sister Sledge's 'The Greatest Dancer'.

Mark looked at Amanda and smiled. 'Sorry, I know that's not me, even though I wish I was.'

They were having so much fun, time flew by ridiculously fast, and when Amanda looked at her watch she couldn't believe it was nearly 11. She could have danced disco all night, but the DJ had other things in mind for the last hour or so, and with the onset of slower songs, the mood changed from light-hearted to passionate. Barry White's deep baritone version of Billy Joel's 'Just the Way You Are' gave Mark the courage to hold Amanda close to him and the two danced together slowly. By the time Dionne Warwick's 'I know I'll Never Love This Way Again' was playing, Amanda felt an affinity with the words. Sam sat out the slow songs, turning down the young lad who had asked her to dance. Instead, she drank a cool glass of water, silently watching and feeling pleased she had acted as matchmaker for two very important people in her life, who were now evidently falling in love.

But Sam wasn't the only one watching, and when Amanda lifted her head from Mark's shoulder she caught sight of Nick. He had the most terrifying gaze she thought she'd ever seen, his eyes narrow and clearly seething with rage and jealousy. Amanda turned her face away, shut her eyes and tried to focus on Mark.

With the song over and another soft piece of music playing, Mark and Amanda held hands and walked over to join Sam for a refreshing drink of water, but before they had the chance to sit down, Nick headed straight towards them.

'That drink I promised you, the offer still stands you know.' Nick stared at Amanda, blanking out Mark completely, his voice slurring and his teeth and fists clenched. Unclenching his hand, he was desperately trying to appear relaxed. All three were astonished to see he still hadn't given up, despite it now being clear that Amanda and Mark were an item.

'I'm fine thanks,' Amanda replied awkwardly, hoping that Mark would intervene and come to her rescue. However, clearly bemused by Nick's audaciousness, Mark didn't utter a word.

'Suit yourself,' Nick said, failing to hide his suppressed rage. He sidled up to Amanda, and as he opened his mouth, she could smell alcohol on his breath.

'I thought them two … Well, you know what I mean, them two being the same sort, I thought they were together, if you get my drift. Never knew that all this time it was really you and him. That's really disappointing, Amanda, really disappointing. I thought you were a decent girl.'

Leaving her with that chilling comment, he walked away, heading back to join his friends, and Amanda was left shaken but determined to ignore what happened.

'What the heck did that creep say to you, Mand? You look terrified,' Sam said, worry etched on her face.

'Oh, nothing much, at least nothing important,' Amanda shrugged, trying to keep her composure. 'He's never taken no for an answer and I think the penny's finally dropped that he hasn't got a chance, and he can't handle that.'

'Well, I hope he leaves you alone now,' Sam replied, looking unsettled.

The final dance was over and Sam had turned down the fresh-faced boy one last time, but he still insisted on giving her his telephone number. As he handed Sam a piece of paper, Amanda noticed her friend saying something to him, and she couldn't wait to find out what had happened, although by the look on Sam's face it didn't look promising. They picked up their jackets and walked out of the pub. With the lad no longer around, Amanda wanted the low down.

'So, Sam, I saw he gave you a piece of paper. I'm guessing he's asked you out and that was his telephone number.'

'Amanda, or should I say Sherlock Holmes, you're right, but it's a no-go, I'm afraid.'

'Why not?'

'I asked him how old he was.'

'And?' Amanda asked. Mark leaned in, also waiting to hear the reply.

'16, he's 16!'

Mark tried his best to stifle a laugh. 'Three years isn't such a massive gap, Sam, is it?'

Sam gave a sarcastic smile. 'It is,' she retorted, 'especially when his birthday was less than two weeks ago.'

'Surely you didn't ask him when his birthday was?' asked Amanda.

'I did, I'm that desperate,' Sam replied. 'At least the lad's got confidence, and I admire him for it, but I simply can't stretch to that.'

Amanda and Mark gazed at each other and smiled.

* * *

The night air was crisp, and the sound of disco music still rang in their ears while a host of memories filled their minds. Amanda felt like the luckiest girl in the world, whose dreams had at long last come true, as she held Mark's hand, just as she did at his father's funeral, but this time not to console. Was it just the cool summer night air, or was it also nerves mingled with excitement which made her legs tremble and teeth chatter? Whatever the case, while these telltale signs of blissful tension were painfully apparent to her, Mark and Sam didn't appear to notice.

'I ordered the taxi for a quarter past midnight so it should be here any minute,' she said optimistically, and before long a car with the sign Hailsham Cabs pulled up, and out stepped the driver. Amanda had noticed that she and her companions were not the only ones waiting for a cab. Two of the ladies from the 'around the handbag' dancing fraternity were also watching the car eagerly.

'Car for Amanda,' the taxi driver hollered.

'Yes, that's me,' Amanda replied. He opened the car door, glancing at everyone, including the two women, before Sam clarified it was also for her and Mark.

'When's the next car available?' one of the women asked him.

Looking frazzled, he scratched his head. 'We're fully booked at the moment. Saturday night is always our busiest, and for some reason there are parties all over, as far away as Bexhill, so some of the other drivers are having to pick up from there. This is my last shift, but I'd say someone else will be along in an hour or so.'

This comment was met with cries of protest and frustration from the two women.

'Which way are you going?' Amanda asked, wondering if there was anything she could do.

'Stunts Green,' the less frenzied one replied.

'Stunts Green,' Amanda repeated, 'I'm not sure where that is.'

'Just a little bit beyond where you're going, love,' said the taxi driver. 'Trouble is, of course, I can only take one more.' The women looked at each other, both believing themselves more deserving.

Then Mark, feeling chivalrous and glad for another opportunity to impress Amanda, spoke to the women. 'Look, why don't you both take the cab?' Turning to Amanda and Sam he added, 'I can wait for another, or I'm even happy to walk. I remember, Amanda, you said it's only, what, half an hour or so?'

Amanda felt uneasy. 'It is, at a good pace, but I usually like to give myself at least forty-five minutes, plus it's dark and there's hardly any street lights once you're out of town and—'

'I'll be fine, Amanda, don't worry. If I head off on foot I won't get lost. I know it's a straight run. I'll see how I feel, and whatever I decide I'll get back to the guest house in no time.'

Amanda hesitated. 'I'd ask Dad to come and pick you up, but I'm sure he'll be asleep by now.'

Mark gave her a steady look and smiled. 'I'll see you tomorrow.'

With the cab driver impatient and the ladies already thanking Mark, it seemed the deal was done, and Sam, Amanda and the two women were soon settled in the car. As she waved goodbye, Amanda's mind was already thinking ahead to the beach trip tomorrow and spending more time with Mark. What a wonderful night it had been, and she now had every reason to believe tomorrow would be just as good.

Mark stood watching the last of the pub patrons leave before deciding he would set off for the walk back home. In all truth he wasn't keen – walking would be long and lonely, not to mention dark and unfamiliar, but on balance he was even less enthused about standing around doing nothing for an hour or more. He had forgotten to make a note of the cab number, and didn't know where a telephone box was, although he was sure finding one in the centre of town wouldn't be difficult, and if he had any trouble there was bound to be someone to ask, but rather than more delay, he decided to get going.

After leaving the centre of town he started to find his feet, especially as it was so easy to entertain himself with thoughts of Amanda, her warmth and beauty. Yes, coming to Sussex had been a good move, and now he could see a future with her, and that was a fantastic feeling.

Suddenly his thoughts were abruptly interrupted and he turned in fright as a car screeched up right beside him, stopping him in his tracks. That surely wasn't a taxi that Amanda had managed to arrange, was it? It was feasible because she should be home by now – just about – but it didn't look at all like a taxi. So who was it? The window slowly wound down and Mark found himself staring into the face of Nick, his eyes filled with hate as he chewed gum. In the passenger seat and back seat, were the friends he was with earlier.

'Hi,' Nick said in a mocking tone. He smirked. 'Fancy seeing you here, mate. Wanna lift?'

'No thanks,' Mark replied, realising he could soon be in trouble. Even worse, up until then he'd noticed that every once in a while a car would drive past, but now it had become terrifyingly quiet.

'Come on, you must wanna lift, you're all alone. What's happened? Has your white woman abandoned you, or has she cried rape?'

Now with no doubts, and realising what was happening, Mark decided his only option was to quickly walk on.

'Not so fast.' The car edged forward, more than a match for his walking speed. Mark swung round boldly to confront his aggressors.

'Look, I don't want any trouble, just leave me alone please. Just go.'

This was met with guffaws all round.

'Hear that, fellas? Leave him alone, he says.' Nick laughed, 'Yeh, we'll do that, we'll leave you alone alright, but not until we've finished with you, you black bastard.'

The car parked, and all three got out. Mark, who had now started to run, felt feelings of intense fear, desperate to see another person – anyone.

'Don't let that wog get away.'

'Go Kunta Kinte.'

This was followed by peals of laughter. One of the men who had caught up with Mark shoved his face close, eyeballing him, and despite the darkness of the night he stood close enough for Mark to notice he had a scar above his left eyebrow. The other man impatiently pushed him aside, and then, with relish, seeing the way was clear, knocked Mark to the ground with one blow. Mark instinctively reached out his hand and managed to stop his forehead violently hitting the pavement. While Nick stood watching, his two friends administered vicious punches and kicks, directed mainly against Mark's torso, arms and legs, until he thought he would pass out or even die. The only thing he could see was the night sky, and the only sounds the thud of Doc Marten boots, accompanied by four-letter words, delivered with each blow. After what felt like an age, although in reality it was little more than a minute, Mark was rendered motionless, although not quite left for dead, as the three men fled the scene.

Chapter 13

Amanda opened the bedroom curtains and the sunshine streamed in. On the porch roof below, several sparrows chirped, and she breathed in the fresh country air blowing through the net curtains. She felt ecstatic but also apprehensive. What if Mark had thought things over last night and changed his mind? Granted, he didn't have much to drink, but it's one thing to fall in love with a girl wearing her glad rags, over a lager and pounding music, and another to still feel those same flutters the following morning in the cold light of day. She chastised herself for being fearful again. If Mark had been interested yesterday, which he clearly was, then surely nothing would change today. For the first time she found herself wishing Sam wasn't always around, and felt guilty about that, but she was also longing for some time alone with Mark before they were both gone in just a couple of days.

Remembering they had left him at the pub, she wondered if he had managed to get a taxi or had chosen to walk instead. Then it crossed her mind, she'd forgotten to give him the number of the taxi firm, but she was sure he would have asked someone.

Heading to the bathroom, she brushed her teeth and got dressed, before lightly knocking on Sam's door. It had been a late night, and although Amanda didn't want to wake her friend, it was now nearly half past nine and she was keen to speak to her. She also didn't want her parents, who would have been up for several hours by now, to think Sam rude. Amanda knew full well that Joan in particular would be frustrated if the girls were still in bed after a certain time. She liked to get going in the morning and would be itching to prepare breakfast for them.

After knocking, Amanda was pleased to hear a cheerful, 'I'm up, and I'll be five minutes.'

'See you in the kitchen, Sam,' she called back, before making her way downstairs, but once there, she was surprised to find her parents sitting in the living room, looking burdened and nervous.

'Mum, Dad, is something wrong?'

Amanda had a sense of foreboding, and her heart started to thump loudly in her chest. As was usually the case during tense moments it was Robert who spoke. 'Earlier this morning, about an hour and a half ago, Mum and I heard a knock on the door,' he said with deliberation.

Amanda interrupted her father nervously. 'I didn't hear it, who was it? Was it Mark? Is he okay?'

Robert hesitated, 'Yes Amanda, it is to do with Mark, but it wasn't Mark. It was Rhoda Bailey from the guest house.'

'Oh yes, the owner, I spoke to her when I booked the room. Why was she here so early, Dad? What's wrong?' Amanda began to tremble, unsure she could cope with the answer.

Joan's countenance quickly switched from subdued to irritable. 'Calm down, Amanda, please,' she said brusquely. 'You'll start to get me in a panic too. Your father will tell you what happened, just stay calm and sit down.'

'Sorry Mum, I'm sorry.' Amanda sat down slowly. 'Dad, what's happened?'

'Mark's hurt,' Robert answered. 'As soon as I opened the door and saw Rhoda's face I knew something had happened. She said he was picked up and dropped off by Alison Mills—'

Before he could continue, Joan asked, 'Wait, Robert, don't you think Sam should be here?'

'I am,' came an unexpected reply. Sam was standing at the bottom of the stairs and nobody had heard her come down. Amanda ran to her best friend, held her hand, and led her to the sofa where she sat next to her.

Robert looked heavily at Sam. 'I would normally say good morning, but I'm afraid it's anything but.'

Sam immediately burst into tears and Amanda hugged her in shock. 'Please don't cry, Sam.'

'It's not that bad,' Robert said, holding out his hand in a desperate attempt to reassure. 'Although serious, it's not grave news. How much did you hear before I stopped talking?'

'You were saying that someone had picked up Mark?' said Sam, trying to compose herself.

'Yes, that's right. Rhoda said Alison Mills, who is a nurse, was coming back from a late shift and saw Mark at the side of the road unable to stand, badly beaten and bleeding. It's such a blessing she came across him. Being a nurse she immediately knew what to do, and she also had a first aid kit with her. Anyway, Rhoda said they got back at about 2 a.m. Although she had left a key for Mark, knowing he'd be back late, she hadn't expected it to be as late as that. For some reason she hadn't been able to get to sleep, and so she was awake and able to see to him the minute they arrived.'

Sam's and Amanda's eyes were wide with horror as they absorbed the news.

'Rhoda said Mark was badly hurt, with injuries to his face and body, but of course she could mostly see his facial ones.'

'Oh God please help him!' Sam cried out.

'And unfortunately,' Robert said, his brow furrowed, 'Mark felt he had to go home.'

'What?' Amanda said, her voice heavy with disbelief. 'He's gone?'

'Rhoda said he insisted on getting a taxi back to London at about six this morning,' Robert added bleakly.

'Gosh, what must that have cost?' Amanda's body slumped on the sofa and she looked lifeless. Then Robert handed her a letter.

'Rhoda said he wanted you both to have this.' The envelope was sealed, and the words on the outside, 'To Sam and Amanda', were evidently written by an unsteady hand.

'It's okay, you open it,' Sam said to Amanda. 'I don't think I can.'

Amanda tore it open, pulled out a sheet of folded paper and began to read out loud:

Sam and Amanda,
I'm sorry it's ended like this, but please don't worry. I've had to go home. I've been beaten by Nick's friends but I'll be okay. Don't do anything silly like go to the police. I'll be fine and I'll speak to you both soon,
Love Mark

Amanda sat motionless, trying to process it all. Everything started to make horrible sense when she saw the word 'Nick'. Her growing rage was ready to spill out from her lips. 'That evil—'

Joan interrupted her. 'I can imagine how you feel, love. It's not good. In fact, it's really bad, but there's no point upsetting yourself like that.'

'How could he, how could Nick do this?' Amanda repeated in disbelief, tears falling from her eyes at the sheer injustice and wickedness of it all. 'I want to call the police ... I must.'

She rose to her feet but Sam held her back. 'No, you heard what Mark said, don't do it. Let him talk to us first.'

Amanda sat down again, feeling helpless.

Joan eventually broke the silence. 'I'll put the kettle on, I imagine you're both hungry. What about some toast and eggs?'

'I *was* hungry,' Amanda replied, 'but not now.'

Over breakfast several minutes later, everyone was quiet, until Sam stood up after taking a few bites. 'I'm really sorry, but I have to go home too.'

Amanda felt dejected. 'Why, Sam? I mean, I know why, but do you really have to?'

'Yes Amanda, I do. He's probably home by now and it sounds like he's in a bad way, and I can't just carry on as if nothing's happened.' Sam's breathing quickened. 'Can you imagine Geraldine on the phone to my mum after he turns up in that state? I need to be there to give some sort of account of what I know, even though that's not much, and besides, I've got to see him. Mum will worry about me and my safety too after all this. If that's what has happened to my cousin …' Sam's voice trailed off. 'Anyway, I've got to go, Amanda.' Becoming tearful again, she rushed out of the kitchen. 'I've gotta leave, I'm so sorry.'

* * *

It wasn't an easy goodbye at the station. Amanda hugged Sam before waving her off, stony-faced in the carriage as the train pulled away. Robert hugged Amanda while she buried her tearful face in his chest. 'Hey, love, hey, look at me,' he said, gently stroking her cheek. 'I know you, don't you dare go blaming yourself. None of this is your fault.' He smiled and raised her chin. 'Tell you what, why don't you spend the afternoon at Hillbrook Farm tomorrow instead of moping around the house and worrying, eh? It might take your mind off things.'

Amanda took a brief moment to consider. 'You're right, Dad. I could go, couldn't I? They know Sam and Mark were supposed to be here, so they're not expecting me, but I can always pop by.'

'That's my girl, and today the three of us can still go to the beach as planned. How about that?'

'No Dad, I couldn't possibly,' Amanda said, shaking her head. 'Someone needs to be at home in case the phone rings with any news about Mark.'

Arriving back at Marshywood, they found Joan sitting in the living room watching the tail end of *Morning Worship* on ITV.

'You're back,' she declared energetically, turning off the television.

'No need to switch off, Mum.'

'I wasn't really watching it anyway. There's naff all on telly Sunday mornings, which isn't such a bad thing if it encourages people to spend time with family. Anyway, you didn't tell me if you enjoyed yourself last night.'

'I couldn't, could I?' Amanda replied, surprised by Joan's offhand and chirpy attitude. 'Mark and I … we … I think we started to get close.'

Joan's eyes narrowed, but Amanda's heart was too filled with emotion to care. 'Yes, Mum, I think we fell in love. Well, that poor excuse for a human being who goes by the name of Nick, he was trying it on with me all night and saw us together. He said something pretty nasty and then we left. Some girls wanted to share our taxi so Mark said he'd walk and ...'

'I know you're upset and you've lots to say, love, but try to slow down, just a bit,' Robert urged her.

'She doesn't have to say anything else,' Joan responded curtly. 'I think we get the gist of it. Didn't I tell you this was going to happen, Robert? I knew it! What were you thinking of, Amanda? That might be *it* for you now.' Joan's tone was direct and bitter.

'What on earth do you mean, Mum?' Amanda's mouth fell open. 'Is that all you can say?' She turned to Robert. 'Dad, is that all she can say? "I told you so". What about Mark? Don't you care about him?'

'Of course your mum cares, Manda. She's just worried about you, that's all.' Robert smiled weakly, trying to maintain peace.

'Dad, she's being so insensitive.'

'Oh grow up, Amanda,' Joan snapped. 'I thought you had more sense.'

Having now reached breaking point, Amanda ran upstairs and slammed her bedroom door behind her.

Joan looked unfazed.

'Do you think that was fair, love?' Robert asked tentatively. 'I mean, she is hurting a lot right now, and so is Mark.'

'Okay, call her down then,' Joan replied blandly, and within minutes Amanda was reluctantly descending the stairs.

Joan looked up and smiled. 'I'm sorry, love,' she said, with a degree of genuine remorse. 'I've just been finding it stressful having Sam here, and to be honest I'm glad we've got the house back to ourselves now. I don't mean to be unsympathetic, and I'm sorry about what happened to Mark, but I'm only thinking of you, love, and your reputation.' She patted the sofa and beckoned Amanda to join her. She looked seriously into her daughter's eyes. 'Victoria tells me people round here talk, and I don't want them talking about you, that's all. Do you understand?'

Amanda's response was delayed and she sat quietly for a moment. 'Yes Mum,' she said, breaking the silence and accepting her mother's apology. 'I do understand.'

* * *

Not even Joan could have anticipated how quickly the news travelled, and when Amanda arrived at Hillbrook Farm the next day it was obvious everyone had heard. Although Cecil, Victoria and Dean were civil as always and happy to see her turn up unexpectedly, there was also a stilted atmosphere, and it wasn't until lunchtime, when Amanda and Dean were alone, that they finally had a chance to talk openly.

'I'm really sorry about your friend.' Dean's eye contact was steady, and his concern was real. 'Mum had a phone call from Alison's aunt and she told her everything. It's disgusting,' he said, looking down for a moment. 'She said he was badly beaten, and I think we all know who did it.'

'I definitely do, yes,' Amanda replied. 'Mark's gone home now, but he left us a note.'

'So was it really Nick and his mates then? Mike, the landlord of the Old Sussex pub, spotted one of them around town yesterday with blood on his T-shirt, and put two and two together. When confronted, he said your friend laid into him first and it was a fair fight, but I doubt anyone believes that. Has he gone to the police yet?'

'No he hasn't, and doesn't want to either – but I don't know why, because I've not spoken to him.' Amanda felt anger welling up inside her again. 'I can't believe your brother's friend did that to him!' Her voice quivered with emotion but then she immediately regretted her outburst.

'Oh whoa, hold on,' Dean exclaimed, his posture straightening, 'friend is a very loose term, and anyway Stuart feels guilty enough. He told me he wished he'd never talked to Nick about you. He said he knew Nick was a bit rough and ready but never thought him capable of that kind of brutality.' Dean's facial muscles relaxed. 'He's asked me to apologise on his behalf,' he said slowly, 'and to mention something else. He feels bad about not getting the chance to speak to you and your friends. I'm telling you all this because he had to rush away yesterday to visit Emma's parents.'

'Emma? Was that the girl with him on Saturday night?' Amanda asked, sounding calmer.

'That's right. He met her at Cambridge and now she's working in personnel management. Apparently her parents are a pair of hippies who own a tumbledown cottage and some land in Devon. He and Emma are staying for a week in a caravan on the land. They've gone on his motorbike.'

'She must be brave, travelling all that way on the back of a motorbike.'

'Either brave or insane,' Dean chuckled.

Amanda smiled back. 'Please thank Stuart for his apology when you next see him. We were dancing and chatting with other people, so I wasn't offended that he didn't get the chance to come over to say hello, although to be honest, perhaps I did think it was strange at first, but it really doesn't matter.' A shadow of remorse fell across her face and she put her sandwich down. 'And I'm sorry I vented just now. I can't blame Stuart for what happened. In fact, I feel it's my fault, I really do. If I hadn't invited Mark to the disco – or even to Sussex – he wouldn't have been attacked, and I'm afraid that by being polite to Nick I may have unintentionally strung him along, which resulted in all of this.'

'Don't blame yourself, Amanda. It's nothing to do with you, at least when it comes to the attack. I hope you can see that. No decent person would have done what they did, not under any circumstances.'

'I guess you're right,' Amanda replied. She appreciated Dean's encouraging words, despite still feeling culpable.

'I'm sure Stuart told you all about the disco, but how was your Saturday night in with Carolyn?' she asked, trying to shift the focus away from herself.

Dean slowly placed his mug on the wooden tray. 'My evening in ... it was fine ... well, okay, I guess.' He was quiet for a moment before adding casually, 'But Carolyn admitted to me she's not happy with the ring.'

'Really?' Amanda was baffled. 'I thought it sounded like a beautiful ring, and didn't you say she really liked it?'

'I did, but we were sitting on the sofa here at the farm watching *The Incredible Hulk*, and she said she didn't want to hurt my feelings but wondered if it was too late to exchange it because she preferred diamonds.'

'But there are diamonds in that ring,' Amanda said, noticing a tenseness in Dean's smile.

'I know, but she said she wanted *just* diamonds, a solitaire, or maybe a collection of smaller ones. She also said green wasn't really her colour. Just then the Hulk threw a man across the room and I said, "If green's not your thing, how come you fancy the pants off this geezer?"'

Amanda grinned. 'What did she say?'

'Nothing, and I'm not even sure she found it funny,' Dean said, bringing his coffee mug up to his smiling lips. 'Anyway, so much for my failed attempts at chivalry, but at least I tried to get it right. Who can get into the mind of a woman? They're so complicated ... present company excepted, of course!'

'I think I'll take that as a compliment,' Amanda said with a playful tone of indignation, 'but then again, if you're saying I'm simple ...'

They sat silently for a moment with relaxed smiles. Then Dean continued, 'I did telephone the jewellers – Hoffman and Sons – first thing this morning. They said it was too late for an exchange but it would sell second-hand for a good price. So what I'll do is take some money out of my savings and buy her another ring. And this time she's coming with me,' he said with a firm nod and a smile. 'Then I'll try to sell the emerald one and put the money back in the bank before the wedding.'

'Sounds like a sensible plan,' Amanda said, impressed by Dean's efforts to please Carolyn. 'I think you've been very understanding, which is a good thing. She's going to live with the ring for the rest of her life so she ought to be pleased with it. It's also fantastic that she felt she could be honest with you.'

'Yes, I really appreciate Carolyn's honesty,' Dean said confidently, 'and that's not the only thing I appreciate. We are all glad you were able to come today, after all, Amanda.'

'It's nothing,' she replied dismissively, 'and, anyway, it's far better than sitting at home waiting for the phone to ring. When I get back, Mum and Dad will update me with the news about Mark, if there is any.'

She wanted to open up a bit and now seemed like the right time.

'I haven't been back to London since we moved, but I'm going to travel up to visit Mark – if he wants to see me, that is – probably within a week or so.'

'Of course he'll want to see you.' Dean sounded surprised. 'You're dating, aren't you?'

'Not really, no. There was a spark at the disco and now that might be gone forever. And not only that, Mum thinks I've lost something else too.' She paused, unsure whether she should say more.

'What Amanda?' Dean asked, looking at her solidly.

'My reputation. She thinks I may have lost that as well.'

Dean's eyebrows drew together with empathy as Amanda's voice wobbled and she turned her face away.

'You do worry, don't you, Amanda?' He smiled gently. 'Far be it for me to contradict your mother, but I really think she's massively overreacting if by that she believes anyone will think less of you ... or your friends. Most people round here are well meaning and can sniff out a nasty character like Nick a mile away. On the other hand, I've heard many good things said about you, and I see no reason for that to change. Things will get better. You'll see.'

Closing her eyes for a second, Amanda managed to steady her emotions long enough to mutter a faint, 'Thank you.' She could tell he was speaking from the heart.

Just at that moment, Millie came running towards them. 'Dean, Dad wants you in the barn.'

Amanda had met Millie for the first time several weeks back, an energetic 14-year-old, today wearing her long dark brown hair in two large plaits. She was glad to see her again. 'Hi Millie, are you enjoying the school holidays?'

'Yes, but I would even more if Dad and Dean weren't working me like a shire horse.'

Amanda smiled, thinking the peppy teenager didn't appear particularly over-exerted.

'Too bad, munchkin,' Dean said, tickling Millie rambunctiously, 'you should never have been born a farmer's daughter if you can't handle it.'

'Hey, stop it will you, no more, please!' Millie begged, between fits of laughter before managing to escape. 'Come on, hurry up, Dean,' she shouted, heading towards the barn, 'Dad needs you.'

* * *

On Sunday morning almost a week later, Amanda was heading to London by train. Although unaware of the current state of Mark's injuries, it was a good sign he had agreed to see her at last, so she remained quietly optimistic things were not as bad as she initially feared. Although what she had heard about Geraldine's panic when he came home concerned her, she reasoned it was natural for mothers to be anxious, and hoped there was no real cause for alarm. One thing was for sure, she couldn't wait to see him.

Regrettably, unbeknown to Amanda, the situation wasn't so simple. Mark's Good Samaritan, the nurse who found him, had pleaded with him to go to the casualty department at Eastbourne hospital, but he had refused, instead opting to return to London as soon as possible, hoping his GP would confirm that his injuries weren't serious. When his doctor saw him, he was amazed that Mark had coped without hospital treatment, saying it was nothing short of a miracle that he'd managed to avoid a single broken bone. Despite this, he was not left unscathed. His injuries included nerve damage to his face, a bloodied and black left eye, a deep cut on his face, which would inevitably scar, severe bruising on his body, swelling to his lips, and a minor concussion, which fortunately would have no long-lasting effects. In time, the doctor was confident Mark's injuries would heal, but he was concerned about possible psychological damage, so much so that he suggested a referral to a psychiatric nurse. Mark said he'd think about it, but in truth he'd already made up his mind. Medical records mentioning assault was one thing, but a history of psychological instability was quite another, and he could never allow that to happen.

* * *

As Amanda walked down a wide road in an unfamiliar part of London, she easily managed to find Mark's house. 'Number 52, that's the one,' she said under her breath. Mark had told Sam he wanted to buy a place of his own, but so soon after losing his father, he decided he couldn't do that to his mum, at least not yet. Amanda was glad he had postponed buying somewhere. If there was any future for them at all, one of them would have to move, and if that turned out to be him, it would be easier if he had no home to sell. She looked at the three-storey terraced house, which was much larger than Sam's – and Amanda's old home too. Now that it was only Geraldine and Mark at home, Amanda thought they both could do with moving one day, Geraldine to downsize and Mark to a new home of his own. But where would that be? It felt good to be back in London; after all, that was where she was born and had lived for nineteen years. But it was no longer home, and would Mark ever wish to leave it? There were a number of solicitor's firms within striking distance of her new locality, and Mark was so bright and successful he was bound to be snapped up, but even if at one point he would have considered moving to Sussex, would that still be the case after all that had happened?

Amanda walked up the stairs leading to the front door, rang the doorbell and waited. No one answered, so she rang again, and soon there was the outline of a familiar tall figure behind the opaque glass. The door opened, and Amanda could see her fears had not been unfounded. She blinked hard, trying to hold back her tears. Mark attempted to fashion his swollen lip into a smile, and despite his eyes being hidden under sunglasses, she soon saw signs of swelling, scarring and discoloration. His whole demeanour was hunched over and subdued. There was something lost in his spirit.

'Come in,' he said listlessly, ushering her towards the living room. 'How was your journey?'

Amanda noticed he was hobbling slightly as he walked. 'It was fine, but it felt a bit strange. I haven't taken the train to London from Sussex before. I enjoyed it, though, and it's true what you said about the views around Wivelsfield.'

Mark pointed a finger upwards. 'Yes, that was the name of the station I'd forgotten, just outside Haywards Heath, wasn't it?' he said, sounding more animated.

They sat down, and Amanda had to speak about the obvious, or felt she would burst.

'Mark, thanks for seeing me today. I'm so, so sorry about what happened. If only I could do something.'

'No Amanda, please, don't feel that way,' he said quietly, 'there's nothing you can do or could have done to change things. Life can be a bummer sometimes.'

'But you didn't deserve that, nobody does. Sam told me some of the sickening things they said to you. That Nick, he's a …' Amanda checked herself, trying not to get het up again. 'I just want to do something, I have to Mark. Have you changed your mind about contacting the police?'

Mark took a deep breath and held it in. 'I have already said, Amanda, that's not what I want to do. Look, I am about to qualify as a solicitor. Do you think it will help my career if I'm involved in a prosecution case where I'm the victim? It could be reported in the press, it could ruin everything. I don't want that sort of publicity. Besides, cases like these can take forever to come to trial, and even then there's no guarantee there will be a conviction.'

'But at least there's a chance they will be convicted and jailed. If you do nothing they'll just get away with it, won't they? And if they're let off the hook, scot-free, they might do it to someone else,' Amanda pleaded.

'I just don't see it like that,' Mark replied hesitantly. 'This might be a funny thing for someone with a career in law to say,' he said, his hands lying still in his lap, 'but I believe that justice will be done, even if I don't do anything. My mum also wanted me to go to the police, but now she understands how I feel. And she told me just yesterday, she believes that no one gets away with evil, that what goes around comes around eventually, and they will be punished somehow. Do you believe that's true, Amanda?' he asked, his voice lifting.

Amanda paused for thought and swallowed. 'Perhaps Mark, and I hope she's right, I really do.' She tucked her hair behind her ear and looked around, noticing his mother's absence. 'Is your mum home?'

'Sorry, no Amanda, she's out.'

'Do pass on my good wishes, if I don't see her before I leave.' Amanda was trying to put on a brave face, all the while paranoid that Geraldine was avoiding her because she blamed her for the attack. 'I think it's good she can see your point of view, and I also know how much your career means to you.' Amanda stopped short and her muscles tensed briefly. What had Mark told his boss and others at the firm? 'Sam said you had to take time off. Are you back at work yet?' she asked, trying to sound matter-of-fact.

Mark gave a resigned sigh. 'I'm back tomorrow. I had to inform my boss that I was attacked, I mean, what else could I say, I walked into a brick wall?' Overlooking the irritation in his voice, Amanda wanted to touch him – to calm him. 'It will be obvious when they see me anyway,' he said sounding softer. 'A colleague phoned me at home and said he was sorry to hear I'd been mugged. I was confused at first, but now I'm wondering if my boss told everyone I'd been mugged to protect me from being criticised in case people assumed I was drunk and got into a fight.' Mark shuffled his feet. 'Or maybe Mr Berrington just assumed it was theft motivated, although I don't think I gave him that impression. I only told him I'd been assaulted. Anyhow, I didn't correct George.'

'George?'

That's the colleague who phoned. It seemed so much easier to let everyone carry on believing it was a mugging by random strangers, and I suppose that's what they were, at least as far as *I* was concerned.'

Despite wondering if she had heard a hint of disgruntlement, Amanda refused to believe that Mark was trying to insinuate that she had any sort of relationship with Nick and his associates, but she still felt uneasy, and what he said next didn't help her feel any better.

'I just want this to be forgotten, but making progress in my career is already at risk because of this.'

'Surely not,' Amanda exclaimed, gripping her hands together tightly in her lap.

'I'm afraid it might be,' Mark continued. 'It was extremely bad timing. I was going to move over to civil litigation this week and it had to be postponed. The Senior Partner in that division is not known for being accommodating. I'm fortunate Mr Berrington was such an understanding boss, so I'm sure he'll try his best to smooth things over.'

'I'm glad to hear that,' replied Amanda, giving Mark an affectionate smile, but he didn't reciprocate. She also noticed he hadn't offered her a drink. Not only was there no offer of tea or other refreshments, but everything seemed perfunctory and there was no affection. No hand holding, no warm smiles, no laughter. It was as though the light had been extinguished, not only in Mark, but also in their relationship. 'It'll all work out, you'll see,' she said encouragingly, remembering Dean's words to her just a week earlier. But instead of looking heartened, she could see only a blank expression under Mark's dark glasses and she was met with silence.

'Are you seeing Sam today?' he asked after a while.

'Yes, assuming she hasn't changed her mind about having me round,' Amanda laughed lightly, trying to sound more upbeat than she was feeling.

'Would you give her this for me, please?' Mark got up and robotically picked up a small umbrella and handed it to Amanda. 'She asked me to hold it after we left the cinema. I put it in a carrier bag with the chocolates I bought for Mum and forgot about it. I ended up taking it home. I meant to bring it to the disco.' His face contorted as he finished his sentence.

Seeing his anguish, Amanda scrabbled around for positive words. '*Moonraker* was good, wasn't it, Mark? I really enjoyed watching it with you and Sam. Please remember, I'd love you to come back anytime you want. I know it may not be for a while, especially after the experience you've had, but you're always welcome, you know that.'

'Thanks, Amanda, I'll bear that in mind.'

His feigned willingness to visit again did little to convince her he would be returning to the village any time soon. He must be suffering from trauma. Who wouldn't be in his situation? She felt convinced that in time things would improve for him, and hopefully for their relationship too, but how long would that take, and would he allow her to be part of the healing process, even in some small way? She just couldn't tell.

After another long silence, Amanda began to wonder whether handing her the umbrella had been a subtle hint for her to leave. She decided it was time. 'I think I'll head over to Sam's now. Please keep in touch and let me know how things go for you at work, won't you?' Mark sprang to his feet when he realised she was about to go. 'Oh Amanda, I'm really sorry. I don't think I offered you a drink, did I? Can I get you a tea or coff—'

Amanda interrupted him. 'I'm fine, Mark. I'll have a drink at Sam's. You've got a lot on your mind, I'm aware of that, so please don't worry about me.' She walked towards the front door with Mark behind her, and after leaving the house she turned around to face him. Standing on the first step leading down to the pavement below, she was now too far away for them to comfortably touch and this was a strange relief to her. Now was not the time to suddenly start showing physical affection, and as she gently waved goodbye, she began to wonder if physical contact, the way it had been at the disco, would ever again be a part of their relationship.

* * *

Smiles, laughter, and plenty of jollof rice and Nigerian chicken stew was a great comfort to Amanda as she sat in the lounge, plates on laps, with Sam's family. Not only was she starving, having forgotten to eat lunch, she was also hungry for human warmth and affection, and with Precious this was offered up in bucket loads. Amanda never felt uncomfortable or judged by Precious but only experienced warm acceptance. In contrast, Sam, although clearly pleased to see her friend, seemed distant. Amanda had known her far too long, and valued the friendship far too much to ignore it.

'Sam, are you okay? You're not your usual self.'

'Sorry, Amanda, I'm fine. It's just …' she looked downwards for a moment, 'I suppose it's the shock of it all. What happened to Mark, and everything. Geraldine is in a state, as you can imagine, and I still don't know how well he's coping. How did he seem today?'

'Not his usual self either, but I was expecting that.'

'Mum and I went to see them Friday night. I couldn't stand seeing him like that, Amanda. It all seems so unfair.' Sam relaxed her tense shoulders. 'Mum prayed with him and Geraldine, and when we left she told them she'll pray for him every day. I know she does, but as for me, well, I'm really struggling right now. It's thrown up so many questions in my mind, and I'm not sure how safe I feel after all this. I'm probably not making much sense.'

'I think I understand what you're trying to say,' Amanda replied, taking care with her words. 'Look, Sam, I know it's easier said than done, because I fell into the same trap when I was younger, but please try your best not to let anything knock your confidence or make you become insecure. Also, I don't know if you appreciate how lucky you are to have such a caring family. I was thinking when I watched you all praying together before eating tonight how special that was. I'd love it if Mum, Dad and I did that at home, but that's not something we've ever done. You're very lucky, Sam.'

'You're right,' Sam said, glancing at her brothers wrestling with each other. 'I do have a lot to be thankful for, and I'm sure Mark will be okay. It could have been so much worse.'

Amanda was of the same opinion. Although she was desperate to tell Sam her own worries, she decided to refrain from talking about her fears for her relationship with Mark, but almost as though she could read her friend's mind, Sam decided to raise the subject anyway.

'He did tell me though, Amanda, when I saw him on Friday, that … well … he didn't think that you and him …'

'I know,' said Amanda, stepping in to save her friend from an awkward moment. 'And it's okay,' she said quietly.

'I'm sorry, Amanda. I really had high hopes for you both.'

* * *

As Amanda walked to Leytonstone underground to catch the tube to Victoria station, she took in the sights, sounds and smells of her old haunts in East London. She walked past her senior high school, the shops which sold wonderfully interesting ethnic foods from far-flung places – the Caribbean, South America and Asia and the Indian restaurant where she had celebrated her 18th birthday. Despite it being a Sunday, East London was brimming with activity, and she felt a real sense of nostalgia, as though she'd left years ago and not mere months.

She couldn't help but feel there was a change in the air, not just in her life, but in the national psyche too. With the launch of the Two Tone record label, black and white kids were uniting like never before, under music inspired by ska, reggae and punk, while at the same time there were growing signs of ethnic unrest with debates in the newspapers about things she didn't understand, such as 'sus laws', and there was even talk of racial tension which could one day lead to rioting. And now, in her own life, Amanda had witnessed race-related violence. As a result, her hopes and dreams had been shattered and her heart torn to pieces.

As she travelled home on the train, she couldn't get The Specials' song 'Gangsters' out of her head and the lyrics were now poignant. Would Mark always dread the future? Would his scarred face always be a reminder of his experience? The words seemed cruelly apt.

Chapter 14

After a few weeks, Amanda found herself settling back into her old routines, including her work at Jimmy's. At first, every time the café door opened she would freeze, fearing Nick would walk in, but after several days passed she came to realise it was increasingly unlikely he'd be coming back. *Too ashamed to show his face*, she seethed inwardly, but then she began to sense that her anger towards him was hindering rather than helping her. Nick had developed into an ogre in her mind, the cause of all her disappointments, until she realised that attributing that power to him was ridiculous.

Sam had told Amanda that Precious had urged Mark to forgive rather than hate, and that although Mark confessed he would find that very hard, he had said he was willing to try. Amanda could see why he might struggle. Even though she hadn't experienced anything close to what happened to him, just thinking about Nick and his friends was starting to affect her physically. Evidently she too needed to let go, and if Mark was able to do it, she certainly could.

One morning Jimmy announced that he had something important to say. One of his long-standing friends had recently died and he was shutting the café for four days to travel to Glasgow for the funeral. Although Amanda wasn't going to be paid, she fully accepted the loss of earnings, realising that it must have been a difficult decision for Jimmy, since he and Pat would also lose four days' income.

With the café closed from Wednesday to Sunday, Amanda had five days of freedom. She was looking forward to recharging her emotional batteries and catching up on things she hadn't had time to do. But what about Hillbrook? While Amanda didn't want to stop going to the farm in those five days, she also wanted a proper break from everything. Instead of her usual afternoon sessions she decided to devote an entire day to the farm and take the remaining time off. Today she would let them know that she would volunteer all of tomorrow, but after that she wouldn't be back until Monday.

She arrived to see Dean dashing towards his car, and although she wanted to tell him her plan, he was clearly rushed.

'Sorry Amanda, can't stop now. I'm really late for the egg delivery, but Dad's around somewhere. He's got a few jobs for you. Maybe see you tomorrow.'

'Yes, of course,' Amanda called after him.

They hadn't spoken much these past few weeks. Although she didn't get the sense he was avoiding her, he just didn't talk or hang around as readily, and she was missing their chats. Occasionally he seemed down, and she hoped nothing was wrong. He was beginning to feel like a friend to her and she wanted him to be happy. Yes, Amanda often told herself that she very much wanted him and Carolyn to be happy.

When she told Cecil her plan for the week he had no objections. 'Dean's going to Hailsham cattle market tomorrow morning,' he said, locking the farm gate. 'Autumn's coming and so he's there regularly, looking for a good supply of store cattle.'

'Store cattle?'

'I apologise,' Cecil replied, 'it's easy to forget you don't have a farming background. Store cattle are fattened up over the winter until they're ready for slaughter.'

Amanda nodded. She had seen how well cared for the animals were at Hillbrook. Dean would talk fondly about his cows and their differing personalities – something she too was discovering. All the animals, including the cows, had a good life and she knew Dean and Cecil would do all they could to ensure they also had a good death, free from pain and suffering. 'Thanks, Cecil. I've got so much to learn,' she said.

'As you're here all day tomorrow you're welcome to go along with him, if you'd like.'

'I'd love to go. I've never been to a cattle market before.'

'And it's not just cattle, but sheep and pigs too. The market's been around since 1252 and was given a Royal Charter by King Henry III.'

'Sounds amazing!' Amanda didn't know what receiving a Royal Charter meant, but it sounded impressive. She would ask her father later. However, sensing Amanda's lack of understanding, Cecil explained that a Royal Charter was equivalent to a modern-day land deed.

'I believe Henry allowed the market to trade exclusively and gave it privileges, a bit like the rights companies have in this day and age,' he said, 'but I'm a farmer, not a historian, and certainly not an expert on these matters.'

'Thanks for explaining, Cecil. I think I understand. I'm looking forward to going along tomorrow,' she said, before setting off to begin the day's tasks with a light spring in her step.

* * *

The next day was a beautiful sunny September morning, and Amanda arrived at the farm to find Dean leaning against his Land Rover.

'Morning Amanda, how's things?' he said cheerfully.

'Very good thanks, Dean. How are you?'

He lowered his eyes, and for a moment there was no answer. Amanda could only hear a crunching sound as he shifted his foot awkwardly on the gravel beneath. 'Something happened last night, which I'll tell you about in a moment, but apart from that

I'm fine,' he said, and then he smiled. 'I'm glad you've agreed to come with me today. Should be fun. We won't be back until after lunch, though, so the plan is to grab something at the café.'

'I'm sorry I haven't got any cash on me ...'

'We wouldn't expect you to pay, Amanda. Lunch as always is on us. It's the least we can do.'

'That's really kind of you, thank you, Dean.'

'Absolutely no problem at all.'

Amanda sat in the passenger seat wondering what had happened last night. She remembered the last time she was in Dean's car and the fun they had had listening to music, but she didn't expect that today. Not only was the journey significantly shorter, but Dean had something on his mind.

'Is everything okay? How are things at the farm?' she asked.

'Not too great at the moment,' he said, his voice sounding unsettled. 'Yesterday Dad found one of the sheep on her back, bloodied and mauled by a dog. She was in a bad way. Mum said she'd seen a man with a pit bull terrier type dog near the field, and if he was the cause of all this then he's a disgrace.' Dean gripped the steering wheel a little tighter. 'Irresponsible dog owners disgust me,' he added, with palpable frustration. 'Dad called the vet, which cost us quite a bit. He cleaned the sheep up and gave it penicillin, but since this morning we've not seen it and Dad thinks it's gone somewhere secluded to be alone to die.'

'Oh that's horrible, Dean. I'm so sorry,' Amanda flinched when she pictured the injured sheep dying.

'It isn't good, but it's part and parcel of farming. Never mind, you have to accept these things and move on. I hope today will be better and I'm able to find some good livestock at the market.'

'You're looking for store cattle, aren't you?' Amanda said, showing off her newfound knowledge.

'That's right,' Dean replied, looking more positive.

'Is everything else okay?' Amanda asked, seizing the opportunity. What happened to the sheep wasn't good, but it happened only yesterday, so it wouldn't account for Dean's apparent change of mood these past few weeks.

Dean didn't answer for what felt a long time. 'Oh, you know, just been busy making plans for the wedding.' The silence which followed and the look on his face suggested there was something more. Dean tried to relax his tight shoulders, but could see that wasn't going to be enough to convince Amanda everything was fine. 'I'm probably worrying about nothing,' he continued, 'but I'm getting concerned about Carolyn's best friend Tracy. I'm starting to think Carolyn tells her a bit too much about our relationship. Tracy is apparently surprised that ... well, that Carolyn and I are waiting until marriage to sleep together and said that her boyfriend Brian wouldn't be such a wimp.'

Amanda pressed her lips together tightly. She wasn't expecting this depth of sharing and was slightly taken aback. Although Tracy's remark was rude and disrespectful, it was also mildly amusing, but she kept a straight face, appreciating that Dean had taken her into his confidence. And for his sake, she tried to ignore her own feelings of awkwardness.

Dean, too absorbed in thought to notice anything untoward, continued, 'I have a high regard for Carolyn and her values so we haven't had sex. She said her parents told her the trick is to avoid spending long periods of time alone together, and we've found that does help. You would think it was her parents telling her what to do, wouldn't you, but it was actually her decision to wait, although to be fair, how she was brought up does have a lot to do with it. Her dad was an elder at the Ebenezer chapel in the village. I'm sure you've seen it.'

'Yes, I have.'

'It's a strict Baptist church, and although they no longer go, her parents still have certain morals which they taught Carolyn from an early age, and I respect that.'

Amanda nodded, still slightly taken aback to be talking with Dean this intimately, but feeling much more at ease.

'I also think sex should be special,' he said, pulling up at a red light. 'I know it's not a popular view nowadays, especially if you're a man, but I could never understand why some people are happy to sleep around or go with someone who they end up never speaking to again.'

'I totally agree,' Amanda replied as he lifted the handbrake to move forward.

'Stuart, on the other hand, not to put him down or anything, but put it this way, I don't think he shares our opinion. Despite his many relationships, and believe me he's had a few, I'm not sure he's happy, even though he's currently with Emma. I've never wanted lots of relationships, which is a good job, because if I had I wouldn't have found the time. Seriously though, all I've ever wanted was a good woman I could rely on. It helps of course if she's a looker, and Carolyn is a looker, don't you think?' He smiled and swiftly turned to Amanda who, having no choice but to agree, made an affirmative sound.

Dean was on autopilot, having driven this route many times before, and Amanda was glad that he hadn't shared something like this during their last car journey together, because it was clear that baring his soul was making it harder to concentrate on driving.

'Not only does Carolyn tell Tracy a lot,' he added, 'but she really values her opinion as well. Tracy thinks we should go abroad for our honeymoon, for instance, but I can't afford that, and I'm not keen on those resorts anyway. I was thinking about Scotland, perhaps a cottage by Loch Ness or something, but it'll have to be later in the year when the weather warms up a bit. Let's face it, Scotland in January isn't the best choice.'

'No, probably not.'

'So, I plan to book a couple of nights at a nice hotel immediately after the wedding, just somewhere close, and then a proper honeymoon, maybe in the Scottish Highlands, in the spring.'

'That's where Jimmy is now, Scotland,' Amanda said, noticing the smell of newly laid tar on the town road.

'Yes, Dad mentioned about the café closing, which is why you're spending the day with us, of course.'

'I think Scotland sounds lovely for a honeymoon, Dean.'

'I'm sure Carolyn would have been happy with that too, that is if Tracy hadn't sown seeds of doubt in her mind. Although, I must be honest and admit it's not just Tracy's influence. I know she'd happily honeymoon in Bognor as long as we're together,' he smiled, 'but at the same time Carolyn would easily travel the world, if she could. She always said she wanted to, but even if I felt the same, how could I? I've got the farm.'

Amanda initially unsure of an appropriate response, quickly thought of something. 'My aunt and uncle, they've travelled around the world, and they're off to Kenya on safari soon. We, by that I mean Mum, Dad and me, have never really wanted their jet-setting lifestyle, but Mum's always fancied a safari, so she has to admit she is envious this time.'

'We're here.' Dean pulled into the entrance of the cattle market and found a space in the car park, but before getting out he appeared troubled. 'I've just realised, I'm doing the same thing,' he said, looking rigid.

'Doing what?' Amanda asked, perplexed.

'I'm complaining about Carolyn telling Tracy things I'd rather she didn't, but isn't that exactly what I'm doing, sharing things with you? You could say I'm guilty of doing the same thing.'

Once again, unsure how to respond, Amanda had to think on her feet. 'I suppose that's true, but a lot depends on *why* you're doing it. I think it's because you want things to improve, and that's not a bad reason, is it?'

Dean seemed satisfied, and Amanda, surprising herself by her wisdom, felt relieved.

They were soon inside the main market area. She looked around. There were men with flat caps and neutral brown, grey and beige clothing, some smoking pipes. There were also several large animal transport trucks and metal pens, not to mention a variety of healthy looking sheep and cattle. Almost the instant Dean left the car, he was waved at and greeted by several people, many of whom he chatted to as he made his way around. He looked comfortable among his fellow farmers and seemed to know everyone.

A man was standing by cows in a pen with an assembly of farmers around him, speaking at rapid speed, using rural bidding phrases incorporating several strange pitches and tones. It was clearly auction speak, leaving Amanda unable to decipher individual words let alone sentences, and so wonderfully traditional, it felt like she was witnessing a taste of days gone by. She followed Dean as he walked towards the auctioneer and watched him inspect the cattle.

'I'm not sure any are suitable today, unfortunately,' he concluded. 'They're not what we're looking for. Oh well, perhaps next week.'

'That's a shame,' Amanda replied. 'Does that mean we have to leave?'

'Not just yet, there are a couple of people I'd like to speak to before we go, and don't forget lunch, they do great cakes in the…'

'Dean, hey Dean!' someone called loudly, interrupting him. Fast approaching was a young man with olive skin, black hair and wearing a big smile.

'Flavio!' Dean exclaimed. Soon the two were greeting each other with enthusiastic pats on the shoulders and warm smiles. 'What are you doing here, Flavio?' Dean asked, stepping back.

'We're refurbishing our restaurant and I'm looking out for new local suppliers for quality meat. We normally buy from wholesalers, but I know some slaughterhouses get their stock from here … hold on a minute, Dean, if I remember correctly your Dad's farm used to supply meat for butchers.'

'We still do.'

'Do you supply restaurants too?'

'Not currently, but I don't see why we couldn't. I'll go back and speak to Dad about it.' Dean suddenly realised Flavio and Amanda hadn't been introduced. 'Flavio, this is Amanda, she volunteers on the farm. Amanda, this is Flavio, we went to school together and his parents own an Italian restaurant down in Eastbourne, and a very good one at that, although I'm ashamed to admit I've only eaten there once.'

'And I'm ashamed to say I've never bought any of your meat,' Flavio smiled and sucked in a quick breath. 'Hello Amanda, nice to meet you.' Amanda took Flavio's hand and he firmly shook hers before turning to Dean again. 'How long since I last saw you?' he asked.

'Let me see … it must be five years, or coming up for that.'

'Easily, so what've you been up to?'

'I'm still working on the farm. I do have a bit of news, though. You probably don't remember Carolyn Mitcham, although I think you met her just before we left school. We're getting married in January.'

'Congratulations,' Flavio said with a grin. 'I always thought you'd tie the knot young. Yes, I think I remember your pretty girlfriend. When in January?' he asked, tilting his head to one side.

'We haven't confirmed the date, we'll know within days, but it's looking like the 26th.'

Flavio slapped his forehead in mock despair. 'Lucky for you, I can't come. January's our quietest month so we always close the restaurant for two weeks and travel to Italy to see my grandparents, otherwise I would be expecting an invitation.'

Dean laughed. 'Typical Flavio, still as cheeky as ever. What about you? Any girlfriend yet?'

'My lovely Italian mama is always trying to marry me off, but I've managed to duck and dive so far. I work in the restaurant day and night, so no time anyway. I'm really glad we've almost finished the renovations. It's been such a major project we've been shut for nearly a week, but we're opening again on Monday.' Flavio paused and then said brightly, 'Hey, do you want to come and see? That is, if you're finished here for the day.'

Dean pondered. 'Do you know, I think we *have* finished although I was going to chat to a few people but that can wait until next week. Yes, that would be fantastic, I'd love to. How about you, Amanda?'

The prospect of an unplanned trip to Eastbourne sounded exciting, but Amanda was unprepared. 'Right now?' she asked, her eyes widening, 'Well, yes, if you think that'll be okay with your dad.'

'Of course! I'll make sure a message gets to him.'

Amanda and Flavio stood awkwardly while Dean rushed over to another young farmer, and before long he was back. 'Alan is going to pop by the farm to let Dad know I've had no success with the store cattle and that we're going to Eastbourne for the afternoon.'

'Terrific! Let's go, shall we?' said Flavio, and he set off for the carpark.

Dean's radio was once again the source of happy entertainment as they followed Flavio's car southwards towards the sea. 'This is a good song,' Amanda said enthusiastically as 'Girls' Talk' by Dave Edmunds played, and afterwards she and Dean screeched their way through Janet Kaye's high-pitched long note in 'Silly Games', with Dean quickly conceding defeat. After their recent conversation, both were amused by the line in Supertramp's 'Breakfast in America', expressing disappointment at not getting much, when it came to his girlfriend and, according to Dean, the Ska rhythms in the song 'The Prince' by a new band called Madness, 'was cracking.'

'Isn't music a wonderful thing?' Amanda said, pausing to catch her breath. 'I couldn't live without it, although if I don't like a song I can find it really annoying.'

'I know what you mean.'

'Sometimes I can't switch it off and it drives me round the bend. Advert jingles, especially, get stuck in my head.'

Dean took his eyes off the road for a second and glanced at Amanda. Her high spirits were entertaining. 'Sounds like that might get a bit irritating,' he smiled.

Amanda was on a roll. 'My love of music can make me look like a ninny sometimes, and what if Flavio sees us bopping in our seats in his rear-view mirror? He'll be wondering what on earth we're doing.'

When the intro to Cliff Richard's chart-topper 'We Don't Talk Anymore' started up, they finally found a song to split their opinion. 'Boring,' was Dean's verdict.

'Do you think so? I quite like it,' said Amanda singing along before her eyes became drawn towards the coastline. 'Look, doesn't the sea look beautiful,' she exclaimed, looking out of the window.

Very soon they parked outside Mozzarella Italia where Flavio was beckoning to them through the glass restaurant doors.

'Come to the kitchen, Mama will be there. I don't know if you remember, Dean, but she can't speak English too well, but come say hello anyway.'

Amanda and Dean shared a glance. 'After you,' Dean said, and Amanda, suddenly feeling more nervous followed Flavio into the large kitchen. There they were greeted by a short, plump woman with a small gap in her teeth, which was only visible when she smiled widely. Flavio spoke to his mother in Italian, and Amanda heard him mention her name.

His mother responded by grabbing Amanda's hands, saying, '*Bella signora, bel fidanzato.*'

'No Mama.'

'What did you say to each other?' asked Dean, looking mystified.

'I told her you were Dean from school, and that you were having a look at the restaurant with Amanda who works at your farm. I then said you're getting married, but Mama, who gets very excited when I mention marriage, didn't wait for me to tell her who to. She thought I was talking about you two!'

'*Scusami per l'errore,*' Flavio's mother said, looking apologetically at Dean and Amanda.

'She's saying sorry for her mistake,' Flavio translated.

'Seriously, that's no problem,' Dean said warmly. 'Tell her it was an easy mistake to make.'

Later, in the main seating area, Dean and Amanda were impressed by the restaurant's interior, but Amanda, a first-time visitor, couldn't tell what had improved, and Dean had forgotten what it looked like before. Flavio offered them a drink, and Dean accepted an Italian coffee, while Amanda settled for a glass of lemonade.

'How's your dad, Flavio?' Dean asked, enjoying the strong brew.

'Fine, in fact he's doing great. He's driven to Brighton to buy some artwork and will be back at about three. Flavio looked at his watch and his eyes became wider. 'It's nearly ten past one already, time's flown. I promised I'd help Mum with the cleaning this afternoon – after floor sanding and decorating there's a lot of dust to wipe down.'

Dean glanced around. 'It's looking really good, Flavio. Where's the dust?'

'It's definitely there, so don't look too hard,' he laughed. 'Boy, I wish I could have offered you lunch, but since we're closed the kitchen's pretty empty. When you're married, Dean, you and Carolyn must come and have a meal on us.' Flavio paused and raised his hand warmly. 'You too, Amanda.'

'That's far too kind of you,' she replied.

'He's always been generous,' Dean said. He patted his friend on the back as they said goodbye, promising to keep in touch. 'Oh, and Flavio, I'll remember to talk to Dad about supplying you meat.'

'Please do, my friend,' Flavio replied. 'Bye for now, and see you again.'

With fresh sea breezes filling their lungs and seagulls calling loudly above, Dean and Amanda stood by the car for a moment.

'So here we are,' Dean said, taking in a deep breath.

'Yes, it's great to be in Eastbourne, especially since I'd planned to go with Mark and Sam, but we never made it.'

'Amanda, how hungry are you?'

'Very,' she breathed, with a light sigh.

'Fancy fish and chips?'

'That sounds extremely tempting. I love fish and chips and it's ages since I last had it.'

'Well, head this way then. I know a fantastic place where they do very big portions. Would you prefer to eat inside or on the beach?'

'Oh, definitely on the beach!' Amanda said, smiling eagerly.

'Better watch out for the seagulls then.'

When they had bought their food, Amanda and Dean took their tasty bundles, settled on some rocks and began to tuck in. For a time all that could be heard were the waves crashing and seagulls squawking above, while others perched on the pebbles, looked on expectantly. The only other sound was that of munching as they enjoyed what Amanda thought was possibly the best fish and chips she'd ever had.

'I've got to tell Mum and Dad about that chippy,' she said, almost finished. 'I'm stuffed. I don't think I can manage any more.'

'I think he can.' Dean pointed to an impatient looking seagull by her feet.

Amanda threw a chip and immediately the area was filled with several birds all fighting for the booty.

'Oh Amanda, what have you done?' Dean teased.

Amanda smiled. 'That was lovely, Dean. Thank you.'

'You're more than welcome.'

Gazing at the horizon, Dean started to reminisce. 'I used to love coming here as a kid. Mum and Dad never went on holiday, you just can't when you farm, but we did come to the beach when we had some hours to spare, me, Stu, and Millie, when she was just a baby.'

'You were lucky having the seaside so close. We only saw the sea when we went away to Wales, although we did go on a couple of day trips to Walton-on-the-Naze and Hastings when I was older.'

'I know I'm lucky, and I'm really glad that when me and Carolyn have kids they'll be able to enjoy all this too. I'd love a big family, I'm thinking four kids or more, but not sure Carolyn's keen, even though she is one of five herself.'

'Wow, that's a big family.'

'What, Carolyn's?'

'Well yes, but I also meant you wanting at least four. Perhaps Carolyn's not keen because she is the one who has to give birth to them.'

'Quite possibly.' Dean smiled, picking up a large pebble and feeling its smoothness. 'But I think it's more that she loves her job and would like to travel. Apparently in China it's going to be illegal to have more than one child. Can you imagine being forced to comply with that? And how those poor lonely kids are going to feel.'

Amanda shook her head. 'I can't understand how governments can make laws like that either, but I'm an only child and I don't think my life is all that bad.'

'No, I didn't mean to suggest it was,' Dean said quickly, his tone apologetic. 'Perhaps I've an idealised view of big families, and so much depends on the individuals involved. Carolyn says she sometimes hated being one of five when she was younger, because she felt she had to compete for so many things, but at other times she felt lucky to have lots of siblings to play with.'

Dean sprung to his feet. 'Fancy a little walk?'

'Sounds nice, if I'm able to move that is, after all that food. Where do you have in mind?'

'Somewhere mysterious and beautiful,' Dean replied.

Amanda followed him across the pebbles, intrigued. They walked along the beach and soon found themselves at the foot of a hill leading up to the cliffs. There, they came to a shallow cave, tucked away in the white chalky rock face, and Amanda had the feeling she had stumbled across a secret hideaway, especially as she could see no one else for quite some distance. Looking closer, she saw a spring of water pouring out of the rock. It trickled down, producing a delightful and gentle sound, which contrasted perfectly with the powerful and dramatic roar of the sea.

'Where are we?' she asked, feeling moved and inspired.

'This, Amanda, is the Holy Well. It's a hidden gem, known by locals, and has plenty of history. Shall I fill up your drink bottle for you?' Dean held out his hand. Amanda pulled up the flap and delved into her satchel for an empty Cresta bottle and handed it to him. 'It's frothy, man,' he joked, thinking of the advert, 'although it's not really. The polar bear would be disappointed. He stands a much better chance of getting froth in the seawater than here.' Amanda found herself increasingly enjoying Dean's silly humour and smiled to herself as she watched him fill her bottle with the crystal clear water.

'Can you drink it?' she asked curiously.

'Of course. It's filtered down through the rocks from the cliffs above, and people have been drinking it for centuries, some believing it has medicinal qualities, although that's unlikely to be true.'

'I'm sure it makes for a good story, though,' Amanda said. She felt totally at ease, as she put the bottle to her lips and sampled the cool, refreshing drink. 'You would think, being so close to the sea, it would taste salty but there isn't even a hint, it's incredibly fresh,' she said, savouring its purity.

After they had both had a drink, Dean suggested walking further along the coast. They approached the base of the cliffs, which would lead to the dramatic scenery of Beachy Head and then shortly beyond, the iconic Seven Sisters cliffs. Clambering across the beach, small areas of sand and shingle soon gave way to larger boulders of rock; some were granite, with sparkling flecks which glistened in the sun.

'I always thought there was only shingle on Eastbourne beach, like most of East Sussex, but there's sand here,' Amanda said, marvelling at the yellowy beige coastal strip and feeling the softness below her feet.

'Yes, it is largely shingle, but you do get small patches of sand here and there, depending on the tide.'

'I didn't know that. It might sound weird, because people tend to love sandy beaches, but I definitely prefer shingle. Sand in the house after trips to the beach is annoying, it takes forever to get it out of your hair, and when you're at the beach and the wind whips it up, it gets everywhere … Oh, and don't get me started on sand sandwiches!'

'I totally get your drift,' Dean said with a gentle laugh.

It was at that point that he noticed Amanda's deep red tresses blowing in the wind. She turned to look back at him and their eyes met. The smile fell away from Dean's face. He suddenly felt afraid that she could see something in his eyes that he would have preferred her not to see, something he immediately chose to ignore and forget. He quickly turned the conversation back to nature.

'There are limpets on those rocks,' he said sounding breezy, 'Dad has brought some home for us to eat before, and if we turn over rocks on the sand, we'll probably find all sorts, tiny crabs, sea anemones, and you see those mounds of sand? They're signs of lugworms.'

Amanda closely examined the little piles of sand, and then something Dean said started to register and she began to look peaky. 'Urgh, you eat limpets? They're molluscs, aren't they?'

'Sure do, and they certainly are.'

'That's one thing I can't eat. Fish and shellfish, like prawns and crabs, are fine, but snails, whelks and squid-like things literally make me throw up.'

Expressing her disgust, Amanda wrinkled her nose and poked out her tongue, and Dean couldn't help but be amused by her cute facial expressions.

'I'll bear that in mind and make sure that if you come for dinner Dad doesn't serve you up a plateful,' he said smiling, before noticing other things were competing for Amanda's attention.

'Let's look for some more creatures.'

She hurried on, unaware that the green algae on the rocks was very slippery. Almost slipping himself, Dean thought to warn her, but it was too late. He turned and in an instant she was down. He instinctively grabbed her, holding her tight to catch her fall. And there they stood, Amanda almost on the ground, her shoes wet with seawater, clinging to Dean. He held her close, trying to steady her, but now, standing eye to eye, faces almost touching, they both realised they were holding each other far beyond what was required to simply get Amanda back on her feet again.

After the moment had passed, time went much more slowly. They walked back across the beach, this time very carefully in order not to slip. No words were said until Amanda broke the silence.

'I think we'd better be getting back now,' she said, trying to avoid eye contact. 'By the time I get home it'll be late, well, at least, it'll be the usual time I leave for home.'

'Of course,' Dean replied, seeing how uncomfortable she appeared, knowing he probably looked the same. 'We'll head back now.'

In the car, neither were in the mood for pop music, but the awkward silences became almost unbearable, so Dean flicked on Radio 3, but to their dismay the romantic classical pieces simply made them feel worse.

'I'll drop you home,' Dean said eventually and after clearing his throat. 'What are your plans for tomorrow?'

'Not a great deal, but I was hoping to do some painting, go to the library, and spend time in the garden. What about you?'

'The usual. There's still much to be done on the farm, and now Millie's back at school we've lost our little helper. I'm also hoping to find some time to do a bit of carving and woodwork, I've got a few projects on the go which I've neglected, and I'm keen to get back to them.'

Dean soon parked outside Marshywood, and Amanda stepped out of the car.

'Thank you, Dean,' she said.

'No problem at all, Amanda,' he replied casually. 'Thanks for coming out today, and we look forward to seeing you on Monday.'

'Goodbye. Have a good weekend.'

'You too, Amanda.'

Slamming it shut, the metallic clang of the Land Rover door rang through her body. She watched the car slowly drive away and grew more worried and confused, and those feelings stubbornly refused to retreat as the days went by. Robert and Joan noticed a change in her, but despite her father's efforts to get her to open up, she had no words for him, or her mother.

Monday soon arrived, and on that afternoon, after her shift at Jimmy's, Amanda didn't return to Hillbrook Farm.

Chapter 15

'Passports?'

'Yes.'

'Camera?'

'Yes, I packed it last night, remember? We decided against taking the Polaroid.'

'Of course, I remember now. What about sun cream, mosquito repellent, anti-malarial tablets?'

'Look Charles, I thought it was supposed to be women who nag. Yes, I've got all those too, and we went through this yesterday. Come on and stop fussing, we'll be late for our flight.'

Pauline could hardly contain her excitement as they drove to the airport, although she really wasn't looking forward to the nine-hour flight. She wondered why, despite years of travel, she was still so anxious about flying. Conversely, Charles found getting on an aeroplane as easy as catching a bus and thoroughly enjoyed the experience.

'I swear this Gatwick car park gets busier each time,' he remarked, shaking his head while finally manoeuvring into a space.

After checking in, and with the flight not due for almost two hours, Charles and Pauline waited in the airport lounge with little to do. Charles slurped a coffee while reading *The Daily Mail*, and Pauline, anxious and bored, combed through the Kenya travel guide again, disappointed there was nothing new to read.

'How about a walk?' she suggested.

'Not sure there's anything to see, but okay, if we must.' Charles put down his newspaper and placed his cup on the saucer.

They had walked past the airport chapel and prayer room several times before, but never thought to step inside. This time, Pauline paused and lingered outside the door.

'Let's have a look, Charles.'

'What do you want to go in there for, love? You can pray the plane doesn't crash out here, you know.'

'Charles, don't even joke about such things,' Pauline hushed. 'I want to see inside because there's nothing else to do, that's all.'

'That's a first. Never seen you step into anything resembling a church before, but if you insist.'

Once inside, they discovered a small room with twelve wooden chairs set out in groups of four facing an altar – a wooden table covered with a white tablecloth. On top of the altar were two large candles sitting in gold-coloured candlesticks. There was only one other person in the room, a woman sitting in the front row, head bowed as though in contemplative prayer, but there was no sign of a chaplain. It was completely silent; so quiet that you really could hear a pin drop, Pauline thought.

'Come on. Let's go, love,' Charles whispered. 'There's really no point stopping here. Like I said, there's nothing to see.'

'It's not as if we've much else to do, though, is it? Oh, Charles, this is one of the worst things about flying. All this hanging around makes me so nervous. I can't wait to just get there.'

* * *

Joan and Victoria were having tea in the kitchen at Hillbrook Farm. They hadn't had the chance to get together for some time and Joan had decided to call round to tie up any loose ends left behind by her daughter's sudden departure, even though she herself was at a loss as to why it had happened. Amanda simply told her and Robert that she felt it was a good idea to stop because the arrangement couldn't go on for the long term. She also hinted that once Dean was married she didn't think she would be needed any more. However, this baffled Joan. Why so sudden? Did Cecil, Dean or Victoria imply she wasn't needed? The wedding was still some four months away, and what's more, wouldn't they still need volunteers when Dean got married, because Carolyn worked at the surgery? Why did Amanda look so flustered when she talked about it? Why did she *not* want to talk about it? Joan suspected there was more to it, but she wasn't very good at getting her daughter to open up. Robert was much better at that, but not even he could fully get to the bottom of it. It did briefly cross his mind that Dean may have made a pass at Amanda, or something like that, but going by what he knew about Dean and his family, he believed him to be a thoroughly decent young man and quickly dismissed that thought. Consequently, Robert didn't dare mention anything along these lines to Amanda, and besides, she continued to speak very highly of Dean.

'More tea?' Victoria lifted the pot.

'That would be lovely,' Joan replied. 'How are Stuart, Dean and Millie?'

'Millie's doing well, enjoying being back at Moira House, and studying hard. Poor love, she gets that school bus without fail at half past six in the morning and isn't back until after six, sometimes even later, depending on her activities for the day.'

'That's a long day,' Joan replied.

'Stuart's still dating Emma and they're not long back from Devon where her parents live. Unfortunately it sounds like they rowed the whole time, but he told me her parents were too stoned to notice. Victoria's lively eyes became wider, 'Imagine that, people our age behaving that irresponsibly.'

'Oh dear, that doesn't sound good.'

'And Dean, he's working hard, as always, and he and Carolyn are getting all the final preparations done so they'll be naming the day any minute now.' Victoria lifted her chin and smiled. 'I'm so glad they're doing the traditional thing and getting married at St Mark's with the reception at the village hall. With so many people chipping in with the catering, everything's cheaper all round. Talking of the village hall, are you going to the fete next Saturday?'

Joan nodded. 'Yes, I'm looking forward to it.'

'That's good, because attendance is non-negotiable if you want to be accepted as a true Magham Down villager,' Victoria laughed. 'It happens every year about this time, and it's great fun. It's easily the highlight of the year, although that might be because there's not much that goes on the rest of the time. There's usually a cake baking competition … let me think … there's also a tombola, morris dancers, stalls such as coconut shies, and this year there's a talent competition, whereas some years, it's fancy dress.

'It sounds like there's a lot going on. Are you baking a cake for the competition, Victoria? Your cakes are fantastic.'

'That's nice of you to say, Joan. Yes, I am actually. I confess I did win two years in a row, but not last year, so I need to up my game this time'

Joan placed her teacup down in front of her. She hadn't forgotten the reason for her visit and thought this was a good time to bring it up.

'I just wanted to say I hope Amanda didn't leave you high and dry when she left. I thought she'd stay longer, but, well, you know young people when they make up their minds about something.'

'That's no problem at all, Joan. We were so grateful for all Amanda's hard work. It was so good of her to volunteer her time like that.'

'She really loved it.'

'And we loved having her here,' Victoria smiled. We also appreciated the beautiful handwritten thank you card she sent through the post explaining her reasons. She really didn't need to go to all that effort to explain, and it is us who should be thanking her, of course.'

'That's our Amanda for you. She's always been so well-mannered.'

'Yes, clearly you and Robert have done an excellent job as parents. Please tell her, when she said she was reviewing all her commitments, we totally understood, and to be honest I'm amazed she could do so much in the first place, what with working so hard at Jimmy's. I believe I told you before, Joan, I always tell Cecil that I can help run the farm or I can manage the home, but I can't possibly do both, so I take my hat off to Amanda.' Victoria picked up another jam tart and took a bite. 'It was a little sudden,' she said, her words muffled as she chomped, 'and none of us were expecting it, but I do realise that sometimes people just reach their limits, although it's a pity we haven't seen her since she went to the cattle market that day with Dean.' Victoria looked Joan steadily in the eye. 'We sometimes joke that the real reason she left was the farming mob scared her off,' she chuckled and poured more tea into Joan's cup.

'Oh, not at all. She told me the market was very interesting,' Joan replied.

'And Dean mentioned they bumped into Flavio, a lad he went to school with,' Victoria added. 'Then they went to his restaurant in Eastbourne – just to have a look.'

'That's right. Amanda told me Flavio was a really friendly chap.'

'So, how is Amanda? Is she all right?'

'Oh yes, she's doing well thanks. Still getting on fine at Jimmy's.'

Victoria's face soon took on a more sober expression. 'I'm sorry about what happened to her friend ... Mark, wasn't it?'

'He's not really Amanda's friend ... What I mean to say is, Sam is Amanda's friend, and Mark is Sam's cousin.' Joan was rushing her words and beginning to squirm in her seat. 'Yes, that was a dreadful thing to have happened, but he's safe in London now.'

Victoria, thinking this was a slightly odd response, decided not to mention she thought Mark was Amanda's boyfriend and instead changed the subject.

'I must tell you about some good friends of mine from Ipswich who are coming to visit soon. But first, why not have another jam tart?'

'I really shouldn't, but they're very good and the pastry is so short. You really know how to bake, Victoria … Oh, go on then, just one more. Tell you what, I'd do well to avoid the cakes at the village fete, though!'

* * *

I can't believe it's nearly over.' Pauline and Charles were spending their last night at the safari lodge at the Masai Mara National Reserve, hot, bothered and spreadeagled under a large ceiling fan.

'How can two weeks fly by so quickly?' said Pauline, shaking her head. 'I'm glad we made arrangements to get those postcards posted, imagine flying home with them in our luggage. All that effort for nothing.'

'You could have posted them back in the UK, you know.'

Pauline tutted, 'That would look stupid, Charles, now wouldn't it.'

'You didn't show off too much to Robert and Joan, I hope. She tried to hide it but it was obvious she wanted to come.'

Pauline smirked. 'I agree she wanted to be here, but perhaps not with us. Wasn't her face a picture when we told her. I did try to be considerate in the postcard but I couldn't help saying how fantastic it was to see lions, black and white rhinos, elephants and zebras, up close and personal. At least I didn't skirt over the more unpleasant things and was honest enough to admit the food made me throw up and gave me the runs. She can hardly envy me for that now, can she?'

'No, I don't suppose she will, Pauline, love. It's at moments like these, I'm grateful for a strong stomach that can cope with any old rubbish. I'm so glad you're on the mend now, princess.'

'Yes, I'm definitely feeling better Charles, so much better.'

* * *

'I wonder how Pauline and Charles are getting on. They'll be back soon,' Robert said while Joan slipped on her shoes.

'I imagine just fine,' she replied flatly before rolling her eyes, 'and we'll have to tolerate endless photos and tedious chat about Kenya for years to come. Is Amanda still upstairs? She'd better hurry, the fete's started.'

While mustering up the courage to leave the house, Amanda heard her mother calling. The thought of bumping into Dean, or even worse, Dean and Carolyn together, was terrifying. She even hoped to avoid Victoria and Cecil, but she knew it would be near on impossible, at least when it came to Victoria, who at some point would be spending time with Joan.

'Down in just a sec, Mum,' she shouted, turning her head towards the open bedroom door.

Amanda reasoned with herself, Why am I being so silly? I can't hide forever, plus I've got nothing to be ashamed of. I need to get a grip and stop acting like this, I'm behaving like Maria from *The Sound of Music*, running away, back to the convent.

Amanda certainly looked the part, perfectly dressed for a country fete in her green floral Laura Ashley dress and floppy straw hat. On leaving the house, they could hear the faint sound of chatter and music in the distance; the festivities were already under way. Striding along and holding on to her hat, a gentle breeze blowing through her dress, Amanda took a deep breath and vowed she would be brave, whatever happened today.

The large field, usually bare apart from grazing animals, was now buzzing with human activity. In the centre were morris dancers, dressed in white, waving their handkerchiefs, with bells attached to their legs which jingled as they danced to the music of the melodeon and drum.

'Such a great tradition,' Joan said in Robert's ear, 'but it looks funny, doesn't it? Bearded men, hopping about like girls.'

Robert smiled before becoming distracted. 'Look Joan, there's Pat and Geoffrey. Shall we go over and say hello? I must ask how the get-together in Nottingham went, and let them know the ramble was cancelled so they didn't miss anything.'

'Of course, yes. Manda dear, we're just off to say hello to a couple we know.'

'That's fine, I'll stay here, Mum,' Amanda said, furtively glancing around.

'Have you seen anyone you recognise yet? What about that nice girl you got chatting to the other week? What was her name?'

'You mean Charlotte who works in the bakery in town?'

'Yes, her.'

'Haven't seen her yet, but I'm fine just waiting here on my own, I'll see you in a bit.'

Amanda watched the morris dancers stop and start to the music and felt safe hidden from view among the crowd. The tune continued while the dancers moved apart, and at that moment, to her horror, she saw Dean and Carolyn standing on the opposite side of the ring. As her heart pounded, she calmed herself with the knowledge that they were far enough away not to spot her immediately, especially if she slipped behind someone, but not wanting to take any chances, she planned to move away entirely as soon as it was feasible to do so. Each time the morris dancers separated she was exposed and when they drew together again she had a reprieve. The only advantage of the risk of exposure was that when a gap emerged it gave her an opportunity to take a sneaky look at Dean. How was he feeling, and how was the body language between him and Carolyn? Was he looking happy? Of course he would be. Why wouldn't he be?

Fortunately for Amanda, Dean was chatting to a young man next to him, while Carolyn stood by his side, and so he only glanced at the morris dancers from time to time. He was nodding and smiling as he talked, and Carolyn occasionally joined in. Amanda could see he looked happy and confident and he and

Carolyn were both affectionate towards one another. Every now and again he would extend his hand outwards, touching her waist lightly, and each time it stabbed like a knife, leaving Amanda disheartened by her feelings of jealousy. Obviously Dean wasn't missing her in the slightest, and that was a good thing and simply the way things ought to be. So why was it so hard to get rid of her feelings? He looked so good, so attractive, and he and Carolyn seemed content together. That was fantastic, since she had always wanted the best for him.

After the morris dancing paused once more, Amanda could see Robert and Joan were still chatting with their friends. Again, aware her chances of being spotted were high during an interval, she decided to stay put for now, but as soon as the dancing resumed she intended to make a quick dash to join them. As she looked across surreptitiously to observe Dean one last time before she left, she discovered to her dismay that the window of opportunity for escaping unseen was well and truly over. He was no longer talking to the person next to him but rather looking straight back at her. Gone were the smiles and easy-going composure, and instead of an acknowledgement, he quickly averted his gaze.

Turning back towards Carolyn, he soon reverted to his previous behaviour. His smile returned and he reached out, lightly touching her on her back with an open hand. But it was too late. As far as Amanda was concerned, the communication had been made. His odd manner and failure to acknowledge her suggested something was going on. She knew from her own experience that blanking or ignoring someone often signified the opposite of detachment or disinterest. Perhaps he did care after all, and missed her being around, even just a little bit. If her leaving had been of no consequence, she was convinced he would have waved and headed over to say hello, especially after so much time had elapsed, but then again perhaps he was angry with her for leaving so suddenly. However, the soft, lingering look Amanda thought she had seen for the briefest of seconds suggested otherwise.

Of course any residual attraction wouldn't make any difference to anything, aside from giving Amanda a little satisfaction. She felt terribly guilty even thinking this way, guilty that she felt relieved to see a sign that Dean might have missed her. Until this moment she hadn't realised how desperate she had been for that sign. But what was the use of feeling this way? There was nothing gratifying about it, it was just pointless and wrong, because he and Carolyn were in love, and it looked like nothing was going to change that. In time, whatever he was feeling, he'd soon get over it, and so would she.

The morris dancing resumed and Amanda made her exit. She looked over at her parents, but they were talking to Victoria and so she hastily went in the opposite direction, past the coconut shies and tombola stand. Everywhere people were enjoying all sorts of amusements – children watching a Punch and Judy show, villagers drinking beer and cider or browsing the stalls selling homemade chutneys and jams.

Alone with her thoughts, Amanda was content to wander around solo, without speaking to a soul. As she turned a corner, she spied Cecil, talking to a group of people. She wondered what she should do. If she went one way she would bump into him, but if she went back the way she came she would meet Dean and Carolyn, and then there was Victoria with Joan and Robert, just a short distance away. She felt cornered. Keen to find a hiding place, she saw a quiet area behind the stalls which might be the perfect refuge to catch her breath and cool down. She dived into it and was instantly relieved to be alone at last, but as she stepped back her relief gave way to surprise. There, sitting on a wooden chair on the grass, was old Eddie Walder.

'Oh, hello Eddie,' she exclaimed, practically tripping over him.

'Young lady Amanda, it's mighty gracious of you to remember my name. How are you, my purty liddle lady, and how are you and your family settling in?'

'I'm fine, Eddie, thank you, and we're really starting to feel part of village life now. Today's great. I'm really enjoying it,' she mumbled, immediately feeling guilty for being less than candid. 'There's so much going on, isn't there?' she added, trying to redeem herself.

Eddie looked at her sagely, clutching his walking stick. ''Tis lovely, that's true. This village tradition has been going for many years, ever since I were a young man, that's for sure, but now tis too hard on my feet and not possible with my rheumatticks to stand all day, so I have to take a rest every now and then. But tell me, young Amanda,' he said looking straight at her with his warm, beady eyes, 'if you are enjoying it so well, why are you back here hiding from all and sundry?'

Amanda, realising she'd been rumbled, turned crimson with embarrassment. Thoughts chased through her head. She could lie and say she wasn't feeling well, or she could be totally honest about the reason she was trying to get away. She decided to go for the middle ground. 'Well, Eddie, I just wanted some time by myself. I was feeling anxious about something, but after I've had a break I'll head back and enjoy the rest of the event. At least, that's the plan.'

'Oh, I am sorry to hear you've been suffering from anxious thoughts, my dear,' Eddie said with a warm and compassionate nod. 'You take the time you need to steady yourself, never mind me. I won't disturb yer. Look, there's a chair over that way. Go fetch it and sit yerself down for a while.'

'Thanks Eddie, I think I will.'

All was quiet until Eddie spoke again.

'I see you've got planted some pretty annuals in that old front garden at Marshywood. Miss Baldwin, she let it go to rack and ruin, but that was understandable, a lady of her age.'

'Have you been past our house, Eddie?'

'Oh yes, once or twice. My son-in-law, he does drive me to the lake to fish, on occasion, and we pass Marshywood and I ask him to stop the car and let me look at your front garden and your flowers. It's been a joy to see your poppies, sweet peas and marigolds, fa sure.'

'Thank you, Eddie. That's lovely to hear, especially since I've never gardened before. My parents have worked on it too, so I'll pass on your kind words to them.' Amanda, already starting to feel calmer detected the delicious aroma of meat sizzling on a barbecue. 'Can I ask you something, Eddie?'

'Course you can, my dear.'

'I've been wondering, do you know why our house is called Marshywood?'

Eddie's face lit up and he smiled. 'Yes, that I do, Amanda, that I do. Back in the day, when Miss Baldwin's parr-ents wed, they bought the land Marshywood sits on, but there were no cottage on it.'

Amanda listened, keen to hear more.

'Miss Baldwin's farrther, who were a merchant trader if I recall correctly, then arranged for a cottage to be built, which stood unnamed. Well, he'd grown up in Peasmarsh, and his family hailed from that wild and strange looking region known as the Romney Marshes, whereas Miss Baldwin's marther, she grew up further north of the county by Ashdown Forest.' Eddie paused, and leaned into the chair's backrest. 'So, in naming the cottage, the two young marrieds thought they'd take a part from each of the places they grew up: marshy for the farrther's side, wood for the marther's, and joined them up, just as they had joined up in marriage. Those were olden times where women had no vote,' Eddie said reflectively, 'so by uniting their hist'ries to make a brand new name for a home, it were quite a thing to do back in that day, and folk in the village considered it special and noteworthy. In those days, village folk liked to know how place names came about. Just like Miss Baldwin, I were not born at the time, but this is the story she told me and what her parr-ents told her.'

Amanda had been so engrossed, it wasn't until that moment the hum of people's voices and children's laughter became noticeable again. 'That's a wonderful story, Eddie. Thank you for sharing it with me.'

'Ah, that's my ultimate privilege,' Eddie said, his voice welcoming and unhurried. 'Yes, when two people join themselves in matrimony and bring together their differences, it's wonderful to see. You know, young Amanda,' he said, with a faraway look, 'you remind me some of my sweet Ethel when we first got wed, and she were about your age. She were as bright as a button and wore a kind and gentle smile, just like you. I miss her sorely I do. I remember how, just like Miss Baldwin's parr-ents, that when Ethel and me got our first home we learned to take the best from our old lives to make something new with it. We didn't have a cottage to give a name to, we could only afford to rent, but we set our hearts to only take the best of our old families' ways and leave the rest behind to make up our new way of life.' He slowly blinked his eyes. 'It did us good, since we were married some fifty-eight years, till she passed away.'

Amanda's body was still, but her heart was moved.

'Young Amanda, what are your wishes and dreams? Many a young lady and many a young man has wishes and dreams. I know I did when I were near your age.'

Amanda didn't know how to respond, or whether to share what was on her mind. 'I just hope for good things for the future, Eddie,' she said eventually.

'I wish for that for you too, young Amanda, and I hope and pray you get your heart's desire.'

'Thank you so much,' Amanda replied, her voice rich with emotion.

Eddie looked at his wristwatch. 'Must get back on my feet soon. I've said I will speak a poem to raise money for the village hall. It'll be my turn at two o'clock or thereabouts, and the test is for me to remember all the words. My memory isn't what it used to be, but I reckon I can do it.'

'That sounds great. I hope to be around to hear you – I look forward to it,' Amanda added lifting her chin, 'and I'll donate to the village hall fund too.'

'Bless yer young Amanda, bless yer for certain.'

Amanda turned around. 'Can I ask one last thing, Eddie?'

'Yes, my dear.'

'I'm interested in trees so I know most people think forests and woods are one and the same, and apart from size, I think that's kind of true, but why Marshywood, Eddie, considering Miss Baldwin's mother came from Ashdown Forest? Why not something like,' Amanda pondered for a moment, 'Forestmarsh, or maybe Ashmarsh?'

Eddie rubbed his chin, deep in thought. 'That I don't rightly know, me dear,' he said with a smile. 'I reckon some things are just destined to stay mysterious.'

* * *

Talking to Eddie had lifted Amanda's spirits and she meandered around the fete feeling so much better. She saw Millie with some friends at the tombola stand, but unsurprisingly Stuart was nowhere to be seen. She was delighted to see Pickwick again. He brightened her day as she watched him, true to form, circling around the various stalls and eyeing up food while people watched nervously. *Poor Pickwick*, she thought, but she was soon encouraged to see a well-dressed old gentleman approach and pat him on the back. 'How are you, Leonard, my good man? Nice to see you here today,' he said, while Pickwick returned his greeting with a timorous smile.

Next she spotted Victoria, who was standing behind a stall in the cake competition area. She would have to say hello, she couldn't hide away for ever. As she slowly approached she was relieved to see Victoria waving her over with a cheery smile.

'Amanda!'

'Hello Victoria, how are you?'

'Very well, thank you. And you?'

After Amanda assured her she was doing okay, Victoria rattled on in her usual cheerful way. 'Thanks for your card, by the way, and of course we understand. I hope you're not leaving the fete just yet, Cecil's popped back to the farm and wants to see you when he gets back.'

'Really?' Amanda hesitated. 'I didn't leave anything behind, did I?'

'No, nothing like that. If you had I would have passed it on to Joan.'

'Oh, yes, of course.'

Victoria appeared unusually fidgety. 'He's gone back to sort out a few things and pick up something he'd forgotten – oh no, perhaps I shouldn't have said that.' Seeing Amanda's bafflement, she relented. 'I give up. I'm just so useless at keeping secrets, especially nice ones. He's fetching your gift. We bought you something to say thank you for all your hard work. Now I've blurted it out! When you see him, please act surprised.'

Amanda smiled, gladdened by this unexpected gesture. 'You didn't need to do that. Thank you, both.'

'Not at all, Amanda. Thank *you*.'

Amanda then turned her attention to a large Victoria sponge standing proudly on a cake stand and bursting with filling. 'That looks delicious – so much jam and cream,' she said, keen to sample it.

'Thank you, yes I normally avoid Victoria sponge because I'm bored with the "Victoria's done a Victoria sponge" joke, but this year I thought, why not? It's one of my best cakes. I'm not sure I'll win this time, though. There are lots of worthy candidates,' she motioned with her chin towards a nearby table. 'Mary-Ann's coffee and walnut looks incredible, don't you think? And she told me she's laced it with Tia Maria, which is bound to win over the judges, especially Councillor Parker, who I hear enjoys a tipple.'

At that moment Amanda heard her name being called. 'Manda, we've been looking for you for ages, where have you been?' Robert was walking towards her.

'Hi Dad, nowhere, just looking around. Where's Mum?'

'She's over by the teas and coffees.'

'Oh, that reminds me,' Victoria said pointing upwards, 'I forgot to tell Joan something. Amanda, would you mind standing here for a few moments while I pop over to see your mum? The judges aren't due to come round for a while.'

'Of course.'

'And after the competition I'll be sure to save a goodly amount of cake for the Fernsby household.' Victoria smiled, and walked away to find Joan at the refreshment tent. She had some interesting news to relay.

'Joan, I just remembered …' she started, but quickly noticed Joan seemed troubled.

'Are you okay? The tea isn't great, I know, but surely it's not that bad,' she joked.

'I'm fine,' Joan said quietly, 'but that woman keeps looking at me oddly, and she just mouthed something to the woman sitting next to her. I didn't like the expression on their faces afterwards, and the one who whispered is now smiling at me in a strange way. It's making me uncomfortable.'

Victoria looked over to see who Joan was referring to and the penny dropped instantly. 'That's Gwen Knowles, also known as Mrs Know-It-All, probably the worst gossip in the village,' she said, keeping her head down. 'Don't worry about her, I expect she just said something petty, that's all.'

'I'd really like to know what it was.'

Victoria shook her head. 'No you don't, Joan, really you don't. It's bound to be rubbish.'

'But the body language was so strange, it's making me curious.'

Victoria let out a small sigh. 'Did you say she spoke to her, the one who has just stood up and is getting a drink?'

'That's right, the woman with the grey hair.'

'That's Brenda. I know her quite well, I could find out what she said, I suppose, but I really wouldn't recommend it.'

'Oh Victoria, would you really?' The tension slowly released from Joan's face. 'I'd appreciate that. Thanks so much, you're a good friend.'

Victoria was still hesitant, although pleased to be Joan's ally. 'All right, I'll go over and speak to her now,' she said.

Joan watched as Victoria chatted with Brenda for some minutes and then returned, her eyes lowered, as though trying to collect herself.

'What did she say, Victoria?'

'Joan, I'd rather not have to repeat this, but Brenda told me that Gwen Knowles said …' Victoria stopped and looked uneasy.

Joan searched her friend's face, and although perturbed by the look on it, she wasn't going to back out now.

Victoria inhaled and then breathed out quickly, 'Her actual words were: "That's the woman whose daughter sleeps with black men."'

Joan looked unsteady.

'I did warn you it was better not to find out,' Victoria said, reaching out to touch Joan's arm. 'It's never worth it. I'm sorry Joan.'

'I'm not staying here,' she replied, stepping back hurriedly. 'Where did you say Amanda and Robert were?'

'At my cake stall. Let's go find them,' Victoria said quietly.

Amanda, feeling relieved she hadn't seen Dean and Carolyn again, saw her mother and Victoria approach and soon noticed her mother's wan expression.

'Are you okay, Mum?'

'You're not having another migraine attack are you love?' Robert asked anxiously.

Victoria managed to bite her tongue.

'I just need to go home now, Robert, that's all,' Joan mumbled.

'So soon?'

'Yes, I'm sorry about that. Amanda, you stay if you want to … although perhaps it would be best if you came home too.'

'Well I would, but I promised Eddie – you know, the old man I met in the village – I'd listen to him recite a poem later, but I'll be right home after that.'

'Thanks love, not to worry. I'm fine. I just need some rest.'

Amanda's eyebrows drew together. 'Okay, Mum, hope you feel better soon.'

After they had left, Amanda was very quiet, trying to fathom what could be wrong. Victoria gave an awkward smile, and then exclaimed, 'Drat, I still haven't mentioned that thing to your mum. I did try but got distracted again. Perhaps you can pass on a message, Amanda. It's not majorly important, it's only that I'm thinking of co-hosting a Tupperware party with your mother and I need to run the idea past her first.'

'Of course I will,' Amanda said agreeably.

'So,' Victoria said after a short pause, 'you're staying behind for Eddie's poetry rendition.' Amanda nodded. 'That's his speciality, so you're in for a treat,' she said, arching an eyebrow. Amanda wondered whether she was being ironic.

Just then, Victoria glanced across the field to see her husband approaching. 'He's back!' she announced, and before long Amanda was holding a large bunch of purple and red freesias mixed with pink and white gypsophila, and a box of Dairy Milk chocolates. She walked away from the cake competition area with Cecil to make way for the judges, thinking how easy it had been to face him again.

'But won't you miss the result?' she asked him as he bade a hasty goodbye, ready to go back to the farm.

'Oh, I'll find out soon enough,' he answered, in a deadpan voice. 'She's won it enough times, so it's not exactly exciting any more. But then again, it does make life easier if she wins, she takes it so personally if she doesn't, after putting so much effort in.'

Left on her own, Amanda joined in with the applause as the previous act, a juggling duo, left the makeshift stage.

'And now,' shouted the master of ceremonies, 'Edward Walder, affectionately known as Eddie to us all, will recite a poem without forgetting a word.'

There were cheers, clapping, and even laughter, as Amanda watched Eddie, who was carefully relying on his walking stick, slowly ascend the platform.

The crowd grew silent, and then, without further ado, Eddie opened his mouth and was away.

Some folks as come to Sussex,
They reckons as they knows
A durn sight better what to do
Than simple folks, like me and you,
Could possibly suppose.

But them as comes to Sussex,
They mustn't push and shove,
For Sussex will be Sussex,
And Sussex won't be druv!

Mus Wilfred come to Sussex,
Us heaved a stone at he,
Because he reckoned he could teach
Our Sussex fishers how to reach
The fishes in the sea.

But when he dwelt among us,
Us gave un land and luv,
For Sussex will be Sussex,
And Sussex won't be druv!

All folks as come to Sussex
Must follow Sussex ways –
And when they've larned to know us well,
There's no place else they'll wish to dwell
In all their blessed days –

There ant no place like Sussex,
Until ye goos above,
For Sussex will be Sussex,
And Sussex won't be druv!

There was a brief pause and then an eruption of applause and whistles filled the air. Amanda joined in, doing her best to make her clapping heard above the din, despite being aware

Eddie couldn't possibly discern hers amongst the crowd. The old man stood, with a proud and happy smile, absorbing the applause and cheers. Amanda was sure his recital was word perfect – he sounded so confident. Her presumption was soon confirmed by the master of ceremonies.

'Eddie,' he said, looking at him with a cheerful smile, 'well done, you old rascal, once again, you didn't forget a single word!'

Chapter 16

'I just knew she would!' Victoria dropped her bag on the kitchen table where Dean was eating a slice of toast. In front of him was a copy of *Farmer's Weekly*, but his eyes were distant and elsewhere.

'What did you say, Mum?'

'Mary-Ann, I knew she'd win with her coffee and walnut cake. Hold on ...' Victoria paused, delving into her bag to take out something wrapped in a discoloured, oily paper napkin. 'Here, have a taste, what do you think?'

Dean opened the napkin, broke off some of the cake inside and put it in his mouth.

'Can you taste the Tia Maria?' Victoria asked, clasping her hands together. 'I think it's hardly noticeable. You should have seen her, grinning like a Cheshire cat when she was announced the winner.'

'Really,' Dean replied robotically.

'Yes, but what do you think, Dean? Do you like it? And, more to the point, can you taste the Tia Maria?'

Dean shrugged. 'It's nice, but no, I can't really taste any alcohol in it.'

'What did I tell you!' Victoria exclaimed. She started to tell him about Cathy's banana and cinnamon cake, which was clearly the best entry because you could really taste both flavours, before noticing Dean wasn't listening to any of it.

'Dean, did you hear what I just said?'

'Something about a cake?' he replied in a monotone and staring at nothing in particular.

'Safe bet, but actually I was saying … Oh, never mind, I can see I'm boring you. By the way, where were you and Carolyn all day? I don't remember seeing you after lunchtime – maybe even before that.'

'We left early.'

'Really, why? Where did you go?'

'I took her home.' Dean took in a deep breath. 'We had a slight disagreement.'

'You mean a row?' she asked, raising an eyebrow.

'You could say that, yes.'

'What about? If you want to tell me, that is.'

Dean picked up the *Farmers Weekly* and started to flick through. 'Nothing much, it's fine.'

Victoria paused. 'That's perfectly normal,' she said, hiding her doubts that Dean was being straight with her. 'Your dad and I definitely had a row or two before we got married, and still do, as you well know.'

'True.'

'The important thing is, you kiss and make up and don't let the sun go down on your anger. Have you phoned to apologise?'

'No, but it's not the sort of row that calls for an apology. Neither of us did anything wrong, as such, it was just a difference of opinion – of perception, you could say.'

Victoria, not wishing to pry, decided to allow Dean the freedom to tell her more in his own time. 'Whatever it is, I'm sure it will iron itself out,' she said, picking up some used mugs and putting them in the sink.

'I'm sure it will.'

'By the way, Dean, when are you going to contact Plumpton College for another volunteer? It's been weeks now since Amanda left.'

'I'll get around to it soon,' Dean replied unenthusiastically.

'There's a good lad.'

As she filled the kettle, Victoria couldn't shake off the feeling that something was off. Call it mother's intuition perhaps, but did she see a certain look in his eye when she mentioned Plumpton College and Amanda? Her mind went back to the day she had warned him about spending time alone with her, and the gossip which could result, but she'd had no inkling since that anything was amiss, or that Carolyn had heard anything. Besides, she knew her son. He would talk to Carolyn if anything needed to be brought out into the open. It was a normal lover's tiff, which would right itself, if that was all it was, but despite her rationalising, just in case she was wrong, she decided to probe just one more time.

'Dean, I know this sounds stupid, and please tell me to mind my own business if you want, but the row wasn't about Amanda, was it?'

Dean was silent, but the look in his eyes said it all.

Her suspicions now confirmed, Victoria dug deeper. 'Was Carolyn upset you went to Eastbourne with her? Flavio was with you both, but he drove there in his car, I presume.'

'He did.'

'And you spent time together, alone.'

'Yes.'

'So, as I said on the day you went to Northiam, if you're seen together like that, and Carolyn hears it from someone other than you, that could cause issues, don't you think?'

Dean didn't reply.

'I presume you told Carolyn about your time in Eastbourne as soon as you could?'

Dean nodded. 'Carolyn knew I met Flavio and that I was with Amanda, yes.'

'That's absolutely fine then, she heard it from you first.' Victoria pressed the lid back on to a metal tin containing teabags. 'So that's obviously not why you rowed?'

'No, it's not. As I said, it was nothing to worry about, really.'

'That's good.' Victoria turned around and looked uneasy, 'I'm only saying all this because Mrs Know-It-All said something nasty about Amanda today, and I'd hate for you and Carolyn to become targets too.'

Dean's eyes narrowed slightly. 'Why, what did she say?'

'There's no need to repeat it, Dean, but put it this way, she slandered her – called her loose, you know the sort of thing – and her prejudice was also directed towards that poor lad who got beaten up, and others like him. It's funny, Joan's adamant he and Amanda were never an item, but then again how often does Mrs Know-It-All get things right? And whenever she does, her attitude's all wrong, of course.'

'It certainly is,' Dean replied stiffly, hunching his shoulders.

Victoria decided it was time to move on. 'Dean, I've got to do dinner. It's getting late and because the competition took up so much of my time I could really do with some help.'

'Me? I'm busy.'

Victoria looked dubiously at the *Farmer's Weekly* magazine. 'When I arrived home there was only one person slogging away and that was your father, out in the field.'

'But you know dinner's not my department,' Dean protested.

Victoria maintained steady eye contact and waited.

'Oh all right,' he sighed. 'I'll help, but nothing too hard, mind.'

'Okay, if you can manage to chop the garlic, onions and carrots and also serve up, I'll call it quits.'

'Sounds like a deal,' Dean said, smiling at last.

* * *

'Joan, you've got to get up, love, you can't just spend all day in bed. It's 11 o'clock. You hardly ate any dinner last night and you've not had any breakfast either.'

'Leave the curtains, Robert,' Joan covered her face and held out a hand in front of her, 'you know the sun hurts my eyes and makes my migraine worse.'

'But you said the medication helped. Joan, please don't pretend it's a migraine if you're depressed again. You really have to try, love, it'll get worse otherwise.'

Joan didn't respond.

Robert sat down on the bed and rubbed his hands across his thighs apprehensively. 'Look, I know what happened at the fete was upsetting, but you heard what Victoria said, you need to forget about that woman. She's not worth losing any sleep over, and she's definitely not worth getting depressed about, and besides, didn't Amanda take it well? "I'm not going to let her make me feel bad or upset me with her lies," she said, didn't she, Joan? Our daughter's a toughie.' Robert tried to smile. 'That woman's not typical of people around here, and everyone can see through her.'

'That's what you say,' Joan cried out, 'but every so often I've noticed people looking at me oddly. You know what, Rob,' her eyes widened with fear, 'I sometimes think we made a big mistake coming here. We try so hard to fit in, but I'm starting to doubt we ever will. This insular small-village mentality is getting me down,' Joan stopped to look around her, 'and so is this damp house, not to mention not having anything to do all day, which is driving me utterly insane.'

'But there's so much to do, Joan,' Robert said, gently squeezing her hand. 'We walk with the Ramblers, the house needs work, you have tea with Victoria, and Amanda said she's talking about Tupperware parties, isn't she?'

'Shut up, Robert. Just shut up! Stop trying to make me feel better, because you're just not helping. Tupperware? You think I'm interested in something as boring and dated as that? It's truly pathetic, and I tell you something else that's pathetic … the effort we have to make to ingratiate ourselves … smiling all the time, pretending we're finding stupid, tedious conversation interesting.' Joan stopped briefly, trying to regain some composure. 'You know something,' she added, her voice sounding calmer, 'I'm sorry to have to say this, but I sometimes wish I could have my old life back, my London friends, the shops, the chance to go up West to see something at the theatre, to just go out for a meal.'

'But Joan, there are theatres and cinemas in Eastbourne, even Hailsham's got a theatre.'

'I know, but they're not quite the same, are they? The choice is very limited.'

'But when we were in London we hardly did those things, did we?' Robert hoped he wasn't sounding or looking as concerned as he was feeling.

'The point is, we could if we wanted to. I now realise what people mean when they say you never know what you've got till it's gone.'

'I think you're just upset because of what that idiotic woman said, but it'll be okay, love. You'll get over it and it'll eventually be forgotten, by you and everyone else. I love it here, I know Manda does, and in time you will too, I guarantee it. Come on, give me a hug, will you.'

Joan whimpered, while Robert embraced her. 'I'm sorry, Rob darling. I have to admit, I'm really scared,' she said, blinking rapidly.

'What about, love?'

'That we'll never belong.' Her voice trembled as she turned to look at a smiling photo of herself, Robert and Amanda on the G Plan dressing table.

'Of course we will, these things take time. Also, if I recall correctly, when Victoria first came round, you were the one who wanted space, worried she'd be popping by all the time, remember?' Robert smiled but inside he was worrying.

'Those were the early days, but since then I've tried so hard, Rob. It's exhausting me, and now Amanda's become the centre of attention for all the wrong reasons. Let's just say, that's not going to help.'

Robert opened his mouth to offer up further words of encouragement when the telephone began to ring. 'I'll get that, love. Hold on, back soon.'

However, he wasn't. 'You took ages. Why? Who was that?' Joan said irritably, before noticing the gloomy expression on his face. 'Has something happened?' she asked, swallowing hard.

'It was Charles, he's in hospital. It's terrible news, Joan. Pauline is seriously ill.'

Joan sat upright in the bed, more or less for the first time, since returning home from the village fete the previous afternoon. 'What's happened, Robert? Please tell me.'

'Let's not panic. After touching down yesterday morning and arriving home, Charles said Pauline went to bed with symptoms of the flu. She was hot and cold and achy all over, and just slept, but this morning Charles couldn't believe it, she'd turned yellow.'

Joan slapped a hand over her mouth.

'They drove to Eastbourne hospital where she was diagnosed with malaria.'

'Malaria? How come? Didn't they take drugs to prevent—'

'The food made her sick,' Robert interrupted, 'so she must have thrown it up.'

'Oh my goodness gracious!' Joan tapped her forehead vigorously with her fingers to aid recollection. 'I remember from my days working at the chemist, we'd always advise customers travelling to tropical places to take medication against malaria.' She looked into Robert eyes. 'How is she now? Is she going to be okay?'

'It's bad, Joan. She was taken into intensive care and then she fell into a coma. She's been transferred to a hospital in London that specialises in tropical diseases.' Robert stopped speaking abruptly. For a moment he sat with his head in his hands, then he looked up and continued. 'And it gets much worse. Charles said they just told him Pauline is experiencing multi-organ failure and this may be the end.'

Joan was dumbstruck, horrified by the terrible news. She sank back against the pillows looking dazed.

'I need to go to London,' Robert said soberly. 'He's completely distraught, as you can well imagine, and neither of them have much in the way of family support. As you know, her mother's in a care home up north somewhere, and apparently she hardly speaks to her sister, who is also up north. I said I'd call back after checking it was okay with you, but I've pretty much promised to go. Are you able to manage? Amanda gets back by twenty to three, and so you won't be alone most of the day, and I don't intend to stay more than a couple of days, I hope.'

'Needs must, Robert. You have to go.'

'You could join me, of course, and although it's unlikely to be an enjoyable time considering the circumstances, it would give you a couple of days in London. If you do want to come, I'm sure Manda won't mind being on her own.'

'No Rob, that's alright, I'm better off here. And besides, you're right, I need to forget about London and what I've left behind. Going back now, even for a few days, might make it harder for me to do that.'

'Well, if you're sure. I'm torn, because you've been so down since yesterday. I really don't want to leave you.'

'I'll be fine thanks, honey.'

'Better get packing then.'

'You'd better. This is awful, Rob, just awful. I'm so worried.'

'Me too,' Robert replied despondently, pulling down the suitcase from the top of the wardrobe.

'What will Charles do if he loses her?' Joan bit her lip. 'They've been married even longer than we have. I can't imagine what he's going through.'

Robert glanced at the open suitcase and then stared down at his hands.

'It's at times like this,' Joan said, 'you soon realise how lucky you are. Perhaps I am being daft to get so het up about things,' she added weakly, before finally stepping out of bed.

* * *

It was almost a fortnight after the village fete, and business was as usual in Magham Down. Sufficient funds had been raised for the village hall activities and being the month of October, the autumn season was well and truly underway. Hedgerows were still heaving with sweet blackberries, plump and ripe for the picking, the perfect accompaniment to the apples at Marshywood, and Amanda hoped Joan would help her harvest as much from the hedgerows for the chest freezer as possible, so that together with the apples there'd be a ready supply of crumble and pie filling for months.

It was also mushroom season, but when it came to foraging for fungi, Amanda was less confident. Joan and Robert were never happy for her to cook anything resembling a wild mushroom, despite her diligent study of the *Mushroom Handbook*. Still, when she came across the wonderfully meaty and delicious chicken-of-the-woods, she knew this time she had to indulge.

'It's so distinctive, with that mustard yellow colour and fan shape,' she said, trying to convince her parents, 'and you find it on oak, chestnut and beech. The one I saw was growing on the large oak in the village, and I'm confident it's chicken-of-the-woods.'

She remembered conversations she'd had with Dean, knowing he would have been the ideal person to back her up. He once pointed out giant puffballs on the edge of the farm woodland, calling them delicious. Then one day he showed her an interesting but ominous sight – the death cap. 'I hardly ever see this on our land. It's the most poisonous mushroom in the world, but common in England,' he stated, teaching her how to identify its sickly green colour and swollen base, and admitting that, worryingly, it could be confused with edible fungi. Consequently, Amanda knew Dean would instantly recognise chicken-of-the-woods, but with her aunt critically ill, she doubted even his endorsement could have persuaded her parents to take health risks at such a delicate time.

Work at Jimmy's ticked along well enough but was oddly more tiring since Amanda had stopped volunteering. She hoped this would soon pass, but in the meantime she couldn't help but notice a change in her attitude. Going to the farm after each shift had given her something to look forward to, and now, despite her best efforts to avoid going about her duties in a perfunctory way, she found she had less enthusiasm.

'Amanda,' Maggie called, 'I almost forgot, I'm really sorry. How could I? It's probably because we've both been rushed off our feet.' She reached into her apron pocket and handed Amanda an envelope. 'Yesterday the post was delayed and this came really late, just after you left, and so I told Jimmy I'd look after it for you.'

'Thanks, Maggie,' Amanda said, accepting the envelope. 'Have you any idea who it's from?'

'Sorry, no I don't.'

'Who'd be sending me post here?' Amanda could see from the area and date stamp that it had been mailed in Worthing, West Sussex. 'That's funny, I don't think I know anyone who lives in Worthing.' She began to lift the flap of the envelope while Maggie watched for a moment before realising the content may be private.

'I'd better get back to work,' Maggie said, smiling half-heartedly.

Amanda could see a man waiting to order, so she slipped the letter in her pocket. It was just after midday and the café was starting to fill with customers ordering brunch and early lunch orders. It wasn't until some forty minutes later that she finally had a moment to herself, and standing in a quiet corner she pulled out the letter. She stared at the unfamiliar, scrawled handwriting, and when she caught sight of the name signed at the bottom, her heart sank.

Dear Amanda,

Hope you are well. I miss visiting the café. Most of all I miss you. I'm now finished in Hailsham and have a new job in Horsham in West Sussex, a nice town with countryside around it and I like it so will buy a house there because the building project I'm doing will go on for years.

I need to tell you, babe, I love you and I need you. You've probably heard lots of lies about me but don't believe them, Amanda. Please don't. First of all, I know you're not with that fella any more and I've thought about it and I don't care what happened, Amanda, I still want you, babe, please believe me I never did anything wrong. It was Wayne's idea to rough him up a bit, and I swear I never did lay a finger on him myself, so don't listen to the lies, babe.

You should still have my old number, but I'm moving on Friday, so after that, this is my new one. I will look after you, Amanda, I'll take you out wherever you want to go and I won't ever hurt you in any way. People try to make me out to be a violent man, but that's not me at all.

Remember I love you and I'm waiting for you to ring me, Amanda.

Yours truly,

Nick

Amanda shoved the letter in her pocket and shuddered thinking he really had a nerve, and if he was waiting for her to call he'd be waiting forever. How did he know she and Mark weren't together? Possibly her mum had said something to Victoria, and word must have got around somehow. She stood, immobilized by her thoughts until she heard her name.

'Amanda, is everything okay?'

'Y-yes, Maggie. The letter … it was from Nick, he's still trying it on, would you believe?'

'What?' Maggie frowned. 'Even after what he did to Mark? Oh no, what a nightmare. He isn't harassing you, is he?'

She shook her head. 'I don't think so, no. He's moving soon, so once he's gone I hope it'll be for good.'

'Me too, for your sake, Amanda. That guy seems a nasty piece of work,' Maggie said, picking up empty plates and a full ashtray.

* * *

Joan or Robert would sometimes give Amanda a lift to or from work, unless Joan wasn't feeling up to it, which on this day she most definitely wasn't. More often than not Amanda would catch the bus, especially when she was heading straight to the farm after she finished in the café, but since she had stopped going there she had more time. Robert, once again in London, was unable to provide a lift, and with the autumn weather mild and pleasant, she was looking forward to walking home. A brisk walk might clear her head after Nick's unexpected communication, allowing her to process everything, and as a bonus there were lots of opportunities to forage at this time of year. Passing beech nuts, sloes, rose hips and sweet chestnuts, she found herself wishing she had been more prepared, and resolved to return to various locations with the Sussex trug her parents had bought from the Truggery in Herstmonceux to collect up the bounty.

The natural world fed her soul, even as her heart ached – her aunt was dying, her mother was depressed, and she feared she would never fall in love. When she reached Magham Down at last she saw in the distance the familiar green tractor with the now recognisable figure inside. His facial expressions were too far away to read, but she had no doubt in her mind that with a wedding approaching and an exciting new life ahead, Dean was bound to be feeling happier than she was right now.

* * *

Robert waited patiently outside the intensive care unit until Charles came through the heavy double doors and into the corridor.

'Thanks Robert, for being here again. I really do appreciate it.'

Feeling helpless, Robert observed his brother's bloodshot eyes and gaunt face. He had never seen him like this before. 'Do you want to go for a coffee?' he asked.

'Yes, I do,' Charles replied joylessly.

In the hospital canteen, his heaviness was palpable, as he sat opposite Robert, coffee in hand.

'I can't believe she's been in a coma almost twelve days now. How can that even be real, Robert?'

'I can't believe it either.'

'It's been good of you to spend so much time here with me in London. Please Robert, tell Joan for me, I'm grateful she lets you come.'

'That's no problem, Joan wishes she could be here too. She keeps saying you need someone to look after you and cook your meals. She would love to do it herself, but as you know she struggles with various health issues, and lately she's not been too well, but thankfully she's on the up now, she really is. Amanda would also be up here like a shot, if it wasn't for her work.'

'You don't need to explain, I know you're all doing what you can, and there really is nothing you or anyone else can do. By the way,' Charles said, briefly lifting his chin, unshaven and full of stubble, 'I really appreciated the card Amanda sent me. You've got one amazing daughter there.'

Robert nodded and smiled. 'That reminds me, Joan and I didn't thank you for the postcard. It arrived days ago.'

Charles' eyes lowered. 'Yes, the postcard from Kenya, I'm glad it arrived safely. Pauline was keen to get them posted ... she loves sending postcards ...' He paused for a moment, suddenly overwhelmed, and buried his head in his hands. 'Robert, it's been terrible, just terrible. I've never felt so alone.' He said nothing more for a while until the sound of a toddler giggling at a nearby table brightened up an otherwise sterile but functional canteen. 'Pauline and I,' Charles continued, 'we would have loved to have built a family through adoption but maybe because of all the travel and work commitments we never really settled anywhere. There were so many house moves, things just got in the way. Now this has happened, I've had moments when I've felt totally alone in the world, even though we have made many so-called friends over the years, but where are they now?' Charles began to slowly twist a paper napkin in his hands. 'I feel completely alone, Robert.'

'But you're not, Charles, you're far from alone. Don't forget you've got us.'

Charles tried to smile but then looked down at the table in front of them, lost in thought. 'Robert, do you believe in God?' he asked after a long pause.

'Well, yes, Charles, you know I do, although Joan and I, we don't go to church or anything.'

'Pauline and I were never interested either. I always thought church was full of hypocrites and only good for christenings, weddings or ... funer—'

 Charles stopped short, unable or unwilling to utter the word funeral.

'Before our flight at Gatwick,' he resumed, 'Pauline was bored, so she wanted to visit the chapel. There wasn't much happening in there, and I didn't think much of it, but when she became ill, and especially after she was transferred here, my mind kept going back to that moment, so yesterday I asked a nurse if there was a hospital chapel. She told me that yes there was, and showed me where.' Charles' eyes slowly began to fill with tears again. 'I went inside, Robert, and do you know what?'

Robert shook his head.

'I looked up at the cross on the wall, got on my knees and prayed. I begged. I said: "God, if you exist, please let Pauline live. I know that until now I've not given you the time of day, or cared much about other people, but I want to change all that. Please don't punish us, and please let Pauline live!"'

Although deeply moved, Robert looked on awkwardly, wondering if Charles might be losing his mind. 'Don't be silly, God isn't punishing you for anything, why would he?'

Charles didn't respond, but Robert was surprised to see there was a joyful spark in his eyes. 'Something happened when I spoke to God,' he said smiling, his face taking on a glow. 'I suddenly felt this incredible peace, as though everything was going to be all right. And you know what, Robert, although I still can't stop crying, and I don't know what the future holds, deep down I know that when it comes to Pauline and me everything will work out, and that despite my worries neither of us are ever truly alone.'

'I'm really glad you've found some comfort, Charles,' Robert said at last, surprised and lifted by his brother's words, 'and I'm right by you. I know we've had our differences, many of them going back since we were boys, but we are brothers, and I really do care.'

Charles looked at Robert and smiled before taking the last sip of his coffee.

'I know you do,' he said.

* * *

Dean had a lot on his mind while he finished the repairs on the wooden fencing which bordered the footpath by the farm. Contrary to his mother's hopes and expectations, he and Carolyn hadn't managed to patch things up since the village fete. They were cordial towards each other, and even found time to spend a whole day at the Royal Pavilion in Brighton to see the opulence and showy extravagance of George's IV's palace. 'Not my taste but interesting,' Dean remarked, as he and Carolyn walked around, hand in hand. Distractions like these helped to gloss things over, but when Dean found himself alone, and Carolyn was at work, there were moments when he had to admit to feeling lonely. How could that be? His family were never far away, and he was soon to be married to an amazing woman he admired and was devoted to, but sometimes he'd miss a familiar helping hand, someone to discuss birds with, the wildflowers, the weather, the farm animals, music and song.

The trees were transforming into a riot of yellow, brown and russet, with certain shades of red reminding Dean of Amanda's auburn hair. Even just the sight of particular trees made him think of her and what she said about them. In his head he would hear her voice, or in his mind's eye see her hard at work clearing the animal stalls or feeding the livestock and hens. He'd also hear her laughter every time he told another one of his stupid jokes, and he missed being able to pass the hours with someone who didn't mind in the least being the butt of those jokes. After hours of hard work, fun and activity together, he would visualise her tucking into her lunch as they both sat for a well-earned rest.

He decided to stop. Enough was enough. As lovely and as charming as Amanda was, she was simply too late. Carolyn had captured his heart and would always be the love of his life, he was sure of it. Every couple went through rough patches, and this was the season for theirs. He was looking forward to their wedding day and to making Carolyn his bride at last, but at the same time he was trying to fight doubts which were threatening to sabotage everything. Carolyn could barely find time to help out on the farm, and when she did he wasn't sure she enjoyed it. She said she did, but her actions often indicated otherwise. And lately, he had learned something new; she could be intensely jealous. He had eyes just for her, but having said this, what man failed to notice a beautiful woman? Noticing something and wanting something were two very different things, and Dean knew he would never stray, he just wasn't like that. He was a one woman man, and that woman was definitely his very special Carolyn, a woman he cared deeply about.

Without a new volunteer, tasks at the farm were starting to build up. Cecil continued to do a noble job, but Dean knew his father was counting the days to retirement and the time he could finally hand over the farm to his son and daughter-in-law. Dean's mind was ablaze, and he knew he needed to step off the worry wheel. Normally the sounds of nature were enough, but sometimes music was the best way to keep him going during bouts of heavy work. He picked up his chunky portable radio and turned it on. Catching the tail end of the Rainbow song 'Since You've Been Gone' he sang along to the upbeat rocky hit, and became acutely aware of the lyrics— the singer bemoaning the love he has lost after his woman had gone. *It's funny, if I didn't know better I'd believe those words were mocking me*, he laughed to himself.

Next was Lena Martell's 'One Day at a Time', its comforting message, especially for people going through hard times, made him think of Amanda's aunt who, according to his mother, was gravely ill in hospital. Country and Western wasn't usually to his taste and he was pleased when Sad Café's 'Every Day Hurts' was next up. But why so many songs about breakups? He felt his heart tug as he put away his tools, but felt relief when The Police's 'Message in a Bottle' offered a welcome respite from all that emotion.

He stood back and looked at the fencing. He deserved a pat on the back, it was a job well done. It was time to head home for dinner and he reached over to switch the radio off, but before he could, a familiar tune began to play. It was a song that had been in the singles charts for some time and one which he had grown to like, but until today it hadn't meant much to him. As he listened to the heart-wrenching lyrics about not being able to find the words, missing someone incredibly, and only God knowing how to find solace after losing your love, something resonated. And then, the gentle melody of 'Just When I Needed You Most', together with Randy VanWarmer's mellow voice, finally led to a breaking point. He couldn't remember when he last cried, and didn't know or care who might see him as he stood alone with the radio playing and his heart aching. He crossed his arms and leaned heavily on one of the newly constructed fence panels and, looking into the distance, allowed the tears to fall.

Chapter 17

'Charles, that's incredible news, whoo hoo! I'm so, so happy,' Robert boomed, and within seconds Joan and Amanda were standing at his side in the hallway. Moments earlier when the phone rang, he had solemnly risen to his feet. 'I'll get it,' he said, leaving Joan and Amanda in the living room, tense, motionless and anticipating bad news.

'Is it Aunty Pauline?' Amanda asked, watching her father glance upwards with relief, while gripping the phone.

'Yes, yes, it's Charles. Pauline came out of the coma late last night. Joan, speak to him!'

Joan grabbed the phone and started to repeat everything Charles was telling her.

'She's not totally out of the woods yet … she is on dialysis … she can't talk or swallow, but she's aware of what's going on because she can move her arms to show she understands what is being said … although it seems she is still very confused. Oh Charles, can we come see her? Not yet … that's fine, I totally understand.'

Robert, delighted to hear Joan wanted to visit Pauline, took this as a major sign that her depression had lifted at last.

Amanda was overjoyed at the terrific news, even though it seemed Pauline still had a long way to go. 'Please tell Uncle Charles to give Aunty Pauline my love, Mum,' she urged, bouncing on her feet.

Several weeks elapsed, and by November Pauline had steadily improved, managing a few words at first and then learning to walk slowly with a stick, until eventually she was able to leave hospital. However, it would be a long time before she felt in a fit state to receive visitors at her home, so Joan, Robert and Amanda decided to stay away until she was feeling stronger. Charles became her full-time carer, helping her feed and dress herself. Every day he would hold her steady as she caught her breath walking upstairs to bed, where she would then sleep for hours. At times she still became confused, but there was one thing she could see and understand all too clearly; her full and bouncy head of hair, once her pride and joy, was now thin, wispy and grey. The hours spent highlighting it at the hairdressers, making sure it looked 'just right', were now a thing of the past.

After his experience at the hospital chapel, Charles made the decision to dig out his dusty Gideon Bible from the loft. He found the subject headings useful for guiding him to passages which spoke to whatever situation he was feeling at the time, whether it be fear, worry and anxiety, anger, or even thankfulness. He was encouraged by the passages on sickness and healing, sometimes reading out loud to Pauline, even while she was sleeping.

'Uncle Charles has found God, hasn't he,' Amanda declared, while her father drove her to work one morning.

'It seems he has,' Robert replied pensively. 'Who'd have thought it, eh? I certainly didn't think he'd be the type, Manda, never.'

* * *

It was a bright Sunday afternoon in November, and although it had been a relaxing day, Amanda hadn't been able to dismiss a concern in the back of her mind. It had been some time since she had heard from Sam, and she was beginning to worry their friendship was waning. Letters had been few and far between, and phone calls were even more infrequent. Wanting things to improve, she decided to call Sam after lunch when she'd be back from church. Amanda was also curious to know the latest about Mark. The last thing she'd heard was that he was still excelling in his Articles training. Although he found civil litigation challenging, he had managed to impress the very exacting Senior Partner, which apparently was quite an achievement. Even more important, Sam said his injuries had largely healed, although he would be left with at least one permanent scar on his face. When it came to his psychological recovery, Geraldine said it would take some time for him to get over the trauma, although no one would know how much he had suffered. 'My son hides those sorts of things only too well,' she had told Sam.

After enjoying a giggle and chat with Sam that afternoon, Amanda felt reassured their friendship was back on track. While she listened to Sam enthuse about a Jamaican guy at her church she'd had her eye on for months, Amanda kept quiet. She had nothing of that nature to report, and according to Sam, Mark was in the same loveless boat. That sounded hopeful. He was still single, however, Amanda had now accepted that she would no longer be the one to change that.

It was such a waste. Two people who could have been in love, both still alone. Feeling the temptation to focus on Nick, she stopped herself, knowing that deep down he wasn't responsible for that. If she and Mark had been truly meant for each other, nothing could have put a stop to it.

* * *

In contrast to the unequivocal demise of Amanda and Mark's relationship, Dean and Carolyn's was flourishing again. Dean had fully recovered from the emotional glitch he had suffered several weeks ago. He put it down to being tired and hungry at the time, both known causes of psychological instability. Since then, he and Carolyn had been getting on brilliantly, and he was increasingly appreciating her wonderful qualities. Most of all, she loved him, and he reasoned that ultimately that was all that mattered. As he hadn't seen Amanda for a long time, he was now able to think more rationally, and with the wedding only two months away he was excited about the future. He felt strong enough to take on anything.

Various bones of contention were being ironed out. The decision to go to France for their honeymoon, for instance. This was the perfect compromise, because it was abroad, which appealed to Carolyn, but also not too far away so an easy drive for Dean. He hadn't driven on the continent before, but decided cutting his teeth by going no further than Normandy would ease him in gently. He was looking forward to it. Stuart said driving on the continent was a cinch, although that was easy to say for someone who was totally fearless at high speeds on a motorbike.

The January weather in Normandy might be an improvement on Scotland, but not by much, so in accordance with the original plan they would take their trip to France in the spring. Immediately after the wedding, they planned to stay in the posh Grand Hotel in Eastbourne, and that would do nicely until they could embark on their honeymoon proper. Dean was looking forward to his wedding night. It wasn't easy to wait, and with only a couple of months to go, it was becoming even harder to hold back, especially as Carolyn seemed far less worried about waiting than he did. Thankfully, she had promised to stop sharing details of their intimate life with Tracy. Fortunately for them both, time alone together was hard to come by. At Carolyn's house, there were four siblings at home, and Dean always had at least one parent or Millie around somewhere. Time alone was also limited by the challenges of coordinating their busy schedules, and Dean was committed to ensuring that his car was simply used to transport them from A to B, rather than a place to canoodle.

Now the clocks had gone back and the evenings were longer, Carolyn and Dean enjoyed cuddling up close and watching TV in the living room at Hillbrook Farm. Not only could they relax and laugh together during these times, but it was also a chance to finalise wedding plans, including their gift list and order of service. Other than that, every spare moment was spent doing up the cottage on the farm, their forthcoming home. Although Dean was handy with a paintbrush, and could even make furniture, if given time, Carolyn dreamed about the perfect home, and was keen for everything to be ready the instant they moved in. She knew this wasn't feasible, but reasoned there was no harm in looking, and persuaded Dean to drive her to MFI in Eastbourne, where just viewing the beautiful new kitchens and bathrooms would be all that was needed for an enjoyable outing. Life felt good, and Dean caught himself whistling breezily when he and Cecil brought the sheep and cattle indoors in preparation for the winter. If last year was anything to go by, the season would be long, harsh and very cold.

* * *

Amanda and Maggie had really made an effort at Jimmy's café. Green, gold, silver and red tinsel was draped across the ceiling, and colourful paper snowmen, bells and reindeer lined the café walls.

'Thanks for helping with the decorations, Amanda. It takes time, but once it's done, it's done.' Maggie hung the last few baubles on a small artificial tree, stepped back and smiled.

'No problem at all, Maggie.'

'The customers love to see a bit of festive spirit,' Maggie added, before leaving to take someone's order.

Christmas in only three weeks, and it's not looking very festive outside.

Amanda looked through the large café window at the driving rain. *Our first Christmas at Marshywood*, she reflected. Would it feel any different? Now that her Aunt Pauline was slowly gaining strength, that was the best ever gift for them all. What kind of Christmas would it have been if they had lost her? *Perhaps Aunty Pauline and Uncle Charles are able to come for Christmas lunch.* And then there was Joan. Her mother was growing more positive by the day, and it was very good news indeed when Amanda heard her say she was learning to put everything in perspective. The happier

Joan was, the better her relationship was with Amanda, which in turn made Amanda happier, as did the closeness developing between her parents and her aunt and uncle.

Maggie shouted across to Jimmy, 'Egg, sausage, beans and chips twice, plus one with bacon.' Jimmy gave a thumbs up and slapped more bacon rashers into a large frying pan. After serving the customers' coffee, Maggie approached Amanda, who was busy clearing a table.

'What a mess,' Amanda moaned as she wiped up spilled tea, egg yolk and brown sauce, only to discover toast lying butter-side down on the floor.

'Hey Amanda, what are you doing New Year's Eve?' Maggie asked cheerfully.

'New Year's Eve? Nothing that I know of yet.'

'So you've no plans?'

'None.'

'Fancy a party?'

'Tell me more.'

'My step-sister Tracy is having a New Year's Eve party, right here in Hailsham. She said I could bring a friend, so I'm inviting you.'

Amanda felt honoured, especially since Maggie was older and they didn't seem to have a lot in common.

'I don't know Tracy very well, to be honest,' Maggie continued, 'and I hardly ever see her. My dad married her mum just three years ago. You know, it feels really weird, suddenly having a sister when you're 32 years old, but I've always wanted one, so I shouldn't complain, even though she's a good ten years younger than me. I've managed to scrape the money together to get someone to babysit Becky for the night. My dad and step mum can't resist a knees up, so they'll be there too, so unfortunately no free babysitting for me,' Maggie tutted, 'not that I ever got much of that anyway.'

'If you're ever stuck for a babysitter I'll be happy to help if I can,' Amanda said with no hesitation.

'That's really kind of you, Amanda, I'll bear that in mind next time a gorgeous bloke steps in here and asks me out on a hot date. Chance will be a fine thing, though! No, seriously, I occasionally like a night out with the girls, so that would be great.'

'The party sounds good, Maggie. Thanks for thinking of me.'

'Don't mention it." Maggie brushed the gratitude away with a swipe of her hand. 'I can't bear to think of anyone, especially someone your age, stuck at home on New Year's Eve. Oh, I almost forgot. They're making a makeshift cocktail bar so bring a bottle.'

* * *

The closing credits flashed across the screen for the *Top of the Pops* Christmas special 1979 – 'Oliver's Army', 'Video Killed the Radio Star', B.A Robertson's 'Bang Bang' ... so many good songs that year.

'That was great!' Amanda said, removing her slippers and tucking her legs underneath her on the sofa.

'If you say so love,' Joan replied with notable disinterest.

Amanda glanced over at her father. As usual he was asleep on the sofa after a huge meal consisting of turkey, stuffing, roasties, sprouts and Christmas pudding, while Joan, never one to follow pop music, was finishing off a crossword puzzle.

Charles and Pauline had decided to spend a quiet Christmas at home to aid Pauline's slow and steady recuperation. And now there was less than a week to Maggie's sister's party. Maggie had told Amanda that her step-sister had recently moved into a townhouse with her fiancé and so the celebration was a mishmash of a New Year's Eve and house warming do. Amanda thought a party in town might offer a new social pool to tap into, with the opportunity to make a new friend or two. However, she stopped short of pinning her hopes on a romantic encounter, having gone through an emotional rollercoaster ride these past few months.

Sam had telephoned on Christmas Eve to wish her a happy Christmas, saying Mark and Geraldine were staying, and were due to arrive that evening. Amanda told Sam to send her regards to Geraldine and to give Mark her love, before immediately regretting her choice of words. But she was also happy to find no residual emotion lurking within, or any feelings other than platonic ones. She genuinely wished Mark every happiness for the future, whatever that may hold, finally content in the knowledge that she wasn't going to be a part of it.

Robert's light snoring started to get louder. Amanda shook her head and smiled.

'Dad just can't handle a big Christmas lunch, can he?'

'No, he never could,' Joan sighed, closing her puzzle book. 'I wonder how the Applebys are enjoying their Christmas,' she mused. 'Victoria told me Stuart would be home but Dean was spending it at Carolyn's. Since they'll be living at the farm full time after their wedding, she said it was only fair to share them with Carolyn's parents. She can't wait to have a resident daughter-in-law.'

Amanda shifted uneasily in her seat, disappointed to discover that while earlier, her feelings for Mark had been neutral, in stark contrast, the mere mention of Dean's name had stirred up a hornet's nest. Trying to quash the emotion which had taken her by surprise, she quickly composed herself. 'That's really lovely,' she replied calmly, 'they're so lucky to have all that land and those buildings so Carolyn and Dean don't need to buy anywhere new of their own.'

'I presume so, but I wonder how much space they get to themselves? I mean, you don't want your mother-in-law breathing down your neck all the time, do you?'

'No, but I doubt Victoria will be like that,' Amanda said, noticing the angel had fallen from the top of the Christmas tree.

'I do agree with you, love.'

Amanda fell silent, and after getting up to place the angel back in position, she returned to the sofa. It felt soft and cushioning, but as she sank into it, a discomforting thought crossed her mind. 'Mum,' she said quietly.

'Yes.'

'I can't believe the wedding's only a month away now.'

'Me neither, Manda. It seems like yesterday when Victoria told me they were getting married. Doesn't time fly.'

* * *

'Thanks for the lift, Dad.' Amanda left the car and Robert wound down the window.

'That's alright, love. Now remember, I'll be waiting outside at half past twelve. I hope that's late enough.'

'Yes, I'm sure it will be, and this is the one time I don't feel guilty about keeping you and Mum awake. Although perhaps I should, because even though it's New Year's Eve, I know you would still prefer an early night.'

'That's true, but it's fine. You won't stand a chance getting a taxi tonight and it's not as if you're always out at parties, so it's no trouble giving my daughter a lift on a special night out.'

'Perhaps I'll pass my test soon, which might make things easier.'

Robert feigned horror. 'If you think you're going to be let loose with our car you've got another think coming!'

'I thought I was doing okay,' Amanda said sounding disappointed, 'those extra hours of practice since leaving the farm have really boosted my confidence.'

'That's true, and I'm only joking, love, you're quite the good little driver now.'

'All thanks to you, Dad,' she said, feeling the frosty air on her cheeks and nose. 'You're a great instructor. I'm not sure I'd feel comfortable driving this car without you next to me anyway. It's all we've got, so I'd be nervous about crashing it. Perhaps I should get my own wheels.'

'Don't be silly. The last thing you need is a car to eat up all your hard-earned cash. Now, mind how you go, the ground's still icy and those shoes aren't great for these conditions.'

'Yes, I'll be careful, love you, see you later.' Amanda waved, and Robert drove away.

She could hear music as she walked carefully, trying not to slip, her warm winter coat wrapped around her and a bottle of advocaat in her hand. Standing at the doorway, she listened to 'Another Brick in the Wall' echoing inside. There were certain bands with a cult following that Amanda didn't quite 'get', Pink Floyd was one, and some of the others were heavy metal groups, which in all fairness, was probably due to her not being so keen on hard rock. Before she knew it, she was again thinking of Dean, who once told her he had some Pink Floyd albums. *It might be number one, but it's hardly festive*, she thought, hoping the music would improve, as well as hoping she would forget Dean for the rest of the night.

She rang the doorbell, but thinking no one would hear it above the noise, was about to knock loudly when she saw the door was ajar. It was intimidating to walk into a stranger's house with no one to welcome her. For all she knew, she wouldn't recognise a soul, apart from Maggie. All she could see were shadows accompanied by loud voices coming from the lounge. She stood in the hall, feeling slightly on edge, not seeing a single person until ...

'Hi, I'm Tracy, who are you?'

A young woman with long dark hair, wearing a black dress with thigh-high slits, had emerged from the party room and was looking straight at her.

'I'm Amanda, Maggie's friend,' she said, hoping she'd managed to avoid looking startled.

'Oh, you're Amanda. Hi, really nice to meet you. Ahh advocaat! Fabulous, now we can make snowballs thanks to you. I'll take it to the kitchen in a sec. Maggie's already here. Pop your coat upstairs in the first bedroom you come to and then head this way.'

Tracy rushed back into the living room and Amanda walked upstairs and took off her coat to uncover the blue dress she had worn to the pub disco back in the summer. As she did so, she heard roars of laughter coming from the party room and immediately felt paranoid, although she knew the laughter couldn't possibly be anything to do with her. The thought of walking into a room packed with unfamiliar people filled her with trepidation.

She needn't have worried. After she returned downstairs and entered the room, she was instantly met with a sea of smiling faces. Maggie got up to greet her.

'You made it, Amanda! Wow, you look stunning. Come sit over here, the chairs are filling up fast.'

Amanda squeezed herself in between a woman and a man sitting on a sofa. The woman, who was on Amanda's left, was laughing at the top of her voice. *That explains the noise*, she thought. The man on her right, who had fair hair and glasses, was rather awkward and shy looking. He had a pleasant, not unattractive face, and appeared to be in his late twenties. He turned to Amanda and smiled sheepishly.

'What can I get you to drink?' Maggie asked, looking down at Amanda.

'A coke or something like it would be great.'

'I'm guessing Tracy has coke, in fact, I'm pretty certain I saw Pepsi in the kitchen just now. Are you sure you don't want something a bit stronger?'

'Perhaps later,' Amanda said, smiling with appreciation.

'Coming up. What about you, Kenneth? Do you want your lager topped up?'

'I'm fine, Maggie, for now, thanks.'

Maggie darted away to get the drinks and Amanda couldn't help but listen to the woman sat next to her, recounting a story, in between fits of laughter. It sounded as if she'd had a bit too much to drink already. On her other side, Kenneth looked keen to chat, so she decided to make the first move.

'Hi, I'm Amanda.'

'I gathered that,' he replied, with a tone of voice suggesting social ineptitude rather than rudeness. 'And as you've just heard, my name's Kenneth. Lovely to meet you, Amanda.' He awkwardly pulled out a hand which had been wedged between the seat and the arm of the sofa and reached over to shake Amanda's.

'Nice to meet you, Kenneth. Do people call you Ken?' she asked realising the question which had just rattled off her tongue was possibly a sign of her own social awkwardness.

'I'd rather people didn't.' He then paused, adding with an awkward smile, 'But you can call me Ken if you want.'

'I won't if Kenneth is what you prefer,' Amanda replied, hoping she sounded relaxed enough to put him at ease.

'Are you local, Amanda?'

'Yes, fairly, I work with Maggie in Jimmy's café, and I live just outside Hailsham in a village called Magham Down.'

'So you live rurally. How nice. I live and work in Tunbridge Wells and I'm a friend of Tracy's fiancé, Brian. I'm also a bookkeeper.'

'A bookkeeper, what does a bookkeeper do?'

By now, Maggie had returned with drinks, so while Amanda quietly sipped her Pepsi, she tried hard to follow a detailed explanation of financial data and records, sales and purchase receipts, invoices, cash registers and bank reconciliation.

'So you're an accountant then?' she concluded.

'I'm afraid nothing so grand. Actually, some of the work I do gets passed on to accountants – the more complex stuff. I've never been great at exams, so I didn't try to qualify as an accountant. I'm really lucky though, I've been working for my company since leaving school, and in the new year ...' Kenneth paused, raised his arm and looked at his wristwatch, 'which starts in less than three and a half hours, I'll have been there thirteen years.'

Amanda wanted to share her experience with Kenneth, having appreciated his transparency and humility. 'I wasn't great at exams either,' she told him. 'I liked certain subjects like English, but even just thinking about tests tied my stomach up in knots. I actually didn't turn up for one of my O levels – English, in fact – and after resitting it, I decided I didn't want to keep putting myself through that sort of stress.'

'You and I have something in common then.' Kenneth smiled, his shoulders relaxing.

'I suppose we do.'

Amanda quickly noticed a familiar scent, which she hoped wouldn't become too bothersome. 'You're a fan of Brut aftershave,' she said confidently.

Kenneth stared at Amanda in surprise. 'That's incredible, you've got an amazing sense of smell.'

'I guess that's true, but I can also tell it's Brut because I worked in Woolworths for three years and I got to know certain fragrances.'

'I'm impressed,' Kenneth said, before unexpectedly declaring, 'I'm not one of those, you know.'

Amanda cocked her head to one side, looking perplexed. 'I don't think I understa—'

'Brute, I'm far from being a brute,' he beamed.

Finally getting the joke, Amanda smiled. After her experience with Nick, she was very glad to hear it. Nothing else was said for a while. She looked across at the DJ, who was about to play another record. Things had improved since Pink Floyd, and she was hoping for another good track.

'Brian said he's a professional DJ,' Kenneth remarked, following her eyes. 'I think he's been pretty good so far, don't you?'

'Yes,' Amanda agreed, and when The Nolans' 'I'm in the Mood for Dancing' started to play, she wasn't disappointed. Like a shot, the noisy woman on her left jumped up and bounded towards the centre of the room where people were already dancing, grabbing the man next to her. At last there was more space, and Amanda and Kenneth, no longer squashed, shifted apart slightly. Contemplating whether to get up herself, Amanda wondered if Kenneth was the dancing type, but the room was starting to fill, and there were already many more people than seats. Just as she began to think about at what point she was prepared to lose hers, she was astonished to see a familiar face walk in. It was Stuart, and noticing her straight away, he quickly made a beeline for the empty space beside her. Amanda stiffened, wondering why he was there and whether that meant Dean would also turn up. Petrified at that prospect, she became calmer once she reminded herself that Dean and Stuart didn't tend to move in the same social circles.

'Hi Amanda, I've not seen you for such a long time. How are things?' Stuart was smiling broadly.

'I'm fine, Stuart thanks. How are you?' she replied, nervously glancing at the door before remembering Dean was unlikely to be there too.

'Doing alright,' he said, sounding quietly confident. 'I've completed the final assessment stage for the army and will be starting my training soon.'

'Congratulations! Oh, by the way, this is Kenneth, Kenneth this is Stuart.' The two men nodded in cordial acknowledgement.

'How's your girlfriend … Emma?' Amanda asked, trying to make conversation.

Stuart's face fell slightly. 'Emma and I broke up a couple of months ago, so I'm now young, free and single.' Accurately anticipating Amanda's response he held up his hand, 'But no, don't be sorry, it really was for the best, we were never right for each other anyway. It took nearly two years to work that one out,' he laughed nervously, 'but we got there in the end.'

Amanda wondered if thoughts of Emma had triggered stress. Looking agitated, Stuart reached into his pocket, pulled out a packet of cigarettes and offered one to Kenneth, who declined politely.

'I know you don't smoke, Amanda, and quite right too, it's a rotten, filthy habit.'

A cigarette dangled from his mouth, while he shoved the packet back in his jacket pocket. Flicking his lighter, he was about to light up when Tracy charged towards him.

'Don't even think about it, Stuart!' she said, crossing her arms. 'Smoking is banned in the house, so you'll need to go outside. I don't want cigarette burns on my new carpet and it stinking of smoke.'

'But it's absolutely freezing!' Stuart pleaded, but Tracy stared pitilessly. 'All right, I'll be a good boy,' he conceded, but as soon as Tracy's back was turned, he communicated his chagrin to Amanda and Kenneth. 'Telling guests not to smoke? What the …? Oh, and good luck with the carpet,' he nodded furiously. 'What possessed the woman to get a new one fitted just before hosting a party anyway? I mean, didn't anyone tell her about red wine stains and vomit?'

Amanda was inclined to agree that the carpet might look a little different after the party was over, but responded with just a hesitant smile.

'Are you a friend of Tracy or her fiancé?' she asked, wanting to find out why Stuart was there.

'I know Tracy ... sort of. At least, I've met her a few times before. She's Carolyn's best friend, so I've seen her at various get-togethers,' he replied, matter of factly.

Amanda froze. Stuart had just said Tracy was Carolyn's best friend. She was connecting up the dots and she didn't like what she was seeing. Didn't Dean, all those months ago, say Carolyn's best friend was called Tracy, the same name as Maggie's step-sister? But Tracy was a common enough name, so there would have been little chance of her making the connection. Then she realised the implications. Carolyn was likely to be here tonight, and therefore Dean too, but if that was the case, where were they? It was almost 9 o'clock. As her mind continued to tick rapidly, Stuart put her out of one misery, while catapulting her into another.

'Dean and Carolyn are coming tonight but not until later,' he said. 'You see, when my little brother wants to slack off, he can always blame the farm. I've seen him use that excuse dozens of times when he just doesn't fancy socialising. He can be a bit of a hermit, or I should say introvert, to be kinder, and now, with a wedding coming up, he has another excuse to decline invitations.' Stuart hesitated. 'Perhaps I am being a bit unfair. He did look off colour this morning, saying he had a splitting headache and felt like he was coming down with something, so maybe everything's taken longer and he's behind.'

Although Dean would be the first to admit he was never the life and soul of the party, Amanda didn't think he was a party pooper, and the friendly reception he received at the cattle market wasn't suggestive of a hermit either, so she concluded Stuart was indeed being unfair.

'But Dean told me he likes dancing,' she added, hoping not to sound too defensive.

'That's true. Me, on the other hand, I'm not a fan. Yes, you're right, Amanda, he loves a dance, so maybe he isn't trying to duck out tonight, and I hope I haven't bad-mouthed my little brother too much. That wouldn't do, would it? Being his best man and everything.'

'You're the best man?'

'I am, worse luck, because that means giving a speech. Yes, to be fair I'm not entirely sure what the reason is for their lateness tonight. He just said he'd see me later, and there was no need to mention anything to Tracy because Carolyn had already told her they'd be late.' Stuart suddenly became aware of Amanda's edginess. 'Are you feeling okay, Amanda? You're looking a bit peaky yourself.'

'I'm fine, Stuart … no, really, I'm fine.'

A look of regret suddenly crossed Stuart's face. 'I never got the chance to say anything to you after what happened to your friend that night. I know Dean did the apologising for me, but I want to tell you how sorry I am, now I've finally got the chance.'

'Thank you, Stuart.'

'How is he now?'

'Mark's doing well, thank you, and there was no need for you to apologise. It really wasn't your fault.'

'No, but I still regret having anything to do with Nick. I'm guessing you haven't heard but the bastard's moved away, and I hope he's gone for good.'

Amanda, wanting to avoid going into the details about Nick's letter, resisted telling Stuart she already knew. She looked over at

Kenneth and smiled, and far from looking neglected he seemed content, despite having been excluded from the conversation for quite some time.

The smooth, spooky-sounding intro to Michael Jackson's 'Off the Wall' began, and Amanda knew she couldn't resist a dance this time. If there was one song which could take her mind off Dean for a moment, this was it. Seeing her body language, Kenneth looked poised to join her, while Stuart decided he would brave the outside for that much desired smoke. 'Better head upstairs for my blasted coat, then,' he said. 'See you folks in a bit.'

Amanda was delighted to see Kenneth losing his inhibitions to the funky rhythm, as she watched him transform from an awkward and shy young man to an energetic mover. The magic of the music was clearly getting to him.

The party was now well and truly under way, and although Tracy's lounge was spacious, there was little room for manoeuvre. Maggie shimmied towards Amanda, pointing to the far end of the room. 'That's my dad with Tracy's mum, my step mum,' she said. Amanda looked over to see a man in his sixties, in good shape, silver hair flapping wildly as he shook his head, dancing with a small plump woman with short brown hair, twisting and swirling to the music. 'Didn't I tell you they were party animals?' Maggie laughed, before noticing Kenneth's demeanour. 'Amanda,' she said lowering her voice, 'I see you've made a friend, best leave you two alone then.' She winked suggestively before slinking away. Amanda hoped Kenneth hadn't noticed. It was unlikely he had, because she could see he was concentrating on her and no one else.

'Have you ever been to Tunbridge Wells?' he asked, rocking his arms back and forth.

'Dad drives through on the way to London, but we haven't stopped there yet.'

'So you know how easy it is to get there then. Just up the A267 and north of Heathfield. You really must stop by next time you head that way. It's actually called Royal Tunbridge Wells, thanks to Edward Vll, and it's also a spa town with a historic area called the Pantiles where you can shop and eat.'

'Sounds lovely.'

'Before we go home tonight we must exchange telephone numbers so we can arrange to meet if you're passing, or I could always come down and pick you up and take you for a visit, if you'd prefer.'

Amanda, catching her breath, realised she was being asked out. She was a little surprised how quickly it had happened and wasn't entirely sure how she felt. Kenneth was pleasant enough, but she was yet to see a spark. She knew attraction could grow, so she didn't want to write him off completely, but she also had a feeling that, had it not been for the music, things might have been rather flat, despite appreciating his attempt at humour with his Brut joke and admiring his candour. For now, she decided to put aside her reservations, admitting to herself that after her recent romantic disappointments she was loving the attention and having the most fun she had experienced in a long time. This made it easier to forget about Dean and Carolyn, and anyone who saw her carefree dancing could see she was having a ball. And unbeknown to her, someone had noticed. It was only when she paused for breath, fanned herself with her hand and looked across the room, her heart skipped a beat. Dean and Carolyn were standing by the door.

Chapter 18

Amanda stopped dancing, her feet frozen to the spot. There was no escape. What should she do for the best? Go up to them and say hi? No, that might appear presumptuous and brazen. Wait for them to come to her? That was bound to look bad and make both Dean and Carolyn feel uncomfortable. Should she wave? Wouldn't that seem frivolous? What about ignoring them? That would be rude! What to do? In the end Amanda decided to smile and wait. She looked behind her, and relieved to find her former seat vacant, she practically fell into it, all the time wishing it would swallow her up.

With Kenneth's seat occupied, he decided to grasp the opportunity to get Amanda another drink.

'Thanks, Kenneth, I'll have a white wine spritzer,' she said without thinking, keeping a surreptitious eye on Dean and Carolyn.

'Is that with lemonade or soda water?'

'Uh, lemonade please, but soda's also fine.' Amanda's words were rushed, but she hoped she didn't look or sound as distracted as she felt.

'Okay, I'll be right back.' Kenneth strode away, his arms swinging contentedly.

'Thanks, Kenneth,' Amanda mumbled, watching him leave.

Saved by the bell, or more accurately rescued by Stuart, Amanda was relieved to see him re-enter the room holding a chicken drumstick. He bounded up to Dean and Carolyn and then looked across at Amanda. The three of them immediately started to walk towards her, but with Stuart as a buffer, Amanda felt her panic begin to subside.

'Amanda!' he shouted, Dean and Carolyn following him. 'I was telling these two latecomers to grab some food. Why don't you do the same? The kitchen's packed with goodies, and Brian's busy making cocktails: snowballs, Piña coladas, you name it. Anyway, look who's here.' He pointed at Dean. 'You know what they say, better late than never.'

Amanda felt daunted looking up at the three of them.

'Hi Amanda,' Dean said warmly, his voice uncharacteristically croaky, 'it's great to see you after all this time. How's things?'

'I'm fine, thank you,' she replied, taking care to acknowledge both him and Carolyn, and resisting the urge to look away. She swallowed hard and cleared her throat. 'How's the farm – and how are your wedding plans going?'

Dean's bright smile showed off his teeth. 'The farm's busy ... and freezing! And as for wedding plans, they're pretty much finalised, aren't they, Carolyn? At least I hope so, with less than a month to go.'

Carolyn nodded with a reserved smile, and looking distracted, glared at Amanda's dress. Dean seemed intent on keeping the conversation flowing.

'I think I might be coming down with something,' he said with a sniffle, 'but I'd rather get it out the way now than be ill just in time for the big day.'

'I'd better keep my distance then.' Regaining her composure, Carolyn lightly pushed him away before holding on to him again affectionately.

'How's that possible when you can't keep your hands off me?' he joked, kissing her on the nose. Then, turning to Amanda, he asked, 'So how do you know Tracy and Brian then?'

'Tracy's step-sister Maggie invited me. We work together in Jimmy's.'

'I don't think I know Maggie, do you, Carolyn?' Dean asked.

Carolyn paused for thought, and tapped her forefinger on her chin. 'I believe I met her once, some years ago, maybe just after their parents got married.'

Stuart was looking restless, 'Look, I don't know about you,' he said, 'but I'm off to pick up more grub and a cocktail. Who wants to join me?'

Why didn't I ask Kenneth for a snowball? Amanda thought, annoyed with herself.

'Thanks Stuart, but I'm still full after dinner, so perhaps later,' she said.

'Well folks,' Stuart said, tipping an imaginary cap, 'see you later then.'

With Stuart now gone, it was Dean who broke the uncomfortable silence.

'You and your parents will be there, I hope,' he asked.

'Yes,' Amanda nodded, painfully aware of what he was referring to.

'At the reception, that is,' Dean clarified, 'since the village church is tiny we do things a bit differently in Magham Down. Not everyone can squeeze into it, so the service tends to be by invitation only, whereas it's traditional that if you're from the village, the reception is open to everybody and a team of people help out with the catering. The only limit is how many you can cram into the village hall, and even if it ends up being standing room only, that's hardly a problem. Of course, not everyone from the village likes it this way, and some couples prefer the old churches in Hailsham or Hellingly with an invitation-only reception, but Carolyn and I,' he paused, and gave her an affectionate look, 'we thought, why not? The traditional way avoids drawing up guest lists and seating plans, not to mention all the cash it saves.'

Amanda already knew about the reception-only invitation, since Joan had told her, and far from being disappointed when she heard, she was relieved to not be at the service to witness Dean and Carolyn taking their vows. 'Yes, we'll be there and thank you,' she replied, keeping her voice on an even keel.

'We're also saving money by not bothering with a stag or hen party,' added Carolyn quickly, keeping a wary eye on Amanda as she spoke. 'It seems to be the trend nowadays – I bet it comes from America, but we thought we could do without yet another thing to organise. And besides, because we're getting married so close to Christmas and New Year, we assumed everyone would be sick of parties by the time our wedding rolls around.' She smiled and eyed Dean dotingly. 'We'll just have to make do with Tracy and Brian's stag and hen dos before they tie the knot in June, won't we, darling? By then we'll have been married almost six months, so still newlyweds really. We're going to miss each other like mad that night.'

'You're joking, aren't you? I'll be well and truly sick of you by then, and desperate for a break.' Dean pressed his lips together to hide a grin.

Carolyn gave him a playful slap and then he pulled her towards him for a hug. As she looked on, Amanda thought she was tolerating the flirtatious and loved-up gestures admirably.

Kenneth returned with the drinks. Dean and Carolyn's eyes followed slowly and with interest as Amanda extended her hand to accept the wine glass from him, and for a moment no one said a word. Dean's muscles became taut and he looked confused, while Carolyn looked up at her future husband, studying him intensely. Amanda wanted to introduce Kenneth and say they'd only just met, but before she could open her mouth, Dean grabbed Carolyn's hand. 'Fancy a dance, darling?' he said, with a nervous smile.

'I thought you said you weren't up to it,' she muttered, smiling through gritted teeth.

'I'm feeling a bit better,' Dean said looking flushed, leaving Amanda feeling slightly embarrassed for them both.

'Okay then,' Carolyn nodded, her voice sounding more positive. 'I'd like to eat first, though.'

'Good idea,' Dean replied, lightly tugging at her hand. 'See you later, Amanda.'

'See you, Dean. Bye Carolyn,' Amanda called after them as they made their way through the revellers.

She was alone with Kenneth again, who, happy to have her all to himself, felt his patience had finally paid off.

'Did you know that Royal Tunbridge Wells is one of only three English towns to be given a royal title?' he began.

'No, actually I didn't,' Amanda replied instantly, her thoughts far away. When Kenneth's words finally registered, her heart sank. For more than one reason, she was starting to feel as though she was dying inside.

'Indeed it is.' Kenneth was unrelenting. 'The other two are Royal Leamington Spa, and Royal Sutton Coldfield, so as you can imagine, it's a rare privilege and—'

Amanda sprung to her feet without warning. 'Fancy another dance?' she said, squeezing past people and heading towards the middle of the room where there was more space. Kenneth followed eagerly.

The DJ had proved himself to be worth his professional status. Amanda was loving every song choice, and soon her spirits were being lifted and restored. As the evening progressed, Stuart, who was increasingly unsteady on his feet, regularly entered the lounge before leaving again, looking more inebriated each time. Although both Dean and Carolyn remained in the room, Amanda noticed they were hardly in each other's presence and rarely danced together. Carolyn, always with a cocktail in hand, preferred to spend time with Tracy, while Dean, when he wasn't eating or drinking, danced nearby. It was also around this time Amanda discovered he was a nifty little mover, never having seen him dance before.

All of a sudden the music was turned down and Tracy stood at the entrance to the room, poised to make an announcement.

'It's nearly eleven and there's still tons of food and drink in the kitchen. Brian and I don't want to take any leftovers into 1980, what with it being a new year and a new decade and everything, so please, get inside that kitchen and demolish it all!'

Cheers and laughter followed, with a number of people heading out of the room. Amanda, starting to feel hungry, was about to join them, but when the music was turned up again, she heard the gentle intro to 'How Deep is Your Love' by the Bee Gees. Seeing her excitement, Kenneth swallowed hard and bit the bullet, nervously extending his hand. He and Amanda moved towards each other and began to dance slowly. Around them people were coupling up, including Maggie. Amanda, unsure whether she was doing the right thing or whether she was leading Kenneth on by slow dancing with him, decided to close her eyes, relish the music and enjoy the moment.

When she briefly opened her eyes, she saw Dean standing among the crowd, not dancing himself but averting his gaze when she looked his way. She felt ashamed to find herself gratified by this. Even after all this time, did he care about her, even a little? Surely not. That would be wrong, and she wouldn't let herself think it possible. He was in love with somebody else and their marriage was imminent. There was simply no hope with him, but perhaps there was with Kenneth?

Amanda closed her eyes, and the next time she opened them she saw what looked like Dean and Carolyn having words. She dismissed the thought that it could have anything to do with her, since that would be a highly irrational and conceited thing to believe. After a slow 360 degree rotation, still holding on to Kenneth, she was at her starting position again, the point at which Dean and Carolyn were easily in view, only to find them no longer in the room.

* * *

Stuart stood in the kitchen and knocked back the last of his tequila sunrise. Time for a fag, he thought, and then all manner of unwholesome words filled his mind at the prospect of going upstairs yet again. Why on earth wasn't there anywhere to leave coats downstairs? It just didn't make sense. 'Sod it!' he riled, heading towards the front door, before swiftly changing his mind once he felt the cold air rush through when somebody walked in from outside. Had he known he was going to be banished into the bitter night air, he would have chosen something more suitable than a thin cotton shirt to wear. After resolving to hang his coat over a kitchen chair, to save him from ever having to do this again, he headed for the bedroom one last time.

The repetitive climb up the stairs was proving challenging now he was feeling worse for wear. He reached the top step and lingered for a few seconds out of breath before easing open the bedroom door, only to be met with an unexpected sight. There on the bed, next to a large pile of coats, sat Carolyn sobbing quietly, her shoulders shaking as she wept.

'Is that you, Carolyn?'

There was no answer.

'It *is* you. What's up girl? Where's Dean?'

Carolyn frantically wiped away the tears and tried to compose herself. She turned around and faced Stuart with bloodshot eyes.

'Hi, I'm sorry, I'm just not feeling very good, that's all. Dean's gone home.'

'Why?' Stuart asked, jerking his head back.

'He said he was feeling sick,' she replied, her voice shaking. Stuart moved a pile of coats to make room for him to sit down next to her.

'What's up with him, Carolyn?' His eyebrows drew together as he looked at her.

'He's got a cold,' she replied, trying hard to sound composed, but Stuart had already seen her crying so she could see little point in making the effort to hide her distress any longer. 'Except ... that isn't all there is to it, Stuart. I can't cope any more, I've had enough.' She broke down and sobbed.

'What have you had enough of?'

'Him, and her, and how he is with her!'

'Who?'

Carolyn didn't give a direct answer. It was too painful.

'It was the same at the village fair, he kept looking,' she snarled. 'I could see it in his eyes.'

Stuart fell silent as the penny dropped. 'Are you talking about Amanda?'

'Yes! So you've seen it too?'

'No,' Stuart corrected her hastily, however his facial muscles became slack, 'at least, I don't think so. I always thought Dean only had eyes for you.'

Carolyn clawed at the blanket and then let go. 'He used to, until she came along,' she spat out bitterly. 'You know what they say, the eyes are the window to the soul, and it was clear to me that Dean was hankering after her tonight.' Carolyn's sobs became uncontrollable, and when she buried her head on the bed, Stuart felt he had to comfort her.

'Hey, hey, calm down, that's someone's coat you're soaking,' he teased, putting an arm around her. Letting go briefly, he reached into a pocket. 'Here, have a napkin.'

'Thanks, Stuart,' Carolyn replied, consoled for a few moments, wiping her eyes. 'You're a star.'

'They don't call me super Stuart for nothing, you know. That's better, that's what I like to see,' he said, detecting a weak smile.

Carolyn's eyes widened with alarm. 'Please don't tell anyone else what I've said tonight,' she pleaded. 'I've not told a single soul about this. Not even Tracy, and I normally tell her everything, but not this.' Her eyes lowered again. 'Right from the start I found it impossible to say anything, and it only got worse. It was just far too humiliating and embarrassing to admit, even to myself, let alone anybody else, that I thought my fiancé might be in love with someone else. Tonight I just wanted him to go home and leave me alone. He was being so obnoxious, saying things like "You'd better leave before you cause a scene, like you did at the fete." I didn't cause a scene, believe me, he was just worried everyone was watching us argue so we left. I wouldn't be surprised, though, if a few people could tell something was wrong tonight, but he just made excuses about having a cold and cleared off, leaving me to face the music.'

'Sounds like my brother.'

'Even if I had wanted to leave with him, which believe me, I didn't, because I was happy to see the back of him, how could I leave? It's Tracy's party, my closest friend, and if I left early, especially before midnight, I know her, she'd think it weird, especially since we arrived late. Now I'm not sure how I'll get home.' Her voice became a whimper and she looked lost and confused.

'There are lots of people with cars, I'm sure we can find you a lift,' Stuart said trying to reassure her.

'But are there any who haven't been drinking?'

'I'm not sure about that. I mean, I've had a few myself.'

'Just a few?' Carolyn arched an eyebrow, briefly finding his tipsy mannerisms entertaining.

He smiled. 'I'll get you a lift, don't you worry,' he repeated.

'Thank you,' she muttered, feeling her anguish start to rise up again.

'Stuart, would you believe he was even thinking of her when he bought that engagement ring?'

'Why do you say that? What do you mean?'

Carolyn reined in more tears. 'The ring was an emerald and diamonds, which I thought was an unusual choice, so I asked him why he chose it. He got really flustered and started stuttering, saying drivel like he just liked the look of it. I've known him long enough to know when he's not being straight with me. Something didn't sit right, so I asked him to swap it for the one I've got now.'

'Can I look?'

Carolyn paused before replying. 'Sure.'

Stuart took her hand and examined the diamond cluster ring.

'I thought you'd seen it before,' she said, sounding slightly surprised.

'No, I don't believe I have. It's a pretty ring on very beautiful hands.'

Stuart didn't let go and tried to concentrate.

'Later on, some time after he swapped it, I managed to prise it out of him that Amanda was the reason he chose it and that she had inspired him. Could you believe he used that word? He said she only suggested what to buy, but when he said "inspired", I could guess what he really meant. My hunch was totally correct, he had been hiding something from me all along, and I couldn't work out why she had to become involved. Anyhow, after the village fete, and after I found out about the ring, we kept having rows about all sorts, and everything almost fell apart, until November time when things began to improve. He told me he was really sorry if he'd hurt me, he never meant to, and he swore he had absolutely no interest in Amanda whatsoever. I really believed him, Stuart, so I finally put it all behind me,' Carolyn broke off, looking dazed, 'and then tonight happened.'

'What happened?'

'His eyes again,' her voice erupted, 'the way he kept looking at her. I don't see him looking at me that way, not any more, not since she came along. I'm afraid when we get married he won't stop wanting her, Stuart, and then anything could happen, couldn't it, because …' she stopped short again, this time with horror etched on her face. 'I think I noticed something in the way she looked at him tonight. I'm sure she has feelings for him too. Oh, Stuart,' she said with a light gasp, 'I'm so glad I got rid of that emerald ring. It would have been a constant reminder of her and the look in his eyes every time he sees her.'

'And what about your eyes?' Stuart raised Carolyn's chin with his hand to look into them. 'They're so sad. You deserve better than this.' He studied her face intently. 'I hadn't noticed before but you do have beautiful eyes. I thought they were brown like your hair because they're really dark, but I can see now they're the darkest blue, almost grey. That seems quite unusual.'

'Yes, perhaps they are, but they're not pretty like Amanda's,' Carolyn said dismissively, turning her face away.

'No, they're prettier,' Stuart replied, gently bringing her back to face him,

'But hers are a beautiful clear green. The emerald was darker and more opaque, but do you know what, Stuart? Something insane just crossed my mind. I'm beginning to wonder if her eyes had something to do with his choice.'

'If so, that's neither here nor there, Carolyn. The important thing for you to realise is that you are beautiful just as you are.'

These words were a much needed tonic after suffering what felt like months of hurt and rejection. The emotions currently overflowing and overwhelming her, married with the deceptively strong cocktails she had enjoyed earlier, were beginning to lower her inhibitions. Even when she realised Stuart's hand was still holding hers, she didn't try to recover it. As he maintained his gaze, without looking away, not even for a moment, she saw how attractive his deep brown eyes were, drawing her in – along with his lips.

Neither knew who made the first move, but they soon found themselves in the grip of passion, kissing feverishly and with abandon. After a few minutes Carolyn eased Stuart away, suddenly panic stricken.

'Someone will come in, we'll be found out, it'll be absolutely terrible. What the hell are we doing? What about Dean? We'd better stop this minute!'

Stuart looked at his watch. 'It's twenty to midnight,' he smiled. Who's going to leave the party now? It'll be the countdown to the new year soon. And never mind Dean. As you said, his mind is elsewhere, and at this moment so is mine.' He glanced at the door, stood up and turned the key in the lock. 'There, it's locked.' Next he stumbled over to a large built-in wardrobe and slid it open to find some clothes inside, but also a deep recess. He climbed in and shut the door. Quite forgetting her distress, Carolyn found herself giggling uncontrollably.

'What are you doing, Stuart Appleby?' she asked, watching him climb out again.

'A lock on the door and a wardrobe which I can fit into. Don't you see? Luck is on our side, Carolyn. If the worst happens, and someone does try to get in, you can unlock the door yourself and I can hide in there until they've gone.'

Carolyn's good sense, which had been compromised by the drinks, evaporated as she jumped from despair to unnatural joviality, bursting into laughter at the humour of the situation. 'Why do I feel as though I'm in a *Carry On* film or something?' she giggled. 'We must be mad, taking a risk like this.'

Putting an arm around her, Stuart leaned in and then paused to stroke her face with the back of his hand. 'It is a risk, Carolyn,' he said, his breathing growing faster, 'but the way I feel right now, I think it's one worth taking.'

* * *

'Hurry up everyone, get in a circle, link hands, it's countdown in just a couple of minutes.' Tracy gathered the crowd together and then moments later she saw Carolyn enter the room.

'There you are. I was getting worried, you've been in the bathroom for absolutely ages. Come on, quick, join the circle, link hands. 1980 here we come!'

Amanda didn't see Carolyn come through the door, as she had been deep in conversation with Kenneth, or rather he was sharing more interesting facts about bookkeeping. They were both ushered into the circle, and as she joined it, Stuart walked in and also linked hands. There was something odd about him, she thought. However, at least he appeared to be a lot more sober. She tried to catch his eye, but he seemed reluctant to look in her direction. Then, as the countdown began, appearing more at ease, he looked around at fellow guests smiling once or twice. Amanda wondered where Dean was. Had his cold symptoms become too much? She couldn't shake off the memory of his and Carolyn's uneasiness, plus her own conflicted feelings and remorse when she'd caught him looking at her.

Ten, nine, eight, seven, six, five, four, three, two, one … Fireworks erupted outside and as Tracy, Brian and their guests sang 'Auld Lang Syne', Amanda battled mixed feelings. Much to her surprise, she had promised to see Kenneth again, having decided she didn't have a lot to lose by going on a date with him, even if her heart wasn't in it. She also knew that in a month's time there would be no hope for her and Dean. Tonight she had realised that she still had feelings for him, even suspecting he felt something too. If he had, it would be a miracle if at this late stage he decided to do anything about it. He was getting married, so he just had to deal with any unwelcome residual attraction towards her, which she didn't doubt he'd soon be rid of forever. On the other hand, Kenneth was free, and she tried to stay positive as he kept his eyes on her. 'Happy new year, Amanda,' he said with a shy smile.

'Happy new year, Kenneth,' she replied, watching everyone around her exchange new year greetings.

 Casting his eyes downwards he stepped back awkwardly and scratched his head. 'Can I give you a lift home?'

'No need for that. My dad's picking me up, but thanks anyway.'

'I'll give you a call then, and I'll take you to that restaurant in Tunbridge Wells I told you about.'

'Yes, that would be nice.'

The DJ played 'If You Leave Me Now' by Chicago, during which people began to collect their coats and disperse. Feeling too guilt-ridden to speak, Stuart looked on from the sidelines, his hands hanging limply at his sides and watching helplessly as Tracy arranged a lift for Carolyn without his assistance.

'Mum and Dad will take you home,' Tracy said, touching Carolyn's arm, 'and I hope Dean feels better soon. Such a shame he wasn't well enough to stay until the end.' She stopped, stepped back and looked hard at her friend. 'Carolyn, there isn't anything wrong, is there? I'm not sure you're okay.'

'I'm fine, Tracy. That's so good of your mum and dad to take me home,' Carolyn replied, avoiding her friend's gaze.

She left without speaking another word. Shortly afterwards, Stuart said goodbye, mounted his motorbike and was also gone.

Maggie, slightly disappointed not to be asked out by the man she had slow danced with earlier, was now also ready to say goodbye. 'Great party, little sister,' she said, giving Tracy a quick hug, 'although it still feels a bit weird calling you that,' she smiled. Tracy looked happy but weary, as she stood in the hallway next to her equally exhausted fiancé Brian.

'Thanks. I'm glad you enjoyed it and that you could all come,' Tracy replied, speaking to Amanda and Kenneth as well as Maggie. Brian promised Kenneth he'd be in touch soon and then the three of them walked out of the front door and were gone.

'Looks like Kenneth has bagged himself a bird at long last,' Brian laughed quietly, giving Tracy's waist a gentle squeeze.

Amanda wondered how long Kenneth would linger at her side while she waited for her father to arrive.

'Chilly, isn't it,' he blinked, plunging his hands into his pockets.

Amanda nodded.

'Brian and Tracy know how to throw a good party.'

'Definitely.'

Both looked out towards the road, and after several minutes of silence, Kenneth stirred. 'I'd better be off then,' he said, slipping a hand outside his pocket. For a moment it looked as though he was about to reach out with it, but instead he hesitated, rubbed down his coat and tucked it in again. 'It was good to meet you, Amanda. Goodbye … for now.'

Offering back an encouraging smile, she said quietly, 'Goodbye Kenneth, take care and happy new year.'

'And happy eighties, Amanda,' he replied. 'And let's hope it won't be the decade America or Russia drops the bomb.'

If Kenneth was making an attempt at humour, it had fallen flat. As he walked across the road towards his car, Amanda looked up at the starry night sky and breathed in deeply. Yes, a new decade had begun; the seventies were over, and soon her teenage years would be as well. It was high time she ditched her *Jackie* magazine but what would take its place? *Woman's Own* perhaps? No, too middle-aged. What about *Cosmopolitan*? That was a bit too racy. Maybe she should take a break from magazines altogether. After all, they were hardly a necessity.

Standing under the big night sky, she recalled the evening's events. Thoughts of Kenneth, Carolyn, Stuart, and of course, Dean, filled her mind. Again and again she wondered what this new year and the new decade would bring, hoping with all her heart that she'd find love, which Kenneth had reminded her had better be before they dropped the bomb. Why had he chosen to leave on such a note, thoughtlessly reigniting a fear in her which had been lying dormant? She supposed she should make allowances for him. After all, he wasn't to know what triggered her. Being willing to overlook this blunder was not the only thing she was open to. For all she knew, Kenneth could be 'the one', and this optimistic thought gave her hope as she watched her father's car approaching.

* * *

'You're looking much better,' Victoria said with a smile, handing Dean a mug of coffee across the kitchen table as Millie left for school. 'Have a super day, sweet pea,' she said, waving her daughter goodbye.

'I *am* feeling better,' Dean replied, cupping his drink, 'especially now I've finally got rid of that annoying cough. It's a shame it took over a week to shift.'

'I was going to send you straight down to the doctor's this morning if it hadn't,' Victoria said, pointing at him firmly. 'Talking of the doctor's surgery, I've not heard you mention Carolyn for a few days. How is she?'

Dean's silence spoke volumes.

'You've had another row, haven't you?' Victoria said, trying not to frown.

'We have, and it's not too good,' Dean said, looking pained.

'What's it about this time? Tell me, please.'

Dean hesitated. 'Dad's outside at the moment, and Stuart's not up yet, is he?' he asked, making sure the coast was clear.

'That's right.'

Lowering his voice, his words spilled out clumsily. 'She thinks I'm in love with someone else.'

'Ah,' Victoria said, picking up a box of cornflakes. The light clatter of the cereal being poured into a bowl was the only sound for a while. 'And is she right?'

'Of course not!' Dean shook his head in confusion. 'Certainly not love. I love Carolyn. I'm sure I do, but I can't lie, I did like someone.' His voice trailed off. Did he really say that? Yes, he did and it felt like a relief. 'I'm guessing you know who that was.'

'Yes, I believe I do,' Victoria said quietly, her eyebrows drawing together.

'We got on really well, but I was already engaged when I met her, and Carolyn's going to be my wife.'

Victoria listened until he finished speaking. 'Dean, you do realise that a broken engagement is far better than a broken marriage, don't you?'

Thinking carefully, Dean responded slowly and with deliberation. 'I've made a commitment to Carolyn and I honour my commitments. You know that.'

'Yes I do, and that's one of your best and finest qualities, making you steady and reliable, but this is the beginning of the rest of your life, and arguably the biggest decision you'll ever make, so you've *got* to get it right.'

'I'm sure I have. Okay, I admit, I don't know why we keep rowing. I told her I loved her and I was sorry if I'd ever hurt her feelings, that I would never, ever do that intentionally.'

'Does Amanda know anything about any of this?'

Dean pressed his eyes shut for a moment, lowering the slice of toast he was about to bite into. 'Not that I know of, and I hope she never will.'

'Do you think that's why she left so suddenly? It would explain a lot.'

'Possibly ... I mean probably.'

'And nothing intimate has ever happened between you and Amanda?'

'No!' Dean said emphatically, turning his head away before facing his mother once more. 'Well, nothing more than holding each other at the beach, and that was only because she slipped and fell. That's the ridiculous, crazy thing about all of this. If there had been anything, how could I sleep at night? There's nothing going on, nor has there ever been.'

'Except in your heart perhaps?'

Dean was momentarily paralysed by his mother's words.

'Mum,' he said after a while.

'Yes Dean.'

'There's something else.'

'What dear?'

'I saw Carolyn yesterday and something's not right. I mean, something's seriously wrong. I don't understand it, and although we didn't argue last night, I made a totally innocent comment and she started crying for no apparent reason. She doesn't seem herself.'

Victoria paused for thought. 'Women have moods,' she replied, 'hormones can really make life difficult, and perhaps she's feeling nervous and exhausted with the wedding coming up so soon.' She rested her elbow on the table and rubbed her forehead. 'But you're right, that doesn't sound normal. I hope she's not depressed. How long has this been going on?'

'Around a week or so. After the party I called to apologise for going home, even though the only reason I'd left was because I was so ill and had a massive headache. You remember how rough I was on New Year's Day, but I still went round to see her. I was feeling bad about the argument and I wanted to wish her a happy new year, tell her I loved her, stuff like that, but when she opened the door I said, "Happy new year, darling, but tough! This will be the year you're lumbered with me for life." She didn't even smile, in fact, she struggled to look me in the eye. I'm now wondering if she talked to Tracy at the party and Tracy told her lots of negative things about me which she's letting come between us.'

'Best not jump to any conclusions, Dean. Just keep loving Carolyn, and perhaps keep an eye on her these next few days or so. As I said before, I'm sure it'll all work out.' Despite her positive words, Victoria's less than enthusiastic smile revealed her concerns. If she wasn't careful, her own doubts would soon start to get the better of her.

'And when it comes to Amanda,' she said, pouring milk onto the cereal, 'you've sworn you've done nothing wrong, and I know you're telling the truth. Carolyn will get over her jealousy, plus some jealousy is quite normal and not at all unhealthy. In fact, if you didn't get jealous over someone you loved, then something is wrong. It'll all be ironed out, provided you and Carolyn are prepared to communicate your feelings.'

'I'll give it my best shot,' Dean said.

'Good,' she breathed out, 'I know you will.' Victoria munched on her cornflakes before suddenly stopping to lower her spoon. 'One last thing, Dean,' she said, her voice sounding apprehensive.

'Yes.'

'You're not sticking to your commitment because you're concerned about what people will say if you called things off, I hope?'

'Not at all,' Dean said with a strained laugh. 'I admit it would look really bad to break up just weeks before the wedding, but I would never make what people think or say influence me when it comes to something as big as this. That would be plain stupid.'

'I'm really glad to hear that, Dean,' Victoria said, feeling assured.

'Yes Mum, this is totally about my love for Carolyn – and I *will* marry her.'

Chapter 19

'Western Road Surgery, how can I help you?'

'Carolyn, it's Stuart.'

The surgery was just about to close for lunch and covering the receiver, Carolyn nervously darted her eye across to the patients still sitting in the waiting room. Mrs Parsons, an elderly lady, had come to see Dr Wilson about her hearing difficulties, and Mrs Reed had an appointment with Dr King for her four-year-old son who was burning up with a temperature.

'How can I help you?' she repeated.

'It's Stuart.'

Carolyn lowered her voice to a whisper. 'Look, I can't talk now, can you call back in half an hour?' She glanced again at the waiting patients. Predictably, Mrs Parsons hadn't heard a thing, and much to Carolyn's relief, Mrs Reed's attention appeared fully focussed on her young child and the pages of a storybook.

'This won't take long, Carolyn—'

'You're very loud, sir,' she said forcefully, fearful he might be audible through the receiver. 'Would you mind lowering your voice please?'

'Ah, I get it, obviously there are others within earshot. I should have realised, sorry. Look, I'm ringing to say … well, never mind, I'll say it later. Can we meet in St Mary's churchyard after you finish tonight – say 6.15? It'll be dark and nobody will see us there.'

'Yes,' was Carolyn's brief reply.

'Great, see you by the front porch of St Mary's at 6.15 then.'

'Yes, that will be fine, goodbye.'

Stuart placed the receiver on the hook, wondering if he'd managed to sound calm and collected. It was now over a week since the party, and he was desperate to connect with Carolyn. Carrying this secret alone was starting to take its toll on him and he needed to speak to the only person in the world who shared it. It seemed totally wrong that they hadn't exchanged a word since, and he guessed Carolyn would be feeling the same.

The afternoon surgery flew by, and after the last patient had left and the day's distractions were over, the satisfaction Carolyn usually felt at getting to the end of the day felt more like despair. Tidying up and putting things away just before leaving, she said goodbye to Dr King, who had left his room ready to leave the building. Before opening the door to the outside, he stopped.

'I hope you don't mind me saying, but you look exhausted, Carolyn. Has it been too much for you with Yvette off sick these past couple of days?'

She stopped shuffling papers and looked up. 'No Dr King, it has been harder of course, but I've managed fine, thank you.'

'Yes, I can see you've tried,' the doctor replied. He adjusted his tie and looked uneasy. 'I wasn't going to mention anything until tomorrow, when either Dr Wilson or myself intended to speak to you, but there's no time like the present. Can we sit down and talk briefly now?'

'Of course,' Carolyn said, her voice composed as she took a seat. What was he going to say? Nothing like this had happened before, and she wasn't used to the quality of her work being called into question.

'Dr Wilson and I have noticed you're not quite yourself, Carolyn. A number of mistakes have been brought to our attention recently – thankfully nothing major,' he held up the palm of his hand in an attempt to reassure her. 'A couple of patient records have been misfiled, and a prescription request wasn't honoured. Also, I've noticed you're working through your lunch hour and staying late most evenings.' He looked at his watch. 'Normally you'd be done by now, whether Yvette is off or not. We're concerned about you, Carolyn, and just wanted to check everything is okay.' Carolyn said nothing, while her employer studied her curiously. 'I am sorry to repeat myself but I do think you seem off colour. I hope you would tell me or Dr Wilson if there was anything we could do to make things easier for you, assuming we were able to help of course.'

'Yes, I would, Dr King, of course, thank you. I'm just tired because the wedding's so soon and I've had a lot to arrange, but I'll be fine, and I'm really sorry for the mistakes.'

'Well, if you're quite sure,' Dr King hesitated, 'oh, and when it comes to the errors, don't worry, we've put things right as best we could, so no lasting harm has been done. As long as you're well and things improve, that's all that matters.'

'It has been easier today and I'm about to go. I'm happy to stay behind and lock up. I hope you and Mrs King have a good evening.'

'Thank you, Carolyn. I hope you have a good evening too. See you in the morning.'

Carolyn looked up at the surgery clock. It was 6pm. She had better ring home to ask for dinner to be kept warm again, but this time it wasn't working late that was going to delay her. She wouldn't be able to spend much time with Stuart – not that she wanted to, of course. She couldn't risk missing the last bus to Windmill Hill, but if she did, a taxi would be preferable to telephoning her father, who was bound to lecture her on the journey home for failing to be organised. Even if Stuart had a car rather than a motorbike, she wouldn't dare get in it in case they were seen together. At least it wasn't raining and she felt grateful for small mercies. It was bad enough having to face Stuart again in the cold and dark.

The walk from the surgery to St Mary's church was no more than ten minutes, and Carolyn was soon waiting in the porch, anxious and alone in the dark. Her scarf, hat and gloves provided some much needed protection against the elements, while the warm air from her mouth created steam vapours when she breathed out nervously into the cold night. There were only minutes to go before their designated meeting time, and she kept wondering what Stuart was going to say. The last thing she wanted to do was to face him, the person with whom she had betrayed the only man she had ever loved. But at the same time she would rather face Stuart than Dean. At least she could look Stuart in the eye because he knew something about her that Dean didn't, and that she hoped he would never, ever know. Stuart knew her intimately, but only in the physical sense, whereas Dean was intimate with her soul. When the time came for her and Dean to join together, mind, body and spirit, how could she fully become one with a man she was hiding such a big secret from? There was now a no-go zone between her and Dean, a barrier to closeness which could never be erased. Could a relationship thrive, or even survive, with such a monster of a barrier in place? Carolyn doubted Stuart had any answers to these heart-wrenching questions, but he was the only person in the world she could talk to.

Carolyn jumped when she felt a large hand on her shoulder. She spun around. 'You almost scared me to death, don't do that!' she said. The darkness couldn't hide a familiar face, now close to hers, looking back with a smile. It all came flooding back to her. How she felt at the party sitting next to Stuart on the bed and of course, all that took place afterwards. Today was the first time since then that they stood facing each other, and now looking up at him, tall, smiling and towering over her, everything seemed so different. Nothing was the same now they had crossed a line. There was absolutely no going back.

'Sorry, I didn't mean to scare you. I hope you've not been waiting long out here. I see you're wrapped up well, though.'

'What do you want, Stuart?'

'I just felt we needed to talk.'

'Go ahead,' Carolyn said firmly. Her no-nonsense approach briefly made Stuart uneasy, and he looked down and shuffled his feet.

'I felt I needed to say sorry.'

'Sorry for what?'

Stuart squeezed his eyes shut. 'For everything,' he said, opening them again. 'Sorry that you've had problems with Dean, and now I'm sorry I may have made things worse.'

Carolyn turned her face away, looking detached.

'I also wanted to know what you're planning to do, Carolyn ... if anything.'

She swiftly turned to face him again, fear and fury coursing through her body.

'Do?' She jutted out her chin. 'What can I do? I've already done it, haven't I? I've ruined my life!'

'Of course you haven't,' Stuart said with a fixed smile. 'You made a mistake, I made a mistake, we had too much to drink. You were upset, one thing led to another. It should be forgotten.' He looked into her eyes solidly. 'It can and will be forgotten.'

Carolyn clenched her jaw. 'Much easier said than done,' she said, sounding despondent.

'But certainly possible.'

'How can I forget when I'll be seeing you all the time? You're his brother, not just some random man off the street I never have to face again, and even if you were, it would be impossible to forget. I've not been eating or sleeping, I'm making mistakes at work. I can't even look Dean in the eye any more. I just don't know if I can carry on.'

'I don't like to see you this way, Carolyn, please don't. You really mustn't allow yourself to get in such a state. Everything will work out.'

Carolyn felt Stuart's comforting arm wrap around her.

'Look, you know I'm leaving for the army, and that'll happen in a matter of months. When I'm gone, you won't see me any more, you and Dean will be married and you'll get on with your lives. Don't you think everyone has skeletons in their cupboards? You really shouldn't beat yourself up over one mistake.'

Carolyn pushed Stuart's arm away. 'But this is a mistake like no other,' she said hysterically, 'and it's not a skeleton. It's not old and buried, it's very much alive. I can't seem to bury it, Stuart, it's always there in my mind.' She bit her lip, trying unsuccessfully to fight back tears.

'What's the alternative? Are you going to tell him?' he said, briefly turning his face away before looking straight into her eyes again. 'That wouldn't be clever, would it? It would mean the wedding will be postponed, at the very least, but most likely, it'll be called off. All those months of preparation and planning down the drain. But that's nothing compared to losing Dean.' They stood still for a moment, taking in those words while silently breathing in the crisp winter air. 'I know you've always loved him,' Stuart continued. 'Imagine not spending the rest of your life together. That doesn't bear thinking about, does it? All because his dickhead brother wasn't able to keep his hands off you – if you excuse my French.' Carolyn's angry glare communicated she was not in the mood for humour. His limp smile fell away and he carried on talking. 'And imagine what will happen in our families?' He grimaced. 'Not only will Dean be finished with me, but Mum, Dad and Millie too, plus all my relatives, no doubt. But I don't care about that. I don't care about me at all. It's you I care about. Your dad and mum, they're very religious and I can't imagine how they'll react, let alone if it gets out into the village. None of this will happen if we just learn to live with our consciences and put it all behind us. I don't know about you, but it's clear to me what the easiest option is.'

Unconvinced, Carolyn listened carefully, brushing away a warm tear which fell down her cheek. 'I just wish I could turn back the clock,' she said at last.

'We can't, can we? But we can look to the future. Chin up. You've got a wedding to go to, girl!' Stuart put his arm around her again, and this time she lacked the will or energy to rebuff him.

'I can't eat, I can't sleep, I'm racked with worry, guilt and fear, thinking he's going to find out any minute. I just want this to end, to wake up to find it was all a bad dream and things are back to how they were before the New Year's Eve party.'

Stuart didn't reply, but his face communicated understanding and empathy, and for a brief moment Carolyn felt a respite of calm.

'Stuart,' she said, looking up at him, 'is this the last time we're going to meet until the wedding?'

'I guess so, unless you want to again. We haven't many options for safe and quiet places for a secret rendezvous, and it's far too cold to keep meeting here after work.'

Carolyn nodded once. 'But if we need to talk again, how can I get hold of you?' she asked. 'I can't phone the house because they'll recognise my voice.'

Stuart pondered. 'My friend Tom, I sometimes stay over with him. I can give you his number, and if I'm not there, he'll pass on the message by calling me at the farm to say that you rang and I'll call you back. I'll tell him you're some girl I met and that you're keen on me but I'm not sure about you. I'll call you Sue or something. Have you got a pen?' Carolyn dug deep into her handbag and pulled out a fountain pen and handed it over to Stuart. 'Thanks, I'll write down Tom's number for you.'

After taking the empty cigarette packet with the scribbled number, Carolyn seemed less distraught. 'Thanks,' she said quietly, raising her arm to look at her watch. 'I'd better go, I'd like to get the next bus which is leaving in five minutes.'

'Sure,' Stuart replied, and leaning towards Carolyn to give her a friendly kiss goodbye, he was pleasantly surprised to find she didn't turn away. Both felt awkward and uneasy but also emboldened as they quickly parted company.

* * *

Dear Sam,

It feels great to write again. How is 1980 so far? I just had to tell you some news, although not all fantastic. Well, first the great news. My aunt Pauline was well enough to visit last week. She looks different. So much thinner and frailer, but she can now walk unaided, and what's really lovely is seeing how she, Mum, Dad and Uncle Charles are getting on so much better. Mum's depression has lifted too, and she's much happier than she was before Christmas. And another thing, I wish your mum could meet my Uncle Charles. I'm sure they'd love to talk about God. He seems so happy and full of life now. It's great to see.

More good news. I've made a nice friend, Maggie, who works in Jimmy's with me. We've worked together since I started there but have got to know each other even more lately. We went out shopping in Brighton the other day with her little girl Becky who's really sweet, and we chatted about so many things. I miss doing girlie things like that with you!

Now for the bad news. Remember I told you on the phone about Kenneth? Well, I went on a date with him yesterday evening. He came and picked me up in his car and we drove to a restaurant in Tunbridge Wells. As you know, he's a bookkeeper and when I met him at the party, all he talked about (pretty much) was his job, and it really wasn't that interesting. I thought this was a one-off, but on the way to the restaurant, guess what he talked about? Yes, you guessed it! Then, at the restaurant (it was Chinese) he didn't ask what I might like, but said he wanted to choose the set menu because it was more economical. Despite all this, Sam, I didn't want to write him off completely BUT, at the end, he didn't offer to pay and instead he said (grinning) we should go halves because it had cost him in petrol to drive all the way from Tunbridge Wells to pick me up and drop me back home again. Can you imagine, Sam? I think you can guess if

I'm going to see him again! I know you're still waiting to be asked out by Glenroy, aka gorgeous Jamaican fella – hope he'll ask you soon and that your date will be much better than mine!

Give my love to your family and please say hello to Mark. Oh, I almost forgot, I'm going to a wedding on the 26th. I'm sure you'll remember I told you that Dean, the farmer's son, is getting married to a girl called Carolyn who works at our doctor's surgery. As it's January I imagine it's going to be a cold day but most of the village is going to be there, so I'm sure the atmosphere will be warm, even if the weather isn't. Also, Sam, I promise you, if I see that horrible Know-It-All woman, I'll try not to sock her one! Although I have to admit, I think what she said may have upset you more than it upset me.

Love Amanda x

Licking the envelope, Amanda reflected on how she had managed to avoid sharing her affection for Dean with anyone. Not Robert, not Joan, not Sam, not anyone, and having resisted the temptation to do so for so very long, she was now confident that nobody would ever know about those difficult feelings she had battled with … ever.

* * *

'Who was that?' Dean asked, as Stuart hastily put down the receiver on the phone in the hall.

'Just my friend Tom. Where's Mum?' Stuart replied, looking flushed.

'She's gone to the market and said she'll be back by lunchtime.' Dean paused, opened his mouth to speak and then closed it again. 'Look, Stuart,' he said, sounding hopeful, 'I've got to go to Cowbeech this afternoon to get the tractor serviced. I'm scheduled to pick it up at 5, but they warned me that they're busy with a backlog and that I may have to wait a while. I might not get home until 6, maybe even 6.30. Could you help feed the calves their sugar beet? Dad will need a hand - it won't take long.'

Dean waited for a response, while Stuart, with eyes averted, hesitated.

'I'd really like to, but Tom said he's in the area and he needs to talk to me about something urgently – that's why he rang. I won't be around, I just agreed to meet him in town, sorry about that.'

'I'm sure Dad will manage,' Dean said, unsurprised but trying to sound casual.

To be fair on Stuart, Dean had noticed a change in him lately. He was at home much more often these days and choosing to spend less time staying out late and living it up. Best of all, he was more willing to help out on the farm, and so Dean was inclined to believe he was telling the truth, especially since the dismissive look in his eye that usually accompanied his attempts to shirk just wasn't there this time. Instead, he seemed a little on edge, so maybe Tom did have something important to say.

Stuart was telling half the truth. It was true he couldn't help this evening but it wasn't because Tom needed to speak to him. Why did Carolyn want to see him tonight? Checking Dean had gone back out and the house was quiet, he picked up the phone again and dialled the surgery number.

'Western Road Surgery, can I help?'

Stuart didn't recognise the voice. 'Can I speak to Carolyn please?'

'Who shall I say is calling?'

Stuart was suddenly put on the spot. 'A friend,' he replied, not knowing how to answer but then immediately thinking he may have said the wrong thing. He heard the receiver being placed down, then moments later it was picked up again.

'Carolyn speaking.'

'It's Stuart. You called.'

'Yes,' Carolyn replied, looking over her shoulder to see Yvette busy speaking to a patient.

The surgery was bustling and noisy and Stuart could hear people talking in the background. This gave Carolyn the opportunity to speak quietly but audibly in to the telephone without fear of being overheard.

'Can we meet again tonight?'

'Sure thing. Is everything okay? Tom said you sounded a bit weird?'

'Sorry, I've got to go. 6.15 please, see you there.'

The phone went dead and Stuart stood holding the receiver in his hand, slightly unsettled and somewhat mystified.

* * *

Standing outside St Mary's, Stuart and Carolyn didn't escape the rain this time. The small church porch sheltered them from the worst of the cold, wet, wintry weather, with Carolyn's umbrella providing much needed extra protection, but they still shivered as they stood in front of one another. It had been evident to Stuart the minute he saw her approaching that Carolyn was distressed. Why was she looking worse than ever? What had happened? Had she told Dean, or had he found out some other way? That was highly unlikely. As she stood before him Stuart couldn't distinguish between rainwater and tears.

'Carolyn, this better be worth it. It's a nasty night to meet just to say hi.' His feeble attempt to break the ice with humour failed to provoke a smile. 'What's up, girl?'

'I'd better just come straight out with it,' Carolyn said, a shaky hand reaching up to brush wet hair away from her face. 'I think I might be pregnant.'

Stuart wondered if he'd heard right. Then he realised that only an unhealthy psychological defence mechanism could make him think otherwise. 'Are you sure?' was all he could muster after a lengthy pause.

'Not totally no, but it's looking like it. I've never been this late before, ever.'

'But ... at the party, you just ... you said nothing to me so I just assumed you were on the pill,' he said sounding numb.

'I was ... I mean, I am,' she stammered, 'Dr Wilson said I should take it at least a couple of months before the wedding so I'd just started it, but I've been missing the odd one because I'm still adjusting, still getting used to the routine.'

For a moment Stuart was silent, however his incredulous facial expression said it all. After what seemed like a very long time he managed to say something, sweating despite the cold. 'When will you know for sure?'

'I'll be able to take a test on Wednesday.'

'Where are we today?' Stuart, sounding slightly panicked, looked upwards in thought. 'Monday, that's not too long to wait, but Wednesday's ... what, only three days before the wedding.'

These words were all it took for Carolyn to break down and give way to open sobbing.

'No, sorry, please don't cry, just stop it, will you,' Stuart said, acutely aware of the irritation in his voice. His lacklustre attempts to console by patting her on the shoulder was all he was capable of when trying to hide his own feelings of shock. At that point, they were both startled by a movement from amongst the gravestones. For a brief second, they were frozen in fear, wondering if someone was about to discover them, but were relieved to see a rather emaciated-looking fox staring back at them, its eyes reflecting the glow of a distant street lamp. 'So, if you *are* pregnant, Carolyn, what are you going to do about it?' He stared at her lowered head, placing a hand on each of her shoulders, almost as though ready to shake her.

Carolyn lifted her face sharply, and looked straight at Stuart with indignant eyes.

'What do you mean what am *I* going to do about it?' her voice roared. 'You mean what are *we* going to do about it.'

Stuart hadn't seen her this angry before, and he was initially stunned into silence, too stunned to even remind her to keep her voice down. 'Sorry, I didn't mean for it to sound like that,' he said looking a little shell shocked. 'I really didn't mean to be insensitive.'

Stuart's apology, although accepted couldn't change the situation. 'I can't believe I may have a baby growing inside me, a new life,' Carolyn said, her eyes almost wild with disbelief. 'This means everything changes from now on, nothing will ever be the same.'

'Look, there's no need to panic, something can be done.'

'What does that mean, Stuart?'

Carolyn looked at him intensely, fearful of what he might say. Stuart fell silent for a while.

'I know how your parents brought you up, Carolyn,' he replied, staring blankly. 'Dean said your father doesn't even believe in birth control. Although I can't say I agree with him, I know how strongly your family feels about such things. They're Catholics, aren't they?'

'They're not, no. Dad was raised a strict baptist.'

'So Carolyn, with your background and family values, I'm not expecting you to be anybody other than who you are,' Stuart said tightly, resisting the temptation to blame her for the disaster which was unfolding. 'Do you and Dean think the same way as your parents?'

'About birth control, you mean?'

Stuart nodded.

'No, we don't. Dean and I, we don't agree with Dad. Not that that matters any more, of course. This is all water under the bridge now, but before all this mess, we decided there was nothing wrong with preventing a pregnancy and we intended to space our children out. I never wanted to be like my mum, her whole life just living for her kids. I enjoy my work and I wanted to travel before starting a family – as much as being a farmer's wife would allow – but that's not going to happen any more, is it? How can we get married now? I'm spoiled goods. At least that's what my dad would say, and not just by anyone, but his own brother! Dean and I will probably never have a child together now. As soon as he finds out I'm pregnant, it'll be all over between us, you'll swan off into the army, this baby will be born, and I'll be a single mum, most likely forever.'

Stuart looked strained. While he was absorbing the enormity of the situation he had nothing to say. Then, all of a sudden, his face lit up.

'There is a way around this, you know.'

'Is there really?' said Carolyn flatly. So far she was unimpressed with Stuart's pep talk, but having nothing to lose she listened.

'There is something very positive about the wedding being so close.'

'What are you trying to say?'

'How will Dean know?'

'How will he know what?'

'That the baby isn't his.'

Carolyn's jaw dropped. 'You really mean to say, Stuart, you would want me to lie about that too? Really?' she said, her eyes wide with disbelief.

'You wouldn't be the first.'

'And I wouldn't be the first to have a supernatural conception either, but I don't think if I told Dean I was miraculously pregnant he would think it was possible just because the Virgin Mary set a precedent!'

For some time, Stuart was confused, then he understood.

'You mean ...' he gasped.

'I most certainly do.'

'You and Dean haven't even …'

'No Stuart, we haven't. Dean and I decided to wait until our wedding night.'

Stuart's arms fell by his sides. 'Well I never,' he said with disbelief. 'I always knew my brother was made of stronger stuff than me and had moral standards that could put the Pope to shame, but being able to keep his hands off a beautiful woman like you for so long? I can't believe it.'

'Well, he has.'

'So we couldn't even pass the kid off as his then?'

Carolyn, thrown by Stuart's deceitfulness and callousness, blinked rapidly. 'You mean to say you would stoop so low as to even consider that? I don't believe it. How could you?'

Again Stuart apologised, this time feeling the need to justify himself. 'Carolyn, you have to understand something. It feels like ever since I was a young kid I have been getting away with things. Always finding a way out of problems. I know this isn't a good thing, but old habits die hard. I need time to think and to process all of this. We'll meet on Wednesday, same time, same place, but can you do something for me? Can you please call me beforehand as soon as you know, I mean the minute you find out? The sooner I know where we stand, the sooner I can think of a way forward. Just call Tom and pass on a simple 'yes' or 'no'. He'll just think it's something to do with a date and I'll call you back straight away.'

'Yes ... yes, I can call you ... I mean Tom. I can do that.' Carolyn nodded frantically, before her head lowered again in passive acceptance.

'Carolyn.'

'Yes?'

When I asked what we were going to do about it earlier, it's because my mind can't stop thinking of solutions to problems, and right now it crossed my mind that if you were to tell Dean you conceived on your wedding night that could work, couldn't it? Depending on the dates, I mean. From what I've picked up over the years, and from memories of sex education classes at school, babies do come early, women get their dates wrong, and all sorts. It may be possible to still convince Dean the baby is his.'

'Yes,' Carolyn replied, now sounding somewhat resigned, 'you're probably right. Something like that might be possible. What may not be possible, though, is being able to spend the rest of my life living a lie.'

'I can't stop having ideas about how we can win in this situation, Carolyn. I actually find it almost impossible not to think about overcoming worst-case scenarios and difficult situations – another reason why I've chosen the army, I guess – and, by the way, lying gets easier the more you do it. That's my experience anyway.'

'That hasn't been *my* experience,' Carolyn responded, sounding despairing. 'Hiding the truth from Dean seems to be getting harder and harder each day. Without doubt it's the most difficult thing I've ever had to do in my entire life.'

Chapter 20

Dean hung the picture of the sunflowers on the wall. Carolyn had seen the painting in Debenhams several months earlier and had loved it, so Victoria insisted on purchasing it as a gift from her and Cecil to the newly married couple. It was to be a surprise, and with only days to go until the wedding Dean was counting on Carolyn not coming to the cottage again until after they were married. He had done his level best to prepare everything for his bride, but even after all his hard work, the cottage was still in need of TLC, having stood empty for several years.

The original plan had been for Carolyn to spend the whole of Saturday hanging curtains, giving the place a final clean and moving in some of her possessions, but after just a few hours at the cottage she began to feel dizzy. At least they were not arguing as much, but the reason for that didn't make him happy. Carolyn was usually too despondent to argue, everything was an effort, and her eyes had lost their usual life and sparkle. Dean concluded she had depression, but getting her to go and speak to a doctor, even though she worked at the surgery, was proving impossible.

He struggled to understand how she could be depressed when they were about to get married, but felt confident that as soon as her low mood lifted, things would be back to normal again. In the meantime he resolved to be patient and stoical. He had loved her enough to ask her to marry him, and what had changed? Nothing, certainly not from his perspective. However, his positivity couldn't dispel every doubt, and sometimes he even feared he was the cause of her unhappiness.

But I've asked her more than once if she still loves me and wants to get married, he reasoned with himself, while putting away the hammer and spare picture hook, *so what is there to worry about? I can see she is telling the truth and still very much wants to be my wife.*

Despite being assured of Carolyn's love, to boost his confidence he enlisted the help of his mother. Only yesterday, prompted by Dean, Victoria had spoken to Carolyn's mother, Janice, broaching the subject of her daughter's mental health.

'I ask Carolyn what's wrong almost every single day,' Janice replied, 'and each time she says she's fine. I've told her several times to speak to Dr King or Dr Wilson since her appetite's poor and I've also noticed she looks tired and she seems deep in thought all the time. I really hope she perks up before the big day, but you know what, Victoria? Just between ourselves, if I didn't know my own daughter I'd think she was pregnant.'

When Dean heard this he tipped his head back and laughed. 'If that's the case,' he told Victoria, 'I wasn't there when it happened!'

Stuart knew nothing of these conversations. He'd had conversations with Carolyn of his own, of course, but of late the person he was conversing with the most was himself. As Wednesday loomed, and with Saturday just around the corner, he found himself unable to think of anything else. Carolyn dominated his mind, and in less than twenty-four hours it was likely she would confirm she was carrying his baby. He thought about the fact that nobody knew, and that he desperately wanted to keep it that way. His emotions were starting to take over, and this was something he wasn't comfortable or familiar with. To his annoyance, his feelings of fear and guilt were increasing, and so too were his concerns for Carolyn.

Not only was he sorry to see her plight, but he had come to admire her strength and rectitude, while at the same time appreciating her vulnerability. Yet, it was no good, he couldn't do anything for her. He was in an impossible situation – *they* were in an impossible situation. All he could do was fall back on what he knew – covering up and escaping. Avoiding difficult situations usually got him out of trouble, and instant gratification was something he was used to and had come to expect. With all this reflection came the sudden and terrifying realisation that he only had days to write his speech, just days, and he hadn't started it yet. In fact, he hadn't even thought about it. When he did finally put pen to paper, what on earth would he say?

* * *

Amanda was starting to enjoy the long winter evenings. She had the radio, the TV, and she was now completing her art projects indoors, although still getting inspiration from the world outside, via a window, or from pictures and photographs. Even though there was no foraging and the deciduous trees were bare, she could still appreciate nature. She would look at the shapes of the winter trees, the bark, the catkins, even the thorns. She loved to watch the birds visit the garden at Marshywood – robins, long-tailed tits, dunnocks and goldcrests – and since moving to the country she had come a long way in identifying their songs. Recently she was thrilled to see a common redpoll for the first time, and was wowed by the stunning flash of red on its head. There was only one dampener on her happiness, and it was something she didn't want to admit, even to herself. It was not being able to share what she was seeing and learning with Dean. She longed for his guidance, knowledge and insight. She also missed the farm, the animals, Cecil, Victoria, Millie, even Stuart, in fact, everything and everyone. However, she would be seeing them again very soon, and in just a matter of days she would be saying hello to the new Mr and Mrs Appleby.

Winter could be peaceful and snug, but after her session at Jimmy's was finished, home was all she had. It was the place she would sit with Mum and Dad for hours in the evenings, and where Tabitha, her cat, always greeted her on her arrival. Not until the spring would there be more opportunities to get out of the house, when she could meet new people and be fulfilled in new and exciting ways.

Looking back, Amanda was very grateful for her time at Hillbrook Farm, for the lessons she had learned there and the knowledge she had gained. But life moves on, people change and say goodbye to old friends, and now she could see that's what she and Dean were, simply old friends. She would make new ones. She already felt she had a new friend in Maggie, and as for romance, she thought about Mark, Nick and Kenneth and how, although unsuitable for different reasons, all three had helped her to grow in some small way, to increase her confidence and give her hope. At last she felt she could be strong on Saturday, knowing that she was no longer that inexperienced and awkward young girl reading *Jackie* in her bedroom, feeling woefully inadequate and left behind. No, now she was a young woman with a strong sense of confidence and poise. This meant she now had the strength to look Dean and Carolyn in the eye, and say with genuine affection, 'Congratulations to you both, I wish you every happiness for the future.'

* * *

The phone rang. Stuart's heart skipped a beat. *Pull yourself together, you damn idiot*, he told himself, unused to such intense emotions, and anyway, it could be anyone. Yet he knew it was likely to be Tom.

Picking up the receiver, he noticed his hand shaking and he swore at himself for failing to get a grip. Taking a deep breath he confidently said 'hello,' and his greeting was returned by a familiar, happy-go-lucky voice.

'Hi Stuart, you son of a gun, it's me again, Tom.'

'Hi Tom, what's happening?'

'Plenty. I haven't told you the big news yet, have I? I've booked a skiing holiday in the Swiss Alps.'

'Can't say you mentioned it, no.'

'It wasn't planned, but Constance – you remember her from uni, the really posh one whose dad's a stockbroker?'

Stuart fell quiet, trying to recall.

'You must remember her. The one who could give Dolly Parton a run for her money.'

'Oh yes, of course, I remember now, how could I forget?'

Tom laughed. 'Well, she's invited a whole bunch of us – sorry old fellow, not sure why she left you out, by the way. Her dad's got a chalet out there, so all we've got to do is find the flight money. The lessons are being paid for and everything.'

Not wishing to make Tom suspicious by asking him to get to the point, Stuart listened patiently while he talked at length about the trip.

'That's great, Tom, really fab. I'm sure you'll have a fantastic time. Is that why you rang?'

'Oh no, sorry Stuart old chap, I completely went off track. No, it's about that girl Sue, the one who's after you, she rang again.'

'Did she really?' Stuart said, feigning surprise. 'What did she want this time?'

'She just said she wanted to say "no" before you see her. I haven't a clue what she's talking about, have you? Ah ... Stuart, you disgraceful old bounder, are you putting that sort of pressure on her already?'

Stuart exhaled slowly, a gradual sense of relief sweeping over him. 'Are you sure she said no, Tom?'

'She certainly did. Sounds like you're not impressing her much if she's already telling you no, and I must say, you're very quiet. You're not complaining like you usually do when something irks you. If you don't like her, why don't you tell her to sling her hook?'

'It's complicated, but no, you're right, Tom. She'll soon be history.'

Stuart tried to sound as unemotional as possible as he steered Tom away from further questions and wound up the conversation. Tom had one more thing to add before ringing off.

'By the way, Stuart, all the best for Saturday.'

'Saturday? Oh yes, you remembered, Tom. I'm impressed.'

'Of course I remembered. If I were you I'd be at panic stations right now. I absolutely detest giving speeches, so rather you than me. If anyone asked me to be their best man, the answer would be no. So, sorry, old fellow, if you and Sue do hit it off, don't ask me, will you!'

'Don't worry, Tom, I won't, and thanks for your good wishes. Have a great skiing trip. I'll see you when you get back.'

'You bet, I'll give you a ring then. See you, pal.'

After putting down the receiver, Stuart's relief turned into anxiety. Tom had reminded him that the job of writing a speech was still outstanding, and despite the good news, he still didn't feel capable of such a task.

* * *

What had become a series of clandestine meetings in St Mary's churchyard was soon to draw to a close, much to Carolyn and Stuart's relief. However, with just three days to go to the wedding, there was one final obstacle to overcome, the wedding rehearsal on Friday evening. Here they had no choice but to face each other again, and this time they wouldn't be alone. Not only would Dean be there, but also both sets of parents, and Tracy, Carolyn's chief bridesmaid.

However, all that was to come, and since today was Wednesday there was still time for them to find within themselves the ability to act normally in front of everyone, but for now, they would be alone again, just one last time.

Stuart was the first to arrive, and hearing Carolyn's footsteps he turned around.

'You're not pregnant!' he said loudly.

'Shh, for goodness sake, keep your voice down,' Carolyn whispered. 'What if someone were to hear? No, I'm not.' Despite the positive news, her face was stony and she sounded lifeless.

'What a relief, and what fantastic news,' Stuart said, perturbed by her lack of enthusiasm.

In the distance they heard the mellifluous twit twoo of a tawny owl, followed by an immediate response from another. Since it was a beautifully clear night, the moon provided enough light for them to see each other's faces as they stood motionless under the stars.

'So, what happened?'

'I took a home test and it was negative, but had I waited I would have known, even without the test, because this afternoon things went back to normal again. The stress of everything must have made my body go haywire. Anyway, I'm fine now, and I'm not pregnant.'

'I know, and it's absolutely fantastic.' Looking at Carolyn's face illuminated by the moonlight, Stuart saw intense sadness in her eyes. 'But you still don't seem happy, Carolyn. Why, what's wrong?'

'What's wrong, Stuart? What's wrong? I may not be carrying a baby, thank heavens, but I'm still carrying guilt, and that will never change.'

Stuart grabbed hold of her shoulders, as he had done once before, and looked her straight in the eye. 'Stop it, Carolyn, just stop. I'm not having any more of this. Don't you see? This is our second chance. You're free now. You … I mean *we* can put all this behind us now. After Saturday you'll be married to Dean, and in ten years you'll have a family, a great life, and you won't remember this, I guarantee.'

'And how can you guarantee that, Stuart?' she asked sounding more emotional again. 'Stop trying to pretend this is nothing.'

'It may not be nothing now, but it's still new, it's still raw, Carolyn. Life has a way of fixing problems like this, really it does.'

'How will I cope when seeing you is a constant reminder of what I did? You say you're going away, but please don't forget, there's a wedding before that happens, and also remember, I have to face you on Friday. I'm bound to give everything away then, I just know it.'

Stuart relaxed his shoulders and smiled. 'Carolyn, take it from me, as someone who's bluffed their way through life, people aren't as good at reading you as you think they are. Even if they were to suspect something – which they won't – they'd dismiss it. Can you imagine anyone thinking what happened between us really did happen? I tell you, they wouldn't, and they'd think it unthinkable. So don't you waste precious time focussing on something nobody else would.'

He continued, undaunted by Carolyn's sceptical and troubled face.

'Look, I know you're worried about seeing me before I leave, but I promise the rehearsal will be fine, and you'll be so distracted at the wedding you'll hardly notice I'm there. Then afterwards I'll be gone for good. I'm not staying around here – no thanks, I'll be glad to leave. And before you know where you are, you'll have forgotten about me, and you'll forget about all of this too.'

In his effort to console and convince, Stuart put his hand under Carolyn's chin and raised her lowered head. 'Give me a smile and say after me, "Everything's going to be fine".'

Carolyn managed a feeble smile but couldn't muster any words. Although he was being firm with her, she felt the softness of his hand gently stroking her chin, and looking into those brown eyes, the same feelings of warmth and comfort she had experienced at the party came flooding back.

'Goodbye Carolyn.' Stuart lifted her jaw higher and reached down to plant a soft, gentle and lingering kiss on her lips. Carolyn closed her eyes, and when she opened them again, Stuart was still looking at her.

'Do you know,' she said, her voice quivering, 'since this all happened I've not been able to look Dean properly in the eye, let alone kiss him. Yes, we hug, and we've had a quick peck now and then, but now it feels like he's just a friend, and a distant one at that. And all because I've put up this barrier between us. It's all my fault.'

'No, it's not. It's my fault too, but please don't be sad any more, Carolyn girl. The passion will return between you and Dean one day, I'm sure. You'll see.'

Despite such words of reassurance, Stuart walked away from the church with his mind spinning. He had hidden it well from Carolyn, but he too was exhausted, having struggled to sleep since hearing the news that she might be pregnant. Although everything was over at long last, he still felt oddly stirred up. Evidently, after having one thing dominate his mind for so long, finally getting rid of it completely was going to take time.

He had left his motorbike back at the farm and he set off on the long walk home, hoping it would clear his head and put a stop to the ruminations, once and for all. A little bit of truth he could handle, but too much could break him. This journey on foot was a last opportunity to regain normality and be done with all this reflection, which was way out of character. But could there be a benefit to it? Would refusing to distract himself from his true feelings mean he could bury them sooner rather than later and avoid the likelihood of them lurking in the wings, ready to pounce when he least expected it?

When he got to Magham Down he was disappointed to find himself no closer to eliminating the emotional turmoil he had been desperately trying to suppress. Seeing Carolyn that evening had only made matters worse. He walked slowly through the farm entrance towards the door, gravel crunching under his feet, and suddenly it happened. At long last, words for his speech started to form. Once he was through that front door he immediately headed to his room, grabbed a piece of paper and pen and began to write.

* * *

The wedding rehearsal came and went, and after everyone had left the church, Reverend Barnaby Miller locked up the tiny St Mark's church. He couldn't help but ponder over the night's events, admitting to himself that something about the wedding he would be officiating tomorrow, just didn't feel right. He had known both Carolyn and Dean since they were babies and thought that they and their families were all decent people, so he tried hard to quash these feelings. However, he couldn't deny that experience had taught him that when he sensed something was 'off', more often than not, it didn't end well. Turning the key in the lock, he sighed and muttered, 'Ah well, all in a day's work.' One other thing concerned him, though. He couldn't help thinking it odd that, without giving a reason, Stuart, the best man, hadn't turned up that night, much to everyone's surprise. To his credit he had left a note behind at the farm apologising for not being able to make the rehearsal and saying he wouldn't miss the wedding tomorrow, yet something didn't quite add up. Still, stranger things have happened, the Reverend concluded as he walked home to the rectory.

* * *

'I feel sorry for Dean and Carolyn, look outside.' Robert was staring out of the window at the sheets of wintry, sleety rain.

Amanda wasn't sure she felt the same. There were better days for a wedding, no doubt about that, yet she didn't feel sad for Dean and Carolyn, especially Carolyn. If she were in her shoes, she couldn't imagine needing sympathy, no matter what the weather. The freezing cold and driving rain were trivial. It was Carolyn's big day, and not only that, she was getting married to Dean, so why should she be pitied? For a moment Amanda thought that if there was anyone to be pitied it was herself, but then she made a rapid 180 degree turn. *Scrap that*, she thought stoically straightening herself up, *it's plain stupid to wallow in fruitless self-pity and I've moved on.* She'd had months to prepare for this day, and now she was ready to face up to it – as ready as she'd ever be.

'I think this is the first wedding I've been to in the middle of winter,' Joan said frowning, 'but Victoria said they couldn't wait until the summer. More's the pity. I'd much rather stay wrapped up in front of the fire today than brave these awful conditions.'

'I wonder what her dress will be like, Mum. She'll be freezing outside unless she's wearing a coat.'

'Won't make for great photo opportunities either,' Joan remarked.

'When you ladies are done commenting about the bride and groom and the weather, perhaps we can get going to the village hall and actually see them,' said Robert.

'You're quite right, love,' Joan replied, glancing at her watch, 'we'd better go.'

The weather was far too inclement to walk, so Amanda and Joan dived into the Ford Escort while Robert activated the wipers to clear the windscreen of slushy rain.

After slowly making their way through the country lanes they were disappointed to find no spaces left in the small village hall car park or on the nearby road.

'I'm afraid I won't be able to park very close so I'll drop you off first,' Robert said hurriedly, tugging at his tie. Mother and daughter got out of the car, the rain battering them as he drove away.

'Oh no! My feet are getting wet,' complained Joan rushing towards the entrance.

'And mine,' Amanda said, battling with her umbrella as it blew inside out.

Once inside the building they could see plenty of people already in the hall, but contrary to what Dean said about standing room only, there were still some unfilled seats. They waited by the door for Robert to arrive, and when he turned up minutes later, water pouring off his coat, Joan whispered to him, 'It's nearly one o'clock and it doesn't look like everyone's here yet.'

'Perhaps the weather's put some people off,' he replied looking well and truly soaked.

'As long as that includes that Mrs-Know-It-All woman, that suits me,' Joan said with a crisp nod, making Robert smile.

Stepping inside the main hall with her parents, Amanda combed the room for the bride and groom, who were nowhere to be seen, and neither were Victoria, Cecil or Millie. Although she didn't know what Carolyn's parents looked like, she guessed they weren't in the room either. However, she could see children running around – little boys dressed smartly in suits and small girls with pretty dresses and ballet shoes. Several ladies, old, young and in between, were wearing corsages, while men walked around with buttonholes containing a white carnation. Amanda quickly looked across to the top of the room where she saw the head table. It had to be, since it was more elaborately decorated, but perhaps the greatest giveaway was the big three-tiered wedding cake with silver ribbons wrapped around each layer, and a model of a miniature bride and groom on the top. Sugared almonds were scattered across the tablecloth, and there were candles, delicate china plates, silverware and what looked like crystal glasses across its length. The other tables were decorated with small vases containing a single red rose and were supplied with basic paper plates, plastic cups and cutlery. Amanda looked around at the bunting and balloons thinking it all looked very impressive.

'I think we can sit anywhere we like, can't we?' said Joan. As more bedraggled and drenched people started to arrive, she thought it was a good idea to claim a seat while they still had the chance, all the time scanning the room for Mrs Knowles. 'I can't see the evil cow,' she said under her breath to Robert. 'Anyway, this will do, come Amanda. Let's sit here.'

'Where's the bridal party?' Amanda asked.

'I overheard the woman from the post office saying to someone that they're having photos taken in a side room and how sad it was they couldn't have a single photo outside, but that's what comes from getting wed in January. She also said people had better take their seats as they'll be finished soon,' Joan replied.

The decision to sit was prudent because very soon ladies in aprons, some of whom Amanda recognised from around and about the village, came out carrying trays of salads, breads, quiches, sliced meats, prawn cocktail, smoked salmon and more. It truly looked as though a feast was about to begin.

'I think we're going to eat well today,' Robert said, eyeing up the trays.

'Yes, and please don't embarrass us by falling asleep afterwards, will you, love?' Joan smiled.

'As if I would,' Robert retorted, smiling back. He turned to his daughter. 'Amanda, when – and I mean when, not if – you get married, you must accept the villagers' pot luck reception. Not only will it save Mum and me a packet, but from what I can see, it looks really good.'

Amanda, encouraged by her father's confidence, nodded, having already decided she was keen to follow suit, if that day should come, that is.

Joan continued to survey the room. 'I'm glad we sat down when we did, there are only a couple of seats left now.'

Robert checked the time. 'I'm not surprised, love. It's nearly ten past, and everyone was supposed to be here for one,' he replied, trying to ignore his rumbling stomach.

Amanda could see several people she recognised – the shopkeeper, a gardener she would often see working, Mrs Bailey from the guest house, which instantly reminded her of Mark, and she was delighted to see old Eddie sitting at the other end of the room who gestured cordially to her. However, there was someone missing. She couldn't see Leonard, aka Pickwick, anywhere. *I can't imagine he wouldn't be here, given the chance,* she pondered. *He'd be in his element with all this food.*

Although almost hidden from view by people sitting nearby, Amanda thought she could see someone who fitted the description of Mrs Knowles. Tilting her head in the woman's direction she asked her mother, 'That woman with the dyed red hair and large glasses, is that her?'

Joan craned her neck for a better view, and quickly recoiled. 'Yes, that's her.'

'Thankfully she's far enough away,' Amanda whispered, 'and there's really no point allowing her to spoil things for us today, is there?'

'No Manda dear, we mustn't let her do that.'

At that moment there was the loud clattering of a spoon hitting a table. A man stood up and shouted in a loud, clear voice: 'Please be upstanding for the bride and groom.' Amanda's heart leaped as she and everyone else rose to their feet and watched the bridal party enter the room. First Dean walked in to applause with Carolyn on his arm, and behind her, wearing long pale pink bridesmaid dresses were Tracy, another young woman Amanda didn't recognise, and Millie. Then came Victoria and Cecil, and a couple who were obviously Carolyn's parents, and finally, Stuart. Amanda took a deep breath and swallowed hard as she watched. Dean pulled a chair from under the table and guided Carolyn towards it, who in response looked up at him adoringly and swept her hands under the skirt of her heavy white wedding dress before sitting down.

'Her dress is lovely, don't you think, Manda?' Joan whispered. 'Those full sleeves are perfect for winter, she's planned it well. And don't you think her younger sister looks like her? Victoria said it's her first time being a bridesmaid, which is the same for Millie, and they were both so excited.'

Amanda nodded but couldn't answer. Once again she was so disappointed with herself. She thought she'd got over all this nonsense, but just one look at Dean and everything was in turmoil again. Her heart was beating nineteen to the dozen, the beats so strong she feared they were audible.

He was now finally gone forever, but the gentle smile on his face was all that it took for Amanda to see she still had a long way to go. She thought she had said goodbye and made peace within her heart, her emotions exorcised, accepting the loss, but instead, it was as though she had thrown an emotional boomerang with all the energy she could generate, only for it to return with a vengeance.

Time is a great healer, she thought positively. It had been months, not years, since she had left the farm. If she was still feeling this way after a year had passed, she'd be worried, so there was no need to panic, not yet. She would adjust soon enough. But then, she had to admit to herself that if the passing of five months couldn't stop her yearnings, unless someone new came along in the meantime, what made her think a year would do the trick?

The photographer aimed his camera at the bride and groom, and Robert, who had been designated the photographer for the Fernsby household, also began to take a few snaps. Then, the same man who announced the bride and groom, and who referred to himself as the master of ceremonies stood up again. 'I don't recognise him, do you?' Joan asked Amanda quietly. 'He probably has links to the bride's family.'

The spokesman thanked everyone for coming, before introducing Bella, 'our wonderful village flautist who will be entertaining you while you eat,' and lastly he called on the Reverend Miller to say grace. Once everyone was seated again, he announced, 'Tuck in now please!' No one in the room needed further encouragement to help themselves to the banquet before them.

Amanda kept a keen eye on Dean, watching him whispering to Carolyn during mouthfuls and freely sipping champagne. She noticed that, although he would smile, occasionally his brow furrowed and this was something she had never seen before. His facial expressions appeared incongruous and troubled, and this concerned Amanda. What other people may have missed was obvious to her, because she knew what he looked like when he was happy. But, surely, so did others close to him, such as his parents, and if they weren't concerned, why should she be?

There was something else too. Stuart, who was sitting beside him, looked very odd indeed, and not at all his usual jovial self. If there was ever a time Amanda expected to see Stuart merry and carefree, it was at his brother's wedding. Surely it wasn't because he was nervous about giving a speech? Most telling of all, Amanda didn't see either brother speak to the other, or even acknowledge one another. Was she reading too much into what she was seeing? How could she be sure her messed-up emotions weren't causing her mind to play tricks on her?

Amanda was now looking more closely at Carolyn. She had heard from her mother she had been depressed in the run-up to the wedding, and Victoria confided in Joan that they all thought the stress of planning it had got to her. Perhaps it was because of this that Amanda was expecting to detect at least some signs of sadness or stress, but instead Carolyn appeared content. Admittedly it was hard for Amanda to tell how Carolyn was feeling. She hardly knew her, and had only met her on a few occasions. Carolyn wasn't the most expressive or cheerful person she'd ever encountered, which made her harder to read, but what else could she possibly be feeling than elation? However, as the minutes ticked by, Amanda began to notice that although Carolyn smiled readily, there was something not quite right. Did her smiles appear lacklustre in some way? Amanda stopped trying to overthink things, annoyed that her jealous feelings were obviously making her have unkind thoughts.

'Robert, you can barely hear that young girl on the flute, even with the mic, but it does sound lovely,' Joan commented while helping herself to a slice of quiche Lorraine.

'Do you recognise the name of the piece?' Robert replied, knowing his wife wouldn't have a clue.

Joan thought long and hard. 'No, tell me please, I'm not as good at recognising music as you are.'

'It's "Jesu, Joy of Man's Desiring" by Bach,' Robert replied, glad to impress her with his knowledge.

'Of course, Bach,' Joan nodded, 'and such a famous piece, I ought to have known that. You're a very cultured man, Robert Fernsby and I'm lucky to have you.' Robert felt his chest swell. It wasn't every day Joan gave him a compliment like that.

After everyone had eaten their fill of the main course, the same aproned ladies brought out big glass dishes filled with trifle. Joan looked with delight at the jelly, set with pieces of fruit, and sponge fingers covered with a thick layer of custard, topped with cream and hundreds and thousands. 'Ooh trifle! Robert darling, I knew I'd have to put the diet on hold today,' she said, tucking in enthusiastically, while Amanda, not feeling quite so keen, ate a spoonful of cream and jelly, leaving the cold custard behind.

'Isn't there any alcohol here?' Joan said, pouring herself another glass of water, 'Or at least any fizzy drinks?'

'There's a bottle of wine over there, and I can see people with coke and lemonade,' Amanda said, lowering her voice, worried her mother had expressed her wish for a tipple rather too loudly. 'It looks like you have to bring your own.'

'That's another reason it'll save us a packet if you follow the village tradition, Amanda love,' Robert said, helping himself to more trifle. 'Strong drink is very expensive.'

Sitting next to him was an elderly lady who overheard him. She told Robert that she had been attending these village weddings since she was a child. 'I can tell you many a story of how things have changed and gotten better over the years,' she told Robert with a gummy smile.

Dessert was nearly over, and as Joan scraped the last spoonful of trifle from her bowl, they were again interrupted by the master of ceremonies, this time tapping a glass with a spoon. 'And now for the speeches,' he boomed.

'I can see why they chose him,' Joan said, again a bit too loudly, 'his voice is like a foghorn.'

'Mum, keep your voice down, please,' Amanda urged with a hush.

Carolyn's father spoke first, as was traditional. He was chubby and not very tall, his remaining snowy white hair neatly combed over a large bald patch. The expression on his pudgy face ranged from jolly to serious, as he spoke through the microphone and greeted all the guests and thanked them for coming. He welcomed Dean as his fourth son and recounted how the bride and groom were destined to be married since Carolyn was 'knee high to a grasshopper'. He went on to say how much he wanted to celebrate his 'oldest little girl', who was 'clever, incredibly beautiful and very special'. The guests clapped in response and he sat down proudly, making way for Dean. Everyone looked at him expectantly.

Silence fell as Dean stood up clasping a piece of paper. Amanda held her breath. She was relieved to see that all eyes were on the wedding party, including her parents'. She had often been told that her expressive face was far too easy to read, and even now she didn't want to risk giving the game away to anyone. No one knew anything of her inner turmoil and she wanted it to stay that way.

Dean unfolded the paper, flipped back his floppy fringe and smiled. Immediately Amanda was transported back to the first time she met him emerging from the cowshed that late spring day, which seemed such a long time ago now.

Although sounding confident, he fumbled with his notes as he thanked Carolyn's father and the master of ceremonies, the reverend, the bridesmaids, and both sets of parents, who he described as 'wonderful'. Finally, he thanked all the guests for coming, and then he turned to Carolyn with a look of devotion. 'And now, to my beautiful wife.'

Just at that moment Stuart got to his feet, the movement so rapid and noisy with his chair scraping the floor that it provoked a startled gasp from a number of guests. What on earth was happening? Was it planned? It certainly didn't look like it, going by the astonished look on Dean and Carolyn's faces.

Dean tried to make light of it. 'What's the matter, big brother?' he smiled hesitantly. The room was silent waiting for a response.

Stuart took the microphone. Amanda noticed Carolyn was looking petrified.

'This is the first of many apologies today,' Stuart replied inexplicably. 'I'm sorry, Dean, for interrupting your speech. I know it's not my turn yet, but I think what I have to say may influence the rest of it.'

Dean looked confused, his mouth slightly open. He turned his head towards Carolyn, but rather than meeting his gaze, her eyes were fixed on the table, her body not moving a muscle. Everyone else stayed quiet, looking uncomfortable, not knowing what to expect or daring to say a word. Then Stuart began.

'Hello everyone, thanks for coming today and being prepared to listen to me. I'm aware it's customary for the best man to start with a joke.' He stopped. 'Well, here it is. You're looking at him.'

Stuart pointed to himself, smiling strangely. 'You see, I'm the joke and you could also say, I'm the jerk.'

There was an audible hum of surprise. 'What on earth is he talking about?' Robert murmured in Joan's ear. 'The man's speaking in riddles, has he lost his mind?' but Amanda who was suspended in disbelief didn't hear her father, and Joan was too captivated to respond. The hall was briefly filled with whispers, but in no time a hushed silence returned once more. Cecil, looking furious as well as embarrassed, attempted to get up to stop Stuart, but Victoria held her husband back. She didn't want a scene, although perhaps it was too late for that, but at least she could try to avoid violence.

Stuart glanced at his incensed father. 'I'm sorry, Dad … See? Another apology. Didn't I tell you I would be apologising constantly today? This won't take long, everyone, if you'll just listen, hear me out and allow me to say my piece.'

Carolyn had turned pale and looked ready to burst into tears.

'I came with two speeches today,' Stuart said dispassionately. 'One was written on this piece of paper.' He lifted up a folded note. 'The other is written on my heart.' He then proceeded to tear the paper into shreds. 'You see what I'm doing? This is what I do to women. Rip them apart. That's why I'm the joke. But no more. Enough is enough.'

'You're dead right that's enough!' shouted Cecil. 'Get out of here now, Stuart.'

Victoria tried to hide her distress. Carolyn's parents were clearly appalled, not knowing where to look, occasionally glancing at their daughter, who was fighting back tears and refusing to acknowledge anyone.

Dean stared at Carolyn awkwardly. He was well aware something significant and unavoidable was about to unfold, which might be the culmination of months of uncertainty. Now he was finally ready for the truth, even if it was going to be delivered in front of an audience.

'Let him speak,' he urged his father, sounding deflated and emotionally spent, before sitting down and repeating in a mumble, 'Please, let him speak.'

Stuart turned to address his brother, in his eyes a look of respect. 'Dean, you and I both know that I've spent so much of my life not taking responsibility for anything. Well, last night I decided not any more. No more lying to get what I want, to cover up for my mistakes and failures, no more using people to get my own way and no more running away from the truth. You see, the truth is, I care about Carolyn.'

There were gasps all around the room. Carolyn lifted her head at last, pain etched on her face. 'No, please no, don't do this, Stuart!' she said, shaking her head tearfully,

'Yes, Carolyn, I've come to realise I really do care deeply about you. I took advantage of you when you were vulnerable.' He turned to the stunned guests. 'You see, until just a few days ago I thought Carolyn was having my baby.'

Another gasp filled the room, only louder this time. Everyone sat in shock and Janice looked as if she was about to faint. Amanda was flabbergasted. Was this really happening or was it a dream? She turned to Robert, and then to Joan for a reality check, and yes, they too had stony faces of disbelief. Then she looked around at others and finally to Dean, sorrowful, grief-stricken Dean. Her Dean, at least she wished he was her Dean. Tears began to stream from Carolyn's eyes, and despite her distress, no one attempted to comfort her – not Dean, not Stuart, nobody.

And Stuart hadn't finished yet. 'When Carolyn told me it was a false alarm, at first I was relieved – you've got away with it again, I thought to myself. But no, I got away with nothing, because I realised I was telling her – forcing her – to condemn herself to a lifetime of guilt and deceit, and I was also condemning my brother to a life of ignorance and a lack of intimacy with the one person who should be closest to him.' He paused and lowered his eyes for a moment. 'I couldn't do that to my little brother. He doesn't deserve it, because he's an upright person and a man of loyalty and integrity. If I hadn't done this publicly,' he said, straightening his back, 'I would be short changing not just Dean but also myself. I knew if I didn't take action, drastic action, action that was impossible to shirk and hide from, I would just bow out again, and if I did that one more time and in a situation like this, there would be no going back. That would be the end, because it would be far too easy to return to a life of denial and not taking responsibility for my actions, and if I had chosen to do that, I was terrified that something in me would be broken, forever, and beyond redemption.' Stuart paused and inhaled deeply. 'Carolyn and I had made a fatal mistake at Tracy's party, but the consequences of that taught me a valuable lesson, and I wasn't going to make another equally devastating mistake, which had the potential to last a lifetime.'

After hearing her name mentioned, Tracy held up her hands and stared ahead tensely as if to say – 'This has nothing to do with me!'

'So now, the ugly truth about what happened is out in the open,' Stuart continued. 'Yes, I could have spoken to Dean privately, the wedding would have been called off, and all this embarrassment avoided. But even today, at the last minute, I was fighting my tendency to bail out and escape, and I knew that the best way – no, the only way to draw a line in the sand and start again was to confess publicly.' He suddenly started smiling. Then he began to laugh, as though overtaken by momentary madness. 'And besides, everyone, what would we have done with all the wonderful things to eat that have been prepared by so many of you hardworking folk? I absolutely hate seeing good food go to waste and absolutely *love* a good party!' With more than a hint of pathos, he smiled and lifted his glass as though proposing a toast.

The small diversion into unseemly humour now over, he made a final confession and plea in front of his transfixed audience. 'I coerced Carolyn into a lie,' he admitted. 'I tried to solve the problem by deceiving my own brother, hoping he would believe the baby was his. I've hurt Carolyn, and now I've hurt Dean. But today, I'm going to put it right. Healing will take time, but forgiveness can happen in an instant, so I am asking two questions.' He turned to the distressed bride and the despairing groom. 'Carolyn and Dean, will you both forgive me?' At this, Carolyn's inaudible sobs turned into open weeping, her shoulders shaking as she turned away from the guests in an attempt to hide her face.

'My second question is also an announcement,' he continued. He slowly shifted sideways, turned to Carolyn and got down on one knee, holding up a small velvet box in one hand; the microphone in another. 'This was partly the reason for my absence yesterday, I had to get this for you.' He opened the box to reveal a sapphire ring with a cluster of diamonds surrounding it. 'I'm not sure you'll want me now, Carolyn, but I have feelings for you which I believe will grow into deep and lasting love. I know that genuine love is about commitment, truth and sacrifice – and a choice, and for the very first time in my life, I think I'm ready to choose love. So Carolyn, I have to ask, will you, could you possibly marry me?'

The room was crackling with suspense. Carolyn spoke no words, but immediately got up, lifted her long train and rushed out the room, her eyes so flooded with tears she could barely see where she was going. Silently and with his head bowed, Stuart placed the microphone down and slowly walked out of the hall.

Although shocked and mortified, Dean was attempting to put on a brave face, and this really broke Amanda's heart. She watched as he gathered close those around him, cupping and shaking hands and receiving hugs, while mouthing the words 'I'm fine', again and again, but of course Amanda knew he wasn't. Millie was crying, and Tracy and Carolyn's sister were trying to comfort her. Victoria was speaking quietly to Cecil whose eyes were transfixed with rage. Janice ran after her daughter, while Carolyn's father simply walked out. Within moments, the sound of his car being driven away could be heard.

Amanda was ablaze with conflicting emotions. Although she felt extreme sadness for Dean, she couldn't help but notice other more positive thoughts and feelings stirring within. From the moment she had first seen him, on what should have been the happiest day of his life, she had sensed something was wrong. She hoped that whatever ordeal he had been going through was now over, or that at the very least this would signal the end of his unhappiness. But in many ways, Amanda realised, this would just be the beginning, since his private suffering had now turned into public shame. He would recover from this, of course he would, what other option was there? But how long would it take? It might be years, and in that time much could happen to change him.

And what about her? Could she even dare to believe that what had transpired might mean there was still a chance for her? Amanda felt ashamed. How could she even think about herself at a time like this? Dean had experienced perhaps the worst day of his entire life, losing the woman he loved, the woman he had always believed he would spend the rest of his life with. And not only had he lost her, he had also found out she had been unfaithful to him – and not just with anyone, but with his own brother, who had then humiliated him in front of the entire village. Even if all this meant that she and Dean could become friends again, surely this was neither the time nor place to wish for anything more. Nobody could endure something as devastating as this and then immediately switch over their affections. And besides, how could she assume Dean and Carolyn were finished, when there was a possibility that even after this, all was not lost between them? Could there be a reconciliation? It was unlikely but not impossible. Infidelities have been forgiven, people have even divorced and remarried their former spouse. So she must never allow herself be ruled by her heart, because one more dashed hope, one more shattered dream, especially when it came to Dean would be just too devastating.

As the aproned ladies gathered up the last of the serving dishes and dessert bowls, hurrying to get on with the job in hand while having to delay the conversation they were itching to engage in, Joan and Robert sat aghast like everyone else in the room.

'Bloomin' heck,' Joan said eventually, as the murmurs grew louder and people slowly started to disperse, 'that'll give Mrs-Know-It-All something to chew on.'

Chapter 21

Janice slowly opened the door of the side room of the village hall and cautiously pushed her head through the gap. 'Are you okay, Carolyn?'

'I don't want to talk.'

Janice felt grieved to see her daughter's face buried in her arms, leaning against the back of a chair, her long veil cast to one side. No longer concealed, the previously hidden white cloth-covered buttons running down the sheer material on her back were now visible, but only to her mother who looked on helplessly.

'I'll be fine, Mum, I just need some time on my own,' her voice trembled.

'You can't stay in here on your own forever, love. Everyone's worried about you.' Janice was doing her utmost to sound compassionate and desperately trying to avoid any hint of disapproval in her voice, but her words failed to reassure Carolyn, whose relentless sobbing grew louder still.

'How can I face anyone again? I can't leave this room until everyone's gone!'

'Don't be silly, Carolyn. You have to.'

Carolyn paused for breath and suddenly looked up with fear-filled eyes. 'Where's Dad?'

Janice hesitated, and then replied reluctantly, 'I think he's gone home.'

Carolyn crumbled. 'You see! Even my own dad is disgusted with me and doesn't want to know. I can never leave this room!'

'You know your dad, he'll come round, he just needs time to process—'

There was a knock on the door.

'Whoever it is, please get rid of them, please,' Carolyn entreated, burying her face again. When she raised her head, she saw to her horror that rather than carrying out her wishes, her mother was awkwardly sidling out of the room. There, in her stead, like a solid impenetrable wall, was Stuart, standing at the door looking straight at her.

At first, Carolyn said nothing, and simply turned away, but as she heard his footsteps approach, her indignation soared. 'Get out!' she barked at him, clenching her teeth.

Stuart, undeterred, silently stepped closer.

'I said, get out!' she repeated, but to no avail. He was now standing right next to her, doggedly resolute. 'How could you?' she screamed, gathering up every fragment of remaining strength she could find. She looked up at him desperate for answers, tears streaming down her anguished face. But still, Stuart said nothing. 'You've humiliated and publicly disgraced me. You've effectively ruined my life. My father may never speak to me again, and this was supposed to be my wedding day!' Her knuckles were white, almost translucent, as she gripped her chair hard. Stuart crouched down and embraced her with his entire being, holding her firmly. There, effectively held captive, Carolyn sat on the chair in the corner of the room, while Stuart gripped her as she spat out angry words, but she was gradually losing the will and energy to fight. 'Just leave me alone, I want to die, and I really, really hate you!'

Stuart spoke at last. 'No, Carolyn, you don't mean that.'

'Oh, I most certainly do.' Her body was shaking and she nodded her head frantically. 'You'd better believe I mean it.'

'You're naturally in shock and very angry now,' Stuart said, trying to calm her. Watching as Carolyn's veil slid onto the floor, he picked it up and handed it to her tenderly. She looked at the transparent, delicate material and reluctantly took it from his hand. Now, with her head exposed, he grasped the opportunity to stroke her unveiled hair, which had been secured in an elegant twist but was now starting to unravel. Carolyn didn't protest, so he became bolder and was soon embracing her and rocking her gently.

'It's been terrifically hard for you. You're emotional, you're tired, and you're bound to be angry and scared.'

Carolyn continued to sob, but slowly became calmer and quieter. 'Why did you do this to us, Stuart? To all of us, why?'

'You heard why, Carolyn. I told you, I told everyone.'

'But did you really have to do it that way?'

'Despite all I said about why I had to do all this – and I still stand by those words, by the way – in the end, it doesn't really matter, does it? What difference does it make how everyone found out, if it was only going to leak out anyway? And say we had managed to keep the secret forever, what kind of life would we ... would *you* have had? The answer is, a totally miserable one.'

'Okay. So you were determined to make a spectacle of us both. But wouldn't it have been more sensible to do it at the service and not at the reception? Why did you just sit back and let me marry Dean?'

Stuart shut his eyes briefly, and let out a deep sigh. 'My final act of cowardice I guess,' he said quietly. 'I'm really sorry Carolyn. Of course, I wanted to stop the wedding, but at that solemn, sacred moment,' he paused, his eyes cast downwards, 'I just couldn't do it. Perhaps the champagne gave me that last bit of Dutch courage I desperately needed, but please, don't be alarmed girl,' he said, still hugging her tightly, 'I'm not drunk. Not today.'

Carolyn, now motionless in Stuart's arms, had finally stopped struggling.

'I meant every word I said, Carolyn. I want to marry you.'

'But Stuart, please be realistic. I'm already married,' Carolyn replied, with heavy eyes. Then she added despondently, 'At least I was.'

'Your marriage to Dean isn't final yet. All those weeks ago you married me with your body, and that's something you and I share that you and he never will. We've already started on our journey of becoming one together. I hope you can see that, so now all you have to give me is your commitment.'

Carolyn looked at Stuart with conflicted eyes, wondering if she could ever dare to trust him. He really did seem different, but no, a leopard doesn't change its spots and fear and anger still raged within her. 'What about all your other girlfriends, weren't you "one" with them too?' she snapped back.

'Yes and no,' Stuart replied contemplatively. 'I lacked the will or desire to treat them right. I know I've done wrong towards them, and in many instances they have done wrong to me too, but today, now, I have the chance to do the right thing and grab hold of the happiness I've been searching for, for so long. I really believe you are the one to end my fruitless search. Carolyn, will you help me find what I've been looking for?'

Carolyn remained still and non-responsive. Stuart pulled up a chair next to her.

'I'm tired of running around and I want to settle down, Carolyn – well, as much as you can in the army, that is. In time, I'm sure Dean will forgive us, our parents too, but for now, why don't we just get away?' Snapping his fingers, he immediately looked annoyed with himself for his choice of words. 'Oh no, that sounds like I'm running away again, like I'm trying to avoid facing the music, but I swear it'll be different this time, because I'll be with you. I can't pretend the life of a soldier's wife will be an easy one, but I can promise you, I'll do all I can to serve you, even as I try to serve my country.'

Carolyn's tears were suspended and she was looking intensely at him. Her dark blue-grey eyes reminded him that there was something he wanted to ask again and again, until he finally got the answer he wanted. He pulled out the small velvet trinket box and opened it.

'This was the closest I could get to your pretty eyes, Carolyn. If I'm being perfectly honest, I can't say buying this ring was the only reason I wasn't at the rehearsal. Something I didn't say out there was that I also missed it because I was arguing with myself all day and into the evening, wrestling with my thoughts and constantly going back and forth, back and forth in my mind, until I finally gave in.' He held his breath. 'Now, Carolyn, will you do the same for me? Will you give in ...? Will you marry me as soon as you're free to do so?'

Carolyn looked at the ocean blue sapphire surrounded by sparkling diamonds, and then she raised her eyes towards Stuart. All the turmoil of recent weeks had made her disconnect with her heart, that same heart which she had to admit had been softened and moulded by Stuart, ever since he put his arm around her at the party. And right now, this already assuaged heart was almost ready to admit defeat. Unable to speak, she simply took the ring and slipped it on her finger.

'It fits perfectly,' she said at last, feeling dazed and exhausted. She admired the ring as it sparkled under the light, and after spending time lost in its beauty she had a sudden thought. 'But how did you know my size, Stuart?' she asked, still looking at it.

'Ah, that was easy,' he said with a smile, 'it all comes with best man territory, you get to look after the rings.'

Carolyn exhaled, her eyes tired but no longer tearful. They sat quietly for a while until Stuart spoke again.

'One more thing, Carolyn.'

'Yes?'

'You do realise we need to set Dean free to be with Amanda, don't you?'

Carolyn closed her eyes for a moment, reluctantly absorbing those bitter but honest words.

'If I marry you, how will I know I'm not making a terrible mistake?' she said eventually, looking Stuart straight in the eye.

He smiled as he reached out his hand again and clasped hers tightly. 'The same way I know that this is the right thing for us both. I just know, and so will you ... in time.'

Carolyn's limp hand became firmer and more confident as she responded to his soothing touch. They sat harmoniously for a while, hand in hand, not saying a word. Before long the door slowly opened and Tracy looked in. 'S—sorry to interrupt,' she stuttered, I just came to ask you, Carolyn, if everything is okay ... but I can see it is, so I'll leave you now.' She clearly couldn't believe what she was seeing.

'No wait, Tracy, please come in,' Carolyn said, beckoning her friend over to where she and Stuart were sitting, his large hand still surrounding hers.

Releasing her hand, she then grasped the two rings that were on her wedding finger, the thick gold wedding band and the diamond cluster ring. 'Tracy, please could you give these to Dean, and tell him I'm so sorry?' Carolyn looked up with pleading eyes.

'Sure thing,' Tracy replied nonchalantly, taking the rings. She walked towards the door, pausing briefly before turning to glance at Stuart with a look of suspicion and distrust. Saying no more she left the room.

'She's protective over me, Stuart,' Carolyn said, reading the disappointment in his eyes.

'I know, and I'm quite prepared for an uphill battle to convince everyone that I'm not the same person I was, but as long as I've convinced you, that's all that really matters to me.'

* * *

Amanda and her parents sat by the crackling fire. It was a chilly Saturday in February, and all three were happy to indulge in a mammoth evening of TV. They had already watched *All Creatures Great and Small*, and now *The Dick Emery Show* was on. Amanda was looking forward to ending the evening with *Dallas*, when she could escape into the cut-throat world of Southfork and JR's evil machinations. Losing herself in entertainment helped to while away the long winter hours, and was a way to forget everything for a while. Her life was good, but uneventful. Nevertheless she was determined to make the most of each day, rather than wish the time away. Something would happen soon, she thought to herself, and it wouldn't be long before the weather warmed up and she would be out and about again doing so much more. She'd be able to pull on her wellies and get stuck into all sorts of projects and outdoor challenges. And so it happened yet again, she was reminded of the farm, and therefore, Dean.

The Dick Emery Show didn't interest her much, so now seemed a perfect opportunity to organise her photo album. She opened up the Kodacolour envelope received in the post only that morning and pulled out the snaps again. Glancing over at her parents, who were focussed on the screen and laughing along with the audience, she guessed they wouldn't notice her poring over the photographs for the umpteenth time that day. Why on earth was she still hiding her thoughts and feelings from them, as though she was a lovesick teenager? So what if they knew she had a 'thing' for Dean, especially now after what had happened?

The pictures immediately took Amanda back to that fateful day. She couldn't bear to discard any of them, even the blurry out-of-focus ones. She perused them all, including those with less significance, such as the one with the flautist, or the aproned ladies carrying trays of food. There were pictures of the head table, elaborately decorated, and a close-up of the wedding cake. Then there was the meatier stuff; the wedding party entering the room, the bridesmaids, a photo of Carolyn's father, and various people in the village enjoying their food, as well as one of Amanda herself and Joan, both smiling widely for the camera. Then came a photo of the bride sitting, seemingly relaxed, looking up at her father as he spoke. As she flicked through, Amanda's growing excitement could not be curtailed. She knew she was approaching the highlight of her collection. And there it was, the two photos she simply couldn't stop looking at, pictures of Dean delivering his speech. After that, no more photos were taken. Stuart's interruption followed, and the rest, as they say, is history.

Amanda studied the first photo, Dean's hand lifted, gesturing in thanks. It wasn't a close-up, but it was close enough to see his expression. And then, and not for the first time that day, she turned the pages in her album to remind herself how he had looked when they used to spend time together. Now in front of her was the only photo she had of him before the wedding. It was taken on a hot summer's day and he was standing at the entrance to Starry Gap field, wearing a checked shirt and blue jeans, arms folded casually and leaning against the gate with Bess and Jess at his side. She compared the breezy and natural smile on his face with the forced and stilted one at the wedding, now in hindsight so obvious, and even at the time, evident, at least to her. There was simply no comparison. She thought how much she treasured that early photograph, and she ran her finger over the album's protective plastic film to remove a smudge. As a finger delicately slid across Dean's face and body, for a second it almost felt as though she was actually touching him. Clearly her wishful thinking was now skewing her sense of reality.

'Don't you think it's bad luck putting those photos in your album?'

Amanda was jolted into the here and now by her mother.

'Why would it be bad luck?'

'Well, that wedding was an absolute disaster, wasn't it?' Joan said, wrinkling her nose as though she was stating the obvious. 'And if you put those photos in an album, you might very well attract the same energy for yourself.'

'That doesn't sound like a healthy way of thinking.'

'I'm only pulling your leg, love, but it's no joke what happened, is it?'

Joan enthusiastically recalled what had easily been the event of the year so far. Even though 1980 had only just begun, the chances of something else occurring, even in years to come, which would rival the magnitude of what had started to become known as the 'Appleby affair' were slim.

'Despite it being a fortnight ago, it's still the only thing I hear people in the village talking about,' Joan continued. '*And* I meant to tell you something earlier which slipped my mind, how on earth could I forget? Must be my age. Anyway, Phyllis at the post office said today it's the biggest scandal to have rocked the village since the Hamilton affair in 1963.'

Robert got up and turned the volume button down on the television, and Amanda waited to hear more, photos still in hand.

'The Hamilton affair, what was that all about?' Robert asked, intrigued.

'That's just it, I don't know any other details,' Joan said, sounding shrill. 'Just when she was about to tell me all about it, someone came in needing to cash their pension, and then I couldn't hang around afterwards because they were about to close. Rita had already turned the sign over on the door, and you know what Rita's like, and how she looks at you daggers if you're in there a second after closing time.' Amanda smiled - she could relate to that, having witnessed Rita's displeasure first-hand. 'But not to worry,' Joan added, keeping an eye on the television. 'I'm sure I'll find out what happened soon enough, but I have to say, if Phyllis' tone of voice is anything to go by, it'll be a very juicy story.'

'Careful, you don't want to become another village gossip,' Amanda warned, smiling.

'Rubbish! It happened ages ago, so I can't imagine anyone involved gives a monkey's. Turn the TV up, Robert love, this bit looks funny.'

With her parents happily preoccupied, Amanda returned to the photographs. She was about to turn to a blank page and peel away the film from the sticky album sheet to position the new photos within, but stalled to have one last look at Dean, standing at the gate, looking relaxed, his warm smile beaming back at her with eyes full of life. She found herself gazing at it almost transfixed, knowing there wasn't a single day since the wedding that she hadn't thought about him. How was he? How was he coping and adjusting? Had he at any point thought about her throughout it all?

She wasn't even able to glean any clues from her mother, because Joan and Victoria hadn't spoken since the wedding. Joan was itching to call Victoria but held back, not wanting to appear insensitive. So instead, she waited patiently, but so far there was no contact. Joan reasoned that Victoria was grappling with shame, but Robert wasn't so sure. 'Give her time,' he said earlier that day. 'There are probably practical things to sort out after such a shock, and anyway, a fortnight passing without you two getting together isn't entirely unheard of, is it love?'

The Dick Emery Show had ended, and Robert rose to his feet to make them a cup of tea. As he walked towards the kitchen, there was a knock on the front door. All three looked at each other.

'Who on earth can that be at twenty to nine on a Saturday night?' Joan said, apprehensively.

'No idea, but I'll get it,' Robert said. 'I'm up anyway.'

'Too many people think it's acceptable to pop by late and uninvited around here,' Joan said. 'I just can't get used to it. Maybe it's Victoria, but no, I doubt it, not at this time anyway.'

The world seemed to stop still when Amanda heard her father's voice. 'Dean, young man, hello. What a surprise, please come in.'

Dean, what? Really? No! Amanda's heart was racing and she thought she actually felt it skip a beat. She looked down at her lap and was horrified to see the photos of the wedding spread over the arms of the chair and on the pouffe in front of her. She gathered them up as quickly as she could but she wasn't quick enough. Dean was now in the room looking directly at her, with that endearing smile of his, a smile so similar to the one he sported in the photograph at the farm, the very same photo she hadn't had time to conceal. She had meant to close the album but she was mortified to glance sideways and see it wide open on the coffee table, and worse still, open on *that* page. After following the direction of Dean's eyes there was no denying he had seen it. He had caught her red-handed with his image laid bare, displayed in front of her.

'Dean, how lovely to see you.' Joan smiled, picking up on her daughter's embarrassment. 'Do you want a cuppa? Robert's just putting the kettle on,' she asked, rushing over to the television set to turn it off.

'That's very kind of you, Mrs Fernsby, but no thank you.' Dean smiled politely, still looking at Amanda and failing to hide his amusement as she blushed furiously, clutching photographs in both hands.

'What brings you here tonight?' Joan asked innocently, although her growing awareness of Dean and Amanda's body language told her the likely reason. How in the world had she managed to miss all this up until now?

'We're sorry for what happened, Dean,' Robert said, feeling he ought to say something. 'Everybody is, I'm sure.'

Dean and Amanda kept sending each other tender sideways glances, Amanda with cheeks still flushed, but Dean relaxed enough to send a few lingering looks her way.

'That's okay, Mr Fernsby,' Dean replied, all the while keeping an eye on the object of affection in front of him.

Joan interrupted, 'Oh do call him Robert. Robert, you'd prefer that, wouldn't you?' Robert nodded. 'And please, Dean, call me Joan,' she beamed.

Dean caught sight of Amanda's embarrassment at her mother's excitement. She gave him an awkward smile.

'Thank you, Joan, and thank you too for your kind words, Robert. It's okay, really it is. It came as a huge shock to everyone of course, but people have been so supportive, and I've had two weeks to process everything, so I'm getting there, slowly but surely.' He paused. 'I'm not sure if you've heard, but Carolyn and Stuart are getting married and they're both leaving Magham Down within weeks, so Stuart can start preparing for a new life in the army.'

There was an air of surprise in the room, but not shock.

'Married, really? I didn't know that.' Joan looked dazed by the speed at which everything was happening. 'I knew Stuart proposed, of course, but I didn't know she'd accepted him.'

'Yes,' Dean said, 'a friend of the family who's also a solicitor has been incredible. Our case is straightforward, so he said he'll do what he can to get our marriage annulled within three months. I think he feels sorry for me.' He looked away briefly and managed to smile.

Amanda, her heart still thumping uncontrollably, was delighted to hear the news. She felt happy for Stuart and Carolyn. She was pleased that something good had come out of it, but was this thought disloyal to Dean, after all the trauma he had been through? Yet, as she saw him standing boldly in the living room of Marshywood, she was becoming increasingly optimistic there would be more good things to come out of a bad situation.

Robert thought that now might be a good time to finally make that tea, and being a sensitive sort of man he said tactfully, 'Joan, I've noticed a job to be done in the kitchen. I'd like to show it to you, would you come with me now?'

'What job?' Joan replied clumsily, but Robert stayed silent until she finally cottoned on.

'Oh, of course, I'm coming.'

Following the direction of Dean's gaze, she knew her husband was right. These two needed to be left alone.

'I'll see you in a bit,' she said and smiled. 'Should this "job" take a long time and you've gone before I finish, please give my regards to Victoria, won't you, Dean?'

'I certainly will do, Joan. Thank you.'

At last, Dean and Amanda were alone. Amanda rose to her feet and stood in front of him. After a short pause, Dean spoke first. 'You're looking well, how are you?'

'I'm fine, Dean, and how are you?' she asked, desperate for the answer.

Dean exhaled. 'Much better than I was, thank you.'

'I can see that, and it's really good to hear.' Even though she had only just stood up, she was feeling wobbly on her feet already, as though she had completed a double shift at Jimmy's without a break.

More silence followed until they suddenly spoke in unison, 'I hope things—' began Amanda, just as Dean started saying, 'I'm here because—' Both stopped talking and smiled awkwardly.

'You first, Amanda.'

'I was just going to say, I hope you haven't found the last two weeks too difficult.'

'Thank you. It's been a process, but I'm getting there,' he replied, sounding steady and calm.

'What were you going to say, Dean?'

He was quiet for a while, clearly in deep thought. 'Just that I'm here because ... Well, first of all I'm sorry it's so late in the evening. That's partly because there was some urgent work to be done – broken floor panels in the sheep enclosures which needed repairing, but I won't bore you with the details.' He laughed gently.

Amanda's eyes widened. 'How are the sheep, and all the other animals?'

'They're all doing fine, the sheep are now housed over the winter, and the cattle are almost weaned.'

'Wonderful,' Amanda said enthusiastically, sporting a wide smile and completely forgetting her embarrassment. 'And the chickens?'

'Oh yes, the chickens, I mustn't forget them.' Dean was also in his element. 'They're doing well, as always. At night I try to keep the hen houses covered with old sheets and blankets, but I don't know why I bother really. I don't think it makes much difference to them, they're pretty hardy. And Jess and Bess are as hardworking and as excitable as ever, as I'm sure you can imagine.'

'I was just about to ask you about Jess and Bess. I do miss them all,' she said with a distant look in her eyes.

The focus on animals prompted Dean to head over to Tabitha splayed out in front of the fire. Crouching down, he brushed his hand across her grey, stripy fur. 'I get to meet Tabitha at last,' he said, as Amanda's much-loved pet purred contentedly. Then he promptly rose to his feet again, realising he'd stopped midway through an explanation.

'Sorry Amanda, I think I was telling you that work in the sheep enclosure delayed me. But I was also late for another reason,' he said slowly. 'You see, I was working up the courage to come round today, and that's why it took me this long.'

Amanda felt emotional and dazed. What did he mean by needing courage? She could probably guess. Managing to maintain her composure she replied, 'That's fine, Dean. You're welcome any time, I hope you know that.'

'I think I do, Amanda. Yes, thank you.'

They looked shyly at each other. Amanda felt she needed to sit down, and it wasn't polite to leave him standing. 'Take a seat, Dean,' she said, sitting back down in her chair.

'Thanks,' Dean responded, proceeding to occupy Robert's favourite armchair. He gently lowered his head and his fringe flopped endearingly. 'Amanda,' he said at last. He lifted up his face again to look her. 'During...' he began, and then he paused. 'During these past few really difficult weeks, I've gone through so many different emotions.'

Sitting quietly she hung on to his every word.

For a brief moment, Dean's face became rigid. 'I hate to say it, but at times I got so angry I wanted to...' he stopped short, 'I wanted to hurt them because they'd hurt me. The sense of betrayal was – well, it was just so unbelievable.' Then, following a sharp intake of breath, his sadness appeared to lift. 'But truthfully, I've also felt intense relief,' he said focussing on her, 'so I'm sure you can guess, I've had really crazy emotional ups and downs. I've also had plenty of time to think.'

Amanda nodded, listening with every fibre of her being.

'I suppose the first thing I thought was, what was I going to do, now that me and Carolyn weren't together any more, now that our marriage was over, you could say, before it had even begun. It's as though I lost part of my identity, Amanda. Pretty much all through my life, I thought we'd be married, and so I began to reflect on my entire existence. I questioned everything. Did I actually want to be a farmer? Did I want to live here in Sussex? Was I *really* not bothered about not going to university?' For a moment, all that could be heard was the ticking of the mantelpiece clock. 'But, you know,' he resumed, 'after thinking about all these things, I realised I had no doubts or regrets at all. I was very happy with my life. But – well, there was something I needed to change.' He paused, and looked at her intensely.

'You see, it occurred to me that for so many years I'd played the dutiful son, always doing what was expected, always pleasing everyone, being loyal and being the good guy. Was this a good thing or a bad thing?' He shrugged his shoulders. 'I'm not sure. But, I do know I took it to the extreme and I became trapped. Loyalty and commitment began to trump everything. Even my own well-being. Even the truth.'

Amanda, although unsure what her silence was communicating, felt unable to say a word.

'I was determined to marry Carolyn, but after you left, I knew … well, let's put it this way, I never felt the same. When you left, it confirmed something I already believed. You were different Amanda, there was something about you.' He smiled reflectively. 'You didn't need to go, because you'd done nothing wrong, and neither had I. But you did leave, because - well, I could tell you left because you wanted to do the right thing. With you away from the farm, I thought I could easily forget you, only I couldn't, although I kidded myself that I could. I threw myself into work and I invested everything into my relationship with Carolyn, hoping I'd forget, and focus on just me and her. And it worked, for a while anyway. We were happy, or at least I thought we were, until I saw you at the village fete. That day was a very difficult one for me and Carolyn.'

Amanda swallowed hard, recalling clearly the events of that day. 'Yes, I noticed you'd disappeared,' she said at last.

'That's right. Carolyn saw me looking at you and that kicked off a tremendous fight, so we had to leave. We did eventually manage to patch things up, and fairly well, I thought, until the

New Year's Eve party at Tracy's. And well, you know what happened after that, as does the entire village now.'

Amanda gazed at Dean with overwhelming feelings of compassion mixed with joy and anticipation.

'Amanda, I think from what I'm saying, you're now able to tell that what happened at the wedding actually saved me,' he nodded gently. 'It saved me from myself.' His warm, hazel eyes were now looking intently at her. 'The truth is, Amanda, I've known I've loved you for a very, very long time. I just decided it wasn't something I would accept, or do anything about, because I had made a decision and I was going to stick with it whatever the cost, but - well, all I can say is, I've been rescued from my own stupidity.'

Amanda, wanting to leap in the air, managed to contain her euphoria. 'Dean, do you know how much I've dreamed - how much I wanted to hear you say those words to me?'

Dean shook his head. 'I guessed you felt the same way. That day in Eastbourne, when I saw how you looked at me, I knew there was something, but when you never came back, again, I ignored what was staring me in the face, and I eventually convinced myself that it was all in my head. I talked myself into believing that if you really liked me you would have stayed, but even if you had stayed, I'm not sure what would have changed in all honesty, because I had decided there was no turning back with Carolyn.'

Amanda looked at him unwaveringly. 'Yes Dean, you were right about what you saw that day at the beach, and you weren't the only one to suppress how you felt. I did the same, saying to myself I was over it, never even daring to hope or allow myself to think that one day we could be together.'

'It must have been very painful for you then, when I married Carolyn,' Dean said, looking regretful.

Amanda smiled briefly. 'Yes, there were moments when it was really hard for me to accept,' she confessed, 'but I can't imagine how it must have been for you to be married, knowing things weren't right.'

'I think that was one of the hardest things I've been through. But like the wally I am, I told myself I was prepared to put up with whatever I had to, and for the rest of my life.'

Amanda stood up with a smile, and moved over to Dean. Not caring if her parents returned to the room she reached out to take his hand. Getting back onto his feet, he lightly stroked her hand with his thumb while staring into her wide eyes, which were beginning to fill with tears.

'Amanda, my love.'

'Yes,' she exhaled, feeling her passions rise with every stroke of his thumb.

'The ring.'

'Which ring?' she asked. And then, she knew.

'You surely haven't forgotten,' he frowned, stepping back with surprise.

Amanda shook her head with delight as he drew closer again. 'No, you're right, I haven't forgotten. You mean Carolyn's emerald ring, don't you?'

'No Amanda, I mean *your* emerald ring.'

Amanda stood still, her breath suspended for a while. 'But ... you sold it second-hand didn't you? When you bought her the diamond one?'

'No, Amanda, it was the cluster diamond ring I sold second-hand, only today.'

Looking up at Dean in surprise, Amanda's pounding heart was overwhelmed.

'You see, Amanda, for some reason I kept hold of that emerald ring. I said to myself I haven't got time to sell it, I'll get around to it some day, and I almost forgot about it, but you know, if I examine myself and my motives, deep down I believe I held on to it for a reason.'

Amanda felt a tickle on her cheek. It was a tear running down her face, which she quickly wiped away. Seeing this, Dean pulled her towards him, she felt his heart pulsating as she rested her dizzy head against his warm chest. At last she was where she belonged.

'You know what though,' he said with a smile, soaking up her essence and softness, 'in my hurry to get here after I finally mustered up the courage, would you believe I left the ring at home, sitting in my other coat pocket!'

'There's no rush,' Amanda laughed a little, wiping away more tears, 'anyway, I know what it looks like, and you already know that I very much approve.'

Continuing to embrace, Amanda looked up into Dean's expressive eyes. Their lips were so very close, close enough to meet, but neither felt this was the time or place. Amanda didn't need to kiss him right now, she was quite happy to wait for that special moment. For now, her feelings of soaring like an eagle, as though her happiness had no limits, were more than enough for her, but of course in real life there are limitations, and Joan and Robert were hovering at the door, ready to reclaim their space, making their presence known with a tactful, 'Ahem, ahem.'

'Sorry to disturb you two sweethearts, but can Joan and I possibly sit in here now?' Robert was trying to suppress a massive smile. 'We don't want to cramp your style, but the kitchen chairs aren't too comfortable, especially at this time of evening.'

'Sorry, Mr Fernsby ... I mean Robert,' Dean replied, looking flustered. After they let go of each other, Amanda gave her lover an adoring glance.

'No need to apologise,' Robert replied, 'it's Amanda's fault for tempting you over here at this time of night,'

'Very funny, Dad!' Amanda replied, swiping her father affectionately, before giving him a hug. After laughter all round, Joan realised something. 'Dean, you don't mean to tell me you and Amanda are going to give the village something else to gossip about ... and so soon!'

'Not only that,' Dean replied with a wry smile, 'but they're also going to have to get themselves in gear for preparing another pot luck meal.'

* * *

It was Saturday 10th May 1980, six weeks after Amanda's twentieth birthday. Amanda and Dean left tiny St Mark's church and stepped out into the sunshine to a fountain of confetti filling the air, covering them in a myriad of colours. They held hands and kissed, their faces radiant, as they were met with sounds of celebration, some might go so far as to say jubilation. Even Reverend Miller, normally a reserved and undemonstrative man, was wearing a broad smile along with his dog collar.

Posing for a photograph under a wild cherry tree heavy with spring flowers, a gentle breeze blew, and the bride and groom were showered with dainty white blossoms.

'Beautiful shot,' declared the photographer, snapping repeatedly, 'nature's providing you with confetti!'

In the middle of a pose, Amanda was suddenly absorbed by an unmistakable sound. She stopped and listened.

'Wren!' she piped up knowledgeably.

'Well done, darling,' Dean replied proudly.

Amanda didn't move, and cupped her ear. 'And that was a blue tit, or should I say R2 D2,' she said excitedly.

'You've got it right, yet again. You're a star pupil ... and there it is.' Dean crouched slightly, leaning into his bride as he pointed to a tiny little creature with a flash of blue fluttering in a branch above their heads.

'Come on you two, stop looking at those birdies and watch *this* birdie! Now, both of you, hold on to the bouquet and give us a smile.'

The camera clicked. Dean stood behind Amanda, his arms wrapped around her, while she held on to her flowers – yellow and cream daffodils, red tulips, purple and deep pink hyacinths, and lilac-coloured anemones, some of which were gleaned from Marshywood's spring garden. The blooms perfectly complemented the freesia, sweet pea and peony flower ring in her hair, resting on her red curls which hung loosely over her lace-covered shoulders.

After a wonderful wedding feast, heartfelt speeches followed, and then Amanda and Dean exchanged greetings, warm hugs and handshakes with their guests in the village hall. They sat to eat wedding cake together, and then Dean motioned for Amanda to sit on his lap by the head table. She happily obliged, her arms, covered with delicate white lace, encircling his shoulders. She watched with delight as in the hall, friends and loved ones tucked into slices of wedding cake after having their fill of the bounty served by those familiar and committed aproned ladies.

Joan and Robert were engaged in happy conversation with Victoria and Cecil, no longer just firm friends but now also relatives. Everyone had been moved by the presence of Pauline and Charles, Pauline looking better than she had done since her illness, and Charles, still filled with joy and peace, thanking God for life and love every single day. Sam, Amanda's wonderful friend, was also at the head table, relishing her role as chief bridesmaid, while Precious and the rest of her family laughed with those around them. Amanda thought she would introduce Precious to Uncle Charles, sure they would have a lot to talk about.

Then there was Flavio, who was chatting with others in his usual exuberant way, and Jimmy with Pat, sitting next to Maggie and her daughter Becky. Dean watched Amanda closely as she relished the sight of all their guests enjoying themselves. Even Pickwick was there. Contrary to everyone's advice, Amanda had decided not to deny him entry. Gordon the shopkeeper said he'd keep an eye, and it made her happy to see Pickwick freely enjoying all the food he wanted, along with the other guests.

Dean smiled. The look on his wife's face as she watched their guests was delightful. 'It's not surprising Mrs Know-It-All kept away,' he said quietly, 'but, Amanda, if she had turned up, I bet you wouldn't have turned her away, not even her.'

Amanda moved her face closer towards his, her hair still decorated with flowers. 'I think you're right,' she said, deep contentment in her voice, 'I guess I wouldn't have excluded her.'

Dean looked at his wife, his eyes full of admiration. 'You're the kindest person I know, Amanda,' he said lovingly, 'truly beautiful, both inside and out.'

Neither Amanda nor Dean had forgotten about Mark. He had sent his apologies, a gift and a beautiful card saying that he and Geraldine wished them both all the very best. Dean said he hoped his absence wasn't because there were too many bad memories associated with the village. If that was the case, it would be a great shame, because Dean was sure that if he ventured back, it would be healing for him.

Stuart too was absent, and in his speech Dean told his guests that it was always the plan that Stuart would be his best man, but since he and Carolyn had left Sussex, his father Cecil had been happy to take on that role instead. He made it clear that he and all the family wished Stuart and Carolyn safety, peace and happiness. They would always be welcome back at Hillbrook Farm and he would forever consider Stuart a fine big brother.

As he thought about the love and forgiveness he now felt for Stuart, as well as for Carolyn, Dean still couldn't believe how the worst experience of his life had been transformed into the very best. Four months and two weddings down the road, everything had changed for the better, including himself.

'Dean, darling,' Amanda said leaning her head to one side, gazing at him affectionately, 'penny for your thoughts.'

'Oh, I was just thinking how lucky I am,' he said with a smile, shrugging his shoulders, 'and I was also thinking …'

'What?'

'I can't wait for the party tonight!' he exclaimed, giving her a tickle.

Amanda almost fell off his lap, until he stopped long enough for her to settle down again. Then they pressed their foreheads together and stared into each other's eyes.

'I'm so glad Maggie got that DJ's details from Tracy, but Dean, do you think the village will cope with loud music blaring out from the hall tonight? What will all the little old ladies think once the loud vibrations start shaking their mugs of Ovaltine?'

'Sweet, innocent Amanda,' Dean said, nuzzling her cheek, 'you have no idea, do you? Most of the little old ladies in this village will be the first on the dance floor tonight! Look at Gladys over there, I've heard she's a right one when she gets going.'

Laughing quietly, she tapped him on the arm telling him to shush.

'But Amanda, my lovely, I can't lie. We are the first couple to use and abuse this quaint village hall in this way. I don't think it's seen a disco before in all its years, that's usually a job for the Red Lion.'

'What do you think he'll play tonight?' she asked, discarding the glace cherry before popping a cocktail stick of cheese, hot dog sausage and pickled onion into her mouth.

'All sorts, I imagine. Whatever's in the charts. What's number one at the moment?'

Excitement filled Amanda's eyes. 'It's our favourite, 'Geno' by Dexys Midnight Runners.'

'Oh fantastic, he should play it then, although I'm not sure it's really a party song.'

'That doesn't matter, we both love it, so there's no reason it can't be our party song, which reminds me, we haven't chosen a song to start the dancing off with, have we? Drat,' Amanda snapped her fingers, 'I knew I'd forget something.'

'Oh well, we'll just have to open the floor with a slow dance to 'Geno' then!' Dean laughed.

Just at that moment, Amanda was almost knocked off Dean's knees by Millie, who ran up to them both and threw her arms around Amanda. She gave her a big, sisterly hug, declaring cheerfully, 'Welcome to our family, Amanda. I'm so happy I've got a sister at last.'

'Thank you for your welcoming words, munchkin,' Dean teased. Millie looked distinctly unimpressed. 'He still seems to think I'm 4, not 14 going on 15!'

Amanda gave her a kiss on the cheek, and said with a whisper, 'Thank you, poppet, can I call you that, is that okay?'

Millie thought for a second. 'I guess that's an improvement on munchkin,' she concluded. 'Oh, and Amanda, I like this dress much better than the last one – I much prefer the colour.' As

Millie cheerfully darted away, Amanda smiled, pleased her choice of bridesmaid's dress had been given the thumbs up.

'I'm not hurting your knees, am I?' Amanda asked, checking in with her husband.

'Nah,' Dean replied with a naughty smile, 'surprising really, considering all that cake you've eaten. Seriously, gorgeous, you're super light, and anyway, it's good practice for when I carry you over the threshold.'

Amanda laughed, relaxed and happy. 'I've loved being back at the farm these past months, Dean. I can't wait to be there all day, every day. I'll miss Jimmy's, though,' she said, 'not so much the job, but the people, especially Maggie.'

'You and Maggie are best mates now, so you'll always be in touch.'

'That's true.'

Dean's face suddenly melted as he looked at the object of his love. He tipped his head to one side and gazed at his young bride. 'I'm so thankful that your parents moved you to Sussex, a year ago this very day,' he said softly, suddenly serious. Amanda hugged him extra close while she listened. 'You've really worked your magic on our cottage, our new home. You've transformed it into something beautiful.'

Amanda gave a quick and dismissive wave with her hand. 'Not really, I've only put up curtains, rearranged the furniture and given it a good clean.'

'And the rest. Now, talking of our cottage, Mrs Appleby,' he said sternly, straightening up, 'as you are well aware, you are moving in soon, Monday to be exact, after our return from the Grand Hotel Eastbourne – which I hope you're looking forward to, by the way.'

'I certainly am,' she said with a fiery smile.

'But my dearest, we have failed to give our new home a name, a failure which is a punishable offence around these here parts.' He wagged his finger disapprovingly at her.

'Oh no,' Amanda replied, opening her mouth in shock. 'I'd better sort that out. Now let me see … How about naming our home something that reflects a bit of both of us?'

'What? Beauty and the beast?' said Dean, arching his eyebrow, 'But that might be a toughie, since no one will be able to tell who's the beauty and who's the beast.'

'Very funny, you cheeky so and so, no I meant what about taking something from where we grew up – Hillbrook Farm or Magham Down, for example, and Leytonstone or London. Let, me see ... we could have Hillstone ... Stonehill ... or perhaps Leybrook?'

'Umm,' Dean posed as in contemplative thought rubbing his chin, 'I'm not sure which I prefer.'

Amanda quickly went through all the options in her head again before coming to a decision. 'What about Stoneybrook?' she suggested, and then nodded her head firmly. 'Yes, Stoneybrook is my favourite. It has a Marshywood ring to it don't you think?'

'Whatever,' Dean said blithely. 'They all sound pretty much the same to me,' he added with a smile.

'Then Stoneybrook it is,' Amanda said resolutely. Dean looked at her happy face, lapping up the excitement which was written all over it and thankful to be able to call Amanda his wife.

'I love you, Mrs Amanda Appleby,' he said adoringly, 'and I truly can't wait for the new chapter of our lives to begin at Stoneybrook.'

'I love you too, Dean. More than words can tell.'

Amanda suddenly sprang to her feet and brushed down her crumpled dress. 'But now I've got to do something, I must speak to Eddie.'

Dean looked bewildered. 'Eddie? Oh yes, there he is, over there. He seems to be enjoying his conversation with that couple sitting next to him. I bet he's telling them all about his dreadful rheumatticks. But Amanda, why on earth do you want to speak to that ancient old codger?'

Amanda smiled, 'Ah, you see I want to tell him we've chosen a name for our new home. It's quite a special thing, the naming of our cottage ... and something only Eddie will truly understand.'